THE GIRL WITH THE SYCAMORE SCARS

The Hickory Heart Book 3

LAUREN NICOLLE TAYLOR

OWL HOLLOW PRESS

Owl Hollow Press, LLC, Springville, UT 84663

The Girl with the Sycamore Scars

Library of Congress Cataloging-in-Publication Data
The Girl with the Sycamore Scars / L.N. Taylor. — First edition.

Summary:
Weeks after the complete destruction of Black Sail City, Lye Li is haunted by the message that Luna and Ash have been captured by the emperor. All decisions, all journeys, will lead to the same place: The palace. If they can reach each other and join forces, they might save each other and even change the world.

Cover Illustration: Stephanie Brown, Offbeat Worlds
Typography: Les Solot
Map Illustration: Evin Kierans
Interior Illustrations: Lauren Nicolle Taylor

ISBN 978-1-958109-34-2 (paperback)
ISBN 978-1-958109-35-9 (e-book)

For Molnar; brother and friend.
Who always had my back literary and otherwise.
Who was just as excited when I wrote my fourteenth book as he was
when I wrote my first.
I know Setsu said, 'wishes are a waste' but
I'd waste a thousand wishes to have you here with us again.

DARK WEST
SHEN MAINLAND
RIVER
RIVER
EMPEROR'S PALACE
CROW'S NEXT ISLAND
CHAR
TERRITORIES
MONASTERY
BIRD CAGE ISLAND
ABALONE ISLAND
COCKLE FAN ISLAND
COALSTONE
VILLAGE
PEARL
SHELL BEACH
N
W
E
S

1
LUNA

BRIDGES OF BLOOD
AND SALTWATER

I *feel* Ash.

I *feel* him clutch to his promise to live like a handful of still hot coals. Dropping them on the cold, acid-cleansed floor as they drag him further away from me.

Don't die this time—when they tie rope tight around your wrists and ankles and cut you with their torturous blades . When they kick, punch, and sneer become as impenetrable as a block of ice.

I *feel* the coarse fibers of seagrass rope chafing his skin as they begin. "Don't die. Don't die," I whisper to the blood-red walls of this palace prison. I graze the stone with my fingers, expecting them to stain. Grains of sand trickle down but my skin remains the same. Whatever colored these walls is old and seeping and comes from somewhere deep. I sniff. The scent of iron, blood, and straw.

My Blood sense finds insects, moving desperately, stupidly, between cracks in the floor. It finds death and dying everywhere as bugs reach the air and are poisoned. Nothing can survive here. Every night the woman comes with her pungent mop and brushes acid over the floors and walls, killing every animal as she disinfects and drenching my hope.

I shake as I spread my call to the night while the guard kicks his feet up on a chair, his shadow becoming still. Ash's torturers are working slow today, giving me a moment to summon a white ghost butterfly. It flutters through the narrow bars high above my head, long silky threads hanging from almost transparent wings. As delicate as the thinnest rice paper, she looks as melancholy as I feel. I let her alight on my finger.

"Don't touch the filthy, poisoned floor, beautiful one. You are too good for this place."

A shock of jagged pain passes slowly through my body. I gasp, "Ash." It pulls my limbs against my chest as it radiates from my shoulder to my fingers. The ghost butterfly lifts into the air, hovering just in front of my eyes. I scrunch them closed against the agony, only but only succeed at pulling it closer against my bones. I'm being whittled, grated, until I am nothing but screaming nerve endings.

My lips forms an empty O, knowing it must be even worse for him.

I *feel* every second of his torture. Clenching my fists, I tell myself he is strong. He is the strongest. He can survive this. He promised.

A chair squeaks across the floor. The halo of candlelight widens like the sun rising above mountains. *Oh, how I wish I were home!*

"Ai ya! Gi Shi, come look at this." I open my eyes to two guards staring through the bars, their mouths like tree hollows. Eyes wide and disbelieving. One in Earth brown robes and one in Air white. The candle holder quivers as the guard rolls his gaze over my body. Wobbling, I rise to my feet. Pain cracks through me again and I stumble. I'm terrified, but I need to remember I am also a terror. A dress of white ghost butterflies covers my filthy clothes. A Blood sense wedding dress. I flick my finger and they flutter out like a full skirt. Blood fills and supports me.

The guard holds up the key. Lifts it to the lock and pauses.

My stomach suddenly pulls in as Ash is punched in the gut. I cry out and double over. The butterflies leave my body as I fall to the ground. Swarming through the bars at the guards in a gust. They have no sting. They are not dangerous. They are beautiful and gentle, and the guards stomp their gossamer bodies into the ground. Spraying them with a chemical from a blue perfume bottle on their table. The puff on the end makes a soft, almost soothing sound that contradicts its danger.

They die quickly, wings dissolving into the earth. At the same time, my sense of Ash fades like he's also dissolving, disappearing. My throat dries like a dammed stream.

Gi Shi turns to the other guard and says, "Ah, Wen, maybe we should move her, you know, further down." He points at the ground with a pudgy finger. His tightly bound plait swings like a monkey's tail.

Wen shrugs his narrow shoulders. "We can't do anything without talking to the doctor." The way he says that word sounds more like *monster*.

Doctor. The idea that they care about my well-being seems as far-fetched as a gravel goose flying west instead of south. I'm guessing the doctor is not the healing kind.

I agonizingly pull myself up to the bed. Every ounce of my skin feels sharp hurt but shows no injury. Perhaps this is my penance. I am deserving of mountains of pain after the horrors I performed on Shen soldiers. But Ash deserves none of it.

I lie on my back and stare at the damp, water marked ceiling, feeling every punch, every cut and twisted limb. I have borne it for weeks and I will continue to. In a way, I'm glad to feel it. It means he has told them nothing of the mountain tunnels where the Carvresses, Sun, Guen, and my mother are hiding.

It also means he's still alive.

THE SHADOW of a boy and two guards grows over the corridor walls. His head hangs as he is dragged back to his cell. His knees scrape the stone. He mutters something and gets kicked. I shake my head for the boy who will never learn.

But he lives.

Ignoring my own injuries, I rush to the front of my cell, hands stretching for Ash. My hickory heart cracks like ice when he lifts his face to meet mine. Hope dies like so many crushed butterflies. "Oh, Ash!"

He tries to smile, blood cracking and flaking from his cheek. "I'm all right, Luna," he lies.

The guards scoff as they throw him into his cell. His body makes a sound like spoiled vegetables thrown to the pigs as it lands on straw and stone.

"You're not all right. You're anything but all right." I press to the bars, fingers grasping at his clothes and then his skin. I push comfort into him: baby birds in their nest, warm and safe beneath their mother's feathers. He sighs hard, coughs, and blood spills from his mouth. And in that moment, I wish he had left me to die by the river.

Thoughts of Ben Ni pass through my chest and layer my ribs with both pain and a soft kind of sweetness. If Ash had left me, I would be in the stars with youngest brother and Ash would be safe. I shake my head. It does little good to think of what could have been.

"I kept my promise, didn't I?" He manages a quick smirk, and it kills me. He says this every time he returns. The words are both relieving and cursed because they're getting thinner. Less likely to be repeated.

I cup his face in my hands and it's enough to pull me back from that wish. Because he's here. I am here. Some sort of hard-as-rock, strong-as-sea love links us together. "You did." *This time.* I lay soft kisses on both his bruised cheeks and then his forehead as he shivers and struggles to keep himself upright.

"I should get tortured more often." Ash winks a swollen eye.

I smile, but it's tense and terse. "I love that you can do that." The guards watch us closely. Voyeurs to a painful romance that is not quite blossoming, more like a tight bud wary of opening to frost.

"Do what?" He brings my fist to his bruised lips and brushes them over my knuckles. Filling my wooden heart with bright sparks that might burn me to ash.

"Find light in the darkest place." He found it in me.

The straw should be growing pea shoots for how many tears I have rained upon it. Weeks of weeping water. But then little grows from salt water. And yet he holds me still.

"Luna," Ash whispers, lifting hair that has stuck to my cheek. "You may flood this cell with your grief. As long as you feel it. Hold it."

"Holding it hurts," I blubber. Tasting the salt on my lips. Feeling that sting of too many tears. My heart wants to close over this aching wound.

Ash nods. He knows grief. He has lost a father, a mother, and possibly a sister. "Yes. Until it hurts less and less."

I swipe at my snotty nose and grip his grimy sleeve. "But when will it stop?" The pressure of his loss compresses me to the size of a coriander seed, easily crushed to powder.

Ash shakes his head and I already know what he's going to say. "Your grief for Ben Ni will always be a part of you. It will never stop, exactly. But as time goes on, the shape of it will change and smooth out until you grow around it."

I touch my heart. "Right now, it feels like a throwing star in my chest."

He smiles sadly. A crease in the face of a boy who has been through so much. With me, but also on his own. "Yes."

"I'd like it to become a piece of ocean-polished glass... like the ones Ben Ni used to collect." I manage between the sharp, dagger breaths of someone who is not done crying.

These weeks have changed the shape of my grief. Not yet polished smooth, but not the spinning blade it once was.

Our eyes connect. Bridges of blood and saltwater that are creaking and in need of repair. He looks close to death. I tap my heart and he asks, "What's the shape?"

"Blunted blade."

"Improvement." He touches his forehead to mine and whispers, "We will find a way out of here, I promise. I'm watching and waiting. I saw someone different today. He seemed important." He shrugs his shoulders, a twitch in his cheek. "Maybe I'm moving up in the world." The cheerful words don't match the darkness of his tone.

I shake my head. *Stop making promises*, I want to say. They feel like flesh-wounding arrows, shot to maim. My back stings with the weight of them, but I can't rip away what little hope he has left. "Who did you see?" I ask.

Ash lowers his gaze. Mutters barely audible words in a voice as frightened as a terror mouse facing a cobra's open jaws: "The doctor." He leans against the bars, forehead creased with worry. "He asked so many questions. So many."

My eyes widen with worry, but he's already shaking his head. "I didn't tell him anything, but it made me play those last minutes before we separated from the Carvresses and your family over and over in my head." He taps his temple, a strange seriousness crossing his features like he knows something is wrong but he's not sure what.

I take his blood-crusted hand and squeeze, feeling his anxiety cross into my own chest. "What? What is it?"

The guards strike the bars hard with their batons, patience thinning. We spring apart. "Get back from each other," Wen growls.

Ash retreats to his bed and stares at his hands. There's a scene playing behind his eyes. "I just feel like—like something is missing." He picks at the tattered gold thread of his borrowed uniform. "You know that feeling? When you can't shake the sense that you left something behind?"

I pull my dry lip between my teeth. We did leave something behind: eight Carvresses, a wooden Shen girl, my mother and brother. But that's not what he means and it's starting to scare me. "Try and remember," I urge.

Gi Shi bashes the bars again, his eyes like darts. "Be quiet! Or they'll send the boy up for another session."

We close our mouths, but they can't stop us from *feeling* each other, and they certainly can't stop us from bridging the gap with our eyes. Caramel and saltwater. In that gaze is a ripple over the ocean. Something strong and steady, waiting to rise.

2

LYE

THE CHOICES IN
FRONT OF US

I close my eyes and I see him. Golden, chiseled, and broad. A crown upon his wicked head. Purple silk and rare jewels on every finger. His lip curls with disgust as he stands over the bodies of my brother and Luna. The idea that blood could even come close to splattering his silk slippers would make the emperor gag.

I see their deaths like they're tattooed on the inside of my eyelids, and I can't stand it.

A knock on the thick tree trunk vibrates upward to where I sit, balanced between two boughs. Sitting in this tree outside the monastery, where I watched my brother chained to a post in the square many months ago, brings me strange comfort.

"I'm not sure this is the most appropriate place for a general to be, Lye." Joka's fine-as-silk voice reminds me of where I am and what my responsibilities are. I stare downward into the face of a friend who suffers as much as I do. His sister is captive—imprisoned in the palace miles and miles away. His mother and brother are in danger also. A fragmented family like scattered tea leaves, leaving no future to tell.

Unlike mine, his Atmosphere is focused, a chipmunk checking its winter stores or preparing for bad weather. He's right to be this way. There is much to do.

From my position, I view the entire monastery, overflowing with refugees from the battle of Black Sail City and the progressive attacks on other islands. Tents nudge each other, filling the archery field. Children, many orphans, play in the square where daggers were once thrown at Shen dummies. The Char world is a beautiful mess. I am at the head of the cleaning party and partially to blame for the chaos.

"I was just taking a moment to think." I climb down the smooth trunk and land gracefully on the ground in front of Joka. Cold seeps into my slippers. Winter is approaching, and though snow and ice are not something we need worry about on the Char islands, they are a serious threat to those hidden on the mainland.

The message Luna and Ash sent said the Carvresses were hidden. My fear rises like filthy water in a deep, damp footprint. They are safe from the emperor, but without Ash, they may not understand the complicated nature of their refuge. The mountain can be safe for someone who knows its maze of catacombs and where to shelter from the steady descent of the glacier as winter creeps down its steep face.

Where the chancellor sits among all of this is unknown. Wherever he is, I'm sure his thin body will be a stick in the spokes of any good plan.

"Lye." Joka taps my shoulder impatiently; he's been waiting a good minute for me to come out of my thoughts. "What are you thinking?"

I smile briefly as I run a hand over my ridged sycamore arm, picturing the chancellor as a stick and snapping him over my knee. I let the Char black cloth slip back over my scars. "I'm thinking of Ash and Luna," I reply, half honest. "About how much I want to storm the palace. I'm also thinking my wish is a waste because I no longer operate on my own." How do I leave them to die for the "greater good"? It's an impossible choice, and yet the only option.

Joka nods, a tightness to his jaw. "They are on my mind all the time too." We begin walking back to the monastery, passing through the newly strengthened gates. The Char are impressive in their resilience. Not wanting to sit still and dwell on their loss, they've put much effort into fortifying this refuge. I bow my head as we pass Char of all ages. I take in each face, scrub their likenesses into my memory, and add them to a pile. These lives are on my shoulders now.

"They plague my dreams, Joka. You don't know the depths of darkness the emperor will allow and what his advisors are capable of." A flash of purple silk as I blink. A dull-witted man child, but dangerous in his ignorance. If the chancellor is not whispering oily evil into his ears, stars would wither at the other possible influences in his life. I swallow. Try to focus on the task at hand and the choices we have in front of us.

Joka stops, turns to me. "You can tell me, Lye."

I shake my head. I don't want to fill his head with black clouds of fear and pain. Telling him how bad it could be will not help and I know I must weather the uncertainty alone. "Why would I willingly plunge a knife into your chest, friend? No, it is better this way." I know how to hold hurt against my heart in silence.

Joka closes his mouth, following me into the great hall where a fog of sesame, soy, and garlic welcomes us. I lick my lips. Char food, like the Char people, is heavy and bold in flavor. Every mouthful packing a punch.

Char soldiers salute their new general as I pass. Leaning against the wall slurping noodles from dark broth. Big slices of ginger floating like rootless islands between green rings of spring onion.

In the back of the room, Setsu Yan turns a table over with ease. He works quickly, his thick fingers more agile than I would have imagined. When he sees me, he lifts his head briefly. "General Koh," he says before turning his attention to deconstructing the furniture. Every spare piece of timber is needed to make shelters. Char islands may not get snow, but the wet season is brutal.

"How are you, Setsu?" I stare down at his blistered hands. The man has barely slept nor stilled since we arrived.

"I am well," he grunts. "Ah, Joka, hold this for me." He drops the end of the table into Joka's thin arms and yanks out the pins holding it together with his oak fingers. My eyes blink rapidly and widen, even though I should be used to this bear of a man and his extraordinary strength.

The table collapses into pieces. "Papa, have you slept at all?" Joka asks, craning his neck to search for the weary, avoiding eyes of his father.

"I shall sleep when we are safe. I shall sleep when this is over." Sounds like a mantra. A song that can't find its end.

I breathe in a sad breath full of dying sails and journeys yet to take. "Then you shall never sleep." His brows fall from the ledge of his forehead with sadness. His Atmosphere is the confused, scurrying purpose of a forest hog collecting its unending supplies of flowers and the wind blowing the heads from said flowers. "Setsu, you *must* rest." I place my hand on his tree trunk–sized arm. My hand that holds no magic has become more of a delight than a curse in these calmer days. Because I can touch people without harming them. I understand the reason behind it better now, though the Carvress said it was the "cost." I wonder if it happened this way to bring some balance to my gifts. Give me a Char perspective.

Setsu straightens, a hulk over my slip of a form. My hand drops. "Do *you* rest, General?" he challenges. I stare at the floor as waking nightmares stretch up to strangle me. I sleep, but there's nothing restful about it. How can I rest when my brain swells with my brother's torture? "Hmph!" Setsu takes my silence as confirmation of his assumptions. "As I thought."

I survey the busy monastery with its hall clear of all rows of tables. Soon it will be a defensible fort and the Char refugees will be safe within these walls. It's time to plan our next move. Strands of plans pull me in opposite directions. The palace with Ash and Luna, or my village and the Carvresses?

I think I know the answer.

Setsu faces me, arms full of timber and empty of the wife and children he yearns to hold. His Char uniform is worn and in need of repair. I look up. "I seek reassurance as I plan our next move. What do you think it should be?"

Setsu chuckles. "Not one can make this decision. The leaders of the other islands have arrived. It would be wise to call a council."

I half roll my eyes before I catch Setsu glaring. My experience with councils, bureaucracy, and the like always ended the same way: stalemates at best, executions for those who were particularly stubborn at worst. "Very well, but I am not wasting time discussing this for hours and hours. It needs to be decided swiftly."

Joka and Setsu exchange a glance suggesting a Char council may be nothing like a Shen one, and this both intrigues and worries me.

3

KI ANAH

A LOVE STRONGER
THAN MAGIC

Ki Anah guesses they have been in this strange cave cathedral for at least two weeks, easing into a third. Their only link to the outside, a small porthole punched halfway up the wall, changes from sunlight to moonlight. She huffs. The glow worm light never changes. When they sleep, they cover their eyes with clothing or their own arms, but light pushes through any crack like an illness. She blinks tired eyes. Sleep is like trying to catch a mountain stingray—elusive, precious, almost impossible.

She sits high up on the stone stairs that wind into darkness, looking upon the group of travelers, missing two. One she loved with all her heart. Her care for the other, Ash, spun as slowly as a grandmother spider's web, meticulous and beautiful, sometimes taking weeks to complete. They were only at the start of constructing a bond when he rushed to rescue her daughter. But she could tell it was going to be a very strong web.

Tunnels branch in all directions from the cavernous space, leading through the mountain to who knows where. They haven't looked very far. Waiting near the entrance seems safest. When the Char come, Ki Anah wants to be easy to find. She shivers, hugging knees to her chest. Although she's unsure of how much time has passed, she's sure they cannot stay here forever.

For now, they wait.

Sun bounds up the stairs, long strong legs taking two at a time. He sits beside her, handing her a pink tuber from the pond. "Mama, you should eat." He crunches down on the root vegetable.

Ki Anah takes the root. "Thank you, Sun." At least they will not run out of food for a while, with only Sun and herself needing real sustenance. It's also a relief they're the only ones who need to eliminate waste. She shakes her head, pitying anyone who accidentally explores *that* tunnel. She takes a bite. The taste like radish but diluted. A poor flavor. Her eyes lift to the sky. *Oh, how I wish I had a spice pouch, a wok, some oil!*

Sun lifts his gaze also. "Do you think the porthole leads to the outside?"

She leans her head on his hard shoulder. "I think so, eldest son. I feel the air blow through it from time to time and it smells fresh." She wiggles her fingers in front of her face. "Like pine and frost." It matters very little. It's far too small for them to pass through.

Sun grunts. "Everything smells like frost in this place. It's so damn cold." He holds his foot near his mother's nose. "Even my foot smells frosty!"

Ki Anah slaps the back of his head for cursing, and for putting his dirty foot under her nose. His foot decidedly does not smell like frost, it smells like unwashed, stinky young man. "At least we are safe. The Carvresses are safe. That little girl"—she points at Guen, sitting near the edge of the pond, legs wide, staring at her birchwood hands—"is safe."

Sun wrings his hands, bounces his balsawood foot on the step below. Ki Anah waits for the question that plagues them both. The question they have been holding against their flesh hearts as they went about the business of survival. "Do you think *they* are safe, Mama?"

Ki Anah doesn't know how to answer since she's never been a good liar. Sun will read the doubt in her face, so she answers with the truth. "Luna is formidable, fierce, and smart. If anyone could survive, she could. And Ash's love for her is just as powerful. That kind of love is stronger than magic. It has built-in survival that will outlive any evil."

Sun grimaces as he stands, running a hand through his dark hair that's starting to flop over instead of stand straight as cane crops. "Ugh! But why did he have to be a Shen?" he groans, though she knows he doesn't mean it. She saw the respect between the two boys. It's the reason she accepted the young Shen so readily. Sun's eyes are on the young girl, Guen, who looks lost and scared. He begins to descend. Turning around, he says, "You didn't really answer my question."

Ki Anah smiles sadly. Her whole body aches for not knowing what has happened to her daughter, her husband, her son Joka. But it's out of her control. She has a task in front of her that is solid and known: Protect the Carvresses and stay alive. "No. I did not."

Sun sighs as deep as Ki Anah's favorite soup pot, broad shoulders sagging. She watches him walk with the weight of a thousand stones, right until he reaches Guen. Then he stands straighter, lightens his expression. The stones tumble down his back like grains from a pierced sack. She is a child. An un-poisoned Shen child. Perhaps the most important task is protecting her innocence.

THE COALSTONE CARVESS, Sifah, coasts up the stairs. Wood should be noisy, clackety, but Sifah glides. Ki Anah regards the Carvress with mixed feelings. What she's learned about Sifah's origins, her past as a Shen princess, has made her more approacha-ble than before. Less of a goddess, more of a person. A creature with flaws who has lied and made mistakes.

The wooden woman stands over Ki Anah. "It is cold, no?"

Ki Anah nods. "You feel it?"

Sifah frowns. Wooden mouth creasing and Ki Anah finds herself wondering what she looked like before her brother, the first Shen emperor, turned her to wood. Was her hair coal black like Ki Anah's or golden brown like Luna's? Were her eyes dark or colored? What element did she possess in her Shen form? But she doesn't ask these questions. Tradition holds her back from such impertinence.

"I feel it a little yes, but it cannot easily harm me." Sifah bends down closer to Ki Anah. "It can easily harm you, Ki Anah Yan. You should come down from here and sit by the fire."

A strange yelp crossed with a growl comes from one the many hollows. Sun stomps away from the fire, long knife in hand. That sound means potential meat. The birchwood child, Guen, trails after him like a pup. Ki Anah stands suddenly. "Yes, perhaps you are right. But right now, I must help my son."

She stands, grasping at stray glow worms. They feel squishy but hard, like rubber. She yanks them from the stone, and they glow bright and panicked as she rushes to meet her son.

She catches his shoulder. "Ah, Sun! I'm coming with you." Her blood rushes at the thought. It has been too long since she's been able to hunt. Guen's tiny wooden hand reaches for Sun's. He takes it and looks down at her with a quick grin.

"Guess now's as good a time as any to teach you how we hunt."

With one hand gripping the wriggling, glowing worms and the other tightly wrapped around her knife, Ki Anah enters one of the unlit tunnels with son and girl. Eight pairs of wooden eyes follow them curiously.

The yelp-growl sounds again.

"I don't know this call," Guen whispers. Her little wooden limbs clunking together, she has none of the grace of the Carvresses. She doesn't seem fearful, merely curious, and this impresses Ki Anah.

Sun narrows his eyes and pricks his ears. "Sounds like a small creature. Small and quick, maybe a fox or a rabbit."

Ki Anah frowns. She prays it's not a piranha rabbit. She prays it has enough meat on it for a decent meal. They steal through the cave, wooden foot over wooden foot. Cherry hips cracking. The yelp-growl echoes down the tunnel, and this time is answered by several others.

Sun hands Guen a small dagger. "Never let go of your weapon."

Guen nods her little head with a solemn expression, catching every word Sun utters like they are drops of rain to a thirsty desert. The child has imprinted on him, and Ki Anah hopes her eldest son takes this responsibility seriously. "Why aren't there any glow worms in here?" she asks.

Sun shrugs. "Maybe they're claustrophobic."

Guen's sweet voice lilts over the word. "Clost-o-fo-what?"

Ki Anah giggles and pats the child's hard shoulder. "It means afraid of small spaces."

"Oh," Guen says with a funny little sigh. "I like small places. Makes me feel… safe."

The worms provide wan light and barely hold back the pitch black. Ki Anah shudders; she prefers the open air and the salt spray of an endless ocean. Her elbow brushes the side of the cave and feels ice. This place is as foreign as if she were living in the sky.

Sun taps his mother's shoulder, whispering, "Over there," pointing with his knife. Meat would help her feel more at home. Ki Anah moves the light slowly to where the tips of Sun's knife directs and the red eyes of a creature she's never seen before widen, as do large jaws with rows of sharp-as-sewing-needle teeth. Ki Anah gasps, but Sun edges forward.

The thing growls. Its ears sit straight up like a rabbit, but that's where the similarities end. Its spiked red back bristles and its thick pink tail swishes across the cold floor. It scratches the dirt like it's about to charge. Sun attacks first.

Ki Anah would shake her head if she had time. Sun always rushes headfirst into danger without thinking. The size of the thing is not the problem. The sharp teeth, though frightening, aren't either. It's the spines on its back. The creature shuffles and sways, aiming these spikes at Sun. Guen crouches, knife out and ready. Ki Anah sweeps the space.

The creature yelps and more red eyes appear, glowing in the worm light. Sun snarls as he searches for a place to stab. He lunges and a spike flies at his neck. He falls backward, a long, red quill embedded in his skin.

Ki Anah rolls her eyes. "You are not being a very good teacher, Sun." Dozens of red eyes crawl closer.

Guen pounces on the one who hurt Sun. Spikes fly but bounce off her birchwood skin.

Sun shouts commands, instructing Guen, and she kills the creature quickly and humanely. Ki Anah lifts the light, hoping it will scare the others. Eyes and tails everywhere. *How can there be so many? Where did they come from?*

She turns, and the light reflects back at her. She blinks at a mirror image of herself, Sun with a spine sticking out of his neck, and Guen holding the dead creature by the tail. And what seemed like dozens of other animals shrinks to a few. But still too many. They growl and gather, slowly stalking the trio.

Ki Anah gulps, wondering if she can outrun the little monsters that look like they've come up from the pits of hell.

Sun curses. Guen hisses and waves the dead animal in front of them, but they seem unphased. Sun grabs Guen's skirt and pulls her to him.

Jaws snap at Ki Anah's heels as she steps back.

They are surrounded. Ki Anah's heart beats a proud rhythm. She will not let this be its last song so she grips her knife and readies herself for a fight.

The ceiling rumbles, softly at first but growing louder with every beat. Pieces of ice and dirt rain down on their heads. Drumbeats vibrate through the cave. Their reflections shudder and wobble. The sound is rhythmic, manmade. It is… music. The primal tempo thrums through Ki Anah's chest. The creatures startle and flee, disappearing through cracks too small for an adult to fit through.

Ki Anah steps closer to her reflection. Palm out, she touches her own mirrored hand. It burns with cold. Her hand is coasting over a solid slab of ice. She pushes on it then kicks it with her foot. It's as sturdy and impenetrable as stone.

Sun curses loudly and slaps his forehead. "Ice wall," he shouts, like he knows exactly what it is.

"Eh?" Ki Anah manages as she stares at the rumbling ceiling.

An unyielding *drum, drum, drum* punctuates Sun's words. "Ash warned me. He said something about ice walls and that we needed to be on the right side when winter closed in."

The noise grows louder as Ki Anah shouts, "Are we on the right side of them now?"

Sun clutches the red spine and pulls it from his neck. A thin stream of blood runs along his collarbone. "I think so——" He shakes his head. "Mama, I'm not sure. It was all said in such a hurry." His eyes lift upward. "What in coral and weed is that noise?"

Guen, dragging the carcass of the beast behind her like an over-loved doll, answers, "That's the drumbeat of the Dark West tribe."

4

LUNA

BLOOD EVERYWHERE

"Now that your wounds have healed, it's your turn, little Char girl." The Earth guard chortles with a high and rough voice. Fear reaches around the doors of my hickory heart, managing to get a grip on the frame.

Ash summons strength from who knows where and rises. Rushing the bars like he could break them. His chest hits with a thud and he strains to grab at the guard. "Stay away from her!" he screams, his body struggling to stay together. Fresh blood seeps through his clothes as he tears what was barely clotted.

Gi Shi smiles wide with black teeth like the chancellor's, making my skin crawl. My heart thumps like a shield and I want to hide behind it. I want to, but I can't. He teases Ash, baton hovering at head height threateningly. "What kind of Shen protects a Char girl?" He shakes his head, ashamed. "You must have something loose in that thick head of yours." He sighs and bounces the baton over his shoulder like a fishing pole. "I suppose we'll soon know what's loose and where it is once the doctor is through with you."

Ash breathes hard as the guard places his key in the lock of my cell. I pin myself to the wall, knowing there's nowhere to go. Love pushes one to do foolish, heroic things. I can't stop him, and Ash should know it will do no good. But he lunges at Gi Shi, just grazing his bare arm through the bars. The guard drops his keys, curses, and lifts his baton to strike position.

Love is the wind at my back. I jump up, summoning what I can; a handful of half-dead slater bugs scuttle up the guard's pant leg. He jiggles and hops and it's enough to distract him so he'll listen to me. "I'm sure the doctor doesn't like to be kept waiting." I come to the cell door and place my hands behind my back. "I'm ready," I say, with no conviction and growing dread, because I have a pretty good idea of the pain to come. I've *felt* it.

Ash falls to his knees, strength sapped. Hands bloodied as he hugs his chest. "Luna. No."

"It's my turn," I say, shakily but sternly. "Let me take it." I allow the guard to escort me out at the tip of his sword, keeping my eyes, ears, and Blood sense on alert.

"I *feel* you, Luna!" Ash shouts.

"Shut your traitor mouth," the other guard, Wen, snaps.

I close my eyes, thinking of kisses and heated skin and heartbeats that will never match. *Oh, how I wish you didn't, Ash!*

As we ascend, the world gets grander, heavier. Draped in velvet and gilded with gold. My slippers, once soaked in damp and dirt, brush carpet and warmth. The guard prods me every now and then, but he doesn't break the skin. And I'm not sure if its kindness or simply preserving me for future harm. As we go up, my sense of Ash fades like a thick fog turning to mist. The strand connecting us becoming thinner and thinner until it simply teases apart and dissolves. I count it as a blessing, but he may not feel the same.

We're on the ground floor and I blink as natural sunlight dusts my lashes. My eyes roll up and down enormous tapestries the height of two Char huts depicting graceful and serene elementals beings. There's no hate burning in their eyes. They seem peaceful. The elements they summon help and heal, not fight or injure. Nothing like most Shen I have come across. I scowl as we walk beneath their glowing, I'm-better-than-you regards, wishing I could spit on the floor without having my ribs parted by a sword.

"Where are we going?" I ask as I'm led further and further away from our cells. Wherever it is, it can't be the same place Ash has been.

Gi Shi grunts his reply. "You'll know soon enough." He nudges me through empty halls with painted lanterns the size of our pig pen hanging from the ceiling. Huge rooms with black lacquered benches line the walls. I search for animals, extending my Blood power outward. My heart beats steady, but my body trembles at the exertion. My sense lands upon something but is quickly pulled back as I run out of energy. I pause. The shape of it was large, but its power seemed small, compressed.

Gi Shi uses the flat of his sword to smack my back. "Move!"

I trudge forward, wondering what it was and where.

Finally, I'm pushed into a large kitchen where maids stare with frightened, distrustful eyes. Their superior shouts at them to get back to work, and their eyes drop to enviable cleavers. The familiar sound of chopping vegetables and butchering hens wraps me in a quick dream of home. The strange sour tang of citrus and pepper sting of chili breaks that dream. Food is different here: lighter in color and scent, noodles are clear, and broth is yellow. I admit, it smells delicious. I tilt my head watching a woman shave brown chunks from a palm sugar cake. That, I recognize.

As we pass, I make note of a cage in the corner where several live chickens await their fate.

The guard winds us around tables laden with herbs and spices until he's turning the handle on a thick wooden door to the left of the window. Things may be moving in my favor. I smile. They're taking me outside.

"That smile won't last long, Char girl." Gi Shi opens the door with a nasty chuckle and my fingers tingle with power. I reach for everything all at once. I close my eyes, sensing Blood everywhere, in the trees and galloping across the courtyard. Padded feet come for me. Wings turn to me. Monkeys shriek. Birds call. It fills me and saves me—I am free.

Again the guard laughs, though this one seems nervous. He ducks instinctually as dozens of claws and paws land above his head. I lift my gaze, expecting the sun to be blotted by hundreds of animals, but there is only the *teck, teck, teck* of their hands and beaks knocking on wood.

I hadn't noticed the smell, waxy and new.

The guard prods me with his baton. "You think we'd just let you walk outside? How foolish do you think we are?"

I step into a large timber box. Every crack, every hole is sealed with wax and lacquer. "Do I need to answer that question?" I mutter. My animal companions scratch at the boards, trying to get inside, but they can't. Their hearts cry out, frantic and incensed.

Sitting at the back on a humble stool, draped in an apron flecked with blood, counting instruments that sparkle in the lantern light, is the doctor. He pats the chair in the center of the room as if offering me seat in a noodle bar. "Please, sit."

I shake my head. "I'd rather stand."

The doctor frowns, stroking a long, thin beard like a black rat's tail. "Sit or I shall ensure your *friend* suffers greatly back in his cell. He will wish for death, but it will not be granted. Not until we're done learning everything about you." Outside, the bloodcurdling screams of howling monkeys makes the doctor rub at his ears. They pound the roof of the box maddeningly, and I wonder if they could pull it apart.

"They cannot penetrate this box. It was constructed especially for you, Luna Yan. So we can study your power and physiology without danger to ourselves. It's double thickness, so it is quite useless to attempt to break it." He winces as the screaming reaches ear-popping decibels. "Though I do wish it could have fit inside the palace." I wobble a little at the strain of extending my Blood powers through the walls. He points again at the chair with chipped, stained fingers. "No matter. Sit."

"What are you going to do to me?" I ask, eyes on the various instruments on his table that look like nothing I've ever seen before.

His voice is honey smooth. Too composed for whatever is about to happen. "Today will be a mild investigation. Unbutton your shirt."

I stare incredulous at his clinical expression. His eyes are ashen gray, the color of deadness. "I will not."

The doctor sighs like I'm already exhausting to him. "Guard!" My guard appears in the doorway. "Please return to the boy's cell and begin ripping his fingernails out one by one." Gi Shi's eyebrows rise as does bile in my throat. If I can stop even one sliver of harm to Ash, I must do it. I lift my fingers to my shirt and unbutton it until my wooden sternum is revealed.

"Good girl," he murmurs and I wish to snarl and snap. Sting with venom. Tear with teeth. But I bite down and hold on to my restraint. For Ash. He puts his hand up to the guard. "Never mind, you may leave us now." Gi Shi sighs with relief, revealing even he has limits, and leaves.

Carefully, and without touching my skin, the doctor straps my wrists to the chair. It kills me to do so, but I comply because Ash is in a cell at the wrong end of a spear and the bludgeoning end of a baton. I cannot be the reason he's hurt. Not anymore.

The doctor lifts a long, thin drilling needle attached to a hand winder. "Hold still, Char child. I'd hate to kill you on our first investigation but I am very curious to know where the wood ends and the flesh begins."

I do as I'm told as the forest surrounding the palace screams to the sky like the earth is grieving.

PAIN STRIKES and stretches. My fists scrunch, sweat runs rivers across my forehead and into my hair. But I am quiet. I stare at a knothole, plugged with wax. I stare so hard it begins to look like an eye. A kind, sympathetic eye. I focus on it, pretend it's my mother, watching me, telling me it's going to be all right. The doctor pats my shoulder and I drop my gaze from the ceiling. *Nothing is all right.*

"Very interesting," he says while running a cloth over the drill he just slowly worked into my sternum. "The wall of your heart is entirely wooden." He unties my wrists, and my hands fly to my heart. Expecting a gaping wound, blood gushing out. Instead, I find a small hole and a dot of blood. One dot for pain that stretched over the mountain like a storm. Pain still bubbling and brewing like lava beneath thin crust earth. Something deeper is wrong though. I breathe in small bursts. Deep breaths feel impossible.

Outside, the animals have grown quiet, but I sense their presence.

Every now and then the scrape of their claws on the roof of the box reminds me they're still here. They still listen and wait.

The doctor's eyes rise to the ceiling. "You Blood power is impressive. I wonder if all Char would have similar strength if awakened, or if you are unique." He narrows his eyes, inspecting me like a lizard in a bottle. His lips purse, making his face even more prune like, and he shakes his head. As if me being special is an absurd idea.

I snort. It spreads pain throughout my ribcage like a hundred termites are gnawing their way out of my body. "Without the Keeper, you shall never know the answer to that question."

The doctor strolls to the door like he's just finished a cup of tea rather than a round of torture, and lets Gi Shi in. "Where is the Keeper?" he asks with his back to me.

I laugh, bitter and quiet because it's all I can manage. "I don't know."

"Where are the Carvresses?" he asks as Gi Shi approaches, weapon in hand.

"I don't know."

The doctor turns and frowns, a slight quiver to his lips. "They will be displeased."

I rise slowly from my chair, gripping the arms for support. "I could give a monkey's behind about the emperor's displeasure," I splutter, then draw in a shallow breath.

The doctor's hand flies out, whiplike, and slaps my face hard, stunning me silent. Everything in his manner has been so controlled until now. My cheek stings, but I don't give him the satisfaction of seeing my discomfort. I glare, unaffected.

The doctor wipes his hands on his apron, muttering to the floor, "You will care, mark my words." He orders the guard to take me away.

Gi Shi yanks me by the arm, and I hang loosely from his grasp like fruit about to fall. I have nothing left: no energy, no breath. Only the tiniest Blood.

He marches through the wooden tunnel and inside the palace. As we pass through the kitchen, howling monkeys hammer the window, their wide lantern eyes scanning the room. Their round, ever-open mouths scare the maids. I flick my fingers with my last shred of energy.

A rooster busts through its cage, tearing around the kitchen, traipsing through the emperor's lunch, and crowing loudly. Feathers fly and chaos clatters.

It lifts my lips as we leave.

They do not notice the tail of a baby howling monkey slip down from the chimney on the back of its mother. They are too busy chasing the rooster about the kitchen to see it crawl across the floor and clamber up my leg, hiding beneath my oversized tunic, tiny claws tickling my skin.

My smile broadens. My Blood never fails.

5
LYE

BEAUTY IN BUREAUCRACY

Joka escorts me to a large tent in the middle of the archery field. His dark eyes are on the sky, naming constellations as we pass under them—the Tree of a Thousand Branches, one for every timber the Char use for their limbs. We simply call it the Earth tree. The Nine Sisters constellation is the same. Nine long, lithe shapes like stalks of wheat. He points at another, calling it the Ghost Dagger of Cowardly Soldiers; a knife turning in like a scythe, aimed at the coward's own heart. It's strange that Shen and Char share some names and not others. I look down at my sycamore arm, thinking about the Carvresses and their origins. We share far more than we could have ever imagined.

Joka points his thin arm at a swirl of stars making up what Shen call the Elemental Wheel. "There's the Whirlpool of Hopeless Love. See the way the stars get brighter as they near the middle?"

The grass is squelchy under our feet. The rain has eased for the night but more promises to visit soon.

"Why are so many of your place and constellation names tragic and sad?" I ask.

Joka scratches his bamboo neck. It's beginning to age, turning golden, especially at the rings. I watch him swallow and my heart does a strange little jump in my chest. "I don't know. I never thought of them as tragic, more romantic."

I giggle. "How is 'hopeless love' romantic?"

Joka pauses in the field, blinking up at the bright, unwavering lights we pin our stories to. "You say our names are tragic and sad, but they always start with love. Love doesn't always have a happy ending, but it's romantic nonetheless. It's worth the suffering, right?"

I run my hand over scars forever set in the wood grain of my arm. Crimes done for the love of an emperor. I'm not sure I agree. Love still feels like a foreign thing to me. A strange, shy ocean creature not ready to breach the surface.

I don't answer his question. "Are there any constellations that don't have me wanting to jump from a cliff?"

Joka chuckles. He steps closer and points to the sky. "See there, that group of stars that looks like a heart?"

I squint, leaning closer to see where he's pointing. The ends of my short hair brush his jaw, my cheek touches his bamboo neck. The shy creature surfaces, eyes blinking at a sky it's never seen before. "I can't see it."

When he talks, I feel his deep voice vibrating against my face. "Right there." He traces the shape with his finger, and I start to wish I would never see it. Then he could lean closer and closer trying to show me. I hold my breath.

I see the heart now. I blink, sailing on this moment, this closeness, for a second longer. Just one. His Atmosphere is shaded ferns and spring rain and I wish I could shelter in it. But I can't. I step back. "Oh yes, there it is. What's the story?"

Joka sighs as I move away. And I'd like to think it's because he enjoyed being close to me too, but maybe he's just tired of educating me on all things Char. "It's a tale of a love so strong and enduring that it extended past the couple and into the atmosphere. Actually moving the stars to form a new constellation. And as the stars moved, pieces of the sky fell to the earth and split in two, creating the heartbirds. Two creatures that would forever find each other, their breast only making the shape of a heart when they embrace."

"Pretty tale," I manage with a tightness in my throat, half joy, half agony. We arrive, the tent glowing with color and smells of smoke. Within, male voices rumble and grate against each other like gemstones in a velvet pouch.

Joka steps back from the entrance. "It is a pretty tale. Nothing more. I don't believe real love to be like that."

I turn. "You don't?"

He reaches over my shoulder, lifting the flap to reveal warmth and light. Tradition and brutishness. "No. Real love is messy and flawed. Sometimes tragic. But I think you work at it to make it good. It doesn't just 'happen'."

I stall in the entrance, gathering my strength as Lye, Char and Keeper. "But always worth the suffering?"

Joka smiles, his face a perfectly flawed mess of mixed emotion. "Always."

I breathe in, filling my chest with smoke and hope, and step over the threshold. Joka doesn't follow and I turn to him. "You're not coming?"

Joka dissolves into the night. A talking shadow. A support I don't deserve. "This is for village elders and military leaders. I'm not invited."

I frown. "I could invite you."

"I'm not needed."

I wonder if I could promote him so he could enter. I shake my head at my selfishness. That path only leads to one place. I stop short of saying, *I need you.* Because truthfully, I don't.

The tent flap closes. Heady jasmine, sweat, and timber fogs the air. I am ready; I have to be. Anticipation sparks in my elemental hand.

Char do everything differently and this is no exception. I jump as a green dragon snaps its teeth an inch from my face. A blue murder bird flaps its wings, circling the space. There is color and life in every corner. A small laugh escapes the side of my mouth. Beauty in bureaucracy. Char always surprise me.

Setsu rises from his seat, pipe in hand. I have met some of these men, and he takes me around the tent introducing me to village elders from Coalstone Village, Black Sail City, Sand Otter Island, Crow's Nest Island, and Bird Cage Island. There are no representatives from Cockle Fan, Yellow Fin, Abalone, or Pearl Shell Beach. We hope that's because they are safe and have no need to seek refuge.

I am the only woman.

The Char elders observe me with differing levels of curiosity and trust. But they share the same serious Atmosphere, a need to protect the interests of their homes and their people. A humble beaver doing its best to strengthen a dam that must be preserved.

I swallow my nerves like a bundle of uncooked noodles and move to the center of the tent. I'm the general, I can do this. I clear my throat and swipe my hand over my fluffy hair. "Thank you for attending this council. We have an important decision to make and—"

The elder of Crow's Nest Island, Po Ka, who has been living at the refuge the longest, coughs and grunts. "Apa ini? What is she doing?" he asks, hands up in the air as if asking the sky. He shakes a pipe at me in frustration. "Kelp and kippers!" The exclamation makes me want to giggle, but I force it down.

The men thump their thighs with fists and grumble. "I'm sorry, I don't—" My hands drops as someone starts a Call and they all join, drowning me out. I knew it was too good to be true. Putting me at the head, naming me general, was foolish. Char are patriarchal in the extreme. *Why would they ever accept a skinny Shen turned Char girl like me?* I feel like the kelp the elder referred to, battered and raked by the waves. Unable to move from my sandy bed.

Setsu claps his hands like thunder. Oak on flesh. The men stop their chatter and give him attention. "Elders, please! This is General Lye's first council. Instead of shouting at her, how about someone hand her a pipe so we can get started."

My shoulders are pinned back, my head darting back and forth like a frightened mouse. The men stare with crinkled, sea-worn eyes, shaking wooden arms and feet at me. I slink around the noise and fold under Setsu's welcoming shadow. "I don't want a pipe!" I manage between frustrated, grating teeth. "I want to discuss Char future. We need to make plans. We need to decide how to proceed."

Setsu chuckles. "Then you better take the pipe." The elder of Black Sail City hands me a pipe with a wide grin. I turn it in my palm. It's pink and pretty and covered in carvings of snub-nosed dolphins. I hold it like it's full of gunpowder, liable to explode. The Char elders settle into the rim of the canvas room. Each leader spaced evenly apart. He gestures for me to do the same. "You ready?" he asks.

Ready for what?

"I will be heard first!" the elder of Sand Otter Island states. The round man stomps his foot aggressively, robe swishing over a pair of wooden knees.

Po Ka stands and grins, his wooden forehead glowing in the lantern light. "I have been here far longer than you, Enah En. I shall be heard first."

I await the inevitable, where men stand and raise their fists, scratch circular patterns in the dirt and decorate it with blood. But the men simply sit down and draw smoke into their mouths from pipes, eyes on the space between them.

"Midnight mauler," Enah En murmurs between breaths.

"Vampire owl," Po Ka says with a grin the devil would be worried about.

The first battle begins.

Smoke creatures grow and fill the empty space. The mauler stalks and the owl swoops in large taunting circles. Its long fangs take snippets out of the mauler with every dive. My sycamore arm rests on my knees, my hands clasp together, loose and relaxed. I am transfixed. Emersed in a world I know so little about. But oh, how I want to understand. I want to be a part of it. I want to play.

The mauler fades, becoming more mist than smoke as the owl continues to attack. It arches its back and lunges one last time, but it cannot match the vampire owl, which swoops in and cuts the smoke creature in half. Po Ka stands triumphant. All is quiet and the men turn their attention to the elder of Crow's Nest Island.

"The threat to Crow's Nest is over. But the threat to Char is not. As long as the emperor lives, we will never be safe. I know we are the smaller force, but we have defeated large armies. Plus, the odds are more in our favor than ever before. We have seriously depleted the Shen army. I say we storm the palace."

Some nod agreeance. Some are silent.

I stand, thunder rippling across my chest. Storms swirl in my fingers but I keep them there, cycling upon each other and building strength. "There's nothing I want more than to see the emperor removed from his throne, but storming the palace as we are—"

The men stare at me like I have just insulted their mothers. All of them. Setsu holds up the pipe. "If you want to lead the discussion, you must follow council rules."

I sit down. Light my pipe and try to follow tradition. I concentrate on a vanity bat, black eyes and sharp claws. Chains of gold hanging from its wings. A pink bat extends from my pipe and hovers over the space. It's wispy and not as well formed as the last animals. Its head too big and wings too stout. A large hoarder bear ambles underneath. We begin.

I lick my lips. The smoke tastes like blueberries and coriander. I don't win this battle, but I enjoy it immensely. The elder of Bird Cage Island earns his turn to speak. He talks of the Shen prisoners held on its shores. The immediate danger that the army could return for them at any moment but also the cost of feeding and housing them. It's a very legitimate concern.

We fight, we win, we lose. Everyone is heard and everyone has a point. It's beautiful and fierce and like no council I have attended. And I wouldn't mind if it lasted all night. But it's obvious to me all concerns lead to the same place.

I finish off the liquid eel with a snap of my diamond-back crocodile, clapping joyfully at my victory. The Char men applaud me too, embracing this scrap of a girl. Belonging is a concept I don't like to toy with too often, but this feels close. I put down my pipe. "It seems to me every one of you shares a similar concern. If we don't find a way to remove the emperor, this will never end. We could storm the palace, but even if we succeeded, the Shen won't simply bow to a Char sitting on their throne. The claim must be righteous."

The men listen but I sense doubt like deer testing an icy pond. They're not ready to plunge into freezing water on a whim.

"We must restore the Carvresses to the throne. It's our chance to end the fighting and unite our two territories."

The conversation builds on this idea. On how and when and the number of soldiers needed. Nothing is decided, but at least they're open to it. They are ready to consider putting resources into this plan.

"First we have to retrieve the Carvresses. That must take priority," Po Ka shouts, his thorny antlered stag stamping its hoof after charging my monster squirrel.

Setsu speaks out of turn. But because he's Setsu, it is allowed. "General Lye's idea is a good one. But you are all forgetting what is most important. We face a much more pressing danger that we must address before anything else."

I spin to face him, heart racing at whatever the next big terror could be. "And what is that, Setsu Yan?"

"Starvation."

6

LUNA

LIKE A LASSO OVER THE MOON

Air travels through the hole in my chest, cold and clammy. Blood seeps, rubber sap slow. I cough as I stumble forward, toes catching on the plush carpet running down the monstruous halls like gluttonous tongues. The pain is unlike anything I've ever felt. Like one thousand quick cuts and violence spinning out of control.

I touch the wound gingerly while tiny claws cling to the underside of my shirt. The place where timber meets flesh throbs. The hole leaks air from my lungs like a punctured waterskin, only allowing shallow breaths. I bite my lip and place a finger over the bubbling wound, finding I breathe more easily this way. This won't kill me, but it will make things more difficult.

Gi Shi prods my back gently with his baton. "Move!" I turn around to find him wearing a conflicted expression: mouth hard but eyes turned down at the edges, nose scrunched. His Atmosphere reads like a dog who has chewed its owner's slippers. Small guilt.

I reach for him, just a hare's step forward, and catch a baton to the cheek for my trouble. "Stay back!" he warns. *Very* small guilt. This Shen may feel sorry for me, but it will not translate to help.

I collapse, and the howling monkey infant hides in the hollow of my stomach as I curl to avoid crushing it. My finger slips from the drill hole, and I return to breathing like a wheezy accordion.

This will not be how I go. A slow death like a punctured pig-skin ball. Deflating until I am flat and useless. I cough up pink mucus and it lands on the carpet. It shouldn't, but it makes me smile that I have sullied the décor. "I can… do this. I can." I pat the baby monkey carefully. "Hold on."

"What did you say?" Gi Shi's shushing Shen accent sounds anxious. He looks left and right as maids scurry between rooms. Another guard nods to him down the hall, Fire orange clashing against all the red and purple. He returns the gesture and puts a hand up to stop the guard approaching. As we pass my spit, he rubs it into the carpet with his shoe. It disappears.

"I said…" Words are thin. I can't quite get them out without proper air. My legs are like chicken jelly. I just need to get to the cell and lie down. Feel Ash's healing Water through my veins. I drag myself up, place my finger back over the hole and walk like I've been cut at the knees. Every step burns my energy like I've walked one hundred steps. I count the paces and note the turns. Making sure I know exactly how to get out of this chemical palace.

Plush to sparse to dark and dank. I reach the prison level and Ash's worry hits me like wailing wolves separated from their pack. Their cry like a lasso over the moon. I try to move faster, feet scraping the acid stone, tripping and bracing against rust-colored walls until I can see him. *I'm fine. He'll see I'm fine.*

I step into the murky candlelight and Ash's face can't even muster half a saltwater smile.

I tilt my head. Maybe I'm not fine.

Ash does show his teeth then, but it's a growl rather than a grin. "What did you do to her?"

The guard unlocks my cell door and I stumble in on my own, my bed calling.

"I didn't do anything," Gi Shi says defensively. The bruise on my cheek suggests otherwise. "It wasn't me, it was the…" He seems to wrestle with his words and chooses to aim blame in our direction. "Perhaps if *you* cooperated, they wouldn't have to touch her at all."

Another lie.

Wen stands from his lazy chair. "Don't expect the traitor to behave rationally, Gi."

My cell door closes, and the two men leave us. If Gi Shi was regretful, it was fleeting. I hear him laughing and joking with Wen around the corner. I snort. There was little hope of an ally in this place.

The bed seems far away. I take another step and Ash watches as my knees buckle and my hands fly out to stop me from hitting the ground with my face. Air is not doing what it needs to do and only part fills my lungs.

Ash's fingers stretch desperately through the bars. "You know that's not true, Luna, don't you? If they would guarantee your safety, I would cooperate, but they were never going to do that." He shakes his head, sorrowful. "They were always going to hurt us both."

I gurgle my response. "Of course… I know. And no… you wouldn't. We can't… let them win. We can never tell… them where they are. No matter how much… they torture… how much they take." The words wear me out. I wipe my mouth with the back of my hand, and it comes back smeared with pink.

I shuffle toward Ash and his Atmosphere of shelter. His eyes are sadness and seaweed, powerless against the ocean's control. "Why do you sound so out of breath? What did he do to you? Where did they take you? I lost you, Luna. One second I could *feel* you and then you were just gone."

I press my finger to the hole again. "You sound… a little out of breath… yourself." I try to smile. I'm sure it looks nightmarish with my blood-stained lips.

His chuckle is as vital to me as rain on a rooftop after the driest summer. "You do that to me, Luna."

I shuffle through straw and dirt to get closer. I show him the wound. His eyes widen. "I'm finding… it hard… to breathe… because of this." I reveal the small hole and the bloody foam oozing from it.

Ash curses, eyes slanted to the ground, then he lifts his gaze, focusing only on me. And even though we're in the worst place, in the most harrowing circumstances, he makes me feel like the stars are dropping to the earth just to crown my head. I lean into his warmth.

The howling monkey crawls up my stomach and peeks between my shirt buttons. Ash does a very good job of pretending he's not startled, and I flick my finger, urging it to hide beneath my bed. It quickly and quietly does as I ask.

"Can you… help me?"

Ash touches my sternum, fingers softly brushing over the wood and brass. "I can, Luna, but you should know by now you don't need my help. You can help yourself."

I look up from his fingers to his sea breeze eyes. Greenish blue today with sun splashes of gold. "I can?"

He nods. "I'm pretty sure you can do almost anything. I know the soldiers are trained to push elements outward to harm, but powerful Shen can mend themselves from the inside. I shall numb your pain so you can concentrate." He closes his eyes. "Then you can answer the rest of my questions."

Maybe Shen and Char magic is meant to come together. Coexist. Because when Ash touches me, sending ice into my wound to hold it together, it feels like a pulse under waves. A signal of good things to come. Of peace. Like it's supposed to be this way.

I inhale long and loud, thinking of tiny wick spiders building beautiful web cities. I channel them through my system. Feel them taking up residence in the wound. Spinning and spinning. Creating a spun silk plug. Air fills my lungs, and I finally catch my breath. He smiles, cheek pushed up, caught in our moment of Blood and Water. "Thank you," I whisper with redness in my cheeks.

He bows his head. "I'm not doing much."

"Yes, but it helps." I grab his hand and hold it to my chest. "Maybe keep it there, just in case." I don't know if it's his power meeting mine or that we might die in here, but I feel bolder. If time is running out, I'm going wrap what I can of him around my fingers.

He keeps his hand on my chest, brushes his fingers back and forth across the wound, keeping it numbed while it heals. "My questions?"

I tell Ash about the large wooden box outside, and how the doctor drilled a hole through my sternum. "I called the forest."

His eyes move to my bed and the tiny creature hiding beneath it. "And I guess the forest answered."

We can plan an escape.

Closing my eyes, I dare to dream we might soon hear the shake of trees and feel earth under our feet. "We must wait until night," I whisper, motioning to the small rectangle of light punched in the wall above us. Ash nods solemnly. The sun will set soon.

I put my hand over Ash's. Air bubbles and blood pushes at my wound. The wick spiders are used to building and rebuilding. But it's taking much of my concentration to keep them in place. Possibly too much.

THEY GIVE us the night but not as a gift. They only let us have these shared hours so we can share pain. They wish to use our love to manipulate. Sometimes I feel like it's a splintered breath away from working, but then I remember, love is strength. Love stretches beyond these thick walls and coats my bones in liquid iron, keeping me straight and sturdy. It will help me tonight.

The guards don't sleep much, but they do get distracted. To save themselves from boredom, they play Mah Jong on a barrel. At least I think it's Mah Jong. I hear bone tiles clink against each other and men brag and hustle.

After playing for an hour, they are deep in the game. Wen exclaims loudly, ribbing Gi Shi when it doesn't go his way. I stare at the keys hanging on a hook opposite our cell. A spear leans next to them, left by Wen before he settled in to play. For once, luck is on our side.

"Are you sure about this, Luna?" Ash asks, hand still on my chest. We'll have to separate when we run. The wick spiders busily mend and re-mend. Mend and re-mend. Ash removes his hand for a moment and flicks it. I've accidentally sent spiderwebs through his skin.

"Sorry," I whisper. I try to restore balance. It's getting easier every time we combine. "And yes, we have to try."

I coax the little monkey out from under the bed. She clambers up my folded legs and into my palm, gazing up at me with rectangular yellow eyes. Her mouth a tiny "o." Howling monkey's always look permanently surprised. I stroke her velvet head, conveying what I need.

Ash shakes his head and runs a hand through his golden-brown locks. "I'm not sure I'll ever get used to the ease with which you use your Blood power."

To me it's as simple as the way my hickory heart beats like a clock. As natural as the knife-shaped grief I feel for Ben Ni and the aching for the rest of my family, scattered to all ends of the land like the pins in the corners of a map. "Lye taught me well," I whisper with affection and gratitude.

At the mention of his sister, Ash's expression changes. Everything from love and distrust to trust and fear flashes across his face.

I lower my hand and the tiny monkey, barely the size of a bao bun, easily slots between the cell bars and to the base of the spear. She halts and blinks like she's forgotten what she was doing, and I flick my finger again. Slowly, she winds up the spear like she's climbing a tree. We hold our breath, hoping it doesn't shift and clang to the ground. My wound begins to throb as I do too many things at once. I tap my heart and Ash steps in, icing over the hole.

The monkey loops the keys around her neck and slides down the spear. I urge her to halt, awaiting noise from the game to cover her jingling.

"Aha! Bad move, friend!" Wen shouts gleefully. Tiles clatter as the game ends and they scrape them into a pile to start again.

"Now," I whisper, sensing her tiny heart, barely the size of a button, fluttering.

She runs the short distance to our cells and brings the keys directly into my hands.

I hope I can move as fast as I need to.

7
KI ANAH

SCHOOLED IN FEAR AND PARANOIA

Sun grimaces as he gnaws the tough meat, picking spines out as he goes with a disdainful look. Ki Anah would normally slap his head for being picky, but as she moves the meat around her own mouth, trying to work up the nerve to swallow it, she can't really blame him. It's dry and sinewy and tastes vaguely of dirt. But the fish have stopped coming. Her eyes coast over the pond they swam through to get here. Ice has taken over most of it now. Soon the tubers will die also.

She holds her hand to the fire. The heat doesn't reach far enough, eaten by this enormous cavern. The Carvresses sit back from the fire. They don't need the warmth like a flesh body does. Their wooden eyes stare straight ahead. All except Shei-Shei, whose gaze seems permanently glued to the floor since she turned the Shen peasant girl, Guen, into birchwood. Damning the child to an eternal life as an eight-year-old. Ki Anah feels sorry for Shei-Shei. She banished herself from her sisters, yet she's never able to get away from them. It's a pitiful existence.

Again, the drumbeats rumble through the cave, and they all look up as glow worms lose their hold and fall onto the pond, bouncing unnaturally instead of plunging in. Char are not built for this kind of cold. Ki Anah never thought she'd miss the constant sogginess of monsoon season, but she would give much to hear the rain bucket down on her shingled roof. At least she has her son with her; shuffling closer to Sun she grabs some of his warmth. She blinks, visions of Luna haunt her and silent prayers float to the ceiling that her daughter is not alone. That Ash found her. All these unknowns leave splintered arrow heads in her chest.

Guen sniffs a little and looks out at the frozen water. Ki Anah guesses she misses her family. She nudges her son in the side.

Sun beckons the girl to sit at his feet. "Guen, why don't you tell us something about the Dark West tribe, eh? Are they as intimidating as the Char?" He winks.

Guen leans against Sun's leg like it's the most natural thing in the world to do. And he pats her head roughly. The birchwood girl swallows and makes circles in the dirt, shaking her head.

The ebony Carvress, Mi Asha, kneels in the dirt, approaching the girl. "Yes, dear. What do you know of this tribe? They did not exist when we lived in the palace. Please, tell us."

Guen blinks at the almost black wooden woman and bows her head. It impresses Ki Anah that she gives the Carvresses respect. She would expect bratty rebellion from a Shen child. But then, every expectation she had about Carvress and Shen has been torn to shreds like old washing.

Guen's voice, usually as light and colorful as a soap bubble floating in the sun, becomes the monotone of someone reciting a lesson learned. "The tribespeople of the Dark West are as tall as two men. They have teeth that have been sharpened into fangs. They live deep in the mountains where there's hardly any light, and it's always covered in snow. But they only wear slivers of skins." She clasps her little wooden hands in her lap and continues. "They kill for sport, sliding unused carcasses down the steep cliffs to frighten villagers. They carry five weapons at all times. They never sleep. The drumbeats are a warning: If you ever cross their territory, they won't just kill you, they'll torture you for weeks. Then when you're screaming for death, they will feed you to the tiger wolves that live in Dead Pine Woods."

Ki Anah's eyes are wide. Not with fear. With something more dangerous and important: Revelation. The child has been schooled in fear and paranoia. Just as Char children are told to memorize awful stories about Shen.

The Carvress of Yellow Fin Island, Fe Shein, laughs, and when Guen's neck twists her way, she covers with a cough. Ki Anah doesn't find this funny, but disturbing. Sun, to his credit, doesn't join in the ashy, blue-coloured Carvress's giggle, but several other Carvresses snort.

"Ai! Fe Shein, do not laugh at the poor girl. She is only reciting what she was taught," Sifah scolds.

Guen's little limbs crack and lock as she tenses. "Why is it funny?"

Sun taps Guen's head gently, seemingly immune to the odd way her wooden plaits clink again each other. "They're not laughing at you, kid. It's just that whole spiel sounds very familiar."

Guen picks up a stone and tosses onto the frozen pond. It tap, tap, taps across the ice, lonesome. "Oh yeah?"

The Carvresses smile, and it's hard not to get caught in their glowing, mystical beauty. Ki Anah shakes her head. Leaning down, she begins to explain, "You see, young Shen—"

Sun cuts her off. "Mama, let me." Ki Anah bows and opens her palm to him, the meat not sitting right in her stomach. Guen crosses her legs and faces Sun while the Carvresses click and clatter behind him. "The description you just recited—well, it's pretty close to what the Char say about the Shen."

Guen shakes her head. "I don't understand. We're nothing like that."

He scoops her up and puts her on his knee. Handling her with care like she's delicate and vulnerable, easily broken. Ki Anah recognizes the girl's strength and doubts she's any of those things. Though perhaps a little on the inside.

"It's all right that you don't understand, you're learning new things. We all are. I think what is amusing to the Carvresses and eye opening to me is the things we tell our children start them on a path. You believe the Dark West tribes are bad people because you have been taught this. And though I have evidence of Shen cruelty, I'm coming to understand they're not all bad." He taps her nose, and she smiles with birchwood teeth. "No group of people is all bad. It cannot be."

"Do you want to know what we say about the Char?" she says wickedly.

"That they're fearsome, handsome, awe inspiring, I bet." Sun flashes a wide grin. He pokes her in the belly and Guen giggles.

Sifah, eldest of the Carvresses, speaks with grace and humility. "I think the lesson is those holding information tightly in their hands hold the power. Be careful not to lap up all that drops from between their fingers. It is likely tainted."

Guen looks at Sun with confusion and he explains, "Don't believe everything you hear." She nods decisively.

Ki Anah worries over the bond between these two. It's father and daughter. A jam in the cogs of Sun's life. For it would take a special woman indeed to take this wooden Shen child into her home and raise it as her own. She shakes her head, chastising herself. There's no room for that kind of concern right now. She rubs her arms. The cold feels like a solid thing, nudging her closer and closer to the fire, cramping her stomach, and making her shiver.

Sifah looks upon Ki Anah with concerns of her own. "You don't look well, Ki Anah Yan."

Ki Anah shudders as her stomach seizes. "I will not be well until my family is whole again," she manages. Then she collapses to the earth like a frayed, felled tree.

8

LYE

HEART STILL HOLLOW

It has been weeks since we've ventured down the mountain and into the city. When we traveled to the monastery, the city was still smoking like a forgotten pipe, the damage hidden under thick, black clouds. We didn't notice as we hurried toward safety.

Now, rain has killed the fires and suffocated the smoke. My feet reluctantly tread over the line between where jungle ends and city begins. All Atmospheres shrink to one feeling: grief.

I'm not sure this can even be called "damage." There should be a bigger word for what has happened to Black Sail. Something that explains the pure devastation of this once vibrant, colorful place. It is in shambles. Unrecognizable.

Black soot stains our slippers as the group steps over the charred remains of homes. The sun shines on this mess, only making it more plain how uninhabitable the city has become.

"We should try Feki's," a soldier suggests.

I turn to Joka, questioning, as we descend a steep incline of gray silty mud mixed with city remains. He explains, "Feki sold mostly pickles and preserves."

I hoist the scratchy, empty hessian sack over my shoulder and nod before pointing at two soldiers. "You two go to Feki's, collect everything you can carry." I knock my head eastward. "The rest of us will spread out and head toward the harbor front." I'm praying for rice, sugar, tea. Staples I hadn't realized we are running out of fast.

Joka, Setsu, and five others stay with me. The rest do as ordered, branching out like small creeks from a river. At least the Shen are gone. The only danger is in the collapsible nature of everything around us.

We slide down slick-with-charcoal streets. Closing our eyes in pain and quick prayer every time we pass another burned body. *I am sorry, dear Char. You deserved better than this.* I scrunch my hands and keep them close against my hips. The aftermath of battle is a sight I don't want to become used to.

Setsu shakes his head. "I am glad Ki Anah is not here to see this. It would break her heart." He thumps his chest along with Joka and the other soldiers. I copy them, lifting my sycamore arm to my chest and thumping it once.

I place a hand on Setsu's load-bearing shoulder. "I am so sorry. I wish—"

Both Joka and Setsu say simultaneously, "Wishes are a waste!" just as we hear a very encouraging sound. The *cluck, cluck, cluck* of a hen.

We scan flattened buildings, trying to pin the source. Just on the other side of a wall, standing on top of the roof of a collapsed building is a reddish-brown shape that will either serve as a delicious meal or lay some much needed eggs. Either way, I must have it. I charge toward the hen just as Joka shouts, "General Koh, wait!"

I storm across the feathery structure, eyes on the hen stupidly pecking at nothing, seeming dazed and confused. I'm about three yards away when it suddenly notices my presence and flaps its scrawny wings.

I halt, easing my coat from my shoulders. Readying to throw, I inch closer on my haunches. Its clueless eyes stare. "Stand on the beams," Setsu shouts, far too late. I have one chance to catch it and I spring onto the roof, throwing my cloak over the bird. As it flutters beneath the fabric, caught, the roof creaks for one protesting moment and gives way beneath me. Men shout as I plummet, landing with a thud in a Char kitchen. Pots and pans bang against each other and me.

Setsu grumbles, "Ah *dia bodoh*, she didn't stand on the beams." I probably deserved the label of "stupid" in this case.

Joka's face appears in the patch of sky above my head. "You need to—"

"Stand on the beams?" I manage as his concerned gaze makes me uncomfortable. I shoo him away. "I'm fine! Get the hen."

He grins in a way that shows he's out of practice as he holds up a squawking weight in my bundled cloak. "Got it."

I scan the maze of tumbled down buildings leaning into and crossing over each other. It reminds me of the emperor's toy city. The way he'd sweep his arm across it when he'd finished playing and stand there, impatiently waiting for the servants to pick up all the pieces. "I'll find my way out on this level. Meet me on the next street," I order, though I don't know whether the next street is even able to be found.

"I'll try." Joka salutes and I hear the creak and crack of him carefully working backward from the roof.

Standing, I pull my elbow out of a broken bamboo steamer, my leg from between two chairs. I've fallen into a slice of time; a life ended abruptly. I don't know why I do it, but I right the toppled chairs and tuck them under the table. I place the dishes in the sink. I allow the grief of this home, this family I never met, to sink into my skin, scratch marks into my bones. Then I shed a tear and move forward. Keeping my eyes out for food, drink, and unlikely survivors.

BLACK SAIL CITY was built with every home leaning against the other like a group of good friends. When supports collapsed, the whole thing spilled over like a house of cards. It also left angled pockets of space between buildings. Little triangles of room I can squeeze through like a rat in a maze. I duck under a fallen beam into another such space. Tiny metal tools are strewn across a tilted table. Crumbly shavings of cork coat the workspace. I lean closer, lifting a frame with a pane of glass on one side, a cork carving exposed on the other. Tiny rosewood cranes the size of my littlest fingernail stand in the foreground of an intricate bridge. The detail is exquisite. I peer at the carving, eyes drawn to a juniper tree that starts out beautiful and fine but degrades into an uncarved lump at the top. The carving is unfinished. I tilt my head, drawn in by its beauty. It's like so many things in my life and reminds me there's much I still need to do. I pick up the carving and wrap it carefully in a cotton scrap, placing it in my breast pocket.

This carver was also fond of preserved plums and though the thought of them makes my mouth pucker, I pile them into my sack with other salvaged items.

I pass through this home and into the next one, feeling as if the buildings are like the chambers of a wooden heart that's breaking. And I'm seconds away from being crushed.

"Bok Ah, Bok Ah." A murmur so soft it could be the wind. "I will wait for you. I will." I follow the female voice. A tone like cut steel cable, strong and dangerously frayed at the same time. "What did they do to you? Where did they take you?"

Weaving over fragments of destroyed lives, I find the face belonging to the voice. A small Char woman with salt-streaked wooden cheeks, sitting on the edge of a bed, clutching a cane ball like it is a child. She rocks slowly back and forth, and I wonder if the war has snapped her mind; it would be understandable. But then she says again, "I will wait for you." And there's a toughness in her tone telling me there's more to this picture.

I approach her slowly, hands out, sycamore arm obvious. It's my white flag to those who don't know me. A way of telling Char I am safe. "Excuse me." The woman lifts her head, eyes as dark and liquid as oil wells. "I am General Lye Li Koh, are you—I mean, do you, need help?"

I hear rustling, materials being thrown aside. They're coming for me. I'm close to the outside. Light punches through a broken window. I made it to the next street and through the rubble. The woman looks at me and then past me. Searching for a face she cannot find. "I know who you are." Her face is split between grief, hope, and anger, unevenly balanced like a hurried meal.

The buildings squeak and shift. This place is not safe. I hold out my hand. "You should come with me. This place is unstable." My eyes lift to the shaking ceiling, which is probably the wall of another home for how topsy turvy everything is.

The young woman shakes her head, one hand tightly on the cane ball, the other scrunched in the bedding. "I have to wait. If he escaped, if he's looking for me, he will only know to find me here."

I kneel at her feet. She's not much older than me. Her long brown hair cascades untied to her elbows. Her Char dress is a swirl of green and yellow batik flowers, which she tucks neatly under her legs. One look shows she is dehydrated and starved. I need to get her out of here. "If your husband is missing, he will know where to go. Everyone knows to go to the monastery. It is posted at the city center."

She releases the cane ball. It falls to the ground and rolls fast downhill, demonstrating how precarious our position is.

"General!" I hear a soldier shout.

"He cannot read, General Koh," she whispers, staring at her empty hands. "I was going to teach him, but then—"

Small carved toys on a chest. A tiny, padded jacket with a dragon embroidered on the side. Slippers the size of rabbit's feet. This is a child's room. She's waiting for her son. There's a stone in my stomach—jagged and heavy. It cuts deep, telling me before she does that something horrible happened. A fear I've held against my heart for a long time and is now about to be confirmed. I place my elemental hand on her wrist and send calming lagoon waters, blue skies and impossible-to-imagine things when you have lost your child. Her wooden cheeks remain as tight and tense as they did before. Her breath still shallow, heart still hollow.

Wood crashes, glass smashes, as Joka, Setsu and the other men open the side of the building revealing the cold light of the outside world. They see a young mother wasting to nothing but holding stubbornly to her place. They hear me say, "Where is your child?" through trembling lips.

Their eyes widen and mouths gasp. Silent and stunned as she answers, "They took him."

9
LUNA

TOO MANY EYES

I stretch up, lifting the infant monkey to the tiny grate in the wall. She squeezes through the bars, turning back one last time. "Go find your family," I say, heart like a clock, soul like a storm. "Go find them and tell them I'm coming."

We're quick and quiet, despite our injuries. Holding each other together like human bandages. Power passing back and forth in equilibrium. Wen has his back to us, and Ash presses his hand to the nape of his neck, disabling him easily. Gi Shi stares, disbelieving. He goes to stand but I summon all my strength and launch across the table. Mah Jong tiles fly, and I send the paralyzing venom of an opal snake into his veins. He pushes back briefly with a tangle of tree roots but the snake winds and burrows around them. Gi Shi's head falls onto the table with a satisfying clunk.

Ash extends a hand, pulling me from the table and like those roots, we wrap around each other.

Time to leave. Time to go home.

AS WE CREEP up the stairs, I dream of the jungle. The bend of palms that lead to the beach and then to sea.

My heart beats to help focus my power and keep my breath even. A seesaw of magic and will. Ash's hand squeezes mine, his power sapped too. I manage a grin as I think about the guards' foreheads imprinted with Mah Jong symbols when they wake.

I can almost taste the sweet, cold air. Almost feel the change from stone to dirt beneath my feet. We emerge from the prison, ragged and filthy and full of hope.

"Do you know which way is best to get out of here?" I whisper, my head swinging back and forth, long hallways stretch in both directions, cavernous, dark, and empty.

He nods, pulling me in the opposite direction to where I went the day before.

I reach for Blood and the animals that could help us in this place. Stretching my power through walls and under doors. Nothing. This place has no life save sleeping servants. The occasional bored guard marching down corridors. We walk across carpet that conveniently covers our footfalls. Tiny circles of candlelight dot this enormous home, bright spots in the gray and shadows.

I feel the big and mysterious presence on the edge of my Blood sense again. My power wishes to know it, wrap around it. It blurs and comes clear. Blurs and comes clear. A barrier between us. A growl and white fangs the size of my fingers. A tongue like sandpaper lolling to one side. I reach. I reach until my blood thins and strains. But this magnificent creature is controlled by another master.

We reach heavy doors made of iron and thick wood. "How do we… ?" A dam breaks inside me as I separate from the mystery animal. My repairs come apart stitch by stitch. I shouldn't have gotten caught up in reaching so far.

Ash catches me as I buckle. I lock my knees and push to my feet, spinning webs as fast as I can. But I'm losing. We drag each other closer to the outside, closer to escape.

Ash stalls, suddenly dead still. I sense his heart racing as he stares at the thick-as-a-cave-wall door in front of us. His eyes track up and down slowly and he murmurs, "Oh no."

My head would snap to him if I had the energy. "What?" I hiss. We cannot pause.

His arms wrap me tighter, making it even harder to breath. "Forgive me. We were rushed, there was little time to relay the instructions. I—"

The smash of metal against bone is the bleakest of sounds, conjuring images of war. It means only bad things. Pain. Anger. The end.

Ash falls, his hand on the bolt. Whatever he was going to say must wait.

I spin around, my shoulder meeting the tip of a baton, hard. I fly backward, hitting the door with an insubstantial thud. Nasty stars burn and bite across my vision. My hand searches for Ash's, finding it cold and limp.

My Blood sense lays its fingers across a large paw before it recedes. I blink and see a strong, made for contemplation, jaw. A creature that only uses its strength when necessary. Then the feeling dissipates. The sense of the creature pulling away from me with a snarl.

A man stands over us, dressed in Fire orange robes. From our viewpoint, he is a speaking shadow holding a weapon and all our chances. "Ash Ki Koh. I'm surprised you got this far."

My hopes dive into the sea like suicide maidens from Ghost Lovers Cliff. Thrashed apart by sharps rocks, hammered by waves. The squeal of a baby howling monkey being constrained and taunted splinters what's left of my ragged heart.

A far-off voice chuckles heartlessly. "We could feed it to Mulia!" *I am so sorry, sweet creature.*

The man grabs Ash and yanks him to standing, slapping his face to wake him. I lunge, pushing piranha rabbits chomping up the man's leg. In a flash, he sticks a knife to Ash's throat before I can blink. Tense and angered, he threatens, "Release me, young Blood Shen. I only need a slice of a second to kill the boy."

I release the man. My wound burbling like a brook. The knife to Ash's throat remains. "Luna, go!" Ash says, crackling from lack of air. "Leave me and escape."

But I cannot. I will not leave him to die in this place.

And they know it.

The man chuckles darkly when he sees me slump away from him. "Congratulations, you two. You have been demoted. You shall be sent where no light can find you and no one can hear you scream."

Ash looks at me with graveyard dirt in his eyes. "You should have run."

THE MORNING sun pokes spokes of light through the double-height windows of the ground level of the palace. Peach-colored light runs smoothing hands over my hair, brushes the grime and tears from my cheeks. I pause in the cut-out piece of light, the red carpet warm beneath my feet. I need the golden touch of the sun, one last time. I close my eyes, feeling the air disturb behind my head as the guard lifts his baton.

"Please," I whisper. "Please give me one moment."

The guard allows us these seconds of pleasure before hours of pain. Ash reaches for my hand, and I take it. His Atmosphere is snow building on a branch. Growing heavier. He's angry I did not run, but love outweighs it.

Drinking in the sunlight, I store it in the creases of my eyelids, between every strand of hair. I believe the man who said we were going to a dark place. I will need this memory.

"Who was that Fire Shen?" I ask Ash. "It seemed like he knew you."

Ash shakes his head, high cheeks scrunched like cast away paper. "He knew me once. He does not know me now. He was one of my trainers."

We have new guards now, and it's pathetic that I miss Wen and Gi Shi.

My moment in the sun is over and one presses a baton in my back, shoving me into the rusty belly of the palace.

The steps grow wetter and slimier. We move like fragments of what we once were. We are malnourished and injured. I shiver and hold my wound closed with the beeswax I conjure in my veins. I feel it mending. Blood power is healing power and I breathe as well as I can, given the stench and staleness.

Ash sniffs the air. The smell of iron is strong. The walls are part stone, part dirt, and all darkest brown. It's so dim I can barely make out shapes. I only notice the bamboo cage when my back is pressed against it.

The guards untie our wrists and throw us in neighboring cells. "Good luck finding your way out of this," one of them sneers.

The other seems nervous, holding his candle close to his chest, eyes moving up and down the walls. His hair is half tied in a messy bun with long lengths falling over his shoulders. "Let's get out of here, Qi Sha. I don't like it. Too many eyes." He shudders in his Water blue robes.

"Ah, Sho Sen, you're so jumpy. They can't hurt you."

I frown as they bound up the stairs and close a creaking iron gate. The sound of the lock sliding into place feels like the final chapter of a book. They take the light with them so there is no way to read it anyway.

I pad my hands around the muddy floor, searching for the side of the cell. "Ash, where are you? I can't see." I hear a familiar sound in the background, though the contentment it usually brings is lost when I can't tell where it's coming from—the powerful rush of water, churning and smashing against rocks.

"I am here, Luna." His voice is dug deep in the cavern of despair. He's making a home there. I need to not let him get comfortable.

My hands run up and down bamboo poles, searching for him. "I don't *feel* you."

"You should have left me. You could have been halfway to the sea by now."

How can a darkness be this complete? I feel as if I have been made blind. "Ash, please, come to me. I couldn't leave you. I will *never* leave you, do you understand?" If I'd left him to die, I may as well have died myself. I cannot lose any more. The loss of my little brother, Ben Ni, is always with me, graduating to the shape of an iron pike in my mind and a crack in my hickory heart. I can't go back to the emotionless monster I became to cope with that pain. "You don't get to be the only one who sacrifices for love. The only way we are heroes is if we are heroes together." I strain for his hand.

I imagine he smiles his broken smile. His "I love the girl with the hickory heart" smile. I hear him sigh and shuffle to the sound of my voice. "Are you saying I'm your hero?" he asks, doubt in his voice. "You may change your mind when I tell you what I did."

I groan, finally feeling his fingers on my arm, creeping up my shoulder and coming to rest beneath my chin. I rest my head in his hand, sending the quick nip of a wolf cub's razor-sharp teeth through his skin. "I'm saying you are my hero, and I am yours. We have to promise to keep saving each other." I kiss his palm. "Whatever you have to tell me won't change that."

He squeezes my fingers softly, like he's afraid to hold me too close. "I don't think I told Sun everything about the ice walls in the mountain."

"What do you mean?" My mother, Sun, and the others are safe. It is the thin thread from which my faith hangs.

Deep breath in, truth breath out. "In my haste to chase after you and the chancellor, I threw instructions about the hiding place to Sun. I can't remember if I told him that they would need to travel deeper into the mountain. I know I said something, I'm just not sure if I was clear. Ice walls seal the tunnels in winter and unless they move to the center, where it is warmer and there are routes to the outside, they will be trapped." His voice climbs upward. "Luna, they will freeze to death."

An ice wall of my own is forming around my heart. But I don't allow it to enclose completely. I don't let blame cool my love. I feel he is doing enough of that himself.

"Mama is smart. Sun has good instincts. Even if you didn't tell them, they probably worked it out." I hold tight to this. "We have enough to worry about without you punishing yourself for something you don't even know if you did."

I hear his hand run through his hair. "Maybe I did, I'm just—not sure."

"Then I'll be sure for you. You told them." I'm not sure. But I can't see what good it would do to think otherwise. If I start picturing Mama and Sun slowly freezing, I won't survive.

Ash's chuckle is as soft as a trampled moth's wings covered in dust. Hard to rouse from the floor, but he's trying. "All right, Luna." If there were no bars between us, I could collect his unhappiness in my arms and tease it away. I put the thought aside and place it in the clouds until later.

I move my hands through his hair and bring his lips to mine in a desperate, dirt-smudged kiss between bamboo bars. We take what we can, knowing time has been pulled from the clock and lies in the emperor's hands.

A cough, as tiny as a sesame seed caught between floorboards, pulls us apart just as swiftly as we connected.

"What was that?" Ash whispers. I shrug, though he can't see it. "Luna, search for light."

The cold bites my back and I shudder. "What do you mean?"

Ash's voice is echoey. "This is like a cave. Caves have—"

I close my eyes, reaching for creatures who make their own illumination. I sense glow worms, reluctant and sleepy, and pull their spirit to me. I ask them to try to light this dark world that smells of old blood and dashed hopes.

"Stars to sea!" Ash exclaims.

I open my eyes to ribbons of light stretching across stories-high walls, multiple cages pressed against the edges of a canyon with rushing water below. And blinking between the bars of these cages—eyes. Dozens of pairs of eyes.

If my heart were not hickory, if it could stop and scream until the muscle burned and bled, it would.

10

KI ANAH

UNRAVELED LIKE THE END OF A ROPE

Ki Anah clutches her stomach as pain like a clawed hand squeezes and twists her insides. The sounds of Sun vomiting and crying out in agony all night meant she had very little sleep. But now he stands over her, hands on hips, worry occupying every crease of his frown.

"What's wrong with Ki Anah?" Guen asks Sifah, who holds Ki Anah's head in her hard lap, blotting her sweaty forehead with a cloth.

Sifah's melodic voice is of small comfort. "The creature you killed had bad blood."

Guen's birchwood face is squished with confusion as she points at Sun. "But he's fine. Why is he fine and Ki Anah looks so bad?"

Sun pats the top of Guen's head. "I'm just real strong, kid. Ki Anah is old." Ki Anah manages to kick Sun in the shins, despite her weakened state. "Er, older than me."

Sifah shifts her legs. They feel like a warm tabletop under Ki Anah's ear. "No, child. It is because Ki Anah has not expelled the poisoned meat quite so enthusiastically as Sun."

Ki Anah wishes she could vomit, but she has always had a stubborn stomach. When she does get sick, it is severe. She groans and rolls to her side.

The little Shen child squats down to Ki Anah's level and purses her rose petal carved lips. She reaches out and strokes Ki Anah's cheek. "I hope you feel better soon," she whispers.

Ki Anah tries to speak but manages only a flattened, dried leaf kind of groan.

It will pass. It must.

AFTER DAYS of barely being able to lift her dark head from the ground, Ki Anah finally feels some strength returning. She manages sips of water. Her stomach rumbles with hunger, but the tubers harvested from the pond sit in a sorry pile of only three. They're running out. Carvresses sit on either side of her shaking body, trying to keep her warm. They have shed their colorful printed robes and cloaks, wafting about in thin slips. Their outer garments now hang from Ki Anah's small frame and look laughable on Sun, but he's not too proud to wear them. It's simply too cold for vanity.

Sun stomps the dirt in front of her and grumbles. His face glows, enhanced by the rich green silk wrapped around his neck. "We need food." His eyes move to the pond and a small circle of water right at the back towards the outer wall of the cavern. Closing over fast. Too fast.

Ki Anah lifts a weary arm. "Perhaps you could hunt again?"

Sun shakes his head. "I'm not putting you through this"—he points at his mother angrily—"again." He twists toward the water. "No. I need to get out of this cave and bring something back. Something we know is safe to eat."

Guen's rattling body claps over to Sun's leg and holds on. "Won't you freeze?"

Sun sets his chin. "No. I'm an excellent swimmer." He begins pulling the Carvresses clothing from his body, stalking toward the pond.

The Carvresses wooden eyes follow him. They may doubt he will do it, but his mother knows. Ki Anah reaches out, tries to shout in her dry, starving voice, "No, Sun. It's too dangerous."

Shei-Shei stands as he reaches the ice's edge. "Sun Yan, no!" The others grimace and clap their hands trying to get his attention. But of course, he ignores them.

Her heart stammers and shivers with dread. Can't move, can't breathe.

Anger begins to bubble and steam. The boy never listens. Not when it's important and not when it's for his own good. He slides clumsily over the pond ice like an eel trying to slither on land, making his way to the small, circular hole that reminds Ki Anah of a howling monkey's mouth. He glances back at his mother once, and before she can protest again, he jumps in.

Are some traits born into children too strong for removal? No matter how hard a mother tries, she cannot scrub them away, scratch them from their bones, shout through their ears so hard unwanted qualities come flying out the other side. They hang on like ticks.

For Sun, it seems no matter how many times it ends poorly, he cannot help but run headfirst into danger. He believes he's being brave. Ki Anah grimaces. It's just plain stupid. And when he emerges from the ice water, which should be any second now, Ki Anah will tell him so. She composes her scolding speech. Building word after word as time gathers into a frightening shape.

She runs a shaky hand through her hair, which is getting messier by the day. She hasn't the bonus of tangle free wooden tresses. Her hair hasn't seen a brush in over a month.

Any second now.

They've all migrated to the edge of the frozen pond. Nine women and one little girl, hands clutched together. Curses, prayers, wishes under their breaths. They didn't get the chance to tell him the simple truth. If it's almost frozen inside the cavern, the outside would be completely solid. If he'd waited, they could have explained. But he never waits.

Guen is the first to speak. "He wouldn't have got through on the other side. The ice is too thick."

Dread like death creeps up Ki Anah's throat to lie alongside the scorching anger. "I know, child." She places a hand on the young girl's bony birch fingers.

Now.

He should emerge now.

They wait.

Until Ki Anah can't wait any longer. She starts onto the ice with Sifah and Shei-Shei following. "Why didn't you stop him?" she snaps, surprised at her tone.

Sifah purses her lips and gazes upon the Char mother with sympathy. "I am sorry. We are used to observing, advising. It does not come naturally to interfere."

Shei-Shei braves a word against her sister. "But we should have, sister. We should have restrained him." Sifah nods, acknowledging her younger sister.

Guen doesn't move. A soft sob coming from the bank.

Ki Anah crawls on her hands and knees toward the hole. Mother's strength filling her when real food can't.

The Carvresses slip and slide behind her, not even their perfect posture and poise able to maintain elegance out here.

They reach the hole and Ki Anah shrieks, "Apa!" Tapping her hands on the plate of ice formed over the water. The cold has moved like a slit throat. So fast. So deadly. It burns against her skin. Above, hanging tree roots seem to groan and shudder with anticipated grief.

They hear a knock and see a shadow beneath. Ki Anah swipes at the ice for a clearer view.

Sun's horror-filled face stares back at them. He's trapped.

Ki Anah screams. Scratching at the ice as her son punches the thick glass over and over. "Sun!" He pushes his feet, thrashing as he both freezes and begins to drown at the same time. "No!" She thumps the ice. She cannot lose another child.

A panicked scream full of sorrow and loneliness comes from the bank. A birchwood child losing her chosen parent.

Shei-Shei, the disgraced Carvress, shuffles to Sun, his thumping becoming slower and more labored. Ki Anah's own breath is being robbed from her lungs. Stupid, stupid boy. Her family is already unraveled like the end of a rope. She can't, she can't, she can't. *Eldest son, live. Live!* She collapses flat onto the ice. Eye contact with her terrified son, the only comfort she can offer.

Shei-Shei shouts at her sisters, "Throw me his spear!"

The Carvress of Crow's Nest Island, Sho Pa, throws the spear beautifully and Shei-Shei catches it in her strong wooden hand. She gives her eldest sister Sifah a look. And it seems to Ki Anah to be halfway between goodbye and sorry. "But sister—" Sifah starts.

"Get off the ice. Now!" Shei-Shei lifts the spear high above her head.

Sifah grabs Ki Anah under the arms and half runs, half skids to the edge. They both fall, sliding the rest of the way and landing in the grasping wooden arms of the others, who pull them to safety.

Guen watches Shei-Shei, eyes wide. "Can we drown?" she asks. The Carvresses nod. They are grim and silent as Guen stares at her wooden forearms with new and frightening clarity.

They allow their sister to make amends for her crime. Ki Anah allows it also. She would never stop her.

The spear comes down once, twice, three times. Each strike spreading cracks like the veins of lightning. Shei-Shei is impressively strong. On the fourth strike, the ice breaks apart and Shei-Shei drops into the water like a pin.

Ki Anah lifts her head to the ceiling. To characters she can't read but hopes are prayers of protection. Guen curls into her lap, breathing like she's forgotten how. Like she might run out of oxygen.

"He has to be all right. He is—" Ki Anah knows because it is the same for her. He's all Guen has. Her chosen family. She swears she will care for the girl if he doesn't survive. She hates that she makes such a promise.

Shei-Shei's head bobs up in the water, clutching the shape of Sun, but not her son. This is a frozen body, blue and rigid.

Her sisters hold out a staff for her to grab and pull her into shore. The cold is like glue. Already freezing back together in razorblade shards. As Shei-Shei tosses Sun onto land, her feet become stuck. The water hardening around her ankles.

Ki Anah uses what little strength she has to run to the fire, now more like darkening coals. She grabs a pot of recently boiled water, carefully carrying it down the steps and tossing it on the Carvress's feet to free her. She falls forward and they yank her from the ice.

They flip Sun onto his back, and Mi Asha presses her ebony head to his chest while Ki Anah's stops beating all together. She pictures Setsu's face at the news that their eldest son is dead. It's enough to break an already wounded heart.

Long seconds pass. Seconds in which she dies over and over again. Mi Asha straightens. "His heart beats but slowly, like a hibernating bear."

"But he's not a bear," Ki Anah whispers.

"No, and he cannot survive for long like this. We need to warm him."

Guen suddenly animates and stumbles to Sun, thumping his chest and screaming, "You can't leave me here. You hear? You can't!" His frozen chest does nothing in response and its hollow sound hurts Ki Anah like a crushing weight is being slowly lowered upon her.

Ki Anah sways. A solitary stalk of wheat in a harvested field. "Guen." She bites the air with her words. "Get all the firewood."

"All of it?" she asks, rising as they drag Sun's body to the fire.

Ki Anah nods. "Every last piece."

11
LUNA

UNDER COVER OF FLAME AND SMOKE

Dozens of dark eyes in grime-rimmed sockets. I find Ash's hand and hold it tightly. He grimaces as I accidentally shoot the anxious claws of a caged sea falcon through his skin.

"Luna," he whispers, eyes narrowed. "Ease off."

There are not spies before us, though their eyes are as wide and surveillant as vampire owls at dusk. More like ghosts for how vapor thin they are. I bite my lip, my own eyes swelling with tears. My pain seeming small compared to this horror.

Beside me, a small hand wraps around the bamboo bars of my cage. The voice of the tiny waif is distinctly familiar. Rough and choppy. Beautifully brutish. Char. "Who're you?" she asks.

I release Ash's hand and shuffle closer. She can't be more than ten years old. Her long black hair looks like an old rope. Twined together but matted. Her clothing, if you can call it that, is simple canvas, like the remnants of a sail. I tap my chest. My heart beats steadily, giving me the strength to bear this atrocity.

I reveal my wooden sternum and answer, "I am Char Luna Yan of Coalstone Village. What's your name, young Char?" Ash draws in harsh breaths. I *feel* his anger building.

Her eyes dip. She squints. They all do. Shielding themselves from the light like it is the first they've seen in a long time. "I'm Char Lu Leng of Black Sail City," she says proudly, thumping a brittle chest.

I reach for her hand, but she pulls away, narrowing her eyes. She coughs as I speak. "How long have you been here, Lu Leng?" My gaze sweeps over the dozens of other cages. At least forty children.

She looks down the gulch beside us at the water rushing beneath the palace. The iron smell rising in the mist. "I've been here a while. I'm not sure." She purses her tiny lips.

In the next cage over, an older boy, maybe a teenager, answers, "She's been here about three weeks. Some of us have been here for months." He points to the wall at the back of his cage where strokes and slashes are carved into the rock, reminding me of Lye's scars. "My name is Char Ha Fun of Bird Cage Island. I keep the time." He points at the wall proudly with a bony arm. They are all very pale for Char, but their spirit is Char through and through.

Ash is quiet. His heartbeat fast and uneven. I turn to him. "Are you going to introduce yourself?"

He shakes his head. His sea storm eyes looking electric under the glow worm light. "How can I speak to these children? How can I even breathe their air after what the Shen have done to them?" he whispers, dishonor throwing a weight around his neck.

The children's voices rise as they speak their names, their islands, and how they came to be here. The stories are very similar. Their home or village was destroyed, and Shen warriors took them under cover of flame and smoke. Some ask after their parents, though I have no answers. The younger ones don't even remember where they came from or what their parents' names are. Ash reacts to each tale like an arrow to his chest. He's already in so much pain. His wound barely having time to stop bleeding before he's tortured again. But he takes this on willingly, like it is his duty. It makes me love him more.

"Ash, this is not your burden to bear," I say. He doesn't listen.

Lu Leng presses her little face to the bars, staring at Ash, who holds her eye contact for a moment before staring at the ground. "What's your name?" she asks, pointing a dirty finger.

"Ash Ki Koh," he mutters.

She laughs, a strange sound in this well bottom of a place. "You're the defector, aren't you?"

He lifts his head to her curious eyes. "How in streams and falls do you know of me?"

She crosses her arms. "I know things. I'm from Black Sail City. The biggest and brightest of all the Char islands." A few children groan exaggeratedly.

"Here she goes again!" someone shouts.

Lu Leng lays a leveling glare at them. "*I* know that Lye Li Koh is your sister and that she tried to save the city."

I lean into the girl's voice, lay my head against the roughness of the word "tried." "What of Black Sail City? Did they get there in time?"

The girl nods and then shakes her head. "It's gone."

Pieces of a much bigger story start to come together. Many children mentioned Black Sail City as their home. I raise my voice over the huge black space to confirm the smoke of my hunch. "How many of you are from Black Sail?"

About twenty hands shoot up.

More parts fall into place as the children talk, each page filled with a child's perspective. A home destroyed. Parents dying or disappearing. Shen arms wrapped around their middles, carrying them to a ship. When we collect it all and order the pages, the truth reveals itself. The Char chased the Shen from the island, but Black Sail City was destroyed in the process. Lost or orphaned children were scooped up by Shen in the mad dash to escape.

Ash pulls himself to standing. "I am so sorry. For this." He sweeps his hands around the space. "For so many things. I want to—"

I close my eyes. I know what he is going to say. I know he has no choice but to say it. And I agree with him with all of my Blood and my hickory heart. We must make this promise. We must keep it. Even if we die in the process.

"I want to promise you, we will find a way out of here. We will get you home."

The children clap and shout and stomp their feet.

Our responsibility has grown like the midnight flower, stretching its long slender petals toward the stars. Growing and growing and never reaching them. But somehow, we have to catch the stars. If we didn't have enough motivation before, this has sealed our intention like wax to a war order.

The noise of premature celebration grows, and Ash grins when he has no business to be grinning. I let the warmth of it reach me, if only for a moment.

Shen footsteps echo down the slippery stairs. I flick my hand and the glow worms dull and darken.

Four guards appear in the doorway with a lantern. Faces like tombs and striped by iron bars. They bash their spears against the gate. "Quiet! Or you'll all get an extra visit with the doctor."

The children are instantly silent, as if the threat pinched their lips closed.

Somewhere, through levels of stone and earth, the stars are stretching toward us. I can feel it. Hope strangling me at the same time as it fills my lungs.

"You're all lucky we have other business to attend to today," the guard Qi Sha snarls. He has the face of a bottom dwelling fish. Ugly and twisted. A face the sun would refuse to touch.

The iron gate is unlocked, and four guards approach my cage. I raise an eyebrow. Why so many?

Ash grips the bars, shouting a warning like the bellow of a snubnose dolphin that has lost its mate. "Luna! Look out!"

But there's nowhere to go.

Like something from a nightmare courtship, their hands are gloved and clutching posies of black flowers.

12
LYE

PULLED LIKE MAGNET

They took him. The phrase immediately tried to drag me under, wrapping around my arms and ankles like lead wristlets of guilt. But then the word "general" offered a rope to my sinking body. The Shen took the Char child. My worst fears are confirmed. But I can do something about this. I must.

Standing in the empty mess hall, we stare at the large pile of scavenged food. Treats we haven't had in weeks. Pork sausage. Kecap manis, sweet, sticky soy. Yellow fin tea. But no one feels like eating. We also found several laying hens to add to the monastery coop. Setsu chased down two carts with zebra donkeys still tethered to them. The creatures will need fattening, but once they're well, food trips can be made daily and with only one or two men if needed. I place my hands on my hips and blow a wisp of hair from my eye. Hair I had wished for and now seems like a foolish thing to waste a wish on. This food will do nicely. It will feed the refuges and give us the means to produce more.

In a room usually filled with the gruff noise of hundreds of Char, no one speaks. Questions linger on the tips of tongues, brushing the dried skin of their lips. But if they ask, then they will know the unbearable truth. And it cannot be unlearned.

The woman we rescued sits on the floor, sipping droplets of broth from her spoon. Other Char care for her, encourage her to eat. They bring her into their family without a second thought. That's their way.

I wring my hands, feeling the opposite of relish in telling them this next piece of horrible news. The Char don't deserve this latest tragedy.

Setsu hefts a bag onto his shoulder. "They don't want to know," he says as he stomps to the kitchen. Joka copies his father, though very overburdened by his sack.

"But I have to tell them?" I say. It's half a question and Joka understands.

"Yes." He follows his father.

I straighten, tightening my fists. Holding predicted storms inside my fingers. "Will they hate me?" I call after him.

Joka slips and grunts under the weight. "Maybe."

I look up at the vaulted ceiling. The rain pecking the roof rhythmically. It wants to come in. We won't let it.

I shrug, trying to mean it. I am accustomed to hatred.

I clap my hands loudly, slowly gathering attention until all Char eyes are on me. "I need to ask a question," I start. They lift their eyes, though none pause in slurping noodles and crunching bok choy. "By show of hands, how many of you lost a child during the siege on Black Sail City?" Shaky hands rise. Too many hands. I swallow, feel those storms swirling through my veins needing a place to strike. I press my hand to my thigh, pushing a painful hurricane in. The hands sway like reeds in a breeze. "I need to tell you that your child may not be dead. The Shen collected Char children to aid their efforts of creating a Char-Shen hybrid. If your child went missing during the battles, they may have been kidnapped by the Shen army."

The hands fall and then form fists. Some Calls sound out, angry and staccato. Not the usual musical harmony. A man with a wooden neck like Joka's but thicker, shaped from something rich and almost purple, stands up. "Are you telling me my daughter could be a prisoner of the emperor?" I nod. The man twists his neck, looks like he's readying for a fight, but then he whispers in the saddest voice, "Oh Lu Leng. My beautiful daughter." A woman strokes his back, and he sits down heavily. His neck cracks as his head sways from side to side. "She's only ten years old."

Others talk about their children. Some as young as three or four. Stolen under a cloak of smoke. Setsu returns and stands by my side. Joka leans against the wall, listening to every name and age and writing it down in a compact book.

I crack the shell of my idea, hoping it's full of nutrient rich egg and not a rotted corpse. "This violates every honorable rule of war. The Shen empire has ordered the kidnapping and torturing of children." The words hurt them but they're necessary. I aim my words at various village elders. "I know you may not believe me, but the majority of Shen people would take issue with this abhorrent behavior. I'm sure of it."

"Did you know about this?" Lu Leng's father asks in broken and blunt speech.

Deep breath in. No lies. You cannot be their general dishonestly. "I suspected but I never saw them. I was a prisoner in the palace. I had no rights, no freedom. Even if I had known, there was nothing I could do."

This starts a raucous chant of disbelief and anger.

"Why wait until now to say something?" someone asks. A valid question.

My head falls to my chest. I run my hand over the scars on my sycamore arm. Do I add more? Do I take on the harm others have caused because I couldn't stop it? I shake my head. "I truly didn't know for sure until now. I didn't want to start a panic without cause. Look…" I pump my hands. "Before, I was powerless. I couldn't have stopped it then. But now we can do something."

Setsu stomps his foot. "Listen to the general. Char do not punish those who have suffered enough punishment to last a lifetime. General Koh has proven herself over and over. You owe her your respect, and at the very least, your ears." He claps his oak hand against his flesh one. The Char quiet at the behest of Setsu.

Trying not to quiver, I act like I know what I'm doing. *I do. I do. I do.* "We must restore the Carvresses to their rightful place on the throne as Shen princesses. It's our only chance of restoring peace without more war."

"You wish us to give up our Carvresses, our only protection?" someone shouts.

"Don't you see? If the Carvresses sit on the throne, you will no longer need protection."

The Char argue and throw doubt my way. They don't want to lose the Carvresses. They don't believe the Shen would support the princesses on the throne. It goes on and on. A cyclonic Atmosphere, spinning in powerful circles.

The young mother stands, climbing slowly and determinedly onto a bench, rising through the clouds of opinions and fear. She turns to face the crowded hall of people and pounds her chest with her fist. We reciprocate and are silent. Her wooden cheeks shine glossily beneath the lantern light.

"*They* have our children. It matters not what you think you know. What you want or believe. *They have our children.* The Char must do everything in their power and give up everything they are asked to give up, to bring them home."

She is right. This changes the approach completely. Children's lives are at stake. We must do this now and we must do it well.

Agreement is reached.

The call of the palace is a blood-coated, iron-tasting thing. I am pulled to it like a magnet. Luna and Ash just need to hold on a little longer.

But our journey to the rust-red building must start at the very tip of the country, where the Carvresses hide. We will cut down from there and hope the blood of change spreads across Shen land like monsoon rain.

I lay out my plan once the villagers have turned in and the elders blow smoke across the tent. The animals they create are small and vulnerable. Cubs and kittens. Calves and chicks. They have only children on their minds. We must travel directly to the northernmost village, where the glacier meets the ground and red rice grows. My home. We shall retrieve the Carvresses. They are formidable, bewitching women, and I have no doubt they will be able to convince many Shen of their royal status. Solid proof would be nice, but we don't have time to find it. I'm banking on Luna and Ash.

I point at the river neatly and accurately drawn by Joka from my description. "We'll sail straight up the western arm of the great river. The canyon is deep and virtually unused in winter. It won't take us long to reach the village. Then, once we have the Carvresses safely in custody, we will walk to the palace."

"You want to walk across the Shen mainland with nine Carvresses and a troop of Char? Won't you be discovered?" one of the men asks.

I smile. It grows as I begin to understand the possibility of this plan. "Yes. That's the idea."

"What if they're not there? What if the Yans have failed to protect them?" Enah En asks.

Setsu stands, oak hand compressing into a fist that would feel like an anvil. But then Po Ka laughs heartily as if Enah En just told the world's funniest joke. "There are many perils to this plan. Many ways in which it could sink to the seafloor like a broken dish. But the Yans failing in their duty to protect the Carvresses is not one of them."

Setsu bows his proud chin, a small smirk in the corner of his mouth.

13

KI ANAH

THE WORD "NEVER"

Blue. Her son is blue when he should be caramel tan. Flames reach high. Worms drop from the ceiling into the fire, squirming and sizzling until they're nothing but black ash. The heat and threat of fire pushes Guen and the Carvresses to the walls. But Ki Anah stays by her foolish son's side, pulling icy clothes from his body and wrapping him in dry ones. Her cheeks are waxy and peeling from the intensity, but she won't move.

Guen cries loudly. Not with sadness, but anger. "You better get up, or I'm gonna, I'm gonna…" She doesn't know how to finish. Fear breeds fury in all people, wooden and flesh alike. Fear of losing someone we love creates a sea of roiling rage. Guen shakes her tiny wooden fist as Ki Anah leans over Sun, swiping wet locks from his proud forehead.

His strong jaw is rigid, the rest of him limp. Ki Anah sees much of Setsu in him, though a refined, whittled-down version. None of her children have her husband's bulk, but Sun has his square jaw. His brutish, beautiful features.

Ki Anah waits for a breath, the tiniest rise and fall of his chest. She doesn't cry. There is no room in her heart for the possibility that he won't survive. She tosses more wood on the fire while her son's head lolls in her lap. He's dry now, blue fading to a faint grayish purple.

A rattle of birchwood bones, strong and flexible. Delicately tough. Guen breaks free of Mi Asha's grasp and rushes at Sun. Clenching her fists, she comes down upon his chest like a hammer. Once, twice, three times. Ki Anah reaches out to stop the girl but her wooden eyes are intense, focused—calm. The calm makes Ki Anah pause. The calm makes Ki Anah listen rather than dismiss.

Guen pushes down on his chest again and orders Ki Anah to blow air into Sun's mouth. Ki Anah pulls a face but does as the eight-year-old demands.

They repeat the pattern several times until they hear a faint wheeze from Sun. He turns and coughs water, but his color matches that of a rotting purple mango. He's still halfway to the sky. Ki Anah searches the Carvresses faces. "Help him!" she begs. "Please. There must be something you can do."

Sifah comes to the edge of the fire, folds over and places a hand on Sun's neck. She bows her head with sorrow. Moving her touch to his ribs, she says, "His lungs are polluted. There is only one thing we can do to help him." She stares at Ki Anah, asking permission of sorts. Ki Anah nods.

Guen pulls back, wiping imaginary sweat from her forehead. "What're you going to do?"

Sifah lifts the last piece of firewood from the floor and hands it to Guen. "*I'm* not going to do anything, young Carvress."

Guen shakes her head. "I am not—You take that back. I'm not what you say."

Sifah laughs quietly and it sounds like the brush of felt on a brass bell. "I feel your power, child. You were created in the moment of Shei-Shei's purest and strongest fear." She looks to her sister, who Ki Anah imagines would blush, if such a thing were possible. "It is how my sisters and I were created so very long ago. From pure hatred comes the opposite." She gestures at the eight

Carvresses. Eight Shen princesses. "We are love. You were created from fear and so…" She points at Guen's heart. "You are bravery."

Ki Anah learned long ago not to gape with surprise. Her mother always tapped her chin up like she was closing a door, saying, "You'll catch flies, Ki Anah." She forces her mouth to stay closed though it works against her. This ancient magic has so many secret openings and strange consequences. She feels both honored and cursed to learn more about the Carvresses. She wonders where it all ends. But then, that is not for her to know. Her duty is to protect them and her family. She stares at the ground, knowing what she finds confusing and overwhelming may save her son. She places a hand on Guen's warm, birchwood shoulder.

"Please, Guen. We cannot lose him." She places all her trust in the Shen peasant girl, who sang naughty songs about the emperor in the forest and had her life changed forever.

Guen nods solemnly and awkwardly. She doesn't know what to do, but the Carvresses instruct her. Ki Anah is asked to step away, place Sun's life in the hands of dark Shen magic. Love and bravery—there are not two more admirable qualities than those.

Dawn sun streams through the small porthole and the last piece of firewood is held to the light.

Ki Anah turns and faces the wall, choosing to trace carvings instead of breaking her world further apart by witnessing what is supposed to be a solitary and sacred ritual between Char and Carvress. She hears the old song. A song she thought was Char but now knows grew from Shen soil. Rich tones of magic that act like shadow and smoke. Winding around them. Protecting them. And— oh, how she prays—healing them.

She understands some of the characters chipped into the wall. The word for women is repeated over and over. As is the word never. "Women never." Words that go together and don't because women don't say never. Not the women she knows. Unless the characters after "women never" mean "give up."

"Apa ini!" Sun's shocked voice is a lasso to Ki Anah's nerves, bundling them into a more manageable switch. She spins as the Carvresses pull back in a widening circle, leaving Guen squatting by Sun's side, hands rising from his chest.

Ki Anah swallows and approaches as Guen shuffles back, sniffing. She seems pale, if that's possible. Her usual rosy timber a little gray.

She stares at her hands. "Did I do it right?" she asks, blinking big eyes at her teachers.

Mi Asha smiles, rows of black wooden teeth. "Why don't you ask Sun Yan?"

Sun blinks fast and taps his chest. Ki Anah comes closer. What did she do to him? She peers, unable to see anything obvious. "Sun?"

Guen tilts her head, eye narrowing. "Take a big breath."

Sun does as he is told. Very unlike him. "Ooh, that feels strange." He flattens his palms over his rib cage.

Ki Anah comes to his side. Grateful. Relieved. Curious. "What do you mean?"

He stares at his chest as he breathes. "Um, kind of like I don't need the air, or…" He taps his chin. "Like the air needs me?" He looks to the Carvresses, who nod.

Sun grins and Guen smiles. "You gave me wooden lungs!"

He lifts his shirt and reveals just the edges of his ribs showing through his flesh, red and rough looking. Redwood pine.

Ki Anah frowns as Sun jumps up, trying out his new lungs. "They feel great." He flexes. "Like I could run all day and never get tired."

The women watch him disapprovingly. Ki Anah marches over and slaps the back of his head. "You idiot!"

Even Guen nods in agreement. Sun rubs his head. "Hey! What was that for?"

Guen storms over and pushes him in his newly wooden chest. "You nearly died. You nearly died and I had to save you." She shakes her tiny angry fist in his smirking face.

Ki Anah shakes her head. "Sun. *Son*. You owe Guen an apology and a thank you."

Sun finally registers the disapproval surrounding him and his face planes into seriousness. He takes a deep breath into lungs that bewilder Ki Anah in their mechanism. "I am sorry. To all of you." He opens his arms and the child falls into him, exhausted. He ruffles her wooden plaits, a very strange image. "Thank you, Guen. I promise I will never do anything that foolish again." There's that word again, "never." Ki Anah doubts he can keep his promise. But she is *never* without hope.

The once raging fire has died to red coals that will soon be dead.

"Your apology does nothing to help us right now, young man," Sifah says sternly. "We have used all our firewood to warm you and save you. We have very little food." She beckons to the strands of tree roots hanging down from the ceiling like wet hair. They lift Guen up and wind the roots around her fingers so she can recharge. The roots begin to change color as many have around the cave. Patches of gray like a middle-aged woman's hair spot the cathedral space. The Carvresses will survive for longer than Ki Anah and Sun, but they will run out of sustenance soon too. "And we are trapped."

Shame paints Sun's features but so does resolve. "I'll find a way to get us out of here."

The drum beats above shake the cave ceiling and small pieces of ice slide down the tiny porthole that brings them fresh air. They land on the stairs and bounce down, *clink, clink, clink*, sounding like glass on tiles. The Dark West tribe bellows across the mountains as they do every morning, noon, and evening. The sound could be a warning. It could be a message. For all Ki Anah knows, it could be a welcome. None of them know how to decipher it.

Like a blanket ripped from her shoulders, the cold bites suddenly. They will likely freeze to death before they starve. Ki Anah has an idea, but she will hold it to her heart until later. Until everyone has had a chance to forgive.

14
LUNA

SURRENDER BLOOD

Three Shen guards enter my cage while Char children watch, fingers gripped around their own bars. Air, Earth, and Water. The Fire Shen stays on the other side. I wonder if they were chosen this way on purpose. One of each element to cover all possibilities. In one hand they clutch bunches of black violet, their other hand buzzing with elemental power.

Ash grips the bamboo bars, coaching me as they approach. "Remember your attacks. You have several in your arsenal for every element. Use them."

I nod but the violets in their fists strike two-pronged fear through my body. One, because I don't want to be without my power for even a moment. Two, because I'm afraid of what horror awaits me that would require crushing my power so heavily. I feel a little like the bruised flowers in their hands. Powerful and dying at the same time.

I spread my fingers as Shen fan out around my cage. The glow worms above flicker on and off. Light, dark, light dark. Guards' eyes lift to the ceiling with trepidation.

"Ash," I whisper. "Which one first?"

The Shen arch eyebrows. I notice they're scratched and bruised already, the loose end of a bandage trailing from under the Earth Shen's tunic. Returned soldiers I have maybe fought before. I smile darkly. In the flickering light, their faces read all kinds of confusion.

"Earth." Ash coughs, gripping his side.

I wriggle my fingers and launch. Earth it is.

I take him down easily with a termite attack. Burrowing tunnel after tunnel until his Earth power is weakened and collapses. And as I ready myself for the next opponent, knowing I won't get to face them one at a time, a chant starts around the huge space. "Parut merah, merah. Parut merah, merah." Red, red scar. Char children roar, rattling cages and stomping little feet. The light and dark changes nothing in their brave, defiant expressions, and they fill me with Char pride and power.

Ash slips to the floor, his strength stretched to its limits. His life hanging by a hook next to torture devices. But he joins the chanting, eyes glowing like luminescent algae over a whitewashed sea.

I strike and kick. Scratch and punch. My Blood element bites and strangles. Sea snakes dripping with poison. Murderbirds cutting through the wind and slicing veins with razor-sharp feathers. Soon the Shen are dragging themselves backward, begging to be let out of the cage. I am triumphant. Rewarded by Char childrens' eyes on me, their hope in my fingers, their future in my heart. The glow worms light the space brightly. Shining like stars about to explode.

I feel—

I stare down at my arms, streaked with black violet sap.

I feel weak.

The Shen crawl to the front of the cage and I follow them. I am weak but not done. Not yet. I focus on their cowering faces and their arms in the air, ready to concede.

The flutter of a heart, smaller than my own but of my people, has me turn toward another cage.

"You better do as I ask, Blood Char." Qi Sha, the Fire Shen grimaces as he presses a knife to the young Lu Leng's thin throat. I sense blood pumping wildly through her veins. Almost in a hurry to come streaming from her skin if he presses a tenth harder.

Hands up. Palms outward. Surrender is not in my blood. But I must surrender my Blood.

The Fire Shen laughs, and it's cruel and icy even though he brims with heat. "Come to think of it—" He drops his blade. "I don't need a knife." He pinches Lu Leng's shoulder, teeth glinting green in the worm light as he torches her with his Fire.

A scream that hollows out the darkest corners of this space. She has no wooden part and therefore, no defense. She is pure and he's scorching her insides. Hickory beats like a protest march. She will not die today.

"What do you want?" I ask, though I know. She quivers in his arms, veins ashy from the constant flame attack. "Release her and I will do anything."

Ash whispers a half-felt, "Luna, no." Because he knows I have no choice.

"Do what I want and *then* I shall release her," Qi Sha growls, not giving an inch as Lu Leng squirms listlessly, very little fight left.

"Fine." I bow.

Qi Sha's smile is sick and twisted. "Good girl. Surrender. Consume the black violet and step out of the cage with your hands up."

Snatching the flowers from a cowardly Shen on his knees in the dirt, I press the bitter flowers to my tongue. They work quickly and soon my Blood power is lost like a pearl dropped into the ocean.

I step out of my cage with my hands raised. They are thrust behind my back, and I'm bound as the glow worm light goes out in a snap. Just the lonely circle of the guard's torch lights the bars.

Lu Leng is released and tossed into her cage. She tries to sit up, but her chest hits the ground. Ha Fun reaches through and pulls her up to lean against the bars.

Ash's eyes follow me as I am shoved toward the stairs. "Where are you taking her?" he shouts.

The guards limping and nursing their wounds laugh but it sounds forced. It sounds like they are balloons inflated with stale air and they can't keep themselves afloat. "*He* wants to meet her."

More forced laughing. "Don't you mean *she*?" the Earth Shen adds.

"Look after them!" I yell before a bag is thrown over my head.

I don't need an answer; I know he will.

15
LYE

A GIFT

Diplomacy feels more challenging than going to battle. Fighting, wounding, and killing come more easily to me. It's what I've been trained for. It's what I try to shake from my body every day like dragon's scales. They decorate my path wherever I tread.

We know the Shen army is depleted since we took many prisoners from the battle of Crow's Nest and the numbers that fled from Black Sail City were small. I know the chancellor would be using villagers and farmers for protection. Tying ropes around their necks and yanking as many as he could closer to the palace. I hope those forced to serve are unwilling and inexperienced. They also don't have me. Their elemental army has shrunk like a preserved animal in a jar. Without the Keeper it cannot grow.

A knock on the door gently pushes it open. A face appears, of which I've come to know every slope and curve. Joka's eyes crinkle. He looks tired. I suppose we all do. I fold clothes into my pack along with as many weapons as I can fit. As Joka turns to close the door, I pull the rosewood and cork carving I found in the ruins from under my pillow and tuck it into the front pocket of my pack.

"I thought this was a peaceful mission." His arched eyebrows frame intelligent, observant eyes. Warmth pools in my stomach, slow and gentle like ginger candy.

Knives clatter against each other as I shift my bag. I run a finger along the edge of a blade. "I'm not taking any chances."

Joka comes to stand by my side and stares down at the arsenal. "Do you suppose that in preparing for the worst outcome, you could bring it about?"

I purse my mouth, contemplating this philosophical notion. "I will try not to be the first one to attack." I do not promise anything.

"On our way to the Carvresses, will we to come close to the palace?" His voice is hopeful. I don't allow it to last.

"Not close enough," I reply, feeling just as he does. How painful it will be to pass by the palace, knowing our siblings are inside suffering. "I am sorry. The Carvresses must come first." My heart grows a little heavier in my chest.

The corner of his mouth lifts just slightly. "We must trust that they live and that they can wait. Luna is tougher than anyone I know. She'll survive this."

I bow my head, praying he is right. Hooking my fingers into his hope and allowing it to carry me across the sky like a kite caught in the wind. Is Ash tough? I wouldn't have thought so six months ago, but now, though I don't believe him hard, I do think he's resilient.

Joka runs a hand through his spiky hair. I watch the action, imagining what it would feel like to brush my fingers through that hair. Would it feel good, or would it feel like trespassing? He notices me staring and pauses. "Do I have something in my hair?" He pats his head frantically as color rises unwanted to my cheeks.

I shake my head. "No. I was just wondering what it would feel like to touch it." My thoughts tumble from my mouth before I can stop them.

I shut my mouth tightly, but the words are out, floating on an awkward and embarrassing cloud. I await disapproval or rationalization of why that would be a bad idea. But he simply smiles and takes my hand. I enjoy the sense of him wrapping around me like a feathered wing to a chick. Warm, reassuring. Not a golden slap of heat and intensity. Slow. Careful. "Lye, you need not wonder."

He places my power-less hand in his hair, and I thrill at the simple treasure and pleasure of just my skin, no elemental interruption, ruffling the wiry strands. I close my eyes and smile.

When I open them, he's watching me in the strangest way. Like hunger but also like he's full and this is almost enough for him. As his lips curve, he reaches for my hair, which is still shorter than his, but at least I'm no longer bald. I bow, pulling back a few inches. "I could hurt you."

He hesitates, tilting his head, eyes on mine, sea blue to midnight black. But then he continues, threading his thin fingers through the hair at the back my head. "I don't think you will, Lye. You have more control than you think." I concentrate, but not very hard. It's difficult to think of anything other than his cool hands on my skin and the way he's pulling my head closer to his. Fire is smothered by spring rain. Snow is melted by a warm wind. Four seasons come to balance within me as I allow him in. Truly and without prejudice.

He doesn't kiss me. Like a seedling, splitting its seed and slowly working its way to the sun, we're not rushing. He merely touches his forehead to mine and murmurs, "See."

I manage a nod. I also manage to hold back tears, but they live in the creases of my eyes. They wish to spill joyfully over my cheeks, but control works both ways. And emotions are still a medium I'm unfamiliar with.

"Your hair feels like wire," I whisper.

He chuckles. "Yours feels like cornsilk."

This makes us laugh and we lean back into our own personal space again. The moment is enough for us right now.

Joka stares at my elemental hand with that deep thought look. Like I'm a page in a book he's trying to translate. "What?" I ask.

As if startled from a dream, he rattles his head. "Oh nothing."

I know he's lying. "Joka, you can tell me."

He purses his lips. "No anger. No judgement?"

My chin pulls in. Now I'm worried, but I promise. "Of course."

He strokes his bamboo neck. "It's just—I know you refused Fah, but do you ever think perhaps that was a mistake? Do you think you might change your mind about giving Char elemental power?"

I'm taken aback by his question. Blinking rapidly, my lips tremble as memories of control and abuse storm the walls of my mind. The strangling fear of being dragged back into that world. "I promised I would never be a weapon again and that I would never be a slave to death and destruction."

Joka pushes. Like poking a bruise to see if it still hurts. It always does. "Your power is remarkable. I know you've only ever known it to be a weapon, but I can't help but wonder whether it could be a force for good. For balance."

"Balance?" My hands shake, upset at the turn in this conversation, and Joka can tell.

He flaps his hands like he's fanning flames. A rather contradictory action. "I'm sorry, I've upset you. I didn't mean to. It just occurred to me that the one thing we're fighting about *and* the one thing that could bring us together, well… it's you."

My head keeps shaking no. "You're oversimplifying a very complicated problem."

Joka chuckles and sighs, but the sound is lighter and airier than it should be. "Yes, I suppose I am. It's just… I know you think of your power as a weapon. Did you ever stop to think maybe it's nothing of the sort?"

It has always been a weapon. A way to make a stronger, more deadly soldier. A way to lift some up and keep others down in the mud. "If not a weapon, then what?" I ask. Fearful of the answer, I put up a hand. I don't want to hear what he has to say.

But he says it just the same. "A gift to be shared."

A gift to be shared. It's the kind of idealistic notion I would expect from Ben Ni. Not his logical brother Joka. But something in his excited, dawn-breaking eyes begs it to be considered. I look down at my hands, the deep grain scars up my arms. It feels too late. Too much damage has occurred. Even if I am unfinished like the cork carving, perhaps that's for the best. What if the completed sculpture is an ugly disaster?

"I am not a gift, Joka. I am a curse."

He places a soft hand on my rough sycamore arm. "And curses are meant to be broken."

16
KI ANAH

THE RIGHT SIDE

Ki Anah watches her son talk to the birchwood child. Guen is far more powerful and capable than Ki Anah thought. She saved Sun's life. Sifah said Guen is bravery. Ki Anah needs to believe this since she has a task for Guen requiring much bravery. Probably all the eight-year-old has.

Her son takes deep breaths with his new lungs. Ki Anah frowns. He has been blessed with two wooden parts which is a rare honor. But it was only given because of foolishness, not because he earned it. She has a task for him also, and like Guen, it will require a brave, faithful heart.

Sun laughs and plays with the girl. It fits him to be that kind of father, the playful, child-at-heart kind. And she does not begrudge Sun his childishness from time to time. He is only eighteen. But she's furious at his recklessness that led them to this dire situation.

Stretching her neck, she rubs her frozen fingers together, preparing for a very difficult conversation. Like removing the seeds from a ghost chili pepper: Difficult but necessary.

She calls her son. Guen follows and Ki Anah raises a hand to stop her. The girl pouts but the quiet, kind Carvress of Bird Cage Island, Fe Lin, connects with Ki Anah and beckons the child with her golden elm hand.

"You called, Mama?" Sun jogs up the stairs, showing no ill signs of his near drowning. She wonders whether there should be something. At least then he might feel a little humbler.

"Walk with me," she says, the air coming out her mouth in sorry little clouds. She clutches the Carvress's dress of pink and yellow hibiscus flowers closer around her shoulders.

He breathes long and loud. "I could run from end to end of this place a hundred times with these new lungs and I wouldn't feel tired!" He shudders. "Though I do feel the chill."

She frowns, cherrywood hips cracking as she leads him down the stairs and to the tunnel where they hunted in what seems like an age ago. "You need to come with me." Her eyes take on that dark and serious gaze as she stares up at her son, and his demeanor instantly changes.

"Yes, Mama. Just one thing."

He runs to the Carvresses and gathers a few more garments, racing back to drape them around Ki Anah's shoulders. He is a good son. A silly one sometimes, but he has a noble heart. She shivers even as more clothing is added. It's so very cold here. Her arm and leg joints feel glued together, her movements stiff and unwilling. And even though Sun moves better, she can tell the cold is working its way into her son's bones too. His spasming shakes played as purposeful are not easy to hide from a mother.

Worm glow lights their way as they tread the earth with a heaviness they both feel in their chests. Ki Anah taps her heart. She misses the sun on her cheeks. The sea air filling her lungs. She had a simple life but a good one. *How did it all come down to this?* A housewife with wooden hips, tasked with saving her people from extinction. She sighs deeply and Sun throws a cool arm over her shoulder.

Keeping an eye out for spiky rat creatures, they sweep their gazes from side to side. Thankfully nothing hisses or scratches, and when they arrive at the mirror-like ice, they see why. It is completely closed over.

"They had more sense than us," she mutters running her hand over the solid slab, hands already so cold she barely feels it.

Sun stops, hands on hips and frowns. "How do you mean?"

She tries to peer through but can see nothing. "Ash said we needed to be on the right side when it closed over." Her heart feels sluggish, bashing against her ribcage like a depressed, captive animal. "Sun, it's clear we are on the wrong side."

He frowns and clasps his hands behind his head. His eyes move from one end of the thick ice to the other, looking for a gap. "How can you be sure?"

Ki Anah purses her lips at the vast faith they have put in the Shen boy with the strange smile and great love for Luna. But she does not think he would have left them here to freeze to death. "Ash would not have sent us here to die. He had a plan that stretched beyond weeks. If Luna hadn't been—" She can't finish her thought. Some things are too painful to say out loud. Sun squeezes her closer. "I think we have made a grave mistake staying so close to the edge of the mountain."

Sun's eyes crinkle with pain and recognition. She knows he came to respect the Shen boy. He certainly trusted him. He curses. "Oh Mama, of course, you are right." He clenches his fist and thumps the ice wall behind them. It reacts like an emperor to a peasant: indifferent.

Ki Anah sits on a boulder by the wall and pats a seat beside her. He eagerly takes his place, and it brings a frozen tear to her eye as she remembers him as a boy. His bouncy enthusiasm as he pulled up a chair and tried to help her pinch dumplings at the table. The misshapen blobs looked like they'd already been chewed and spit out, but he was so happy to be working by her side. She never had the heart to correct him and now wonders if she did him a disservice. Now she must be truthful, and this truth is a harsh one. "I have things I must tell you. And you will do me the courtesy of keeping that smart mouth closed until I am finished."

Sun lets out one more hushed curse before agreeing. Ki Anah rolls her eyes; he does make her feel terribly old at times. She runs a tongue over her teeth, not intending to dust her words in sugar. This truth is as sour as an unripe cherry feijoa, and he must swallow every last bite.

"Sun. You have always been confident. Your strength and size afforded you an advantage, but you let it fill your head with falseness. You believe yourself invincible. You show off and act silly, especially to the young Shen girl. You make out as if you are the strongest and bravest of all of us."

She watches her son's face for a reaction. To his credit, he simply listens. Expression tense but not defensive. "You dove into the pond without thought. Or perhaps one thought? And now, because of your rashness, because the women of this group had to save your life, we have no firewood." At this his chin falls. Shame captioning his dark eyes. She pats his leg. She's Char, so she's not gentle, and it comes out more like a thump. He startles. She's strong too, preferring not to bandy it around as he does.

"I need you to stop slipping into boyhood. You can't dive into icy ponds without thought, you can't launch at creatures you know nothing about. Sun, my dear, you need to accept responsibility for your mistakes and grow up. You must firmly take your place in manhood. And stay there."

She stares up at the young man she raised. Tears sting her eyes, freezing hard as diamonds before they fall. She knows he would have come to this on his own if he had more time, but that's not something she can give.

"May I speak now, Mama?" She nods. "You are right. I've made a mess of things. But please understand, I dove into the pond not only to find food, but to get help."

Ki Anah uses her words like stones to his pockets, keeping him on the ground and feeling the weight of what he has done. "Your motivation matters not. You acted without thinking and without consulting the rest of us."

He inhales deeply, soaking in her words as he does the thin air. "I did. I will say one thing. I only act silly and show off to Guen because she's a kid and I don't want her to be scared." Sun leans his head atop his mother's. "I have been in battle. Don't mistake my play for immaturity."

Ki Anah's voice is stern, solid as an oak. "I do not mistake anything. You may have seen some terrible things, but your heart is young and has much to learn. You have responsibilities. Not only to me and the Carvresses but to Guen. She relies on you like you are her father. You scooped up that title, wearing it around for weeks. It has sunk into your skin and cannot be undone."

He sighs then, big as bellows. "I am sorry."

"Sun, your recklessness has led us here. Without firewood, we're going to die in this cave. You and I will freeze very soon if we don't do something and then Guen will be left with no one and the Carvresses will be unprotected."

His eyebrows rise, legs jitter. "What can I do? I will try anything, risk everything, if I could save us." So ready to throw himself into danger again. Ki Anah sighs, a bedraggled, exhausted sound born of repeating oneself over and over.

Ki Anah shakes her head. "There is only one person who can save us now and it's not you."

Sun blinks, short dark lashes frosted with white. "Then who?"

Ki Anah puts both hands on her son's shoulders and acts as a scaffold, holding him up so he can make the hardest decision of his life. "The girl Guen is small enough to fit through the porthole." His head sways from side to side as she speaks. "She does not feel the cold as we do. She must go in search of help."

"She is a child. You cannot ask this of her," he argues.

"I'm not going to ask her. You are."

Sun's voice cracks. "Mama, how can you suggest this to me?"

Ki Anah is firm in her plan. "You think yourself brave, and you have been many times in the past, but right now is a test of true bravery." She pounds the boulder, punctuating her words.

He wipes his nose, shoulders straightening, anger tingling at the edge of his voice. "How is that?"

She smiles sadly. "Sometimes, the bravest act is letting someone else, someone you love, save you."

His head falls in his hands. She knows he wishes there were another way. She does too. But they are out of options.

"What if she says no?"

Ki Anah does not hold this question in her heart. "She won't."

17
LUNA

THE THREAT TO THE LEFT

She? Am I to be tortured by someone new today? I picture a female doctor, readying her tools, wiping blood on her apron. I shrug. Male or female, torture makes monsters of us all. A stain on the soul that cannot be erased. It lives on my heart like black oil. A permanent shadow next to the split from losing Ben Ni. Oh, brother, the children remind me of you in a hundred different ways. It makes me even more determined to save them.

From under my head covering, I hear the guards separate. The wounded limping down a different tunnel branch, leaving me and the Fire Shen, Qi Sha, alone. He grips my wrist tightly as we twist and turn, turn and twist, head upstairs and down. All the while, he makes little puffs of exertion as he uses Fire to singe me repeatedly. Small scalds that are painful but leave no lasting damage.

I clench my teeth, determined not to give him the satisfaction of hearing me suffer.

"You're not much without Shen power, are you, little girl?" he remarks as he drags me, my knees grazing the rugs.

"I am Char Luna Yan," I say through the fabric. "I am ten times the warrior you are with or without my Blood sense."

The Fire Shen emits an ugly laugh. Like the sound got twisted and coated in darkness as it passed his heart on the way from his lungs. A warped, bat-winged thing.

He yanks my arm up violently and I can't help but let out a small cry of pain. "You are ten times weaker than me. And right now, ten times more likely to die." He relishes his words. He's the Shen we know best. In a way, it's comforting to know my enemy. I snort and get a kick in the side for my trouble.

The air is heavy with jasmine and cherry. I hang from the guard's grasp for a moment before he swings and throws my body like a sack of garbage. Landing on a soft tufted rug, a dragon's eye glares at me through the weave. A woman's sharp tsk of disapproval sounds as the bag is yanked from my head.

"This her?" I blink up at a servant woman, who stares down at me underwhelmed. Sun streams through a second story window, stinging my eyes. My lungs ache for the fresh air rustling the emerald canopy of a forest I never got to step foot in.

Qi Sha nods and steps back from the threshold. "Good luck washing the Char stink off this one!" he remarks, thinking himself hilarious.

I sit back on my heels, taking in the octagonal, gold-leafed room. Every panel intricately carved with flowers and woodland creatures. A large sunken bath sits in the center. Jasmine and cherry blossom petals float on the water like funeral garlands. Water torture is only something I've heard of and was hoping was a myth. Swallowing anxiously, I'm thankful Ash is spared from *feeling* me now. I stand and retreat from the edge of the bathing pool.

Several female servants crowd around with narrowed eyes to corner me against the wall. They're unmarked by elemental tattoos. Hair pinned tightly into buns. Dull lavender dresses sweep their ankles. It shocks me to see the batik sashes around their middles. So very similar to Char patterns. Their gazes track upward from my filthy toes, my torn tunic, to my clumpy, dirt-crusted hair.

I ready my fists and an elderly servant shakes her ginger root finger at me. "We're not going to hurt you, girl." Then she claps her hands and orders, "Off with your clothes."

THIS *IS* torture. Intended or not. Having my arms pulled this way and that, my toes parted and scrubbed. Every portion of my body inspected and found lacking. They clip my nails, scrub my hair, and rub at my face until it feels as if they've removed several layers of my skin. I'm a shell bashed and scraped against the sand by waves until I'm as smooth and polished as a gemstone. Staring down at my bare, scratched, and bruised legs floating above turquoise tiles, I am clearly no gemstone. I like my rough edges, cracks and barnacles, and I like that they make it obvious I don't belong here.

A servant girl leans toward me with a small brush in her hand, eyes on my hickory heart, wearing an expression of horror and fascination. My hand goes to my chest. "Don't even think about it." She frowns and looks to her superior who nods. She scrapes the bristles along my sternum, and as she tries to reveal the shine of the brass, she discovers my limit. I've had enough. I stand suddenly, perfumed water dripping across my heart and down my naked body.

I step out of the bath, picking the petals from my skin and flinging them to the floor. "Where are my clothes?" I yell when I have no right to. The servants startle at my bark but soon turn deaf ears. Fussing around me like they're decorating a cake. Patting me down, redressing my wounds, hanging silk from my arms and chains from my neck. I struggle against them, but it only makes things worse as they put more effort into restraining me, tugging my bindings tighter.

A woman comes at me with a paint brush in one hand and a puff covered in white powder. I lean away, teeth bared. "You touch my face with that stuff, and I'll shove that puff down your throat," I growl.

And I must look like a rabid animal, every bit the brutish Char I hope to be, because she stops dead in her tracks, hands shaking. Her eyes shift to the senior maid who shakes her head and puts up her hand. "She has the luck of the young and does not need such embellishment. Besides, she's not a potential courtier, she's a prisoner." She waves her hands over my small frame. "This will do. It's a vast improvement from what we started with."

My breastbone is showing. Hickory arms and brass joints like a Char shield against this Shen nonsense. I tug the red silk dress they shoved over my head tighter, trying to close the gap. A young maid holds some oil and a polishing cloth up to me. "They want to see it," she says, eyes lowered.

I snatch the oil and cloth. "The doctor has already seen my heart," I snarl as I work the oil into the brass joints.

All this scrubbing and cleaning has bought me time. And my hickory heart has sped the black violet around my system quicker than the average Shen. So quickly the effect is starting to wear off. Blood sense creeps back into my body, but not enough to do anything. I can faintly sense the maid's Atmosphere vibrating with both fear and awe. Like a twin-tailed squirrel captured by a jewel snake. Mesmerized by its beautiful, glistening skin, unable to look away even though it knows it's dangerous.

She steps back, eyes on the floor. "They wish to meet you. And anyone who meets them must be clean and presented at their best."

The elderly maid frowns and shoos the maid from the room. Again, I tighten my dress, which trails in ribbons of red-as-blood silk, engulfing my feet in satin slippers with beaded rubies. My skin crawls beneath all this opulence. I feel comfortable in my brother's old tunics tied with a cord. The old woman tells the guard I am ready, and he enters the room. Eyes widening at the sight of me.

"What?" I challenge, chin jutting out proudly.

He grabs my arm. His Atmosphere similarly apprehensive: fear and awe. Though I don't think these feelings are for me. He chuckles cruelly. "It's just I've never seen lipstick on a pig before." I wish I could bash his stupid mouth with a bear claw, but I need to wait. I close my eyes and think of the children. I must be smart. Besides, I don't entirely disagree with him. This is not me. I trip on my skirts as he pulls me from the room.

I glance up at him. "What, no sack?"

He grunts. "We're not going far."

In this short corridor, the windows are covered by thick velvet curtains the color of an old bruise. Behind me and ahead of me rest heavy bolted doors. Apart from being on the second floor, there's no way to place where I am in the palace.

As we approach the door ahead, I sense the same impressive creature as when we tried to escape. Fangs and fur and a sort of regal-ness setting it apart from regular animals. I run my tongue over my teeth in anticipation. This could be a golden opportunity.

Qi Sha draws me close so his lips tickle my ear when he speaks. "You say one word about the Char children to him and I will make sure they all suffer. You understand?"

When I don't respond, he shakes me violently until my adornments jingle like the bells on an oxen's harness. "All right, I understand," I manage, my mind ticking over the reasons why whoever is in this room needs to be lied to.

Satisfied, the guard knocks sharply on the door. Iron slides against iron as bolts are released on the other side. I brace myself for more torture. Knives and needles. Chisels and vices.

The door swings open, and I'm met by four faces, only one I recognize. I search for the creature but only see two women, one young and ridiculously decorated, the other older and more refined. Sitting between them is a man in purple silk.

The doctor climbs carefully down a couple of wide steps, hands clasped together with glee. He strides straight for me and places his hand on my chest. I try to jerk away but the guard holds me tight. I must suppress my Blood power for the moment. It is agony not to bite back. "Remarkable! See that? She has healed herself within the day. This has marvelous implications for future hybrids, if we can find a Carvress and retrieve the Keep… " Someone coughs and the doctor ceases his babbling.

I'm shoved to the ground. A woman whispers words I can't quite make out and is followed by a strong voice like the bass notes of a mandolin. "Yes, she *is* special. Make sure you treat her as such." Another hushed female whisper and then, "Mmhm. Each part of her must be analyzed carefully. I wish to see your progress notes. Now."

The doctor's voice is high and quivers like violin strings at the bow when he answers, "Yes, emperor," and scuttles away.

18
LYE

BARKING UP THE WRONG OAK TREE

"Are you ready?" Joka asks as we stand in the doorway, rain streaming from bursting gutters in a cold curtain.

His words haunt me. Throw me back and forth like a crab in the waves. I have nothing to hold onto and so I tumble and turn, getting dizzier and more confused by the second. I rise and sling my pack over my shoulder, concentrating on what I am sure of. "I have made long journeys before. I can do so again." My stomach shakes its head, reminding me of my seasickness.

Joka laughs like a broken flute. "I'm not talking about the journey." He pulls back the door and allows me to walk through first.

"What are you talking about then?"

He knocks his head toward the barrel-chested man currently tightening his army vest and awaiting the rest of us slow mortals. My back stiffens and I pump my hands. I'm not ready for this and I'm not sure I'll ever be. I chew on my lip as I watch the father who has lost so much and keeps giving.

My fear comes at me folded in points like a kite, set to pierce my heart. On one side of the crease is my deep, unwavering respect for Setsu Yan. In making this decision, his respect for me may wither as quickly as it has grown. On the other side is a sharper, angled fold: The selfish fear of wondering how I can possibly do this without him.

The small crew is ready to leave. They await my command, packs at their feet, weapons in their sheaths. Sheltering under the eaves of the main hall, backs pressed to the mossy, gray wall.

Setsu stands separate from the others, looking over the monastery barricade. The new additions obscure my view, but I imagine the great warrior sets his eyes on the black stone sails, the rock reflective and magical, the three remaining sentinels of a city that's been reduced to ashes.

I clear my throat to interrupt his thoughts. His oak hand rests upon the bricks and he points out from our fortress while rain thoroughly soaks his clothes. "We should tell the refugees to send people to the lower forest. There are fruit trees and a good fishing spot at the beach. As long as they look out for pebble backed sea lizards."

My eyebrow quirks at the mention of the creature that tried to drag me into the ocean so many months ago. A hopeless, edge-of-death version of myself I was ashamed of. She fought so hard to get herself back up the mountain and to find purpose. I am ashamed no longer. That version of Lye brought me here.

Setsu huffs a sigh and his moustache flutters from his lips. "Stupid, stubborn creatures."

I bite my lip and turn to Joka, who's watching us from the doorway. His worried expression makes me more uneasy. I take a deep breath. "I was attacked by one once," I say. Skirting around what I want to say.

Setsu tilts his face halfway toward mine. "Really? They're not easy to defeat. Their young are delicious though and worth the struggle." My lips purse at the idea of eating a smaller version of that monster. "Ki Anah makes a wonderful pebble back curry. Coconut, turmeric, lemongrass. Just the right amount of chili." He licks his lips.

I stand on my tiptoes, trying to see what he's staring at, but it's pointless. "I wouldn't have thought they made good eating."

Setsu chuckles a sound like the sea in a bottle. "Ki Anah knew how to prepare them. The skin is good for chair backs and water skins too." His broad chest seems to grow even broader. "Ah, she is a good wife. An even better cook. I am looking forward to seeing her again." His mouth curves up at the thought of her and his shoulders relax.

I wind up my fist, ready to deliver the blow. "Setsu."

"The islands look so small from up here." His eyes move from side to side. "I imagine she took the wide mouth and the northeastern arm of the river. The narrow river runs too close to the palace."

I'm surprised of his knowledge of the mainland. "That was the plan, yes."

"Will we do the same?" he asks.

I nod slowly. I need to just spit it out. "Joka, me, and the others will take the northeast river, yes. But Setsu, I need you to stay here—with the refugees."

His oak hand scrunches into a fist, bringing scrapings of rock and moss with it. The sound not unlike how my nerves feel. "I will not."

Stand firm. Be the general he appointed. "This is not a request; it's an order."

Setsu has been the guiding light of even temper. Wise and calm and—and now he's turning red.

His Atmosphere reads of a volcano, bubbling over. Cracks of molten orange showing through usually impenetrable stone. "You expect me to stay here while you take my last son and go to rescue the rest of my family?" His voice is as loud as a shrieking elephant, its wide coconut-storing trunk designed for maximum capacity and volume. "You expect me to hang back with the women and children while you march to the palace where my daughter is imprisoned?"

I straighten my shoulders, rake my skeleton over ice so it's frozen in place. "I *expect* you to listen to your general. I need you here. Your people need you here." I point to the ground. Gray cobblestones sprout all manner of green fuzz in the ever-present drizzle.

He turns to face me, looming over me like a great shadow, brows pointing down like spears. "My girl, you are barking up the wrong oak tree. My family needs me. If someone must remain, let it be you."

I shake my head. "You have no knowledge of how to get to my village. You don't have the connection to the Shen or the palace that I have. I'm sorry, Setsu, but we cannot use you on this mission." I don't say what wafts over my body like a second spirit. *I am the Keeper.* Or was. That will still mean something to Shen peasants.

His nostrils flare. I have insulted him. I shouldn't have insulted him. "You know nothing of my experience, child. Nothing. This is my family. My responsibility."

I inhale deeply. Sadness surrounds me like the funnel of a water tornado I will soon be sucked into. Storms follow me wherever I go. I place my elemental hand on his forearm. I convey my feelings of loss and longing for my brother and his brows drop by millimeters. "Setsu, my family is under threat too."

He grunts, shirking my touch. "I will not refuse orders, General. But I ask you, I—" His faces scrunches in pain. "No, I beg of you. Don't make me stay."

Leadership comes with making hard decisions, balancing needs and wants. This decision hurts me like a thousand fangs dipped in poison but I do not wrestle with this choice. Setsu is far too skilled, wise, and brave to not be the first person I would think to replace me. It could be no other. "Setsu Yan, as your general I am ordering you to remain here and protect the monastery. Your people need a wise and strong leader. It can only be you."

His head bows as he listens to my orders. His eyes do not lift when I am done. "General Koh, as your soldier, I accept your request." My heart swells a quarter degree. Perhaps he sees the sense in this. But then he takes my heart in his oak fist and squeezes it like a sca sponge when he mutters, "But as a father, I will never forgive you."

He lifts his proud chin, eyes on the sky, and stalks from me like I am vapor.

I watch his broad back grow smaller but still enormous as he leaves. His anger washes over me like the downpour above. *Unforgiven* is a badge I've had sewn onto my clothing so many times it takes up most of the space on my uniform. This one stings greatly upon its application. I touch the imaginary patchwork. My aching heart wishes for a different outcome. But it should know wishes are a waste.

Joka grabs my hand and tries to pull me under shelter, and I scratch him with eagle claws. He doesn't let go. "Lye, come inside. We are to have one last meal before we leave."

Glad for the rain covering my silly, un-general-like tears, I sniff. "Your father hates me."

Joka pulls me again, but I shoot him an icy look and he drops it. "Yes, I suppose he does. Can you blame him?"

Am I not allowed to grieve the friendship I have lost, the counsel I leaned on? "No, I guess not. But I've lost my friend." My hair sticks to my head like banana leaf.

Joka shields his eyes from the torrent of water. "If you are *his* friend, you have to let him hate you."

I cross my arms over my chest. "Very well. Go eat your last supper and leave me be."

Setsu can have this last meal with his son. I gift him the relief of not having to look at my pathetic face across the table. Reluctantly, Joka retreats.

Shivering, I taste bitter tears. If I am ever to make it right with Setsu Yan, I must bring his family back. Every member. I laugh hard, thinking of the obstacles in my path. Of purple silk and a golden headdress; an emperor and those that would control him. Vanity and stupidity combined with evil and greed. These qualities colliding give little hope. Like the last flutter of a crushed butterfly. *Shouldn't be too hard at all.*

19
GUEN

OF BRAVERY

Guen doesn't see much sense in waiting around. Though her funny wooden arms and legs tremble at the thought of going up *there* without Sun; he said she needed to. His face went all serious like it does when he really means it, so she knows it's the right thing to do.

A pack hangs from her hands. It isn't very heavy. She doesn't need water or food. Just a knife and a message to deliver.

"The knife is for cutting wood. Nothing else," Sun says gruffly, shaking his finger. "Cut as many branches as you can reach from trees nearby and send them down the hole." Guen nods, trying to write these words into her brain. She wants to make sure she does exactly as she's asked. The last time a grown up shook their finger at her, it was her mother threatening another beating if she didn't bring back enough firewood. There's a weird heat in her stomach that swirls around and grows when she thinks of her parents. She misses them, but she doesn't miss the sting of a bamboo stake against the back of her legs, or the way Mama used to look at her like she was a fly that needed swatting.

Watching Sun's finger wave back and forth in front of her eyes, she catches the worry in his expression. He would never hurt her. It's nice to feel safe with a grown up.

Ki Anah pulls Guen into her arms and squeezes tightly. "Be careful. Be brave but not foolish. If you think you could get hurt, return to us." Guen tries to remember all the advice. But there's a lot of words thrown at her. Be brave is the one that sticks in her head more than the others. She thinks she can do that. She'll have to try.

The Carvresses look at her with their funny wooden eyes, which Guen has to remind herself she also has. She touches her cheek. It feels soft as skin to her, but she knows it doesn't feel that way to Ki Anah and Sun. Shei-Shei, the one who made her, sniffs and sways back and forth like a chime in a red dust storm. Guen scowls. The Carvress feels bad for what she did, but it's over now. Guen's still not sure about her or the other wooden women yet. Sun says that it's going to take a while to get used to her new life. She does know she loves Sun, so she will do what she can to save him.

Sun taps her shoulder. "You ready, kid?" She's not sure but nods anyway. He lifts her into his arms and touches his nose to hers. She wishes he could come with her. She knows he wishes that too. "You're going to do great," he whispers. "You're braver than anyone I've ever met. Remember that, all right?"

She takes a deep, unnecessary breath. "All right."

The light from the porthole is white and cold. Sun lifts her up until she gets her fingers into a crack and can pull herself in. The hole is so tight she can't turn around, she can only go forward. If she were flesh, she would run out of air fast. But being wooden makes all her needs smaller. She pants all the same and tries not to scream at the way the walls press against her. Shuffling on her hands and knees, back splintering against the rock.

Their shouts of encouragement reach her squashed ears. Sun's voice is the loudest. "I know you can do this, Guen."

She can do this. She can. Clenching her teeth, she wiggles upward. Voices getting thinner and smaller as drumbeats get louder and louder.

Pieces of ice slide toward her like tiny fragments of glass. Her wooden hands crunch against them pulling toward brighter light. Almost blinding.

Drum. Drum. Drum.

The sun, cold and white like the moon but harsher. She reaches up to what she hopes is the end of this wormhole and her hand hits something hard.

Ice. She pictures the others, waiting at the bottom. Worrying. Freezing. She gnashes her wooden teeth together and hits the ice with her fist. It splinters but doesn't break. Her knees dig into rock, not painful exactly, but uncomfortable and definitely slippery. She doesn't want to skid all the way back down. Not without having tried her best to save them.

She leans back and springs at the ice, birchwood head down. It shatters, probably sending pieces all the way down to the cave. She flies through the opening and onto something soft and fluffy and whiter than a fresh bao bun.

She flips onto her back, eyes shuttered against the harsh white light. Squinting, she takes in the surroundings, emerald pines as tall as palaces with branches almost sweeping the ground. They loom over her like a bunch of disapproving relatives. They point to a dishwater sky.

She made it! She taps her wooden head. "Thanks to you," she sniggers.

In front are acres of firewood just begging to be cut. This world is foreign and wild. Smelling fresh and clean. Unfarmed and untouched.

Drum. Drum. Drum.

Snow falls from branches with a soft plop. Reminding her of her mother's lumpy congee. Guen lifts her head to the sky. She needs to get to work.

She begins cutting small pieces of wood that will slide down the chute easily. One by one. She works for hours until the gray sky begins to darken, and her hands are sticky with pine sap.

She's worried about night coming. Darkness frightens her. As does the drumming that seems to come from everywhere and nowhere all at once. But she's pleased she got them the wood. It will keep them warm. At least for a couple more nights. She pictures Sun's proud expression, warm and waxy from the fire, and it keeps her going. She stomps through the snow, which swallows her little legs up to her thighs, and tries to follow the drumbeats of the Dark West.

Images of men dancing about a large iron pot filled with Shen villagers tries to push into her mind, but she ignores it. She remembers what Ki Anah told her. "They are people. Just like us. We must believe them to be good as we are good. We are all carved from the same bone. Bathed in the same blood." Which sounded kind of gross to her, but she thinks she understood the meaning. Underneath, all people are the same. She snorts. Shen and Char could have saved themselves a lot of effort if they'd worked this out years ago.

Guen touches the trunk of a pine. It surges with energy and fills her. She's careful not to hold too long. She doesn't like taking it all and leaving the tree dead. The pines are very close here, not neatly planted in rows like in her village. Everything thick and twisted and wound around itself so it all feels like one big thing rather than hundreds. She wipes snow from her eyelashes and shrugs her birchwood shoulders. She doesn't mind it really.

She times her footsteps with the sound of the drum. Singing along, "Bong, bong, bong." Stomping determinedly in what she hopes is the right direction. Snow drops with every beat. The mountain vibrates. She keeps walking, unsure of how long it's been. Only that it doesn't feel like she's getting any closer. She feels tired. Maybe she's walked a few miles. She looks up and sees the color of the sky has changed from gray to rotten peach.

The drumming stops suddenly, making Guen feel cold and alone without the comforting sound. The noises that replace it are a mixture of unfamiliar and terrifying—strange bird calls to growls and groans. Darkness is closing in. She taps her wooden finger on the trunk of a tree, searching for a place to shelter. The trees open to a tumble of snow-capped boulders, leaning against each other like old friends. She churns through the snow to the small gap beneath two. Barely big enough, she curls into a small ball like she did at home, pressed into the corner of the room with the flea-bitten dog. She folds her tiny limbs under her chin and nestles into the damp earth. Hoping there aren't other critters behind her. Or in front.

"I am made from bravery. I am made from bravery. I am made from bravery," she whispers under her breath. The deafening howl that fills the night and causes the stars to shudder makes her doubt this whole heartedly, with every birchwood bone in her body.

20
LUNA

A SIGH OF GOLD COINS
AND SILK THREAD

The doctor's feet shuffle away, buried deep in plush purple carpet that smells like ammonia and lemons. My forehead is pressed to my manicured and oiled hands, and I snicker. The guard was right. It is like putting lip stain on a pig.

"Did you speak?" a voice like silk slipping over skin inquires.

Knotted wool in my teeth, I mutter, "No. I laughed."

"What?" The voice seems to lean in. Curious but not so curious that it wants to get any closer to the dirty Char at its feet. And then I feel it. A tamed wildness like the chatter tooth horse coming in to be fed and then galloping free across the white sands of Pearl Shell Beach. Bristled fur and long, white fangs. An intelligence. A suspicion. But it's just the mist of a presence wafting through my mind, quick as a cloud over a tiny island. My weakened power is returning with every pump of my mechanical heart.

Slowly, I lift my chin from the floor so I can speak clearly. The guard's foot still presses into my back. Silk-slippers covered in polished gems tap impatiently in my view, reflecting a thousand little Lunas like a spider's eyes. My mouth says things it shouldn't. My eyes shine bright when they should be dull and submissive. "I said, I laughed." My fingers scrunch the rug pile, imagining a lion's mane. If I could reach something big, something powerful, this meeting would be over before it began.

A woman coughs and drawls lazily, "Oh, let her get up, son. It's no good talking to the back of her head."

A shallow sigh full of gold coins and silk thread. "Rise, Char Luna."

Pulling my knees under me, I take my time rising from the floor. The long sleeves of my red dress flap about like battle flags, and I try to wind them around my jingling wrists. A strange jolly sound considering where I am and what I face. Three pairs of critical eyes judge me. One studies. One seems fascinated. The last pair look right through me, a ghostly film hanging over their aged gaze.

In the center sits the emperor, straight as a rod, opulent purple clothing hanging from his broad shoulders. His hat is small but glints with pure gold beading and a blue diamond at its middle. He is Shen excess, and he wears it well.

His full lip curls as he stares at my wooden sternum, and I bring my hand up to cover it. "So, you're the hybrid." He points from his throne, and when he places his hand back down, he runs his long, elegant fingers over the purple silk sleeves. Attempting to smooth out the wrinkles. His jaw twitches as he carries out the pointless task.

"I am Char Luna Yan. I have a hickory heart and Blood power," I answer, mouth sticky with red wax, eye powder getting in my eyes. He raises a strong eyebrow captioned by an Air Shen tattoo. Lye described him as beautiful and empty like an elaborate hand-painted vase. The handsome part is obvious. Strong jaw, high cheekbones. Skin fair and unmarked. Not a freckle nor blemish. Grayish eyes. Like they took a silver platter and flecked it into his irises.

I wait for the empty part.

"You could have simply answered yes." The woman to his left leans over, her bosom pressing into the emperor's shoulder. Her long black hair is combed into an elaborate bun with gold clasps and pearl strands hanging from her head like she's a stand in a jewelry store. It looks heavy and uncomfortable, and I frown as the various adornments knock against each other and obscure her view.

She whispers in the emperor's ear, and he nods, placing his hand over hers. Hers immediately scrunches like a slater bug. Almost like she's recoiling. She notices me staring and slowly uncurls her fist. "Is it true you can control animals?" he asks, though it's clear the question comes from the jewelry stand at his side. She narrows her eyes and plays with a sharp painted nail as she runs her gaze up and down my body. She bears no elemental mark. Her Atmosphere is a vanity bat desperately trying to increase its collection.

I shrink from her gaze that reduces me to an object, a small pebble caught in the carpet. There's something snake-ish and calculating about her shrewd face. Though beautiful, she twists it into something sour. As if counting the ways in which she can use me. "Answer the emperor, Char girl." She snaps both her voice and fingers.

The older woman on the other side of the emperor jumps in her seat at the noise, gripping a small round cannister in her wrinkled fingers. She carefully loosens the lid and scoops something as red as fresh blood onto her nail. Placing a small blob on her tongue, her eyes spark like a lit firework. She tilts her gray head from side to side as she swallows, revealing an Air tattoo at her temple. She turns to the younger one. "Soo Si, you are not the empress. You are nothing but an easily replaced concubine. Do not speak for the emperor." Soo Si's painted eyebrows rise about three inches up her forehead and she closes her shiny, red mouth.

The emperor glances between these women like he's a weed crushed between two stones. His shoulders curl in. His ears burn and open like dying flowers. It makes me want to smile but I bite down on it. "Yes. Yes. Mother is right. You should not speak to me in this manner, Soo." He turns his back on the furious concubine and addresses his mother, "What did we want from the girl?" He seems easily confused, like the push and pull of these two women disorients him. The "empty" part of Lye's description is starting to make sense.

The empress ignores her son and points at me. "You are not much to look at. But great power can be hidden in plain, small packages." She purses her lips and her eyes roll. "Packages. Small packages." She goes from looking at me to through me again like her thread of thought has been cut with sharp shears.

Soo Si almost tips out of her chair and murmurs, "Small packages are easy to tear open." Her fingers dig into a much simpler seat than the emperor and his mother. Theirs are carved elaborately with a perfect likeness of each at the head. I imagine they would have taken months to create. Soo Si's looks like a borrowed dining chair.

The emperor grips the edges of his throne so tightly it's like he thinks it will be stolen. *If only*, I think. "Mother, you are right. But none is as powerful as me." I eye the elaborate seat. The carved flowers and animals in the arms. All bowing and prostrating to an uncannily accurate likeness of the emperor's face carved into the top.

Soo Si strokes his tense arm. "Of course not, darling. Now ask her about the process. How did she become a hybrid? Was it difficult? Can it be repeated easily?"

My hands scrunch into fists. I wish I had oak and saltwater by my side. I won't tell them anything. The emperor opens his mouth to speak and his mother interrupts, "You have the doctor for interrogations. Do not lower yourself." The emperor nods and clasps his hands in his lap.

I wonder why I was called to the throne room. Was it simply curiosity? Was it to turn me? I shake my head. That will never happen.

"Why am I here?" I ask, feeling like the red peg in a black board.

The concubine, Soo Si, smiles widely like a mauler after a kill. "We wanted to get a look at you whole. Before the doctor takes you apart piece by piece. Isn't that right, emperor?" He stares at me in a way I really don't enjoy. Detached, as if he's already picturing my heart removed from my body. Soo Si elbows the emperor, and his lips lift to match her smile like she hooked her fingers into the corners of his mouth and forced it so.

He blinks. "Yes. That's right. Of course it is." I can't tell whether he's under a spell or so emptyheaded that all she must do is fill his ears with words and move his mouth like a puppet.

He's pathetic and I open my mouth to tell him that when a smooth growl ripples the drapes behind them. Soo Si tenses, adornments swinging like lonely willow branches. My ears warm and my heart beats steady as a clock. My Blood sense reaches for the shape, tracing large paws, four strong legs, and an enormous snout that could sniff out a one eyed mole from a thousand yards away.

The emperor gives a tight whistle. Paws pad forward followed by long, lean legs and a wet black nose. The fur of the creature is striped black and gray like a tiger who has lost its color. But its eyes are anything but colorless. They are a corn moon's liquid gold. The creature warns me with a rippling of its gum type growl and raised ruff.

"What, what is that?" I ask, fingers trembling with excitement as it circles. It holds my eyes, which are level with its lowered head. Every movement is considered and deliberate like it wouldn't waste a scrap of unnecessary energy. Its fluffy, striped tail swishes back and forth as it sniffs the air. I hold my breath in awe of the most beautiful, fearsome creature I have ever encountered. A child's wish come to life.

The emperor grins proudly, showing rows of teeth shining like skulls in a tomb. "This is my tiger wolf, Mulia. The only one of her kind. A treasure. I had her brought to me from the Dark West."

I reach for the wolf with my Blood sense and for a moment the creature stalls in its slow circle. My power hits a wall like the dagger beaks in Shen farmland. The wolf is bonded to a master and cannot be easily controlled. "How do you know she is the only one?" I ask even though I know the answer. He killed the rest or likely had someone else do it for him. Lye left out a few descriptive words: arrogant, cruel, greedy.

"It is not a rare creature if it can be reproduced. So, I made sure she was the only one." Soo Si strokes the emperor's arm and whispers in his ear. Her expression appears wary of the tiger wolf. Her Atmosphere is threatened, like competing male birds performing for a single mate. "I wanted a one-of-a-kind treasure. It has the highest value. You are one of a kind, Char Luna. But soon that will not be the case."

Soo Si rises from her chair, and I want to laugh. It's not unlike what crowded our own table at home. "Yes, enjoy your novelty while it lasts," she says airily. The emperor's mother snorts at the concubine's choice of words. The sideways glance Soo Si gives her could slice metal. The irony is not lost on the women. "It is the only thing keeping you and the Shen traitor alive."

It's my turn to ignore. "I've never seen nor heard of such a creature. She is magnificent." I look them all in the eye, which appears to bother them a great deal. I reach for the tiger wolf again but two obstacles are in my way: the bond to the emperor and the black violet still floating through my system. The wall is made of fear. Each brick carefully crafted from threat and pain. But I think if I wasn't poisoned, I could find a way to build something deeper out of mutual respect.

Soo Si tilts her head, and her headdress jangles. "How did you know Mulia is a girl?" I clamp my mouth shut. Not wanting to give anything away about how effective the dose of black violet was. "Answer me!" She stomps her jeweled foot. Guards lean in with spears.

"I guessed."

"She's lying," the concubine spits.

The emperor beckons me with his finger and a blade prods my back, forcing me forward. "What can you do with that power of yours, Char Luna? Tell me."

Mulia climbs the stairs to the throne when she is called. She settles at the emperor's feet, taking up a large portion of the stage and forcing Soo Si to lift her feet out of the way. When the wolf lifts her head to look at him, he takes a chain hiding in her fur and pulls up hard. The animal winces, the black corners of her mouth tight with pain. When he releases her, she lays her head over her paws, almost resigned. But I sense a rumbling in Mulia's stomach.

Not from hunger but from the desire to break free. I wrap that feeling around my chest, let it sit there until a plan can be formed.

It hurts to see such a remarkable creature abused. My face contorts when the emperor chokes the tiger wolf again. I feel Mulia's pain. It opens a brief window. Not big enough to crawl through but a slit wide enough to see into. The animal is controlled, not cared for. Its loyalty won through breaking, not training.

I stretch my fingers. It could be useful. "I can do nothing while black violet suppresses my abilities." It's a truthful answer that gives him nothing. "If you wish to see the scope of my power, perhaps you should stop poisoning me." Soo Si taps her finger on her chair like she's taking notes.

The emperor's mother waves her hand in front of her face. Her voice takes on a hysterical edge. "Violets! I hate violets! The smell is ghastly. Get them out of here at once. Get them out!"

She flaps her hands, shrieking like a child in a tantrum. The guards exchange a look that suggests this is nothing out of the ordinary. The emperor stretches to his mother with true concern, attempting to calm her as she struggles against an invisible attack. He tries to take the small container from her hands, but she holds it like it's a lump of jade.

"Get the Char girl out of here!" he manages as he takes the old woman's hands and restrains her. She lashes out with sharp fingernails, a single line of blood appearing on his perfect face.

Soo Si doesn't move. Sitting with her arms crossed, her eyes shooting poisoned arrows at the empress. Her lips curve, a smile like the dark side of the moon. I shudder.

The guards escort me away, spears crossed around me like a moving cage. I go willingly. I have learned who I'm up against. And I have a feeling the biggest threat sits to the left of the throne, not upon it.

21

LYE

WHEN THE RAIN STOPS

We shall leave as soon as the rain stops. It floods and dries like a tap here, and we want to walk down the mountain instead of slide. I move around the kitchen, stacking pots and cleaning the benches. I snort. If the chancellor could see me now. The Keeper, cleaning like a maid. I pause, dirty cloth scrunched in my hand. I was a servant of a different kind.

At a light tap on my back, I swing around. "What is it?" My fingers brew lightning. Always ready.

"Excuse me, General." Her voice is mouse-like, but there's a toughness to it. A metal-plated strength. It's the woman I found waiting for her son in the rubble.

I look down at her tiny frame. Thin, young, but awfully strong. Wooden cheeks pulled up with determination. "Oh hello—I'm sorry," I say, nose scrunching. "I don't know your name."

She bows quickly. "Jing Ha."

I smile, trying to look comforting. She quirks an eyebrow, confused, like that's not what I'm portraying. "Jing Ha. What do you need?"

Jing Ha's Atmosphere reads of protection and love. A sheltering wing against the wind. A strong paw guiding along the safest path. "I wish to come with you. They killed my husband. They have my son. I know I don't have your kind of power and training, but you must let me." The pack in her hand demonstrates a mind made up. Eyes speak pure love and grit. A heart untainted by battle. She hasn't lived under the growling chant of a shifu or captain. Her arms are strong from carrying a child, not a sword.

My eyes and heart soften. "You have your own strength and power, Jing Ha." I sense it in her. It's the flexible yet enduring strength of a bamboo tree, bending with the wind and weathering the storm when others would break.

"So, you will allow me to come?" She has inner strength but her clutched hands suggest desperation. I tilt my head.

I turn away from her, running my cleaning cloth over a cleaver in the sink. It shines like new death and sadly, this makes me smile. I clutch the handle and spin around, attacking Jing Ha.

She blocks my arm with hers, looping herself under until we are chest to chest. I hold back my elements, testing her defensive skills. Jing Ha throws her thin arms out, knocking the cleaver from my hands. It clatters to the stone floor, lifting more than a few curious heads from around the fire.

She breathes fast, her wide eyes and wooden cheeks shining brightly. I relax my arms and she steps back, bowing low. "Forgive me, General. I was just reacting."

I smile, a small sigh trapped in my chest. For she may be strong enough to come on this journey with us, but it is going to be a hard one. Harder still is the reality her child may not be at the end of it. "Don't be sorry. I was testing your defenses."

Her face brightens by a half degree. The flash of green before the sun sets. She's still a grieving mother and won't smile whole heartedly. Nothing can lift those lips all the way except a reunion with her child. "And I passed?" She seems to know the answer.

I nod. "Be ready to leave as soon as the rain stops." She thumps her chest and salutes. Trying to behave like a soldier when she's anything but. It's a good thing. There's no killing on her mind. No enemy. Only life and love.

Joka's words come back to me like spinning stars, though instead of razor-sharp blades, they're made of light. "A gift to be shared."

Jing Ha slings a pack over her slight shoulder and moves to join the others. I reach for the young mother. "Jing Ha, wait."

She stops, turns around and looks up at me. Made of steel and soap suds. Strength and fragility. I call her closer. "Can you hold still for one moment?" I ask in my gentlest voice. She does as I ask, trust and curiosity brushing her features. My hand coasts over her face, her shoulders, searching for her Pulse. It calls to me from a protected location. I lift her arm and find it. I press in. Branches bud and sprout new leaves. Creak and groan under the spring sun. Jing Ha reads of Earth.

I let her limbs fall and she frowns. "What did you just do?"

I shake my head. I did nothing. Yet. "Nothing," I reassure. "I was just checking something." She bows and turns away. Atmosphere reading of unfurling fern fronds, careful and deliberate and seeking. Mind always on her child.

The idea that I could gift power to those of my choosing opens a small box of purpose inside me. I was never given the choice. I was only ever told. Even with Luna, I was pushed by my brother. It was not *my* idea. I close the lid of the box for now. I need to think this over.

I reject the Keeper over and over, but she lives in me. She occupies a part of every cell in my body, coats my bones and swims in my blood. The idea she could be a force for good is an enticing prospect. That I could be everything, not nothing, brings unwanted tears to my eyes.

I swipe at them and return to kitchen work.

Joka pokes his head in the doorway, pointing at the sky. "It's over."

I dry my hands and let a twinkle reside in my eye for the time it takes for the soap bubbles to burst. Perhaps it's just beginning.

22

GUEN

A SICKLE-SHAPED MOON

Dreams come to Guen in short clips. A child who went missing from her village, standing in a circle of pines, snow up to her waist. Rusty red-skinned monsters chanting. Animals snapping at her ankles as she runs away. Frozen statues of people she cares about, waiting and waiting for her to return in a dark, cold cave.

The drums feel like her own heartbeat, and also like thunder. They tell her to wake up. They tell her she must keep going. But a sound like air escaping through a small hole makes her eyes scrunch and brings her limbs against her body. Breath. But not hers. Breath that smells like rancid meat. Guen thinks she'll wait until whatever is out there has gone.

She curls inward. Maybe she'll look like a pile of wood. An abandoned nest.

The crunch of snow sounds odd, like grinding salt. She decides to open one eye slowly, taking in the danger in smaller pieces. As her lid lifts, she's met with darkness where she had just felt the weak sun on her face. Something wet and rough brushes her cheek, then a scratch and a growl.

"Ooh, what have you found, Zui-Zui?" a gravelly voice affectionately coos.

Guen opens her other eye. A head is blocking the light. A gray-and-black striped head with golden eyes and sharp teeth. It nudges her body, which clacks as her arms and legs hit each other. She takes a deep breath and holds it. It takes everything in her not to scream. She shuffles backward, but the black nose pushes further into the hole, sniffing her out like dinner.

She should fight back, but those teeth and those eyes. A slimy tongue runs over her face. *That's it!* "Ai! Get away from me!" she threatens, hands to her face. So tangled in her own limbs she can barely move.

"Back, Zui-Zui. Let us see what you have discovered." A gloved hand reaches past the creature and grabs at Guen. Long fingers clamp onto her head and drag her from the hiding place. Light floods Guen's vision as she's lifted into the air. She dangles there, gripped only by her little head while the enormous monster turns her back and forth, inspecting her like a dead rabbit from a trap.

The gray and black creature jumps at Guen's legs like she's a treat. The monster holds her birchwood body out of reach. Guen stares in shock and wonder at its tiger coat and wolfish body. She thought they'd been wiped out with the emperor owning the very last one. "Tiger wolf," she murmurs. She'd be excited if she wasn't so terrified.

The gravelly voice comes from within a gruesome face. Rusty red, with black slit eyes and a hollow-looking mouth. "Indeed, it is." It speaks without its lips moving. Everything the Shen said was true. Guen can't find her bravery. In fact, she might faint. It clicks its giant fingers, and the tiger wolf sits eagerly with eyes on Guen. The Dark West monster swings around and whistles. Several other creatures emerge, all as tall as two men, all with the same terrifying face. The monster shakes Guen's little body, nails digging uncomfortably into her birchwood skull. "Look what Zui-Zui found."

"What is it?" one asks, traipsing through the snow with long, fleece-covered legs.

Guen's eyes dart from creature to creature as the one holding her shrugs. "Not sure."

"Is it alive?" another asks. "It looks like a toy of some kind."

The monster lifts Guen's arms and legs up one at a time, using a single finger the size of her dagger, until Guen snatches her limbs back. "I'm alive!" she snaps. "I'm not a toy, I'm a girl. Put me down!" She kicks her legs and twists her body.

The monster laughs. It's not a bad sound. It reminds Guen of her grandmother. If her grandmother was a tree-sized creature of the forest. "Certainly," it says with a chuckle. It lowers her almost to the ground, toes grazing the snow. The tiger wolf lunges, jaws wide. The monster lifts her from the ground again. "Wa! No, Zui-Zui! We haven't decided what to do with it yet."

Guen swallows. Crosses her arms over her chest. "I am not an it, I am Guen."

The light bouncing off the snow brings a strange sparkle to the scene. The trees glisten and the air smells clean. Guen sighs. It would be pretty nice, if she were not being held by a hellish giant.

Other creatures stalk closer, a group of about ten, dressed in skins and holding spears and knives of various sizes. They poke and prod her in a very unpleasant way. Guen feels a sinking feeling in her wooden belly like she's already failed. Her lip quivers. These Dark West monsters are going to cut her up and feed her to their pet tiger wolf. It will splinter her skin and crunch her bones and there'll be nothing left. Sun and Ki Anah will die. Then the Carvresses will follow. She can't help but let a tear slide down her cheek. "I am Guen," she whispers again. "Please, don't feed me to your wolf."

The monster brings Guen's face so close she could trace the black tattoos across its cheeks and forehead. They sort of remind her of the carvings in the cave. "Oh dear, little one. Don't cry." It pets the tiger wolf, which lifts its head into the monster's palm. "Zui-Zui has had his lunch." She shakes Guen again, her little legs knocking against each other like rhythm sticks. "Don't think he'd want to eat you anyway, child. What on earth are you made of?" She flicks Guen's stomach. It doesn't hurt. Well not on the outside, but Guen feels her pride being thrashed about.

Guen closes her mouth, tired of questions. She simply glares. The monster shrugs and throws Guen into a pack strapped to its back. She lands in a jumble of fur and rights herself to peek out the top. "Lucky we found you. We only returned to the winter village a few days ago."

With eyes that capture everything, Guen notes where she is and where she's going as the huge creature takes long steps away from the boulders with the rest of the group. Pine branches swish against her head as they travel westward. Through the forest, heading down into a snow-filled valley.

She's found the Dark West tribe. But whether they'll help her hangs like a sickle-shaped moon over her head.

The creatures talk to each other in an altered Shen language. Some words sound different, with high notes instead of lows on the ends of sentences. It gives their speech a rather sing-song sound. Guen always thought Shen sounded like the swish of silk on a stone floor. Char sound like they're throwing their words in a bucket and shaking them about. Guen snorts. These things sound like both, but deeper, rockier. The other strange thing about their voices is the tenor. They all kind of sound like her grandmother.

The creature reaches back and pats Guen's head roughly like she's a coconut to be cracked. "You all right back there, Guen?"

She huddles down. Just her eyes poking out the top of the soft fur pack. She makes a muffled "mhm," and the monster stops thwacking her head.

As they descend into the valley, the group fans out and disappears between the trees. Even the tiger wolf bounds away, leaving her alone with her captor. From the monster's back, Guen can only see what's behind them. A rising wall of black rock lined with pines.

Smoke pipes into the sky and Guen searches for the source. As they weave through the trees and her monster swings from side to side to greet others, the village is revealed. Stone and wood huts built into the side of the mountain. Animal pens with bulky sheep moving slowly through the snow. Guen blinks rapidly and disbelieving as she watches one of the monsters crouch down, arms open wide as a young, normal-sized child gallops into its arms.

Drumbeats rattle the chimneys, and they all look up, moving toward the sound like it calls them. Guen shudders inside the pack, wondering what will happen next.

She's swung from the shoulders of the monster, lifted out and placed on the ground. The monster crouches almost at Guen's eye level and places a thumb and forefinger at its chin. Guen trembles. She scrunches her little hands into fists and readies herself. She came here to ask for help. She has to try. "I need your—"

The monster lifts its chin up, up, up. So far up that the chin is no longer a chin. It's a hat. Guen's gasps in shock as the monster removes a carved mask. Showing its—*her*—true face. The woman smiles kindly, fine lines around enormous eyes, and reaches out to pat Guen on the head with a hand the size of buffalo fig leaf. Guen watches others lift masks. Fine, female faces exposed. They smile and laugh. They embrace smaller Shen and paler children who must hail from the Dark West, who hug their legs. Guen doesn't understand what she's seeing. She's doesn't know if she should be relieved. Only that she's confused.

The woman tilts her pale face and smiles. "I imagine you have some questions." She offers a hand. "I know I do."

Guen manages a nod.

"I am Dianh," the giant offers. Guen takes the woman's hand and half walks and is half dragged through the snow on anxious little feet. The words she needs to say caught on her tongue.

The mountain tribe of the Dark West is not what Guen thought at all. It's not what Sun and Ki Anah thought either.

23

LUNA

TRYING TO CATCH A FALLING STAR

Every step I take, I think of escape. And yet with every stair, my feet willingly lead me to darkness and then into my cage. The dynamics of the emperor, his mother, and the concubine have me rolling impossible plans around my mind. The emperor is weak and easily influenced by both his mother and the concubine. His mother is halfway drugged, demented, or both. There were moments of clarity, but a cloud presses into her brain. The concubine, Soo Si, is dangerous, but the level of danger is unknown. If the empress were to die, she would have sole power over the emperor. I need to learn how deeply her nails are embedded in the emperor's skull and what her agenda may be.

I reach the gate and pause. It smells like a memory down here. A warm, happy memory. I shake my head, wondering if I'm losing my mind. I flick my fingers and glow worms light the room in purple-green. The guards curse and blink shielded eyes. I allow myself the broken grin of someone who needs to find the sand grain of good in the desert of bad. Dozens of tiny hands scoop mouthfuls of congee into their starving mouths. My stomach gurgles.

Ash looks me up and down as I'm escorted past his cell. "You look like—" I'm tossed into my cage fast and with an element of panic because the guard knows the black violet is past its usefulness. I keep my feet as my power surges like the drag of the tide before a devastating wave, and I push the flats of my palms at the guard. Small rocks rumble and beetles pour from an opening in the ground. They surge towards him, clamber over each other to get to his leg. *Yes, Qi Sha, you better retreat to where the floors stink of acid and the bugs can't survive.* I control the world in here. The children pause in their meal to point and laugh as he runs up the stairs while trying to shake his leg free at the same time. The laughter is a glorious sound. The iron gate is closed and bolted. A not so glorious sound.

I twirl in a circle, red silk slapping the edges of my bamboo bars. "You were going to say something?" I pose for him, knowing full well how silly I look.

His eyes are a choppy sea and a boat that wishes to ride them. "You look like a dream and a nightmare." I grin. I like that description.

"As long as I am in your thoughts." I kneel closer. He pushes his half-finished bowl of congee my way, and I take it.

"Always."

Reaching for my face, he uses my impractically long sleeves to wipe the red stain from my lips. Children giggle as he leans toward me, but I pull back, conscious of watchful eyes. We smile, though Ash's looks half hitched on a line and ready to blow away in the wind. "Not with an audience."

He nods in agreement, though keeps a hand at my waist as I press against the bars. "I saved you the meat," he says, pointing at a small brown lump in the bottom of the bowl.

I bite my lip. It stirs up feelings long buried and shelved. Ki Anah surfaces in my mind, cherrywood hip jutting out as she claims to be full and pushes the last piece of meat to the skinniest child. It always went to the one who never asked and who needed it most—Ben Ni.

Ash tilts his head, feeling me. "What's the shape?"

I touch my chest, an unswallowable lump sitting above my heart. Thoughts of Ben Ni never leave me. Like blood, he courses through my veins, keeps me alive and sometimes makes me feel like I'm dying. I wonder if the memories will ever stop hurting. "Like that piece of meat if I gulped it whole."

He lowers his gaze to the bowl as I push it between the bars. "I'm full. They fed me upstairs," I lie. "You take it, please."

Ash tips his head, cheek pushed up on one side. "Really?" he asks.

I nod my head. "Really. Don't let it go to waste."

"A lump of meat is better than a dull knife, right?"

"I don't know. At least a knife is quick."

He takes the congee with doubt weighting his hands. "Grief is never quick."

I sigh. The ghost of golden eyes searing my heart. But as I begin to tell him what happened in the throne room, he forgets those doubts and finishes the congee without thinking.

"The emperor's mother is peculiar," I start. "She seems sharp and dull at the same time. She had this red stuff in a tiny container that she put on her tongue." I poke out my tongue.

Ash smiles and then it falls. He rubs his jaw and exhales. "The empress must have succumbed to red lotus. It's a powerful drug used to treat pain, but also for pleasure."

I frown. We don't have such things on the islands. Unless you count over-drinking wine. "So, she's not a threat?"

"Depends on how far she's fallen. Red lotus can make your temper unpredictable. Eventually it will rob you of your sanity, but that takes years. Were her fingers stained red?" I think back, re-membering her nails. They were red and when I tip the image over, I recall the red was bleeding halfway down each finger. I nod. "Then she is most likely lost."

It's not reassuring. She still sits beside the emperor, and he seems to listen to her. "The concubine Soo Si is the opposite. All sharp edges. I'd guess her mind is bright and dangerous. I get the feeling she has her own agenda." Ash nods along.

"And the emperor?" he asks, running his finger along the edges of the bowl to catch the last streaks of porridge and fat. He talks while chewing. "I haven't met him. He never came out of the palace when I was training here."

"He's certainly handsome." Ash's eyebrows rise. "But there's a weakness to him. Like he willingly allows the two women to push and pull him in whatever direction they please. He seems to respect the mother more. And the concubine isn't subtle about her displeasure at that fact."

Ash smirks. "Is he as handsome as me?" he asks, trying to puff up a caved in chest and flick clumped locks. But he's more beautiful to me in this state then the emperor could ever be. Half broken and yet still trying to stand strong, Ash is ten times the man the emperor is. I blink. My heart suddenly fluttering in my chest. Something I didn't know it could do. I tap it. There's no comparison between Ash and that cork weasel.

To Ash, I shrug. "I'm not sure anyone can be as handsome as you think you are."

He grins, adding light again to this dark place. "Perfection has no shame."

Halfway through an eyeroll, I grab his hands in mine, excitement rippling through my body and coming out as pups jumping at a treat. "Oh Ash, did you know about the tiger wolf?"

"The only time I was in the palace was the night I left with Lye. You've probably seen more of it than I ever did."

Children press against the bars as I describe the magnificent animal. The line of her body, and the flick of her tail. Her incredible striped coat. There's something deliberate and majestic about her that draws me in. I tap my fingers on the bamboo as I talk, and Ash takes them in his.

"I assume they brought you up there to intimidate you, but it looks as if it had the opposite effect." His mouth is lifted yet his voice is painted with concern.

Aware that hope can be a dangerous thing, I whisper, "You're right. And I know we are far from out of danger. But for the first time since we came here, I feel like there's a chance. A shot. Even if it's the equivalent of trying to catch a falling star, it's there. Mulia is our chance."

Ash's concern drops below the waves just a little, like a jellyfish hanging close to the surface. "I agree, but this Soo Si sounds like a dangerous woman. You need to be careful."

I'd say, "Aren't I always?" but I already told him one lie today.

POWER FLIES from my fingers like lightning trying to find the earth. Blood has built up in my system from the black violet. When the poison wears off, my Element flows like water from a broken dam. If only I knew how to break that dam at the right time. The children clap and chant as I create patterns and plays for them on the wall with my army of bugs. It feels good to give them this. A brief escape from the nightmare of their situation.

Ash laps warm waves against my hundreds of excitable baby sea turtles. Calm to my agitation.

I create shadow puppets on the wall with black beetles. Bringing some Char-ness to this rusty Shen palace. Silhouettes of men with loopy moustaches and swirling eyes bow to women, offering sharp right-angled arms for a dance. The women pull back as they must, refusing for a reasonable time before accepting.

A little something from home. A home I hope is still there when we get out of this place.

Mama sighs as we pass the little theatre and I tug on her sleeve. "Please, Mama. Let me watch. Just for a minute."

She puts her hands on her hips and shakes her head. "You always say 'just for a minute' when you really mean all the minutes it takes for the performance to be over."

I clutch my hands together and pout. "Pleeeeassse!"

Mama frowns. "That face doesn't work on me, Luna."

My chin falls, my eyes on the shadow puppet play. They're about to fight. My favorite part. I slip from Mama's hand and wander to the back of the stage. You can watch from both sides. Almost all the crowd watches from the shadow side, but I like to see the puppeteers moving their actors. I like to count the dots on the leather puppets and watch the bamboo sticks move up and down.

I grin as the skinny character wins. Then Mama grabs my hand and drags me away. "But I didn't get to see the end."

"Oh little Luna!" Mama grumbles. "It always ends the same way." She walks fast and I struggle to keep pace with her. "Now I will be late to the fish market. It will be three-day-old snap turtle for dinner if we don't hurry."

I like to think she's wrong, that it's not always the same ending. That there's room for something different. Something new to the story.

Lu Leng claps her hands on either side of the bars and whoops to the ceiling. The sound turns into a lung-hacking cough. The guards will come down soon if we don't wrap it up. I summon the shapes to bow and disperse. "Can you teach me how to do what you do?" she asks, big brown eyes blinking with innocence and desire.

I shake my head. "I wish I could."

She pouts, disappointed, lips of pink rose petals smushed together. "I wish you could too. It looks like a lot of fun."

It strikes something at my heart. Like the scraping of a match against a door frame. My power never felt like fun. It felt necessary. Then overpowering. Then a weapon and instrument of cruelty. That it could be cause for laughter and joy lays more purpose on top of my crown of feathers and fangs. Instead of making it heavier, it makes it easier to bear.

24

LYE

TAKE A BITE OUT OF THE MOON

Rose gold beaches glisten as we approach the mouth of the northwest river. Pink salt making the sand look as if a sunset wept onto the land. Water sprays our faces as I grip the mast of our small but conspicuous boat. Blood-red sails dragon-defiant against the sky. The sea's up-and-down motion is still not my friend, and my other hand clutches my stomach like that could keep the contents from spilling out. It cannot.

How strange it is to be home.

I picture two faces like bookends to the body of water separating Shen and Char territory. Setsu's worn and worried expression as he waved a regretful goodbye to Joka and me. And Ash's smile for a thousand different reasons, landing here many weeks ago. I twist to the east towards the palace and the horrors lying beneath the lavish carpets of the ground floor. I want to believe my brother is still alive and that maybe the chancellor kept him from harm. I'd like to think our bond is so strong I would feel if something had happened to him. I shake my head, running a finger over the salt layer on my sycamore arm. The further west we go, the more my heart stretches for the palace. But it cannot be.

Joka taps my arm. "What are you thinking, General Koh?"

I sigh, torn but knowing the tear must run one way. "General Koh is thinking we made excellent time, but soon we must row against the current." Jing Ha nestles into a space, hands at her oar, desperate to prove herself. I smile. "Not yet, Jing Ha. We will need to drag the boat across the sand and into the river."

Joka squeezes my bony shoulder gently. "What is my friend Lye Li thinking?" he whispers so the others can't hear. I turn to him, allowing myself to absorb the warmth of his gaze like a lizard on a rock.

I tilt my chin up. The blue sky is a liar. It makes light of the difficulties ahead. The sun, the pink beach, the deserted entry— they all give us too much hope. "I was thinking of family. Yours and mine. Every part of me save one wants to turn this boat and head for the palace."

Joka's face scrunches with the same pain. Separation and guilt. Two strands wound tightly together and then around our necks. "What does the opposing part tell you?" he asks, tone low and knowing with a small streak of doubt.

I heave a sigh of river rocks and mountain ice. "It tells me we have to do it this way. That without the Carvresses, we stand no chance. But—"

The boat beaches. Jing Ha and the men jump out, cursing and hopping up and down at the frigid temperature. "But—" Joka continues my train of thought like he's driving it. "It's killing you not to rescue your brother first." I nod. Killing me in the slowest, most painful way possible. A slow working poison that feeds on heartbreak.

My small voice, the one reserved for self-pity, comes out in a croak. "I don't know if I can bear it."

Joka bows his head, takes a deep breath and when he looks at me, he's a mess of emotions. A dish with too many ingredients. His Atmosphere reads like a bird that's lost its nest. Twisting and twirling, looking for a place to land. "You can and you have to. As do I." He cups my face with his hand and gets panda wolverine spit for his trouble. A favorite creature of mine for its ferocity and tenacity. Eating only black bamboo because nothing else will do. It also spits the poisoned juices at any creature or person who comes near its grove. Joka holds still, knowing I need a moment to concentrate on control. And I feel like I am resting in a place I don't deserve but would fight a hundred Fire Shen to keep.

"We'll help each other. I'll keep you on the right path and you will do the same for me," he murmurs, tapping the small notebook in his pocket. Names of kidnapped Char children. "Remind each other of what is most important."

I lean into his touch for one perfect second and then pull back. "Yes. We can do that for one another. Just as I'm sure Ash and Luna are looking after each other." Like I'm sure the emperor and those close to him will do their best to corrupt them. "Their love is like gravity. Keeping them together despite all outside forces trying to pull them apart. Its strength is beyond any evil they might face."

"Do you really believe that? Luna was so—" Joka starts. His mouth grim as he remembers what she was like when they left.

"Desolate and detached?"

He shakes his head. "I was going to say grief stricken. Maybe numb."

I don't know why, but I feel like this is no longer a concern. "What Luna was doing couldn't last. I feel certain, wherever she is, she is herself again."

He tilts his head, ever thoughtful. "How can you be sure?"

"I can't be sure, but remember the moths?" I ask, my mind going back to that room and the dinner plate-sized moths fluttering frantically after being sent across the sea.

Joka shudders. "How could I forget?"

"Magic leaves a trace. A sort of imprint. I felt it when those moths entered my room." Joka's eyes light with interest.

"What was imprinted?"

I smile as I climb from the boat and land in the soft pink sand. I stare up at the knowledge-seeking Joka. "Love."

The water is icy. I stare across the river mouth. The mountain isn't visible, but the temperature means the glacier has reached the ground. I swallow hard.

The group shivers and shudders uncontrollably, and I move between them as they wind ropes over their shoulders and around their middles. I do something I've only ever done for Ash. I concentrate on warm earth and thick fur and touch each Char on the back of their necks. It's temporary comfort, but one I am uniquely qualified to offer. Instantly the Char relax and can drag the boat across the shallows, over the sand bar, and into the inlet of the river, which is colder still.

I pull beside Jing Ha, red-faced and straining her tiny arms as the others pull with more ease. She's the face of all Char: outnumbered and unwilling to give up.

Once the boat is deep enough, we climb back in.

The sun is setting, creating colors so bright we shield out eyes.

Jing Ha settles against a barrel, lifting her head to the sky. "General Koh, is it safe to just float out here? What if a Shen sees us?"

I smile. "If they see us, they will report it. But don't worry too much, Jing Ha, there are no settlements here. The water is too salty to drink or use for irrigation."

Quick minded, she tilts her head and says, "So we will encounter more Shen as we travel away from the sea. Once the water becomes drinkable?"

"Yes."

She grips her knife and I search her Atmosphere for signs of hate or revenge. But it's mostly alertness. Curiously, there's little fear for her own safety. Only for her son.

She pats the deck beside her. "Tell me the plan once more." The others crowd around. There are only ten. Soldiers I selected for their strength but also their restraint. Captain Ipoh, Luna's favorite teacher, helped me choose, and he stands at the bow, quiver on his back.

"The northwest arm of the river leads directly to my village. Once we pass the mouth, the bank rises high and will keep us hidden. With sails folded down, I hope to pass through unnoticed. We're not to hurt any Shen. We're not to get off the boat for any reason. When we reach the village, we will find the Carvresses,

Sun, and Ki Anah, and that is when we will make ourselves known to the Shen."

Teh Bo clicks his wooden elbow and frowns as he chews on a white bun, dipping it in a jar of preserved fruit. "Then what?"

This is where faith takes over and the "plan" sprouts dragon scales and leather wings and threatens to fly away. Because I don't exactly know what will happen. Only what I hope will happen. "Then we will see if for all our fighting and all the pain we have caused each other, the Shen and Char have some common ground."

Joka finds my eyes and runs a hand over his bamboo neck, thoughts playing through those fingers. "We know they do." He gestures around the group. "You have accepted the Shen Keeper as your general. It is possible."

"What if they kill us first?" Jing Ha asks.

I shake my head. "They would never kill the Keeper."

Ipoh runs an arrow through his fingers and points the head at the first star, shining like a doubtful eye. "You seem very sure…"

"I thought I could be only one thing, Shen or Char. Keeper or general. That I had to leave one identity behind. But I look at Jing Ha, powerful and soft. Mother and warrior. And I understand I can be both. I can be a myriad of different things. I can choose to be a whole, not a half.

"Even if she did terrible things, could you kill a Carvress?" I ask. The group draws shocked breaths at the idea, like it hurts them to think it. "Some things are sacred. They command respect and unconditional protection. I am one of those things."

I gaze across what seems like endless sky with empty land below it. But it's a false view. The land is covered with Shen. Once *my* people. Could they be again? My Keeper power touched so many Shen. And I'm starting to think it could do even more.

Unbuckling my pack, I pull out the gray robe I borrowed from a Char monk. They're not exactly like the robes I let sink to the bottom of the harbor, but they will have to do. I must slip the Keeper skin over my own, at least for now. I slide my arms through the worn felt. Much softer than my old robe. My comfort was never the chancellor's concern. It wraps me like new armor.

Joka clears his throat and taps the bare mast. The boat softly rises and falls, much gentler than the sea. "We should get some sleep while we can."

Lantern light makes for a golden glow over inky water. It reminds me of a tapestry in the palace. A powerful Water Shen raising sky crabs from the sea floor by creating sea funnels. A blanket of stars shakes silver dust in our eyes. All very beautiful and very fleeting. I glance at Joka and his mouth twists in a strange way at my regard. He turns his back to me.

I stand and make my way over to the lanky yet elegant boy, and hang over the stern with him, elbow to elbow. "Does it bother you to see me this way?" I ask holding up my hollow sleeves. Overboard, little pops of water break as fish try to bite the moon.

He sighs. "No and—" I lean my head against his shoulder, and he pulls away. He runs a hand over his bamboo neck. "No. I've always thought Lye and the Keeper could not be separated from one another."

Then why does he look at me with such a pained expression? "I'm starting to understand that to be true."

He straightens his arms as he grips the lip of the boat and nods to himself. Making some decision he will not share with me. His Atmosphere reads of a sapling in the shadow of an oak. He turns, saluting stiffly, and he may as well have slapped me in the face. "Goodnight, General."

I return his bow. Hoping sleep will iron out those creases in his forehead. Wondering why sometimes it feels like the storms are chasing me and other times it feels as if I am the storm, and everyone should run and take cover.

25
GUEN

BIG AND STRONG

Her wooden body has driven a channel through the snow. Dianh takes long strides though the village, legs like an opening and closing ladder. Waving or nodding her head at other women who stare openly at the girl being dragged behind her. Guen glares at the shocked faces and the sharp way they breathe in at the sight of her. She doesn't like how their round eyes grow rounder. She needs their help, and it won't do her any good to scowl or throw a fit, no matter how much she may want to. She scrunches her tiny fists.

Drum. Drum. Drum.

The sound is so much louder, vibrating across the valley. And when it does, the women pause their work and smile. Hands on hips, eyes to the sky.

"I'm hungry," Dianh throws over her shoulder. "Are you hungry?"

She stops and swings Guen past her legs and catches her, holding the wooden girl under her arms so she can peer at her face.

"I don't eat," Guen confesses sadly. Though it has been useful in the cave not to need real food, she misses it. She thinks of spicy pork sausage and fish sauce and lime noodles and licks her lips with a wooden tongue. The giant woman watches, fascinated, poking Guen's face with her finger.

"You don't eat?" she asks, brows raised. "Then how do you live?"

Guen shrugs. "I dunno." That's a question for the Carvresses. Guen has a whole heap of those too.

Dianh laughs, opening her pale mouth wide as a whale. Guen tilts her head. The woman is paler than any person she's ever met. "You dunno? You are a very interesting little creature!" She shakes Guen and her birchwood legs clink against each other.

Guen grimaces. "I'm not a creature."

"What you are then?" Dianh slings the child into the crook of her arm like she's a baby and Guen folds her arms over her chest crossly.

Guen doesn't know whether she's a Carvress, a wooden Shen, or a puppet come to life.

She lifts her chin to the pale woman dressed in skins. "If I tell you, will you help me?"

Dianh stops and chuckles. "Child, I have already helped you. You are a brave one indeed to be asking for more. First, I eat. Then we talk about where you have come from and where you need to go."

Guen has no choice. "I am bravery. I am bravery." She repeats these words quietly to herself as Dianh thunders down a shoveled track, past sturdy stone homes that look cherished and well kept. The dark mouth of a cave at least as high as two great pine trees appears before them. The roaring boom of drumbeats makes Guen cover her ears. The sound reverberating in her head like the worst headache she's ever had. Dianh grins with huge, shingle board teeth. Guen bounces and shakes as they get closer.

Women greet Dianh. Patting her on the back and peering at Guen as she's held up to their big round eyes of blue and green. They *tsk* and pat her head. They part to let Dianh through.

The drumbeats stop and Guen can finally hear the thoughts in her own head. She counts the heads of at least fifty grown women. Very grown. *Over*grown. There are no adult men to be seen. Dianh stomps up gray stone steps, still holding Guen in her arms. Eyes focused upward. Women pass her with sacks in their hands, tapping their palms to Dianh's as they pass.

This is where they throw her in a pot and boil her down to paper mulch. Or chop her into kindling. The walls are lit with torches and Dianh follows the firelight further inside. "Where are you taking me?" Guen asks, voice getting smaller and smaller like a shell eroded by the waves.

Dianh frowns. "I told you, I need to eat." She stops suddenly, feet almost touching the edge of a pool of steaming water. She eases Guen to the ground with a stern expression as she orders with a large-gloved hand, "Stay right there!"

Guen stands still, knees shaking as the long-legged woman moves to the wall of the cave and retrieves what looks like a gigantic hammer. Guen should run. Her mouth goes dry, her hands clammy. The tales were right. This monster of a woman is going to club her to a woody pulp and feed her to the tiger wolf. Guen begins to whimper just as Dianh raises the club high above her head and strikes. One, two, three times.

The sound is huge. Like they're inside a bell. Guen eyes scrunch closed awaiting pain. But all she feels is a tiny splash of warm water against her face. She opens her eyes and blinks up at the pink and purple cave coral high up on the ceiling.

Bong. Bong. Bong. Dianh hits the wall again and pieces of coral fall from the high ceiling and land in the water. She twists to Guen, who would look drained of color if she weren't already homogenous. "What's the matter with you child?" she asks with true concern.

Guen manages to open her chattering mouth and whisper, "I thought you were going to kill me."

Dianh looks genuinely hurt. Touching a heart that's probably the size of a watermelon. "Why would I do that? You needn't worry. I am not going to harm you, Guen. All children are safe here in the *tempat perlindungan.*" Place of refuge. Dianh grasps a long pole with a net attached and scoops the coral out of the water. It pulsates with color as she places it in a sack from a pile next to the clubs. She leaves one piece out, bringing it to her mouth and biting it with a satisfied crunch. "I told you, I needed to eat."

Guen tries to relax but she's being bombarded with information. "You eat cave coral?"

Dianh grins, teeth glowing with strange color. "I do." She crouches down to Guen's level and taps a finger under the girl's chin. "It makes me big and strong!" She winks and extends to her full height.

Guen is baffled. Cave coral has always been seen as dangerous. Dark in magic and intent, the way it grows toward life and tries to skewer it with needle-thin tendrils. And here is Dianh crunching on it like it's a piece of okra. A small giggle escapes her mouth, and she covers it.

"Something funny?" Dianh arches a pale eyebrow.

Guen's little birchwood limbs rattle and shake as she struggles to contain the hysterical laughter bubbling up inside her. "Big and strong. You are certainly big and strong." She points at Dianh and the woman gives her a kind smile.

"You shall fit in here nicely, little girl." She pats Guen's head roughly, though Guen's starting to realize she can't be any gentler. "You are safe now."

Guen freezes. "What do you mean?"

Dianh picks Guen up, throwing her onto her shoulders as she talks. "I mean you can stay here with us. You can have a house and a family and—"

Guen wriggles free of Dianh, sliding the long way down to the ground and landing with a wet plop in the snow. She jumps up and places her hands on her hips, stomping her wooden foot. "I have a family!"

The giant looks upon her with pity and something else—like Guen is broken and doesn't know she needs to be fixed.

"I have a family," Guen shouts again. She has a family, and she needs to rescue them.

A quick bark before black-and-gray striped paws knock her to the ground. Claws dig into her birchwood chest. She may not really feel the cold. She may not need to eat. But when her skin splinters, she feels pain as raw and as real as if she were flesh and bone.

26

LUNA

AN ARMY OF INSECTS

Sleep doesn't come easy in a room filled with tiny coughs and sniffling button noses. It doesn't come easy when the crushing weight of the palace sits on top of you. Ash and I lie on scattered straw, arms threaded through bamboo bars.

He draws small rings of ice in my palm. "We need to make a plan," he whispers.

I dampen the glow worms light at night, but we are not in complete darkness. The children cry more when it's dark. I squint through the soft purplish glow, trying to find those sea-stained eyes. I turn onto my back, staring up at worms, trying to pretend they're stars. Wriggly, squishy, purple and green stars. I purse my lips. "I know we do." I flick my fingers, sensing insects gathering in cracks in the stone, pockets of air under the floor. "I'm building an army."

Ash sighs. "I'm not sure an army of insects will do. So many will die once they leave this level. Maybe if it were just you and me, but we need to ensure everyone gets out."

I roll to the side, taking his other hand and clasping it in my own. "That may not be possible." I imagine taking the children up the stairs and through the palace. I can't picture our freedom yet. There are too many obstacles. Too many guards.

Ash withdraws his hand. "It has to be. I am not leaving here without them, Luna. We must find a way." He grips a bamboo bar in his hands tightly. "Feel this."

I tentatively touch the bamboo. It's ice cold. The timber creaks and cracks and almost, *almost* breaks. Ash's face is contorted with concentration, energy draining from him fast. "Ash, stop." I take his hand from the post. "You're not strong enough. Not like this." I gesture at his wounds, his thin body.

Another cough, wet and juicy. The damp and mold of this place is working its way into the children's lungs. Ash shakes his head, golden brown hair sweeping over his eyes. "Maybe not, but I have to try. I can't stand this place. This is worse than any torture. Watching these children get hungrier and sicker. You hear that coughing? It's Lu Leng. She's fading, I can feel it." His head falls against the bars, and I reach out to stroke his beautiful, tortured face. "It's killing me. My heart feels like a lead weight in my chest." He's all warm blood and openness to my sliding chambers. My tick-tock heart. And I love that he feels it this much, and how he wants to sacrifice everything to help these Char children.

I tap my heart. Mine feels as it always does. I hate that there's still disconnection from emotion. A battle inside of what to keep out and what to invite. I lean into him. Taking a page from his salt-crusted book. Forehead to forehead is all we can manage. "We will find a way."

My heart at least knows I love him. That love is like a boat carrying me over the ocean of indifference. I will not capsize it. I can't.

Six-legged, hard-shelled things teem beneath the surface, but it's not enough. It may never be.

Ash is quiet for a while and then he pulls back. "Tell me again about the emperor and the others." I go over every detail while he plays with the long silk sleeves of my dress, trying to find a weakness or any bit of information to use. And I cling to his tenacity like a bird hitching a ride on a buffalo's back. If he is unwilling to give up, then so am I.

"FLOWERS FOR ME," Ash exclaims. "You shouldn't have. I'm sorry, boys, but I'm already spoken for."

I open my eyes to a spear pointed right between my eyes. "Get up!" Sho Sen tries to growl, though it's more a nervous yap. His blue silks tremble over his shaking body.

Children rattle the bars, shouting at the guards defiantly. "Leave them alone!" Lu Leng rasps, her face even paler than before.

Qi Sha storms to her cell and pokes the spear through the bars. "Shut your mouth, Char scum, or I'll shut it for you."

Ash stands quickly and grabs the black violet being shoved in his face, placing a few flowers on his tongue. "All right, all right, I'll go." I stand carefully, the spear inches from my face. I flick my fingers and Ash says, "Luna, don't waste your… energy."

My eyes dart to Ash, stumbling forward as the guards grab him roughly and pull him from his cage. "Take me," I shout, hands out.

Ash shakes his head. "No, Luna."

Qi Sha sneers. Such cruelty in his features, like he was forged from iron hate. "Very well."

I'm handed black violet also. I take it, crunching down on the bitter stems. I swallow the flowers, and as they slide down my throat, a sweetness follows that I've not tasted before. I frown. But my power recedes as usual.

Sho Sen yanks my arm and throws me in front of him, urging me forward with his spear. His actions are cruel, but I sense regret like the pup that bites its owner out of excitement.

They push Ash forward. "I don't understand," I shout, fears coiling inside me like a sleeping snake.

The guards ignore me and shove us up the stairs to the sound of children screaming, then yelping in pain as another guard jabs at them with his sword. "Shut your stupid mouths!" the guard shouts. "I'll keep cutting until you stop."

But how can you ask a child to be quiet when you've just sliced their skin?

My mouth tastes like blood. My heart swirls with it.

My power is fading fast from the black violet, but I summon every ounce left and send my army scurrying forward. The guard shrieks in terror as he and my insects tumble down the steep rocks and into the rushing river below.

"Luna! No," Ash says, though he knows I had no choice.

"I had to," I reply, power slipping away fast.

"She killed him!" someone yells.

The guard strikes my head with the length of his spear, pain radiating like the sun in my temple.

My army is gone. And with it comes the realization there's little point to building another. It took thousands to take down one man. We will have to find another way.

27
LYE

NEVER ENOUGH

Pink blends to brown like fresh meat to cooked as we row upstream. Everyone puts their back into it, heaving oars against the current. Exhausting work but somewhat peaceful as we glide through the water and watch the landscape change. The river mouth tightens to a throat as we travel north. I look behind me with an ache as the expanse of empty land begins to disappear and the canyon closes in like a secret. Sandstone builds from a small tumble to longer and larger cliffs, giving us shadows and shelter.

The sandstone walls are cut into sharp angles like stairs where large blocks were cut to build the palace. I sigh. Even now, it taunts me.

With sails down we may look like any boat rowing upstream to trade. From the high banks, no one can see our lack of tattoos or hear the gruff Char way of speaking. And though I don't want to hide, I hope to avoid Shen discovery until we have the Carvresses.

I tap Ipoh on the shoulder. "It's your turn to steer." He bows sharply and stands, sweeping a hand over the three hairs he has committed to pretending are a full head. I take his place beside Jing Ha. Her matchstick arms strain to keep up.

Taking an oar, I begin to row, losing myself in the rhythmic stroke. The smell of muddy river water and the pale sun casting light but no heat. The Carvresses should be in the center of the mountain by now where the smoldering dragon heart lies, keeping them warm and dry. I heat the oar with Fire. Lucky for us I have the skills to get us inside the mountain. I should be able to melt a tunnel through the ice. I blow a stray hair from my forehead. It will take a lot out of me.

Jing Ha watches me from the corner of her eye as she rows. "Can you tell me what is on the other side of the bank?" she asks. "I see boughs leaning over the edge. I listen for birds and fish, but the further north we travel, the quieter it becomes. I thought the Shen mainland was crammed edge to edge with people."

I nod. "It is and it isn't. The people don't live spread out across the land. They live in designated villages and those villages are often overpopulated."

Stroke. Pull through the water. Her small voice is a windpipe to an orchestra. Beautiful and necessary to round out the sound. "Designated?"

I purse my lips, wondering if Ash had this same conversation with the Char in his party. "We don't get to choose where we live. We're allocated a home and a profession that we may be suited to."

Jing Ha stops rowing long enough for her oar to catch in the current, and she quickly finds the rhythm again. "You mean your life is decided for you?"

"Yes."

Jing Ha shakes her head and I wait for the typical Char response. That they don't agree. They think we're mad or weak or both to simply accept what we're told to do without question. But all she says is "That must be difficult for a Shen if they're allocated a profession they don't like." Her breathing is labored. She's not built for this. "I value the freedom to choose my own path. And though some things are beyond my control, I would find it hard if everything was. It must make for a strong empire, but also a discontented one?" She phrases it as a question. It's interesting to me that she's curious about Shen happiness.

"For some, yes. Others are just proud to do their part for the emperor." Some of the men snort or grumble at the mention of the emperor. I don't blame them. I add, "They don't understand fully who they serve."

Jing Ha sways a little, then seems to lock her bones, grit her teeth, and continues to row. "That makes me sorry." Her lashes wet with tiny tears. "But it also gives me hope. If the Shen peasants don't know of the stolen children, then they're not to blame. The emperor is to blame."

"It's a sorry circumstance. But we're going to try and change it." I picture the emperor, sitting on his throne, wasting hours and brain cells. He always struck me as weak and easily influenced. But I would have thought torturing children was too far, even for him. The chancellor, however, is capable of anything. I frown. It matters not. The emperor is the Shen leader. Whether he knows of the children or not, he's still responsible. He cannot be absolved. Even if he haplessly and unconsciously stands on the heads of children and peasants, his silk covered feet still uses their bodies as stepping stones. Ignorance can be the vilest crime.

Jing Ha sounds wheezy, and I put up a hand to stop the crew. "Let's take a quick water break."

Ying Yi drops the anchor over with his mahogany hand, so we can stop without losing ground.

"I am sorry," Jing Ha manages, taking a large gulp of water. She coughs and splutters as it goes down the wrong hole. She pats her chest. "Oh, if Bok Ah could see me now!" The mother smiles and grimaces.

"What would he think?" I'm curious.

"He would be both proud and worried."

Joka bends down and offers Jing Ha some dried pork, which she takes gratefully, gnawing as her brown eyes rise to the sky. "He wanted, I mean wants, to be a fisherman, like his papa. Travel the islands and see new things. He'd be amazed to see me here." She pats the boat. "In Shen territory." Her gaze drops to her blistered hands. "Although, I suppose he saw some Shen mainland himself.

At least I hope he did." She takes a sharp breath in trying not to cry. "If he's still—"

Joka places a hand on her back. "We have to believe they're still alive. It makes no sense for them to steal children only to kill them." I know he's trying to comfort, but in saying this, he places the thought of torture in our minds. Because he's right. They wouldn't steal them just to kill them. They had a much darker plan.

I give him a sharp look. He steps back like my stare is a solid, powerful thing. "What Joka is trying to say is Bok Ah is very likely alive."

Jing Ha sniffs, arms shaking. "I am sorry. I'm slowing you down. I'm strong. But not as strong as a soldier. I lack training. If only there were a way to strengthen my body overnight." She laughs half-heartedly.

Overhead, juggling gulls fly in their funny formation. Three looping in a circle, over and over. We must be getting close to a settlement. I tap my chin. *A way to strengthen the body overnight.* She thinks it impossible. It's not. My fingers break storms. My scars seem to pulse a warning.

"I might be able to help you with that, Jing Ha." My voice trembles. The offer almost wanting to jump back in my mouth. It's too frightening to contemplate. I lift my eyes to Joka nervously. He nods, then shakes his head, then rubs his chin in an awkward manner. All very unhelpful, but then no one can help me with this decision.

"You can?" She's soft and flexible like green bamboo. Strongest in this form. I read love and determination. But the biggest emotion blooms like a moonflower on the fullest day: compassion. "How?"

I can do this. I can. I can. I can. Words to convince. The marks on my arm seem to rise and burn as if they were freshly cut. But this is different. This is a choice. I choose, I choose, I choose. This is sharing my power with someone I've deemed worthy. Someone simple and ordinary and so beautiful because of it.

Joka clears his throat. "Men, would you help me with something at the bow." A transparent move, but they follow.

"Jing Ha," I murmur. My voice filling with a confidence that bubbles around my bones like minerals. A feeling that was perhaps always there. "I would like to awaken an Element in you."

Her eyes open like the unwrapping of a sweet gift. "But I am not a soldier, General Koh."

My lips curve. My heart steadies. My fingers tingle with promise. "Exactly."

She bows her head and whispers agreement. "I would be honored."

I say to Jing Ha what I said to Luna what seems like years ago. "Close your eyes. This may hurt a little."

THE BOAT WHIPS around at night, pulling against the anchor to hitch the current back to sea. As if it knows we're heading for danger. If I thought it safe, I would order us to sleep on land. But it's too risky.

Most Char can sleep through this. They're seafaring people. Their blood probably rises and falls like waves.

Jing Ha is sound asleep on a sack of rice. A fresh flush to her cheeks. She is Earth. Unsurprisingly. And she took to my quick teachings well. Strengthening her arms with oak branches, nourishing her body with rich soil. The other men will wonder when they get their turn. They will be disappointed.

I lean over the end of the boat, watching silky water rush around sharp wooden edges.

A familiar elbow knocks mine and sharply withdraws. "Is that what you did to Luna?" Joka's voice is clipped like waste at the end of a paper fold. An uneasiness that wasn't there before.

I drift back to Glass Shard Island. The immensity of her Blood power. "Yes. Though Luna's power was, well, you know."

He stands beside me but with a neat one-foot distance between us. "I know," Joka mutters, deep revel in his tone. "You too, Lye. I've never seen such power. Such unearthly magic."

I tense. "You think me unearthly?"

Joka runs a hand through his spiky black hair, fingers coming to rest at his bamboo throat. His Char black uniform makes him a shadow but for the moonlight bouncing off that neck. "No, sorry. I'm not saying this right. Your power is earthly, it *is* natural and incredible and far more than I really understood. I just feel—"

I reach my magic-less hand to his, trying to grasp it, but he slips from me like an eel through a too-wide net. "What do you feel?" I ask, a familiar lonely sadness growing up under my feet like weeds. Weeds don't belong. Weeds are too strong. They dominate and overtake when they don't mean to.

"I feel like I'm too small for you as I am. Too ordinary." I roll my eyes, though he can't see it in the dull light. "I always knew you were destined for great things. But seeing it is something else." He opens his arms wide like he's tearing a hole in the sky, and I feel like I'm about to lose something before I really had it. "I'm just a Char, a scholar with a bamboo neck. My life will always be limited."

My nose screws up at these words. I don't understand. If his life is limited, it's because he limits it. "But you're the one who told me to share my gift. You started me on this path."

"I did. And I don't regret it." Joka straightens. "But I think the path is too narrow for me to walk beside you. I will walk behind you though, Lye. I will always have your back." He draws breath in slowly. "Unless—"

"Unless what?" I am the heart of a volcano. Dark and brooding, with terrible destruction beneath my skin.

His voice is piped with something like hope, but it's crossed with another feeling. Need. Want. Subtle greed. Things I am very used to. "Unless you could see fit to change me and bring me up to your level."

My chin tucks back with surprise. I reach my hands out and coast around his body. I sense his Pulse. It's right at his crown, a beady, envious little thing right now. He reads Air. His Atmosphere is warm tropical clouds trapped in a valley. Hovering over trees but wishing for open sky. Straining, grappling. It doesn't feel right. I shake my head. He's not ready. His reasons for wanting the change are unworthy. "I cannot, I'm sorry."

He steps back, stroking his chin, eyes scrunched with embarrassment. "Don't be sorry." He leaves me there, hands swaying at my side, feeling kind of angry, kind of baffled. Definitely disappointed. I wish I could change him, but if I'm going to do this, it must be for the right reasons. Not to make up for a perceived imbalance of power. I close my eyes and groan. I never thought of Joka as less than equal. Sadly, in asking me to do this, he has tipped the scales.

I slip down to the floor. I need to sleep, and this lanky Char boy has stirred up my emotions, both sweet and sour, then left me to boil over.

I huff, folding my arms over my chest.

A slight shadow makes its way to me. "Men are foolish, General," Jing Ha whispers.

I knew this already, but I thought Joka was different. "He says he is too small for me." I make an imaginary ball between my hands like I'm compressing the air. "He wants something I cannot give. I don't know how to resolve that."

Jing Ha chuckles quietly. "He *is* too small. And even if you changed him, he would never have your power. Hold your influence. It would never be enough."

I grimace. "Then how do I fix this?"

Jing Ha places a hand on my sycamore arm and pats it. A mother's move though she can't be more than five years older. "You don't fix this. This is his problem, not yours. Women seldom bother with such notions as power imbalance. We don't leave a man because he is stronger. He doesn't understand it's a privilege to be with a woman such as you. He needs to learn that truth."

I feel a little strangled by the sudden inference that we were "together." It had barely begun. But my heart hurts in a new way I've never felt before. Like it's been placed on a high shelf where no one is to touch it. "What if he doesn't learn that truth?"

Jing Ha taps her heart lightly. "Ah, then he isn't the man for you."

28

GUEN

HOME IS WHERE THE CHAOS IS

Guen is getting used to the idea that the world she once knew, where Shen were the superior race and elements and emperors ruled, was a bunch of nonsense. She narrows her eyes as Zui-Zui's lips ripple with a growl and its claws dig into her chest. She lifts her hand to the creature's paw. Guen could probably kill it by turning it into a wooden sculpture. But she's not sure she wants to.

The wolf digs in harder and she gasps. She closes her eyes, counting one, two—Dianh scolds, and grabs its ruff, pulling it back. "Ah Zui-Zui, no! Bad wolf!"

The striped cub whines and rolls onto is back. Dianh offers a huge hand, but Guen doesn't take it. She knows it appears distrustful but Guen's simply afraid she might hurt the giant. Dianh shrugs and looks at the sky. "It's getting dark. Come home with me tonight, little wooden girl. You can tell me about your fa-mi-ly." She drawls the word like she's doubtful of its existence. "I'll make you some dinner."

Guen shakes her head. "I already said, I don't eat."

The woman snorts. "All living things eat."

Guen scowls. "Well, I'm living, and I don't."

Dianh chuckles. "So where do you get your energy from?"

"From the trees."

"Then that's what you eat." Dianh strides from the cave while Guen tries to keep up. Zui-Zui bounds at her side. Guen clambers down the enormous steps, watching the sun slip below the mountains. It still has a long way to go before it reaches the ground. Back home, the plains seemed flat enough to catch the yellow ball before it started digging down into the earth like a piranha rabbit. Though she was never brave enough to try. Her bravery has grown out of trees and ancient magic. She remembers gazing out the window of her hut at the hazy sunsets rippling over the plains, her mother cuffing her ear for being idle. Her father shouting, "Give her another six for good luck."

She rubs her ear at the memory as she runs alongside the woman who's not made of wood but has tree trunks for legs.

Dianh points to a cottage nestled against the mountainside shoulder to shoulder with other homes, golden light and moving shadows within. "Home is where the heart is." She sighs happily and presses a palm to her heart. An angry shout and a squeal rumbles the walls. Guen shrinks from the noise, but Dianh simply laughs. "And also, home is where the chaos is." She puts her hand to the back of Guen's head and steers her to the door. "You needn't be afraid, child."

Guen frowns, joints locking, misgiving swimming in her sap. "I'm not. Is your, er, husband in there?"

Dianh's laugh becomes a trumpeting sound that takes the woman's breath. She slaps her knee with a wallop. "I should very much hope not!"

Guen arches her perfect little birch eyebrow and allows Dianh to usher her inside, to a roaring fire, color on the walls, and happy faces.

CHILDREN OF VARIOUS sizes and shapes rush at Dianh's legs. Some try to climb her like a tree. Others wrap their arms and legs around them like monkeys. Zui-Zui shoves past Guen, who tries to hides behind Dianh and nearly knocks her over in his haste to lick the cheeks of these little monsters.

"You're home!" they shout with excitement. "We're hungry!"

Dianh's laugh is the echo of the mother every kid wants but not every kid gets: Pure delight in her children. She nudges Guen out from behind her like a shy student. "Oh, so did you miss me or my cooking?" she asks, squatting to meet the children at eye level.

The children giggle and bat at Zui-Zui when he jumps at them. Guen would give him a sharper message if it were up to her. She clears her throat and the giggling stops. One by one they notice the wooden girl at the door.

A little boy points at Guen like he's accusing her of something. "What's that?"

Dianh smiles at the boy, who can't be more than five. She pats his head as he crawls into her lap. "*That* is a Guen. She's going to stay with us for a while."

She is? This is news to her. She worries what "a while" means.

"I have to get back to my family," the birchwood girl says resolutely. Hands on hips. The wood she sent will only last them a night or two at best. "I need to ask you—"

Dianh twists on her haunches to Guen with a welcoming grin and pats her head roughly with a hand the size of a concubine's fan. She isn't listening and it's starting to frustrate Guen. But to get the woman's help, she must be nice, right? "It's all right, Guen, you're safe here." She gestures with her spare hand to six grinning faces. "Everyone is finally safe, right, children?"

The children nod their little heads in agreement as they crowd around Dianh when she stands. She lifts a wok, which looks like a toy in her hands, and begins throwing spices into hot oil at a stove as high as Guen's head. The crackle and subsequent smell makes Guen's wooden tongue salivate and her mind turn to home. A place she never really felt safe but there was comfort in it. It was all she'd ever known until Sun scooped her up and ran. She thought family was all about obligation and servitude. But she has safety and loyalty now with Sun, Ki Anah, and the Carvresses. And she's not giving it up!

Guen frowns, retreating to a corner quietly. Questions seething in her mind. Where did these children come from? There are no husbands. In her village a woman with six children and no husband would be an object of pity. Here, it seems they are proud of their way of life. Guen tilts her head. It's as if they do not need men. She snorts as she watches the children wolf down their food.

Zui-Zui hears her and trots over to sit at her feet. Guen presses her back into the wall, holding her breath. She's still not sure she isn't going to end up as Zui-Zui's chew toy. Dianh watches out of the corner of her eye and waggles a finger at the cub. "You look after our new family member, Zui-Zui," she warns. The words "family member" fill Guen with equal parts warmth and terror.

The tiger wolf nuzzles her hand, and she allows herself to sink her birch fingers into its ruff. So soft and alive. She feels the creature's breath rise and fall beneath her palm and sighs loudly. She appreciates the warm welcome. But she is not in need of rescuing. She must do the rescuing.

The scraping of plates and chairs pulling across the floor signify the meal is over. Children zig and zag across the cottage, washing up and changing for bed, while Guen stays pinned to the corner.

Dianh squats down and places a finger under the girl's chin. "I think you should get some sleep, don't you, little birchwood girl?"

Guen shakes her head. "But I have questions. I have things I need to do. I—"

Dianh shakes her enormous head. "All things can wait 'til morning." She yawns loudly and taps her mouth. She scoops Guen up with ease and walks her to another room. It's pretty, decorated with strings of paper lanterns and clumsy characters drawn on torn pieces of parchment. Three girls are already blinking big eyes like toads above the covers.

One bed is empty and Guen feels sleepy just looking at it. Though she needs less sleep than a flesh creature, she still gets weary and today has been one of the most tiring of her life. Dianh points to it. "I had the boys drag a bed in here for you. Pang and

Fen can share until we organize something more permanent." She rolls Guen under the covers and tucks them around her little body. Though technically she has no need for them, it does feel nice to be cared for. To sleep in an actual bed. Guen's eyes become heavy.

She slips into sleep too easily, though she keeps her nails hooked around the task she came here to do. She will just rest her eyes for a few minutes. Then she will explain it all to Dianh.

29

LUNA

DELIGHTED IN A BLOOD-DIPPED DRESS

Ash and I focus on each other as we're poked and pushed up several levels. Past our cell accommodations which seem luxurious compared to the cave of bamboo cages. Until we are back on plush red carpets running through the halls like a lying tongue over the horror beneath. We blink mold and dust from our eyes while the sun tries to open them. Ash sniffs the air as we're forced through the kitchen. The smell of chili and lime, fish sauce and palm sugar makes our mouths water.

In the corner, I hear a small call. I feel the loneliest heart reaching for its mother. A maid pushes a small piece of banana through the bars of an old bird cage. The baby howling monkey snatches it desperately. My heart hammers a strange beat of relief and guilt. It's alive. For now.

I have no time to contemplate before we're enclosed in artificial light once again. The tunnel to the wooden torture box stretches out like a nightmare. "Luna, is this where—?" I dig my heels in, straining against the guards. But without Blood, I cannot overpower five guards, and though Ash also tries to resist, he's in no state to fight.

Eyes bulging with fear at what they have planned, I answer, "Yes. Ash. Hold on. Remember your promise."

Ash's jaw tenses and his mouth sets into hard line. Because of the violet I can't *feel* him bracing for the next bout of immeasurable pain, but I know it's happening all the same.

The door opens and we're shoved inside.

"Treats for me! Wonderful!" Soo Si's high, chiming voice grates against my ears. She points a painted fingernail at Ash and me. Slumped over, dirty rags in this clean, bleach scented room. "You gave them the violet as the emperor ordered?" The guards nod.

"She killed Ka Len." Sho Sen points an accusatory finger at my chest.

Soo Si twists her serpentine neck toward Sho Sen. "Well then…" She waves her hand as if swatting a fly. "Then he died in service of the emperor. There is no nobler death." The guard gnaws on his lip, looking terrified of the swaying stick figure while also looking like he wants to say something more. Her eyes narrow. "How is your wife, Sho Shen? Still enjoying the medicine the palace provides for her debilitating arthritis?" Eyes down, the guard steps back into line. The women bandies the threat like it's dipped in sugar. Like it's a gift, when it's clear she will yank it away at the slightest dissension.

"I wouldn't say death by beetle is particularly noble," Ash mutters.

Her eyes dart to Ash but she doesn't respond. "Did you have trouble with the other prisoners?" Her nostrils flare like she can't bring herself to acknowledge the Char children.

"They're getting rowdy, Lady Soo. Perhaps you could speak to the emperor about moving—"

Soo Si's head snaps to the guard like a trap. "We don't bother the emperor with these things. He doesn't need to be troubled with every… single… detail." She groans these words out like they bore her. "Besides, he's not here today. He traveled to the temple with his mother for the morning. He'll be gone for hours." The relief in her tone vibrates like a gong. She pats her chest and smooths her silk gown. "Pray for the empress. Her health is failing."

They bow and mutter, "Yes, Lady Soo." Backing out of the room like she's the empress, not just a concubine. Ash and I connect, his eyebrow arches. Something is off.

The doctor appears from behind the torture chair, making me jump. "Very right, Lady Soo. No need to bother him about the children until we have something useful to report. I wish Chancellor Koh were here to assist though. He had a plan."

At these words, Soo Si swishes over to the doctor. The crystals studding her long purple dress make little tinkling sounds that bely the raging temper in her expression. She pulls back her thin arm and slaps him hard across the face. He stumbles back from the force of it. "Chancellor Koh and I worked together. And now that he's dead, I am in charge. I have a plan too. Don't you dare forget that!" The snake has fangs and she's not afraid to use them. This new information moves Soo Si disturbingly and terrifyingly up the ranks. She claps her hands loudly. "Now, I came here to review your methods for gathering information. Hurry up. The boy first!"

The doctor's expression flashes in anger as he bows, and Ash is forced into the torture chair and bound. His eyes are storms trying to lift from the ground. Sorry and strength in his expression. With his fists tightened and his mouth curved, he gives me a smile, though the saltwater is dried and flaking.

I'm still crouched on the ground and Soo Si beckons me with her claw. "Come sit beside me, Char Luna Yan." She pats the seat beside her like we're about to watch a play. Her dark eyes alight, readying herself for entertainment. She wiggles in her chair and her head dress dings and tinkles.

I do as I'm asked. I sit beside the beautiful woman, unable to look away as the doctor pulls out his first device. "Now I know I've asked you this question dozens of times, but until you give me an answer, I must continue to ask. Where are the Carvresses?"

Ash grins, his grimy gaze fixed on mine. "I don't know what you're talking about. What's a Carvress?"

I keep my eyes locked on Ash's as the doctor cuts a neat, shallow line right over his heart. Ash grips the chair arms, body tensing. His teeth clamp down. And I want to scream. My body pulses with the desire to tear the doctor apart and send a thousand clawing bats through his blood until he's nothing but a pile of bones.

"Where are the Carvresses?" the doctor asks again.

Ash shakes his head, sweat beading over his bare skin, which is the pallor of dried sage. The doctor sighs and holds a jar of powder over Ash's wound, sprinkling it into the cut. Ash's whole body seizes. He bucks and cries out as the powder sizzles into his blood.

My body rumbles. My heart shrieks like a split tree. "Stop!" I shout. "Please! Stop!"

The doctor checks with Soo Si, who gives a minute tilt of her head. Her expression is serene like she's watching a dance set to beautiful music. Not a crease or wrinkle to be seen as the doctor makes another cut and Ash tries to hold in a cry of anguish only to have it butt against his teeth and fly out anyway.

Tears slide down my cheeks. Rage builds in my breast. I can't stand it. I can't bear it. I can't *change* it. Again, the doctor pours powder into the wound. Ash turns to me, begging for something—strength, love, death. And I try through shaking limbs and bleary eyes to hold him. Cradle what I can. "Ash, look at me. I'm here." Pain ripples through his body and begins to transfer into mine. Blood continues to pour, dripping slow like tar down his chest and onto the floor.

I turn away, trying to catch my breath. Trying to hold on and not scream myself. The concubine looks at me with distaste. Like she's disappointed.

"How much more, Lady Soo?" the doctor asks.

She glares at me, dark eyes penetrating like two endless pits. "Continue until I tell you to stop," her red-painted lips utter.

"It's all right, Luna," Ash sputters. "You don't have to look."

Soo Si's heel stomps into the ground with a crack. "Oh, yes you do." Carefully she slips gloves onto her hands one after the other, pushing down the fingers with meticulous care. Then she takes my chin in her claw and digs in, turning my head toward Ash as another cut is made. This one is deeper. Blood pours from his arm like a fountain.

They're going to kill him.

They're going to kill him and make me watch.

Blood boils hot and angry. "You didn't even ask him a question!" I scream, standing. Soo Si's arm shoots out and pushes me down in the chair.

The doctor ignores me. Going about the gruesome work of tearing my heart, my Ash, apart piece by piece.

Blood fills every space like water. Blood reaches. Blood breaks.

Suddenly, I am acutely aware of the black violet coating my power like a second skin. I sense it in a way I haven't before. And once I do, I find I can remove it. Get my fingers under it and pull it away. Power floods me.

"Stop," I whisper.

The walls begin to shake. The sudden sound of animals shrieking and bashing on the outside builds to the point where it's all we can hear. My hands shake. The doctor ducks at the noise, agitated. He exchanges looks with the concubine briefly and then bends his head down, concentrating once more on his terrible work. Ash screams as tools are gripped to the open wounds and pulled. The sea blue of his eyes turns to a dying gray.

He's dying.

Blood is taking over. Nothing but fur and claws. Death and darkness. "Stop," I say again, in a tone as flat and even as the sea between Coalstone Village and Black Sail City. My hands fly out and walls crack. Hundreds of monkeys and birds, possums and squirrels, peel open the box like it's made of rice wafers. Soo Si stands and steps away from the table, calm and controlled, as planks of wood fly from the box and creatures stream inside, crawling over the doctor. His knife clatters to the floor. The doctor is engulfed in furious tearing claws and fangs, scratching and pulling at his skin. Doing to him what he did to so many others. He screeches high and panicked, begging for Soo Si's help. The concubine does nothing, hands clasped in front, watching chaos reign.

He doesn't plead to me because he knows I would do nothing. I can't control what is happening anyway. I am an instrument. A river of blood that has only one course. Stop the doctor.

Guards run in but stop at the end of the tunnel as the box is laid open like a squashed flower. Ash's eye roll, barely conscious as his life drains away. His hand lifts like he's trying to warn me, but I'm lost in the flurry of feather and fur.

The doctor calls again for help. And is answered. A murder bird dives down, wing out, slicing the doctor's throat before he can utter another word.

Blood of love. Blood of torture. Blood. Everywhere.

Ash's eyes close and slowly the concubine moves to the chair, taking a cloth and pressing it to his wounds. She lifts her perfect chin. "Take him to the infirmary at once!" The guards dodge agitated animals, lift Ash, and carry him away before I can do anything.

My knees wobble and buckle. My hands shoot out to catch my fall. I am wasted. All energy spent. Animals scatter as guards threaten them with spears, leaving the doctor's body exposed. Flat on his back in a pool of blood that's creeping toward my fingers. His eyes open to a sky he never thought I'd be able to bring. I back away, wishing there was still a wall to lean against.

Soo Si's dress is dipped in blood, and she lifts her skirt to stop further soaking. I can barely move, my body sapped of everything, but I manage to murmur through trembling lips, "H-h-how?" I broke the dam. Surpassed the black violet completely and reaching my power further than I ever have.

The concubine smiles so cruelly and so fully I want to run from it like it's a fiery comet coming right for me. She claps her hands, gleeful. "I knew you could overcome it. All you needed was a slight adjustment to the violet and, of course, the right motivation."

The sweetness I tasted—it changed the effects.

"Y-y-you wanted this to happen?" I stutter, staring at the doctor's shredded neck.

"I wanted you to break through the black violet." She steps over the doctor's body like he's a troublesome tree root in her path. "This"—she gestures lazily at the dead man at her feet—"is simply collateral damage." She turns her attention to ordering servants to clean up. They scatter and stoop, picking up the broken pieces of timber. "Quickly now, before the emperor returns. You know how he hates mess."

My consciousness fades. Eyes closing to servants chasing wayward monkeys from the grounds and a concubine twirling around, delighted in a blood-dipped dress.

30

LYE

THE MOON AND THE FALLEN STAR

I thought there were only two sides to Lye Li Koh. Keeper or not. Instrument or independent. But I'm learning I am infinite. Choices stretching before me like rays of a newborn sun. The power of choice comes at a price though. Disagreement, but also responsibility.

My arms burn as I pull the oar through water for what feels like, and possibly is, the millionth time. We're getting close. My exhalations come out in misty clouds. My skin feels dry from the cold. My hair brittle. The men are tired. But they don't stop, they don't give up. The Carvresses are too vital for anyone to slow their pace no matter how much their muscles ache. I frown. If only Ash and Luna were at the end of the river too.

My knowledge of their situation is words on carpet moths' wings. *Captured. Palace.* How did they become separated from the others? How did they manage to keep the Carvresses safe? My fingers spark with lightning. No doubt the Chancellor's hand steered or slapped them down this path. I close my eyes and inhale the cold, cold air. *Live, little brother. Just live long enough for me to reach you. I know it will be hard to hold on, but even if it's by the thinnest strand, I need you to not let go.*

How I wish I wasn't taking the longest road to the palace. But it's the only way.

The men stop rowing suddenly, heads bowed low. Joka whispers, "Above." Though he won't lift his face. I turn to the embankment and the tiny Shen silhouettes waving over the edge.

"Wave back," I order. "Keep your wooden parts from view, but you must pretend you are Shen, at least for now." Jing Ha lifts her face and I push the top of her head down roughly. "Your cheeks." Her neck flushes red and she lowers her face, waving whilst staring at the rippling water.

To the river she mutters, "I thought you didn't want to hide."

I continue to wave until the Shen disappear. Returning to their daily lives of frostbitten farming. "I don't want to hide once we have the Carvresses. But we need to get to them first."

My oar clunks against a piece of bobbing ice. Before it reaches the sea, it will have melted to nothing, becoming part of the river and then the greater body of water that sweeps around the planet. "What if we can't—" *Find them?*

I wave a dismissing hand. "We will. We must." I sniff the air. The sweetness of glacier rice paddies calls me. Red stalks swishing in the briskest wind. "Have faith, Jing Ha. It won't be long now."

Jing Ha pulls her oar with gusto. "I am glad for my Earth powers right now." She casts her eyes at the other Char, shivering from cold.

Standing, I move through the crew, tapping gently and sending hot summer wind through their skin.

Ying Yi, a solid, short soldier, who has been pretty quiet until now, nods his head in thanks. "Would it not be easier to grant us all Elements? It would make for far better soldiers." It would not make him better. Stronger and more deadly perhaps. But not better.

"Jing Ha is not a soldier," Joka mutters. "The general chose her for that reason."

"But why does she get to choose?" Ying Yi persists, and I kind of wish he'd go back to being the quiet one.

Joka pulls through the water, arms gathering muscle with every passing day. I will miss his lankiness. My thoughts drift to lost touches, hands in hair, missed kisses. It was all too brief, almost like it never happened. "To take away her choice would be to return her to a role just like the emperor's Keeper. Is that what you want?"

"No. Of course not." Ying Yi's eyes cast downward, and he puts more effort into rowing with his mahogany hand. Usually used for fine furniture in the palace, it's a strange finish against the roughness of a Char soldier.

Joka exhales loudly and gives a quick, finite nod of his strong chin. I share a glance with Jing Ha for a moment and both her brows rise like goose wings ready to take flight. He defends yet abandons me. I cannot make sense of it. Clearly, neither can Jing Ha.

I want to confront him, but these close quarters make it almost impossible.

WE SIT ON the deck in the dark, so we don't attract attention. Char black covers them well. Keeper gray melts into the air like a cloud pondering rain. We have moonlight bouncing off the sandstone walls. Their crystal composition gives them a starlight sparkle.

Backs against the side of the boat, feet almost touching, we're all getting a little weary of the lack of privacy.

Chewing on rations has become a sport in itself. The tough, leathery dried meat and fish has frozen. My teeth ache as I try to tear off a piccc.

Captain Ipoh grumbles, shoulders hunched and tense. He mutters something to himself and takes a spear to the back of the boat. He's a strange Char. More eloquent than most with a graceful air. I close my mouth tightly even though the words didn't leave my lips. The Char are intelligent, intuitive souls. And I must be careful of old Shen opinions creeping back into my head.

I hear a plop. Ipoh probably gave up on his dried pork and tossed it into the water.

I turn my attention to the others. "How is everyone faring?" I ask no one in particular.

Ying Yi snorts and spits on the deck. "My arms feel as wooden as my hand but without the extra strength." He flaps the shadow of an arm in my face with irritation.

I concentrate on spider webs and lay my elemental hand on his forearm. Sewing his muscles together so they can take a break. He bows gratefully.

"I am sorry I spoke out of turn earlier today, General. I understand why you cannot gift me power. Though I will strive to be worthy of it someday." Ying Yi salutes and then thumps his chest. "And if I am never deemed so, so be it! I am Char. We're made pretty perfect anyway."

I laugh with the others. "You know I believe that's true." I hold up my arm. "And I am honored to be part of your 'perfect' tribe." The men knock their hands, feet, and legs against the wooden deck.

Joka smiles quick, like the flick of an eel's tail as it disappears into its hollow, and then it turns into something more serious. His eyes lift to the stars. The sigh in him rises to the sky, searching for others in its quest to form a storm. He clutches the notebook of missing children's names against his chest. A reminder of what we have come to do.

The conversation soon turns to tales of recent triumphs, or even embarrassment. It's a wonderful song with notes that don't match, instruments out of tune, but it's pure camaraderie. And for once, I feel inside the circle instead of trying to find a way in like a fleece ferret escaping the cold.

Ying Yi elbows Joka in the side and startles him from far away thoughts. "What about you, Joka? Tell us a story."

The boat swishes from side to side as the river tries to loosen the anchor. Joka inhales slowly and purses his lips. "I have no stories worth telling. None that end well, anyway."

My heart doesn't skip, it stumbles. I don't understand what changed. We were always different. My power has always been bigger than his. Why does it matter now?

Ying Yi blows a raspberry and thumps his chest. "Well then, make something up. You're the smart one. You've read all the books. Come on, bamboo neck."

Joka bows his head and clasps his hands over his chest. "Very well. How about the tale of the moon and fallen star?"

The men clap their hands and I shush them. We may be in the dark, but we should still keep quiet. Joka begins in his silken voice, and I find myself leaning in, ready to catch every word.

"The moon, the brightest light in the midnight sky, had a secret. Although her task was to judge human souls and decide if they could join their ancestors as stars in the sky, she had never been human herself. To her it felt like something was missing, and she wished for it desperately. She could throw light across the dark sky, control the position and brightness of the stars, and influence the tide, but she did all of this alone. She felt that very human emotion: loneliness. So, on a dark night, when she usually faced away from the world, she threw her spirit down on a moonbeam. When it landed on the earth, it transformed into a woman. A moon maiden, plainly clothed in white robes, holding all these gifts between her thin fingers."

I barely breathe listening to him speak. The lilt and love in his voice curls around me like a mother's arm. I wish to shuffle to him, lean my head on his chest, and feel the words vibrate through my body. I bite my lip.

"The moon maiden walked the green earth, talking to animals and plants. Touching trees and simply enjoying the pleasure of a human body that could smell, taste, and feel the world around her.

"She wandered to the outskirts of a village, where a man was tending oxen, brushing their hides with the kind of care she would have thought only an emperor would deserve. But this was the kind of man he was. Careful and considerate of every living creature. The man looked up from his work and their eyes connected. It was not love at first sight, but they fascinated each other. The man invited her to sit on the back of his cart, and they talked for hours.

When the sun threatened to rise, the moon maiden returned to the jungle, promising to come again the next night.

"As the sun set, the man waited for the moon maiden. When she stepped out from the jungle, his heart glowed inside his chest. Every night for twenty-nine nights she came to him. And with every night they fell slowly but surely in love."

I understand the hitching of one's heart now. Mine feels like it's caught on a fishhook and someone is trying to pull it through my ribs. At the back of the boat, Ipoh curses after another splash. Perhaps romantic stories are not his thing. The others are enthralled by Joka's story.

Ying Yi leans in, hand clasped. "But she's the moon. How can it work?"

Joka puts a finger to his lips, waiting for the eager man to calm, and then continues. "On the twenty-ninth night the moon maiden glanced at the dark sky and frowned. She needed to return to the sky. Already she had left the stars unguided for too long. The man knelt before her and asked to come too. If she made him into a star, he could be beside her forever. They clasped hands and kissed under the black-as-molasses, moonless sky."

Hung makes kissing noises and chuckles. Joka groans. "Do you wish me to continue?"

My legs bounce agitatedly. "Please! Continue." He arches an eyebrow, a wave of sadness rushing over his smooth features.

Joka strokes his bamboo neck. "The maiden agreed. But her task as the moon was to judge worthiness. She told him he would need to prove himself good enough to sit beside her in the sky. Until then she would return to him once a month on the day the moon hides from the world. The man's hands fell from the maiden's, and he shook his head no. She should not come back to visit him. He understood her job. He even knew it was necessary, but—"

But what?

The boat tips suddenly and violently. Ying Yi pitches over the side, and Hung barely manages to hold on as it hits the water with hard slap. Ipoh exclaims loudly, happily, and a fish slides across the deck, flopping around as it fights for a life it has already lost.

I turn to Ipoh as his expression changes from joy to dread in a second. "What did you do?"

Ipoh runs to the center of the boat, sliding and hitting everything as he goes. "I was fishing, that's all."

"You fool!" I manage. Diamond back crocodiles will be tempted to the surface by fish gathering around a bait.

The boat bumps up and down as if it has a rock underneath. Joka looks at me, eyes wide. "What is it, General?" His hands splayed as he tries to hold onto a flat deck.

I grasp the side as the boat tips again. Ying Yi shouts from the bank, "I'm all right, just so you know!" I quickly count heads. Ying Yi is the only one who was thrown.

"He will not be all right if we don't get him back on board," I tell Joka.

"Why?"

The boat bucks again. "Because Ipoh has called the crocodiles and Ying Yi is a much more rewarding meal than a few fish."

31
GUEN

WHEN NICE DOESN'T WORK

Stars coat the midnight sky like bugs caught in a trap. Guen blinks at the uncovered window and crawls out of bed. She has a phantom thirst, and without thinking she wanders to the kitchen, pumping water into a teacup and placing it to her lips. The water coats her wooden lips, and she remembers. She places the cup down on the edge of the counter.

"Are you having trouble sleeping, Guen?" Dianh's low voice comes from the back of a chair by the fire that could seat three normal-sized people.

Guen wanders over to the woman whose legs rise up like tent poles because the chair is too low to the ground. Zui-Zui snores with his head resting on Dianh's feet. "I think I am getting less sleepy as this"—she points at her wooden forearm—"takes over. They said it would happen."

"They?" Dianh asks, stretching her long limbs and lifting Zui-Zui off the floor for a moment. The pup opens one golden eye lazily.

"The Carvresses," Guen says, head bowed.

Dianh leans forward. "What's a Carvress?" Her voice is suspicious.

Guen doesn't know where to start. Her view of the Carvresses has changed so much since she first ran into Shei-Shei in the woods. Her hands shake a little as she remembers her mother thwacking the back of her legs with a cane and shoving the basket onto her back. She was so mad, but she went because staying would only lead to another beating. She took her time climbing the hill because she was stalling coming home. She zig-zagged up the green slope, singing her made-up emperor song while choosily collecting firewood. When she reached the grove, her whole world changed in one painful and surprising instant. To Dianh she says, "A Carvress made me like this."

Dianh's expression softens. "Did they hurt you?"

Guen shakes her head even though it did hurt, like all her beatings combined. "They didn't mean to hurt me. It was an accident."

Dianh's sigh is as deep and dark as an abyss. "That is what they always say." She gathers Guen up in her arms and strokes her wooden head. Guen wants to squirm and jump away but at the same time, Dianh is comforting. She reminds Guen of Sun.

Guen looks up at the giant woman with sap of frustration in her eyes. "What do you mean 'that's what they always say'? It was an accident. She was frightened. She was protecting herself." Guen's bones feel serrated, ready to catch on anything. "Where are all the husbands? Are they away? Did something happen to them? Did you do something to them?"

Dianh laughs, but there's something bitter and angry about it, like a laugh is not the right sound for how she's feeling but there's nothing else she can do. "Sometimes I hope something did happen to them, I really do. But most likely the husbands are still living and doing what they were doing before we ran away. They probably have new wives, which makes me saddest of all. But if those wives ever need to escape, we will be here, ready to accept them with open arms."

Guen shakes a little. Her traditional beliefs challenged. "So, you ran away from your husbands?" Guen asks and Dianh nods. "Why?"

Dianh taps Guen's nose. "Why do you think, little one? Why do you think the children are here?"

Guen moves her eyes around the room. The warm, joyful space seems to have everything a child could need or want. Everything except a father. But they don't seem unhappy, aching or missing something. Quite the opposite. "You ran away because your husbands were bad husbands." Guen thinks back to her own home. Her father had little patience. Little praise for his daughter, only hard words and an even harder cane to her calves. Her faces scrunches. He was a little man with an even littler heart.

"Isn't that why you're here? To get help because someone hurt you," Dianh asks with a kindness that spreads across Guen's chest like warm blood.

"No." Guen shakes her head.

"All the children here have come from violent or abusive homes. We help all who make the journey. All. We'll help you too." She lifts one of Guen's arms and inspects it with consternation. "Though I'm not sure what we can do about this situation."

Guen snaps her arm back, holding it close against her chest. "I'm not like these other children. I have a family who loves me. I found them, all on my own. I need your help, but not how you think." Her voice loudens. "I like my birchwood body. I like my new life." She bites her wooden lip. "Maybe I needed to escape before Sun and the others found me, but not anymore. Now I've found *my* people. I already have a tribe. Yours is very nice but I belong to another." Guen sticks out her chin. "I belong to the Char Yan tribe."

Dianh pets Guen's head. "You should get some sleep. We can talk about it in the morning."

Guen's frustration grows. "My family is trapped in the mountain, Dianh. They protected me when they could have left me to die. They rescued me from a dull and sorry life. I have to save them." Guen jumps from Dianh's lap and runs for the door, grasping the knob. Nice isn't working. Guen throws nice out the window. "I don't know how to be nice anymore and make you understand me. If you won't help, then I need to get back to them." Sap runs freely down her cheeks. Warm and sticky. She swipes at it and sniffs. "You may be a giant, but I'm a Carvress. I am stronger than you think. I am bravery."

She opens the door and storms out. Snow devours her little legs.

She doesn't get far before she is plucked from the ground by her head.

Dianh holds Guen close to her own face, eyebrows arched. "I've never known one to want to go back to where they came from. I am sorry. When you experience life one way for so long, it is hard to see other sides. Perhaps there is more to your story, Guen."

Guen wants to scream. "That's what I've been trying to tell you, you giant, bone-headed woman." Sun told her not to be insulting. That she would need to be very good and very convincing to get the help they need.

Dianh's fingers squeeze into Guen's head. "No need to be rude."

Guen has had enough, she can't wait any longer. "Put me down. I need to save my family!"

Dianh places Guen on the ground and squats, her furs collecting a dusting of perfect little snowflakes. "Guen, tell me exactly how you came to be here and what you need from us. I promise, I will listen."

Guen folds her arms over her chest and scowls. "I need more than just you. So, if you can get the others to listen, I will tell you everything."

Dianh chuckles. "You don't ask for much, do you?"

Guen smiles, though it's a very wary one. "I would ask for the moon if it would help my family."

EVEN THOUGH HER brain knows it won't happen, Guen's wooden heart stammers like a prize pig about to be roasted on a spit with all these monstruous women staring at her with such interest. Dianh summoned the tribe to the coral cave, placed Guen on a rock in the middle of a circle of giants, and told her to speak. Her birchwood knees knock together as she explains her predicament.

One of the giants, who hasn't stopped nibbling on a piece of cave coral the entire time, says between crunches, "So, you want us to rescue these Carvresses and two women named Sun and Ki Anah Yan." Guen nods, not correcting them in assuming Sun is a woman. "They were very foolish to stay on the outer edge of the mountain at this time of the year. They should have traveled to the dragon's heart. How do you know they're not already dead?"

At this Guen stiffens. She can't leave room for that thought. She has to believe they're still alive. It's only been two nights. If they were careful, they had enough wood for that long. She fists her hands. *She hopes.*

Dianh clears her throat and gives the other woman a funny look. "These women need our help. We've always prided ourselves on protecting those in need. These Carvresses and the Yans are in need."

"A party of six should suffice."

"Also, drills and torches and—"

Dianh interrupts them, watching little Guen anxiously jumping from foot to foot awaiting their answer. "So that's a yes?"

The women nod one by one, pulling their masks over their faces and rising from their seats. "That is a yes. Collect your tools and weapons. We leave in an hour," an older woman states, her mask peeling and more banged up than Dianh's.

Guen feels relief wash over her like desert rain. Sun will be so proud. She can't wait to jump into his arms and pinch his nose and tell him all about the tribe of the Dark West. He was right to say things are not always what they first seem. That what she was taught was not the whole story. She has certainly learned it over *and over.*

32
LUNA

PINES THAT PUNCTURE THE SKY

My eyes throb like a missing heartbeat. My blood swirls sweet and thick. My lips shape and expel one word, one name: "Ash."

"He hasn't come back," Ha Fun whispers.

There's straw at my back. The smell of iron is suffocating. I'm in the belly of the palace again.

Breathing hurts and heals me. My memory returns with my power. Monkeys screeching as a concubine dances in pools of blood. The doctor lying dead among the rubble of a box that looked as if it had been dropped from the sky.

A wheezy rattle comes from the cage beside me. "Lu-na?" Lu Leng's teeth chatter and then she coughs like her lungs might be pushing out between her ribs. A swollen, wet sound. "I'm not—"

"She's awake," an impatient voice snaps: Qi Sha.

Iron creaks. Arms are hooked under my armpits, black violet shoved down my throat.

I'm scrubbed clean, dressed, and perfumed again. Maids give me sorry expressions as they lift my uncooperative arms and legs.

The doors to the throne room open and I'm shoved inside. Three faces greet me. One is furious. One is confused. The other smiles like the slyest snake.

I don't bow to the emperor. I walk straight to the center of the room and glare. My hickory heart polished and shining like a planet set in my chest. A planet that's ready to spin on its axis.

Mulia sets her enormous paws on the steps and crawls forward, lips rippling with a threatening growl. But I know my way around the black violet now. With intense focus, I can peel my Blood power from it like I'm freeing myself of a cocoon. I begin the slow painful process, careful not to tear my wings.

The emperor opens his mouth to speak, and I cut him off. "Where's Ash?"

His angular shoulders pull back into his throne like I've hit him in the chest. Purple silk aflutter. He's so used to speaking first and everyone kowtowing to him. *Well, I'm done.*

The emperor's mother exhales loud and short through her nose like she's a bull about to charge. "Do *not* speak to my husband that way. Guards—" She waves at them. "Teach this peasant some manners." She wipes her nose and rubs red lotus into her teeth. The line between each tooth is reddish pink. I wrinkle my nose.

The emperor shifts uncomfortably in his throne. "Mama, it's me, your son. Papa died a long time ago." To me he says, "If you want answers from me, you best ask nicely."

Soo Si narrows her eyes and leans forward. "The traitor is in the infirmary. Safe for now. Whether he stays that way depends on you." She points her lacquered nail at me.

I put my hands on my hips and step forward. "Why should I be polite to this man? He's not the rightful leader." I push my luck across the line and over a cliff. I want Mulia set on me. I need her focus. The emperor's eyebrows rise, and his fingers dig into the chair arms. *Eyes on me, Mulia.* They follow me as I sway from side to side and wiggle my finger at the man in purple silk sitting unrightfully on the throne. And I begin working my Blood sense around the ties binding the tiger wolf to the emperor. Snipping thread by thread.

The emperor leans away like I'm contagious as I inch closer. A Char disease. I like that he fears me. Though it's slightly ridiculous with ten spears pointed at my throat. The emperor's mother's head lolls about like she's watching spirits flit across the room. Lost in a lotus spell. Soo Si watches with cruel fascination, or is it satisfaction?

"I am the rightful emperor," he states. "There is no one who could challenge me."

Mulia creeps down the steps, stalking me. I clip another thread of connection. "You are wrong. There are eight women who can challenge you. Eight women who would be far better leaders than you could ever be. You"—I point accusingly—"are an imposter."

The emperor's face turns as crimson as the red lotus his mother keeps dipping her finger in, and he thumps his throne with his fist. "Enough!" He clicks his fingers. "Mulia, attack!"

And the tiger wolf pounces, knocking me to the ground and pinning my shoulders. Her perfect teeth bared, her tongue dripping saliva onto my cheek. Flashes of beatings by the emperor rush from her mind to mine. And I calm them. I show her a different way. I show her I could be a kind and respectful partner, not an owner. She snaps her teeth but only because I command it. *That's right, beautiful creature, stay right here snarling and snapping until he calls you off.* I wrap my hand around her ankle, solidifying our bond.

Soo Si taps the emperor's shoulder. "She's no good to us dead. Not yet, anyway." His ear bends to her and he calls Mulia off.

I wrap a thin ribbon from her heart to mine. I have a hold on her, but it's too early to use it.

"So, you're telling us the Carvresses have a claim to the throne." The emperor laughs but it's a guarded sound.

The empress bows her head suddenly, muttering, "The missing Chow princesses."

Soo Si claps her hands loudly to cover the woman's babbling, but flickers of doubt run like paint splatters across several guards' faces.

I stand, chin proud and chest puffed. "I'm saying you are not the only Shen royalty left in this world."

Soo Si whispers in his ear and he says aloud, "Tell me where they are. If what you say is true, then tradition dictates I must give them a hearing." The emperor taps a single finger on the throne arm.

Now it's my turn to laugh. "I will never tell you. When they come, it will be on their terms and to your complete surprise."

The emperor narrows his eyes, his handsome face compressing into something ugly and vain. "You Char are too stubborn for your own good." He claps his hands and a guard steps forward and kneels. "Fetch the doctor. I'm sure he can *persuade* her to tell us something." The guard lifts his face to briefly meet the intense stare of the concubine. She gives the tiniest shake of her head, out of view of the emperor.

"Unfortunately, while you were at temple, the doctor took ill, my love." Her eyes land on me, daring me to expose this secret. Considering I killed him, it doesn't seem like a good idea to volunteer my guilt.

"That is inconvenient," he says, tapping his chin. Again, Soo Si whispers in his ear, and he purses his lips and nods. "Take her to see the boy. Let her understand we hold his fading life in our hands. Perhaps then her tongue will be loosened." The emperor turns to his concubine, cupping her chin in his hand and tracing her cheeks with his thumb. "I missed you at the temple." Soo Si's shoulders lift ever so slightly, a half wince, but she forces them down, tilting her head and gazing into his eyes.

"I am yours always, emperor," she says in a sugar-dipped, wooden tone, but he doesn't notice. They never do. I've seen it in the village, young brides tied to men they have no connection with. Smiling and nodding while looking to the horizon for a better fate.

The guards drag me away and I let them. Mulia rises, wanting to follow. *No, beautiful girl, stay there, protect him as you always have. For now.* She eases back to the ground, golden eyes tracking me subtly.

Mulia is with me now. I feel her enormous heart beating alongside my hickory one. I make a promise I hope I can keep.

That when this is over, if she wishes, I will return her to the Dark West. She shows me pictures of a giant world. Red pines stretching to puncture the sky. Dread white snow that never melts. Her pack running like demons through the forest. Wild. Free. Joyful. Twisting and weaving. Shoulders brushing. Love and trust as bright and sure as the closest sun.

The emperor's mother shouts after me, words deranged and panicked. "Wait! Where is my husband? What did you do to him?" Her voice is curdled and nonsensical.

The emperor turns to his mother, stroking her arm and whispering calming words. "Mama, I'm here. Why don't you give that to me? Just for a safekeeping." He tries to take her pot of red lotus. The concubine rolls her eyes and plants them firmly on me as I'm escorted out of the room. She wants something, and she wants to use me to get it.

I'M LED AWAY from the throne room feeling confused but also like I won a small victory. Though I'm not sure how it will help.

The guards have abandoned the sack-over-the-head farce, and I'm allowed to see where the throne room is in relation to the rest of the palace. Again, I'm not sure what has changed but suspect the concubine has something to do with it.

The infirmary is close to the kitchen. We pass the bustle of pots and pans and maid chatter into a dark and silent space. Narrow beds with white sheets line the walls, but only one is occupied. The boy with the saltwater smile. Ash.

I shirk the guards grip, stinging Qi Sha with a scorpion tail, and run to his bed. His eyes are closed. His face is a mess of misplaced skin, sunken eyes, and soft lips. I touch his shoulder and his eyes open. He gives me a smile. One cheek lifts, but he can't hold it very long. "Luna, you're here," he says croakily like he's run out of water and Water.

The guards step back, forming a human barrier in the doorway. But give us space. It's odd and discomforting, but I'll take what I can get. Something drips from a tube into his arm. "What have they done to you?" I ask, distrustful.

He reaches for my hand. "Shen medicine. It's the one thing we do better than Char."

"Well, there had to be one thing." I clasp his hand. "So, you feel better?" I glance down at the bandages holding his torso together. I can't imagine any medicine is strong enough to fix all of that.

He ignores my question. "How are the children?"

My eyes cast downward. "All right, I think. I wasn't down there long before they dragged me up to the emperor again." I hold back from telling him about Lu Leng's coughing. The drenched, sickly sound echoes in my head.

"Maybe he likes you," Ash jokes, tries to laugh, but pain takes over instead.

I try really hard not to cry, pushing away thoughts that he will die in this place. But he looks closer to the afterlife than I've ever seen him. "Don't be ridiculous. He's just trying to work me out. See if he can use me." I can't tell Ash about Mulia here, not with guards listening.

He lifts his bruised hand to my face, scratching off the make up and running his thumb over my red waxy lips. "Why must he dress you like a cheap concubine? Your face is too beautiful to cover." He taps the freckles across my nose lightly. "These here are like constellations. A map to the most incredible treasure."

He saw beauty when I saw a monster. He sees it now in the worst of times. And though I know I could live without him, *I don't want to. I don't want to. I don't want to.* "Oh Ash, you promised me you wouldn't die. You have to keep that promise." *You have to. You have to. You have to.*

His voice sounds like it's under a foot that's pressing down. "No one is dying."

The sharp click of wooden shoes on the floor parts the guards and a smooth, high voice fills the room.

"Two things." Soo Si holds up one finger. "One, there is nothing cheap about this concubine." She holds up a second finger.

"And two, the only person who can make a promise like that is me."

33
LYE

A BACK BURNER THING

Fat, scaly heads bump the hull, trying to turn it. Rocks still sparkle. Water still rushes, but we are a man short.

Ying Yi shouts again, "I'm coming aboard."

I lunge to the edge of the boat. "No, Ying! Stay where you are. There are crocodiles in the water."

"Crocodiles?" Ying squeals comically high. And I'd laugh if he weren't in very real danger. "What kind of crocodiles? Small crocodiles? Medium sized? Oh, never mind, if they have teeth, I guess it doesn't really matter."

Joka shakes his head and grumbles, "It's like a pin was pulled and now he can't stop talking."

I don't want to answer Ying Yi. Telling him they're as long as the boat and almost as wide will only make him panic. I whisper a secret prayer. At least they are at their winter fattest and slowest.

Joka runs a hand through his hair as the boat sways again. "I'm guessing much bigger than medium sized, right, General?"

I manage a grim nod before I grab Jing Ha's hand and drag her to the ladder. "What are you doing?" she asks, fear shaking her skeleton loose.

I hold her tightly. "I need your help to save Ying Yi."

A nervous laugh comes from the bank. "*Wā* Since no one is answering my question, I'm going to guess big, really, big." Rocks clink as something large and heavy drags its belly out of the water and onto the narrow, pebbly bank. Ying Yi curses loudly.

"Must we save him?" she asks, a slight tinge of humor in her tone, which is impressive given the circumstances.

I pull her over the edge and climb down, freezing water soaking my legs. "We must."

The boat swings over again and we hang on tightly as it springs back.

"You can swim, right?" I ask when it's already too late.

"Of course. I am Char." Silence for one crocodile snap second. "General, I don't want to kill anything," she says determinedly.

I'd laugh if it wasn't so dire. She is my opposite. When all I think is death, she brings me back from the path I've been trained to tread.

We jump into the river and a tail thwacks me in the side. The leathery spines are as hard as plate armor. My mouth fills with frigid water. The channel is deep, and I paddle in the inkiness, hoping a crocodile is not beneath me, jaws open wide. I extend my powers, reaching for the shape of them. There are two under the boat and one on the bank.

"Jing Ha, focus on stunning," I splutter. "But don't you dare give up your life for one of these monsters."

The tail comes at us again, and this time we both press our hands to it. I send sleep-inducing poison from the piranha rabbit's fangs. Used to disable prey so they can chomp and chew at their leisure. I use it to put the creature to rest, choosing Jing Ha's path. The crocodile is strong, and it continues to thrash, albeit more slowly.

Jing Ha's eyes are closed. She whispers, "Weeping willow." The creature's limbs tense and it stops paddling, floating like an unmanned canoe.

"Is anyone coming to help me or am I to be a shared meal for these definitely extra-large-sized crocodiles?" He said crocodiles. Another has left the water and slithers up the beach. The sound is like marbles in a bag. Sweet in any other context.

"Jing Ha!" I shout, treading water, head swinging back and forth searching for her petite face.

"Jing Ha!" Ying Yi exclaims, surprised and not very relieved. She's already on the beach hands out, ready to grasp both tails at once. She won't be able to do it. "Where's the—" His question is cut short as a crocodile lunges for his leg. He screams once and then puts his attention to the beast, throwing rocks, kicking, doing anything to get free. If there are Shen above, they've certainly heard us.

I clamber onto the bank and throw myself upon the beast. "Jing Ha, take just one!" She switches her focus to the other as I climb onto its scaly back. It feels as sharp and jagged as a vengeful dagger. The ridges running down the spine shred my clothes. I need to get to its head. It shuffles backward, freezing water lapping over my already soaked body. I keep moving up the length of the enormous creature.

Ying Yi has stopped shouting, he's probably bleeding out. I reach up and press my hand to the crocodile's head. "Purseflower," I say.

"Parent purseflower?" Ying Yi questions with his last ounce of strength.

The crocodile opens its jaws wide and they stay that way, allowing me to jump from its back and pull Ying Yi to safety.

"Quickly!" I shout to the others. "Help me get him to the boat. They won't stay this way for long."

The crocodile stares at us with yellow slit eyes, unable to close its mouth. Jing Ha has stunned the other one, but it's exhausted her. She sways like the boat, only she doesn't bounce back. She falls to the side, water reaching out to grab her with its icy fingers.

As the others pour down the sides and help us back to the boat, Ying Yi asks again, "Why parent purseflower?" His mouth is bluish, his skin gray.

"Because once it's spread its seed, it opens once and never closes."

Ying Ni lets out a funny little wheeze of a laugh. "Oh, ha, that is true. Clever."

Jing Ha is laid next to Ying Yi, her flesh unbroken but she is injured. Her power sapped, leaving her a shell.

"She will just need rest," I say, scraping her wet hair from her face.

I pull my gray Keeper robes over my tattered clothing, shivering.

If only we could all get some rest.

THE STARS FADE. The orange scattering of dusk begins spreading across the sky.

We have rowed until our arms burned to charcoal to get away from the crocodiles. I roll my shoulders. They crackle like a stepped-on bird's nest.

We stop to drink and breathe. Joka wipes his brow and checks Ying Yi's bandages. Thankfully, the crocodile's teeth did not sink in too far and the damage is superficial, though he will limp for some days.

"You and Jing Ha were incredible out there," he says, patting the soldier's wounds and making him flinch in his sleep.

"We worked together to save him, as a team." I'm not taking credit.

Frowning, he bows his head and then lifts his hand to place it on my leg, stopping to rest it awkwardly on his own. "I'm sorry, Lye. I have not handled this well. I don't know how to."

"You are threatened by my power," I state.

"Yes," he says, and I sense he wants to say more. But he doesn't.

I sigh, frustrated. "You would curse me to a life of loneliness because of your pride?"

"No."

He makes me want to send fire and fangs and everything nasty at him all at once. "Are you now the king of one-word answers?"

"No," he answers, making me growl. He smiles then, which is infuriating. "How about I finish my story?"

I cross my arms over my chest, feeling every bit the rejected woman. The child banished to the corner for no good reason. Blamed for something they didn't do. "Fine!" I snap.

We continue to row as he finishes his tale. Words peppered between labored breaths and yawns we cannot finish.

"The man knew what the moon maiden said was necessary, but it changed the dynamic between them. He could no longer be with the moon maiden because while she stood in judgement of him, they could never have an equal partnership. He could strive to be worthy but eventually he would become resentful. Every time she came to see him, he would know she was assessing his worth. It was no way to be."

"So, there is no hope for them?" I ask, too invested in his answer.

Joka smiles. "There is hope. But it's the kind of hope that grows from patience. You didn't let me finish. The moon maiden was heartbroken. She threw her spirit back to the moon. She still loved him, she would never stop, but he had chosen to be without her. Perhaps it meant he did not love her as much as she loved him. But the man smiled as she left. He did not begrudge her purpose. He knew it was very important, which is why he would wait and see her in the sky when it was time. When he was worthy and ready."

Joka seems comforted by this tale. But all I see is a man who couldn't get over himself to be with his love simply because she had an important job.

"I'm not the moon maiden," I say as the sun strips the gray from the sky like yanking a veil from a reluctant bride.

Joka expression is a blank page with invisible ink. Hiding the truth. "I never said you were."

"I need my friend back," I mutter through clenched teeth.

Joka pats my hand. "I never left."

He's such a liar. But I let him have it. I don't have time for his insecurities or his fear. Love has never been a priority for me, always stuck on a back burner. It can stay that way.

I'd like to seethe a little longer, but I don't get time. The boat cracks and my back jars as wood slams into a solid slab of ice and announces bluntly: You are home.

34

KI ANAH

UNKNOWN FATES,
SCATTERED TO THE WIND

Ki Anah watches the orange glow of the last coal shrink to black. The Carvresses create a circle around Sun and Ki Anah, their movements jerky and slow. They chant old words. They pray in a rich, ancient language that tastes like moon cake and sounds like harp strings. Then Sifah leans toward Ki Anah and Sun and asks them the question. Something Ki Anah both hoped to hear and dreaded at the same time because she didn't know her answer until now.

"Would you like me to change you? All of you." Her Carvress gestures. Part of Ki Anah wishes for a body that could stay warm as her blood pumps achingly slow.

Ki Anah shakes her head and manages to whisper a dry and crackled no. She turns to her son and blinks nearly frozen eyelids. He shakes his head like his spine is fused. It almost is.

"You don't need to choose the same as me." She tries to reach up and touch his arm. It's too difficult. Her energy has melted away. If only the ice would do the same. They hear it coming for them. Crackling over the cave walls like a disease.

Sun's eyes move from Carvress face to Carvress face. "Wood can freeze, Mama. Look at them. They are not going to survive much longer than us. And if I am to die, I want to die as Char." His eyes water but no tears fall. They harden in the corners like sad little diamonds.

Ki Anah has never felt cold like this. So intense it burns. She gazes down at fingers, tips blackened. This is not how she thought it would end. But then, she always tried not to look too far ahead. She hopes Guen is safe. She doesn't blame the girl for not returning. They asked too much.

Sun seems to sense her accepting their fate and locking it into place. He summons what energy he has left to wrap an arm around her shoulders, sharing his warmth with her. It's like waving a candle under a whole raw chicken and expecting it to cook. Not enough. "Don't give up on little Guen yet, Mama. She may surprise us all."

His faith in the girl comes from love. Ki Anah saves her head shake. Keeping it inside. Love sometimes fills you with false hope.

She doesn't say this to him. Let him die with hope and love in his heart. The thought brings her no comfort. Her heart splits open like a pike in a frozen pond.

She plans to spend these last hours in her memories. Dinners with her family. All her boys together and Luna at her side. Ben Ni's golden eyes warming the room as good as a fire. Dancing with Setsu, his huge hands spanning the width of her waist. The tapping of feet against the salty floorboards.

Tap, tap, tap.

The Carvresses slow in their song. Their movements are more and more strained. They thought they'd be able to survive this, but they never tested the theory. Sadly, now they know. Everything freezes eventually.

Shei-Shei lets out a whimper and then a whisper. "Is it time?" she asks no one in particular. Sifah bows her beautiful chin, and it stays there, pressed to her chest, face crusted with ice.

Ki Anah doesn't fear death, but she fears for everything that has been scattered to the wind. All the choices and fates she doesn't know. Her children are adrift and waiting for her to save them. The crown remaining atop an emperor who seeks to destroy the Char. And a husband who will stand at the edge of the boardwalk, scanning the sea until his dying day for her boat to appear on the horizon, her sails to bring her home. Too much unfinished business. Too many things she had left to say.

Her eyes close.

She no longer feels cold. She smiles. Her lips shall freeze this way.

Her last thought is a good one.

Tap, tap, tap.

Feet tapping, whirling about their tiny hut. Joy so full the hut boards creak and rattle like they can't contain it.

The tap, tap, tap, becomes incessant, pulling Ki Anah from her pleasant dream. Is this what it feels like to die? A push and pull as the spirit world plays tug-o'-war with the living one. Ki Anah forces her eyes open and wishes she hadn't. She's surrounded by statues. Carvresses frozen mid movement, eyes darting in panic, bodies unable to move. Sun's lip quivers but soon it will stop. Soon they will all be at peace.

Tap, tap, tap.

The sound echoes through the tunnels.

Tap, tap—a huge thump, just like the drumbeats of the Dark West tribe, but closer. Much closer.

Thump!

Shattering glass. Or ice or—Ki Anah doesn't have the energy to decipher. She has nothing left.

Spirits flood the cathedral cave. Dark, devilish looking things with big empty eyes and long screaming mouths. Ki Anah's heart would beat fast if it were beating at all.

She feels a warm nothingness close over her mind like a neat trap.

GUEN

The ice slab shatters and Guen rushes through the tunnels after the women. Who run, half bent over, talking to each other through the hollowed mouths of their gruesome masks. She listens for Sun's voice or the bell-like sound of a Carvress voice, but she hears nothing. Just the echo of huge feet stomping the earth. A cold so intense she feels her own joints starting to seize.

She follows the trail left by dragged branches and the bobbing orange light of torches lit from a river of fire. She barely had time to take in the dragon's heart as they rushed past it. A red, pulsing stone the size of a house. Her list of marvels is growing longer and longer. But it means little without a family to share it with. She slows down as she reaches the entrance to the great cave with feet frozen in fear. What if they're too late? What if he's already dead? She swallows, throat as scratchy as bark.

The Dark West women shout directions at each other, and light saturates the space like the sun has fallen through the porthole.

"Get the fire high!" Dianh orders, her deep voice booming and bouncing from every wall. Guen longs to hear Sun's voice. His reaction to these giants. But she hears only tribeswomen.

"That's right, warm some water in a pot, we must do this gently. Break the coral into smaller pieces and throw that in there too."

"Where's the birchwood girl?"

Guen shudders. She knows she should be there. Sun may need her protection. She is bravery after all. That's what they said. It runs through her bones as much as the rings of birchwood.

She hears a cough. Could be anyone, but it's enough to force her to shuffle forward. She peers around the edge of the cave wall. The cathedral is lit up like daylight. Orange flames clawing at the roof. Ten figures slowly unfreeze, cracking their limbs and looking up at the Dark West women in shock and awe.

Sun's head moves slowly and Guen's limbs begin to churn like they have a life of their own. She bounds up the stairs and throws herself into his arms. He can't quite hold onto her and she slips, but his eyes move and his mouth twitches.

Dianh rises from her place by the fire. Extending to her impressive height, eyeing Sun suspiciously. "A man. You didn't tell me there was a man here."

Guen grins sheepishly. "I thought if I did you might not want to come."

The other women drape blankets over the Carvresses shoulders. The powerful, magical women inspect one another warily. Giants and wooden sculptures. Slowly, the Carvresses begin to move more easily as heat fills the room.

Sun wraps his arms around Guen tightly. "You did it. You saved us," he whispers with a deep, serrated sadness to his voice. His eyes are not on Guen. They hover over one woman who is not moving. Who is gray and still as stone.

Guen's little heart gallops with guilt. She was too late. She didn't save everyone.

"I'm sorry, Sun," she cries, sap clogging her nose and throat. "I'm so sorry."

He holds her close, rocking the eight-year-old back and forth and Dark West women watch him with less anger and more fascination. He strokes her wooden plaits. "No. No. This is not your fault. You saved us. You did everything you could." Guen's limbs unlock and feel like jelly. She held herself together because she had to. Wanting be brave, she had to find a way to dig out the bravery and leave every other feeling in the dust. Now, here in Sun's embrace, she can let all her emotions wash over her. Flood her heart and mind and know that even though she is falling apart, Sun will help put her back together.

Guen stares at the body in front of her. They all do. Wooden eyes blinking sap. Flesh eyes blinking salt. Warm air fills their lungs like lanterns rising to the sky, but their hearts feel as cold and sinking as the ice that's slowly dripping away. They watch the woman's skin change from the color of bleached bone, birchwood at its palest, to a gray pink color. A corpse color. A small tattoo of a flame at the corner of one of her closed eyes is clear, revealing Shei-Shei as a Fire Shen.

Ki Anah splutters as the tribeswomen hold cave coral tea to her mouth. "N-no! Not another!" she cries, collapsing to her knees at the Carvress of Pearl Shell Beach's side. She strokes the woman's strands of brown hair from her lifeless forehead. The other Carvresses moan. She was their youngest sister. She had flaws but she was trying to make it right.

Shei-Shei, the woman who carved Guen from pure fear and shaped her into bravery, is dead.

35

LUNA

THE DIRTY DETAILS

Soo Si sways into the room, silk dress dragging along the ground. She sounds like rain on a glass bowl. I grimace. The concubine is anything but refreshing. She focuses her kohl-lined eyes on me, trying to look important and intimidating. I know she intends me to feel like dust on the bottom of her shoe, but I'm more the earth shifting under her feet. She trips on her skirts, her face scrunching up like she's just tasted the sourest tamarind. Recovering, she glares at any guards flanking her who dare laugh. I imagine their lives would be quickly turned around if they were to so much as snigger at the concubine. Ash and I have little to lose at this point, and a small chuckle floats from our mouths and joins like two bubbles, bobbing happily to the sky. Soo Si's stomping heel pops the bubble, showering us with soap that stings our eyes.

"Have you ever torn the finest silk just to see how it sounds?" she asks, standing a few feet away. I purse my lips, pretend to think about it and then shrug. "No, I suppose you wouldn't know such a feeling, seeing as you're a vulgar little sea rat."

Ash tries to rise from the bed, but he has the strength of a rice husk, and he flutters back down. "The finest silks and thickest powder can only hide so much if what's underneath is a scheming, scaling wench!" he says before I can stop him.

She laughs, covering her red-stained lips with her hand. Forced through a narrow heart, it comes out reedy and thin. I watch with curiosity. Detaching myself from the insults and trying to see what's under all the layers of finery. She stares fiercely, dark eyes sharp as daggers. She *is* scheming. She *is* scaling. Digging her claws into the palace walls and climbing higher and higher. I sense tenacity and intelligence in her too. She's not just a witless "wench."

"You can insult me if you like, though it won't help you, boy." She steps up to the edge of the bed, extends one finger, and suddenly presses it into one of Ash's wounds. He screams like he's being torn apart, and I lunge at her. Only to find five spears pointed at my throat before I can flick one finger.

"Stop!" I shout. She begins meticulously unwrapping his bandages while he strains against his bindings. Blood flows freely as she runs her pointed nail along the cuts, her polish matching the color running from his chest and stomach and onto the floor. "You murderous bi—"

Very slowly and deliberately, she lifts her sleeve to the corner of her eye and scrapes the powder away, revealing a flame. She is Fire. Shaking a finger dripping in crimson, flecks of Ash's blood landing on my face. "What did I say about name calling? It will not help your cause. Right now, all I'm doing is scalding. Push and you'll see the full force of my power."

Ash's eyes roll back. He mutters as his consciousness drips away with his pulse, "Don't let her—"

"What do you know of our cause?" I challenge.

She extends her hand, and a guard places a clean cloth in her palm to wipe away the blood. The streaks of rust make me gag. She makes me want to forsake all that I have gained in opening my heart and letting emotion back in. Let my hickory heart take over and torture her as she does Ash, tear her veins to shreds in the most painful way possible. Ben Ni's face flashes in my mind, laying a calming palm over my anger. *Don't let them win.*

I move closer to Ash. The guards allow it after a nod of Soo Si's pointed chin. She is not kind. Whatever mercy she's offering comes with many strings attached.

I messily rewrap the bandages while she watches me and talks.

"You wish to be free," she states.

"Of course we do." I don't look at her, since I'm too busy pressing on Ash's bubbling blood. I push the healing power of the ever-life frog through his veins. Regeneration. Growth. Anything to help him.

"And I know you want to take the children with you." Her words are dripping with poison and promise. "I have already helped, but I can help you more."

A nurse comes to my aid, and I step back, allowing her to re-dress him properly. But I keep my hand on his wrist. Using all my power to aid his recovery.

"Don't, Luna. She's a snake," he mumbles.

"I know." But a snake as an ally is far better than one as an enemy. I am trapped. Rocks of responsibility crush me on all sides. To Soo Si, who stands straight and tall and perfect, silly hair adornments clanging every time she moves her head, I challenge, "How have you helped *me*?"

She clicks her fingers twice and a chair is pushed behind her. She sits carefully, arranging her purple silk skirts and crossing her legs. "Did you think you overpowered the black violet on your own? I showed you the way. I added the drops of starlight."

The sweetness.

"It gave you the focus to find a way around it."

Ash snorts quietly, eyes closed. "Starlight is impossible to find. It has been mined into extinction."

She snorts back, as unladylike as a bull. "Not for me! You owe me much, Char girl. I hid the death of the doctor from the emperor when you murdered him. If the emperor found out, you would be executed." She counts all the ways she has "helped" me off on her jeweled fingers. "You have gained control of the tiger wolf, Mulia. Do you think you did that all by yourself? You only had the opportunity after I showed you how to overcome the violet and *my* guards gave you less than prescribed."

"To what end?" I ask, bewildered. I could kill her right now. I want to. But then Ash and the children would be ordered to death before her body hit the ground.

My power is draining away as I hold Ash together by force of will.

"I'm sure you've noticed the emperor's mother is a little, well, let's say off." She taps the tip of her tongue. "But she has influence over him. He seeks her advice, and she does not approve of me." She touches her heart dramatically like that seems preposterous. I snort. "Her red lotus prescription needs to be refilled. Red lotus and blood root are almost identical in color and smell. A mix up could easily occur." The concubine smiles like a mauler in the dark as she refers to the deathly poison used to kill rats and mice. I turn to the guards, Qi Sha, Sho Sen, and the same ones that seem to orbit her fiery planet like obedient little moons, none seem the least bit surprised.

Soo Si climbs her fingers up Ash's leg, pressing down on a wound just to see him thrash in pain. It brings a foul expression of enjoyment to her face.

"Well then, once the emperor's mother is gone, you'll have him all to yourself. What do you need me for?" I feel myself getting sucked into her whirlpool of evil plots. My heart glosses over the horrible details. It tells me I need to play along.

The concubine's mouth twists, disgusted. "You think that's what I want? To have that weak, pretentious little brat to myself?" This time her laugh is true, full, and hearty before cutting off. "I despise the man. Every night with him is one too many."

I can't stand the pain on Ash's face, the way his eyes slip away over and over again. Everything about him is a warning, but what choice do I have? "Then what?" I ask, though I think I know. She needs to say it.

"After the old bat is dealt with, I can finally marry the emperor and become empress. Then you"—she points at my hickory heart which beats steady as a murder plan—"will kill him. Well, Mulia will, under your influence. And I will be free of his body and his pathetic mind." She taps her chin, enjoying the broadcasting of her own plan.

"Why don't I just tell the emperor what you're planning?" I try it, even though I know she will have an answer.

Her hands clasp together and she nods thoughtfully as if this has never occurred to her. "You could do that. Then you and the boy will remain here with the children to be tortured until there's nothing left."

"Does he even know about the children?" I ask, stretching desperately for an alternative to murder.

Soo Si laughs again. A pitying sound. "The emperor both knows and doesn't. He doesn't like to be troubled with the dirty details. He just wants results, and in this case, the result he wants is a Shen-Char hybrid army. He has authorized every kidnapping, every torture, even if he didn't realize it. He will not listen to you, Char girl. He would turn away, ears closed, if you tried to hold a candle to his crimes."

My heart sinks like a waterlogged clock in my chest. She has us trapped in her web. The only way out is by her permission. "If I do as you ask, then you must promise to release all of us, every last child."

She waves a hand, seeming bored. "Hybrids were never my interest. The chancellor cooked it up with the doctor, and the emperor went along with it because he's a spineless fool who hasn't had an original thought in that weak brain of his since he made the decision to stand and walk as a baby. You were good enough to get rid of the chancellor, the emperor's other controlling influence, so that made things a little easier."

She smooths an imaginary wrinkle. "I want the throne and the power. Science experiments and old magic are not the future. Even the Keeper has outlived her usefulness. Specialized warriors are a thing of the past. I have the Elemental soldiers I need to protect the palace, and the rest of the millions of Shen at my disposal have another purpose. I'm interested in numbers, of people and of coin. I already have several countries in trade negotiations, willing to pay dearly for that which our farmers produce easily. Money will pour onto the mountain like rain!" At this, she claps her hands, a child delighted by her own cleverness.

Ash and I exchange a look swirled with her short sightedness. This is where her intelligence reaches it limit. For Lye is more than just useful—she is everything. And to overlook that is a grave mistake. One we will certainly not make her aware of.

"And what will happen to the Char?" I ask.

Soo Si scratches at her scalp, where gold pins dig close. "You don't get to know everything, Blood Char." She narrows her eyes. "But I'd say it depends on what they can produce that will make their existence worthwhile."

"So the Char will still suffer at the hands of the Shen?" She doesn't answer, which is as good as saying yes. It's a crushing feeling. A mountain on my chest, flattening my heart slowly to paper. But the children are here, hurting and dying in front of me. And I can help them. I can save them. I have to do it. "Will you agree to my terms? All of us will be released and seen safely from the mainland."

Ash grabs my arm, ice surging up my veins. "No, Luna, don't."

Soo Si shakes her head. "I cannot agree to that. But I will release the boy and the children if you, my dear, stay here with me. A replacement Keeper, of sorts. I think you could make a powerful and intimidating weapon once we dent that spirit of yours." Her eyes lift to the ceiling. "Just imagine the deals I could make with you there to 'convince' my adversaries."

Kill the emperor, live as a slave to this woman, and Ash and children go free. "If you go back on your word, so shall I. Your dress will be stained with your own blood, concubine," I warn, feeling the blood lust of a murder bird coursing to my fingers.

Tidal waves crash, trying to drown me out. I rip my hand from Ash's grasp as he tries to stop me from making this mistake. I have been a weapon before. He doesn't understand that I would make every mistake, I would slip into a darkness never to return, if it meant I could save them, save him.

Soo Si's face turns serious. "I will not go back on my word. You kill the emperor, and I will set the boy and the children free." She is nasty and conniving beyond belief, but I trust her words.

I hold out my hand. She stares at it for a long while but takes it. I bite at her with snapping turtles—just a small reminder of what I can do. She holds firm and shakes without burning me. She steps back and gives a sly smile. The fox who knows exactly where his dinner is coming from.

"What happens now?" I ask as she turns away from me.

"Now, just try not to get yourself killed before the time comes." She spins, a flurry of purple silk and deathly intention, and clicks away, guards flanking her. Two stay behind. "Let her stay with the boy tonight. It will motivate her." Her order has nothing to do with kindness, but like a bitter, burned *kueh* cake to a starving mouth, I'll take whatever I can get.

I COLLAPSE UPON Ash's bed, tears erupting from my eyes. Saltwater flows from me to him and back again. He strokes my head weakly; it's all he can do to lift his hand.

"Oh, Luna, what have you done?" he whispers.

"What I had to," I mumble into the covers. "What I will always do. If there's a way to save you, I will do it." I hope, deep down, that another option will present itself. But if not, Ash will be saved.

His chest expands with a deep breath. A huge sigh out like he's making clouds to hide a massacre from the sky. "What about me? How do I save you?"

I shake my head, my nose wiping against his arm. Guards shift awkwardly. Someone clears their throat. The darkness seems to close in, making a small, shallow cave of light around us. "You can't."

36

LYE

THE DANDELION ROBBED OF SEEDS

The first ice over the river was always a joyful event in the village. It meant it was time to slow our work. Rake the ground and wait for the warmth of spring to replant. Finally, we could rest for a few months. Those feelings of happiness are lost to me like so many swallowed vows, because if the ice has reached this far down, then the glacier is at the earth. The Carvresses may be warm and safe in the center of the mountain, but it will be almost impossible to reach them until the season changes.

"Do it again?" Ash begs, clapping his hands.

"Oh fine!" I mutter, placing a palm to the hard ice of the pond and concentrating on the blistering heat of a volcano. He giggles gleefully as he quickly places a few sticks in the water to create a character.

By the time I open my eyes, the water has frozen again. The cold so intense it refreezes within seconds, suspending the sticks and Ash's words until spring.

Ash points and rocks back on his heels, so delighted at himself. So far, he has spelled "monkey's butt" and "dung head" in the pond. I roll my eyes.

Among the frozen tips of farm boats breaching the ice like unrolled cigars, we search the bank for Shen villagers. Nothing other than a short, cold wind smacks our eyes. Ying Yi hops to his good foot. "What are your orders, General?"

The others stand at attention, awaiting my decision. There can be no more hiding now. It's time to walk through my village and see whether the Keeper still holds meaning.

My chin wishes to swing toward Joka for reassurance, but instead I set it on the steep stone steps leading away from the dock. "Tie the boat. We shall have to go by foot the rest of the way." I turn my attention to Ying Yi as he hops about like a one-legged gull, pain squishing his features as he tries to gather supplies.

Captain Ipoh offers his help to the wounded soldier. "Give me your pack, Ying," he orders. He doesn't ask or offer; he just takes all of Ying Yi's things and throws them over his shoulder. "Now, give me your weight." Ipoh offers his wooden arm to the hopping man, and Ying Yi gratefully uses his support. I sense more curiosity than fear as the captain's gaze runs along the riverbank and the rusty tin boats gathered like leaves in a doorway. While others struggle to keep their ideas of Shen in check, Ipoh looks upon the stairs with an eagerness that has nothing to do with readying for a fight. I pack the observation away for later.

Jing Ha climbs over the lip of the boat and onto the ice. She slides but manages to keep her balance. Joka and the others are less graceful, feet skidding, legs parting wider and wider until they fall on their backsides. I'm reminded this is their first experience on ice. And wide, panicked eyes tell me it's not a pleasant one. I cover my mouth, but the laugh still escapes.

Ying Yi and Ipoh struggle the most and I jump over to help them to the bank. "Small, shuffling steps," I encourage. "Dig your toes in."

We make it to the base of the stairs mostly in one piece, though there'll be some sore bottoms. The men stand behind me as I stare upward. Above this canyon is my childhood home. The place I grew up and into the Keeper. I pause, fingers itchy for Elements, my rosewood arm grating against my hip. This place is *before*. It occupies the small patch of purity on my heart that's always trying to peel away. This place came before the marks upon my arm, the cruelty and death.

The pure patch begins to throb with worry. Ipoh may not be fearful, but I am. I don't know how to return to a place when I am so changed. *Will it even feel like home?*

Jing Ha taps the space between my throat and my clothing, sending the feeling of sheltering oak boughs over my head. She's taken naturally to her Element. "You've been away for a long time, haven't you General?" I nod, straightening. "Returning home can be difficult." She's cricket sized and just as flexible. I marvel at her ability to spread her compassion.

"It's not just time." I swallow drily. "I have changed so very much." Changed and yet still incomplete. I think of the cork carving in my pack. Can I shape myself into a beautiful tree or will I crumble into something ugly and unnatural?

Jing Ha smiles with a sagaciousness she doesn't have the years for, but there it is all the same. "It's hard to come home when you're not the person you once were, but it can also join the ends of a circle that's been open for too long. A hole that let the bad things in and let the good things fall out can be mended."

Joka comes to stand behind me. "Are we going to move?"

I climb the first step, Joka's voice adding a layer of armor to my back. "Thanks, Jing Ha. In truth, a homecoming was probably long overdue." The chancellor would never have permitted it.

I climb the slippery stairs, determined to walk tall and proud, even if I'm as frightened as a ground squirrel at the mercy of a leopard lynx.

THE VILLAGE IS a mile or so from the dock. We crunch over a light sprinkling of snow, the group fascinated by ice that sounds like salt crystals beneath our feet. We march like we're not expecting a warm welcome.

We're not at all prepared for what greets us.

The lonely tap of single beans dropping one by one into a bucket is the first sound we hear when we reach the outer limits of the village. My eyes bounce over the neat rows of buildings. It's just as I remembered, but then every village looks the same. L-shaped huts, a wide central street. Wet, red clay that sticks to your shoes, adding an inch to your height, though, is unique to my home.

Shen peasants barely lift their heads. The tap of red beans into a bucket is joined by the shake of rice sieves by twig-like arms. The saddest percussion I've ever heard. Ying Yi hops beside Ipoh and I hear him whisper, "What on sea and land happened to these people? They are living skeletons. Maybe not living for long."

Tap, tap, tap.

Shake, shake, shake.

The peasants lift dull eyes from their work, like it uses too much energy. As we pass, suspicious words are muttered, but they do not shift from their positions. These Shen are as Ying Yi says, living skeletons with stick thin arms, skin clinging to their bones, and their eyes retracting into their skulls. My heart hurts at the sight of Shen people in such a state.

We drag through the clay, hands on the hilts of swords that seem unnecessary. I thought this would be difficult, but not in this way. The state of these people on the brink of starvation skimming every piece of a difficult crop that yields little cut deep. I expected doubt and distrust, not dead eyes and disinterest.

Joka leans to my ear. "Why do none of them have tattoos?" he asks, his voice still soothing despite our awkwardness.

"They are peasants," I answer as I count the sorry heads of men and women with very little life left in them. "The emperor only grants elemental power to those who join the Shen army."

Joka swings his head back and forth, expression dismayed just like the other Char. We didn't come to fight, but we weren't expecting this: flattened souls. "Well, I suppose that's one thing that's definitely changed."

I scan the huts for my uncle's home. Where Ash and I lived when our mother died, squashed ear to ear with our cousins. They all look the same, but the Koh family home always had a large jade carving of a dragon key hanging on the door.

The smooth green stone seems to sing to me. "I can't believe it's still here!" Heart leading, I turn sharply toward the hut, my Char party following. The others gather in a circle, backs nonchalantly to the watching peasants. I trace the intricate swirls of the carving. The jade dragon has lost its luster, but the eyes are still fierce. The key it's wrapped around still holds the same pride it once did. This is the Keeper's family home.

I raise my hand to knock.

"Lye Li Koh!" A memory of a voice. A warm ring around my heart like an embrace I always craved. I never thought I'd hear that voice again.

I swing around and so do the Char. I'm shocked at the gathering of dragging bodies that has followed us. Light as hollow bones, they barely made a sound as they trailed us through the village. And in the front, a sallow face with long brown hair rolled into a heavy bun that may be the only thing keeping her eyes from drooping. And cheekbones that sit out like precipices one could fall to their death from.

"Mei." I half sigh, half cry.

"That's Mei Li Long to you, cousin," the fragment of a woman says with a smile that could break my heart.

"Cousin," Joka repeats, tilting his head at the young old-looking woman in front of us.

Shen gather close. Unthreatening, but terrifying in their near-death states. Whispers of "Keeper" float on the icy wind. Shoulders sharp as scythes collide. Eyes pull forward. We are pressed against the door by an Atmosphere of desolation. A dandelion robbed of all its seeds, trampled and broken in the mud.

37
KI ANAH

REMNANT MAGIC

An enormous figure with a face like a demon and hands as pale as dove feathers presses her ear to Shei-Shei's chest. Ki Anah is devastated. She knows it's too late because the Carvress is no longer carved. She has returned to her original flesh and bone body, just as the Carvress of Cockle Fan Island did when she fell to her death. And though Ki Anah had her doubts about Shei-Shei at the beginning, the bone pale Carvress proved herself. She saved Sun from drowning. She tried to make up for her mistakes.

The other Carvresses hold hands in grief as more blankets are draped over their shoulders by the startlingly large creatures.

A bark rings out around the cave and an animal the size of Guen bounds toward them. A handsome creature, the shape of a wolf with black tiger stripes. It sits dutifully at one giant's side like a pet dog.

Sifah sniffs and looks to the ceiling. "Oh sister, we did not know. How could we?" She gestures around the cathedral-like space. "We have never experienced this kind of cold in our wooden form. We thought we would be safe from harm."

Mi Asha, dark as a starless night, voice deep as a grave, says, "But we are not safe, are we, sister." Her eyes bounce from one enormous being to another. "Since we have ventured from our island caves, we have found we are far more vulnerable than we imagined." The sisters huddle more tightly together.

The Dark West tribespeople live up to their legend. Their sheer size is enough to straighten Ki Anah's spine and pin her eyes. They move fast and loud. One points to the wall of characters and drawings. A deep female voice comes from beneath the gaping mouth. Ki Anah realizes as the light grows that their ghoulish faces are masks. "Wa! Look, my drawings are still here. They've barely faded!" She points and laughs. "Still true as the day I wrote it: Women never give up." Ki Anah tilts her head. A mystery solved, though dozens take its place.

The one kneeling at Shei-Shei's side presses her fingers to the princess's neck. She nods then takes a pot of heated water and carefully pours it over Shei-Shei's chest. The Carvresses lunge at her, but there's something about the careful and constant way it is done that makes Ki Anah shout, "Stop! Let them continue." Hands out, waving frantically. There would have been a time, not so long ago, when Ki Anah would never consider raising her voice to a Carvress. But so much has changed. In a way, Ki Anah feels like she's a child, learning everything anew. And what she's learning is she knows very little. This Dark West tribesman is trying to help Shei-Shei, of that she is sure. They keep pouring warm water over her chest and stomach, over and over, never letting it cool.

The Carvresses heed Ki Anah, but one of them demands, "Tell me what you are doing to our sister."

The mask is lifted to reveal a middle-aged woman. Twice the size of any woman Ki Anah has ever seen. Sun curses under his breath at the sight of her.

Guen points at the woman. "Dianh is trying to help Shei-Shei."

Dianh drinks the hot water than lowers her face to Shei-Shei's, blowing steamy air into her mouth. Ki Anah and the others in her party all gape like codfish—too shocked to protest. Sun says something Ki Anah would slap him for if she could reach. Dianh continues to heat Shei-Shei's body, drink and then blow the steam into the Carvress' mouth for several minutes.

Ki Anah and the others lean closer, watching and waiting.

The fire glows golden. The other giants pull off their masks and crowd around Dianh and Shei-Shei, whispering words of encouragement. Ki Anah counts the tribespeople and notices no men in their number.

Sifah steps forward, hand sweeping gracefully through the warm air. "Enough!" Pain takes over the small hope that briefly held her features. She glances down at the drenched Shen princess. Beautiful, no longer timber but no longer true flesh either. "Whatever you are trying to do is not working. Please, leave our sister in peace."

Dianh squints up at the formidable Carvress and bows her head. But she doesn't stop. Instead, she rolls Shei-Shei roughly to her side, pulls back her long arm, and thumps Shei-Shei's back like a drum. The hollow sound makes Ki Anah shudder. She thumps again and a small, glossy lump of amber flies from Shei-Shei's mouth and rolls down the stones toward the frozen lake.

Shei-Shei coughs, knees flying to her chest. Her eyes fly open, green and luminescent like opal. Shei-Shei pulls herself up halfway and wobbles, limbs giving way. Sun rushes to her aid, hooking his arms under hers and leaning her against a boulder. She grabs handfuls of her chestnut hair, running it through her fingers and laughing with a dry wheeze. "I am—" She looks up at her sisters. Green glass eyes, round tanned face. A paint spatter of freckles over her nose. "I am flesh and bone." She smiles, pinching her own skin. Shei-Shei is striking. And young. And elated.

The Carvresses exchange looks of shock and wonder. "How is this possible?" the Carvress of Yellow Fin Island asks, stepping forward as Dianh rises from her knees and swipes her forehead of sweat.

Sifah taps her chin. Glancing up at the giant who just saved her sister's life. "When Shei-Shei's heart stopped beating, it broke our brother's spell." She offers her hand to Dianh, who takes it warily. "Thank you for bringing her back from the spirit world, Dark West woman."

Dianh nods her head. "Her heart stopped beating because it was frozen. She never entered the spirit world. She was simply… suspended."

Guen blinks her wooden eyes. "What was that thing that came out her mouth?"

Mi Asha answers this. "Remnant magic. A small piece of what she once was."

Ki Anah lifts the purple tea she was given to her lips once again, the liquid knocking against her smiling teeth. *Sea and stars!* She has some tales to tell her husband when she sees him again.

Sun stares at the long legs of the women. The power in their muscular arms. "Can I ask a question?"

Dianh turns her head to Sun, eyes narrowing by a degree. She seems instantly distrustful of him but nods her strong chin. A woman of her size need not fear much in this world. "Very well."

"Why are you so tall? Are all Dark West people this"—he gestures the length of Dianh from her boots to the top of her head—"this large?"

Dianh chuckles, her deep voice echoing off the walls. "No, we are not all this size. Just the women of *my* tribe. On the other side of the mountain, in the Dark West valley, the women are of normal height. We are this way because of cave coral." She points to Ki Anah's steaming cup and Ki Anah spits the liquid from her mouth. She has no desire to duck under the door frame every time she enters her house.

The other women chuckle. Guen pats Ki Anah's arm. "Don't worry. You have to eat a lot of it to get as big as them."

Ki Anah places her cup at her feet daintily. She'd rather not take the chance.

The two groups of formidable, magical women stand on opposite sides of the fire, assessing each other. Ki Anah bows, hands clasped. "You have saved us. We owe you a great debt."

Dianh's voice is proud and deferential. "Thank your girl, Guen. She fought for you." She pats Guen's head so roughly her little wooden plaits bang against her ears. "My guess is we are not done helping you though, are we?" The woman exudes warmth, though Ki Anah recognizes a sadness in the corners of her eyes. A sort of hollowing that comes with experiencing trauma.

Ki Anah nods. It is time to come out of hiding. They have waited too long as it is for someone to come for them. "We need to get out of the mountain and back into Shen territory."

Dianh exchanges looks with her fellow tribeswomen. "That is a very dangerous idea."

"Yes, but we must try. We can't stay in this icebox any longer," Sun says as Guen knocks on his chest as if it were a door.

Dianh throws more timber on the fire. Ki Anah had forgotten how glorious it is to be warm. "You misunderstand me. Getting down the mountain will not be difficult. The danger is entering Shen territory. They will kill you, all of you." Her eyes land on little Guen with affectionate worry, and Ki Anah suspects she cares a great deal for the girl.

Ki Anah stands and addresses the giant women. "We know it's dangerous. But these eight women are the missing Chow princesses. I believe we must restore them to the throne. If we don't, our war will never end, and the emperor will—"

Dianh puts her hand up. "Wait, you want to take the emperor's throne?" She stamps her spear into the ground with a metallic clang. The tiger wolf beside her barks sharply once.

"We do." The Char bow their heads.

Her smile is as big as a broken serving dish. She runs her fingers through the fur of her pet. It leans into her touch, emitting a kind of intelligence Ki Anah has rarely seen in an animal. She thinks of Luna and how her daughter would love to meet this creature.

Dianh sits beside them, legs folded, and tells them a story. Of a greedy emperor who attacked their village and rampaged through their lands, killing every tiger wolf except one, which he stole for himself. She pats the pup's head. "We found this little one hiding in the back of the coral cave. He's all that's left." She breathes in deeply and rises. "Please give me a moment to confer with my tribe."

While they huddle by the lake, Guen lifts her little head from Sun's chest. "But I didn't freeze. Why didn't I freeze to death up there?" She points to the roof. To a world only she has seen.

"Perhaps, even though, we don't look it, our bodies are ageing. Perhaps it was colder down here than up there." Mi Asha shrugs her ebony shoulders. "It is both comforting and terrifying to know we can perish."

"Why comforting?" Sun asks, confused.

Mi Asha sighs. "Our family awaits us in the stars. We know we have work to do, but when it is complete, it is comforting to know we may one day reunite with them." Ki Anah knows this feeling well.

Loud footsteps. Dianh and the others return.

"We will return you to Shen territory. We will provide you with food and weapons and clothing. We ask that you do only one thing for us."

"What is that?" Sun asks.

"Succeed! Throw that greedy, murderous man into the street and let the dogs tear him limb from limb." Dianh's kind eyes turn sinister.

Sun swallows drily at the stern-faced woman. "We'll do our best."

Dianh nods. "Tonight, we rest here. Tomorrow, we shall show you *our* way down the mountain." She winks her walnut-sized eye and the other tribeswomen chuckle quietly. Which makes Ki Anah very worried about what *their* way might be.

38
LUNA

No one can save me, but I can save everyone. I can.

I can.

I tell myself that over and over as they carry Ash on a stretcher, down, down, down into the filthy cavern beneath the palace. I tell myself it won't be long now as I hear the children cry for us, and Lu Leng's coughing billowing to the roof like a sickly cloud. Soon we can leave this place.

I correct my thoughts. *They. Not we.* I must stay.

Time is both medicine and poison.

They throw Ash, stretcher and all, into his cage. He moves like a lizard who hasn't seen the sun: no energy and blood running cold and thin. He needs time to heal. It's strange to think that half the time I've known him, he's been on the brink of death. Tortured by both sides. Watching him now, I feel like the pit of a berry peach, hard and bitter but with the promise of growth. He does that to me, works around the sharpness and finds the small sliver of hope.

Qi Sha scorches my arm and I bite back this time. Sending a favorite of mine, fire ants, through his veins. He releases me suddenly and tosses me into my cage, pulling his sword half out of its hilt. "You little piece of Char—"

I grin, mud soaking into my silken elbows. "Do you think Soo Si would approve of you interfering with her plans?" The sword slides angrily back in. Her influence over the guards appears to be nearly absolute. Whatever she's threatening or paying, it must be substantial.

Ash groans. "Leave us!" he shouts, using precious energy. "Or I'll spend my last strength convincing Luna to back out of this plan." He may do that anyway.

Qi Sha growls, "With any luck you'll be dead before the night is through."

I jump up and the shrivel-faced man shuffles back, panicked. I enjoy the fear he has of me. I extend my hands. "I could summon a fleet of worms to devour you right now." He straightens, walk-running away. Trying to maintain dignity while desperately scrambling to get behind the iron gate. I hear it lock with accompanying curse words. Truth is, I couldn't summon anything. Besides harmless glow worms, I've exhausted the store of living things in this space.

My smile dives like a heart bird chasing its mate when I turn to Lu Leng's shaky hand reaching through my bars. She can barely speak, her lungs filled with fluid rather than air. "We… were… scared… that—" She begins coughing. The kind of cough that is halfway to a last breath. I grasp her hand and send the lungs of a giraffe seal to her. Oh, how I wish it would save her, but it won't. It will only help her breathe easy while we're connected. With my other hand, I bring light to our cave world and dozens of grimy Char faces.

The teen, Ha Fun, scratches another line in the wall behind him. "We were starting to worry they'd killed you, like the others."

I swallow. Mouth grim. Heart filling with blood only part way, a reluctant tide. "The others?" I ask and don't want the answer.

"Some don't come back," he mutters, turning to the wall and running his finger over his scratched time markers.

Ash pulls himself up to sitting, arms shaking, his once sun-kissed face as pale as cream silk, and my heart wants to break even though it can't. "That won't happen any—" He starts and I put a finger to my lips. Our eyes connect over saltwater and suffering. I don't want him making promises he can't keep. These children are tough. They have survived this long. But they're flesh and bone. Like sand and wood, these soft and brittle materials can only withstand so much.

THE NIGHT IS dirt cool and moss damp as always. It is as if we live on the underside of a stone. But exhaustion outweighs comfort, stretching to my fingertips and toes, and sleep digs out a little cove for me. Not warm, but snug enough for someone as salmon-tired as me.

My heart beats loudly, like it's impatient. Like it's a gong summoning the whole city to the central pagoda. I tap my chest with my fingers, and they come back sticky and warm. When I inspect them, it's not blood I see but sap. The substance spreading over my chest, up my arms, and down my legs. The hickory creaks and croaks, growing like a tree. Only it's a year's worth in seconds. It is agony. Muscle fibers engulfed by splinters of wood. Bones bulging and breaking, to be born again as branches. I scream, my mouth opening wider and wider, becoming a hollow, a place where vampire owls can make their horror-filled nests.

The concubine's voice is like a metal skewer puncturing my brain. "You shall make a powerful and intimidating weapon."

I shoot up from bed, hand patting my chest frantically. It's wet, but it's not blood or sap. It's sweat soaked from holding onto Lu Leng through the bars. Her hand hangs limply from her cot. Her breath more of a dribble than air.

"Ash!" I hiss, shuffling over to his side of the cage. "Ash, wake up!" My panic grows as the damp, stepped-on sound of the little girl's breathing gets softer and softer. I rattle the bars. He doesn't stir. He's exhausted and caught up in his own need to heal. But I need his advice. I need him.

I grip the bamboo tightly, eyes fixed on the rising and falling shadow of my saltwater love. The ocean that lives in his eyes and heart. I need to touch him. I need to place my hand on his chest and feel his flesh heart beating. The need grows, Blood building but with nowhere to go. My knuckles whiten to bone. I think of otters breaking apart clam shells, their claws built for the task. They do it with ease. Natural. In their blood.

Crack!

My head turns this way and that, wondering where the noise came from. Lu Leng coughs again, and it sounds like the tearing of a bay leaf. Barely a cough. A listless swing at the infection filling her lungs.

"Ash!" I rattle the bars to get his attention. The bamboo poles in my hands give way, neatly split in two.

I check for the shadows of guards. Their candlelight hides around the corner. I quietly push the broken bars apart until I can squeeze into Ash's cell.

Grabbing his shoulder, I send the sharp slap of a whale's tail against calm seas. He jolts as well as he can, given his injuries, and rolls over to face me. "Luna!" he whispers groggily. "How did you get in here?"

I stare at my palms in the faded worm light. These little hands. This little body. Little Luna. Those poles were not broken before. Sometimes I feel like the Blood power is too much to hold. Sometimes I don't know why it chose me. I close my fingers over a growing power I hope I'm strong enough to control. To Ash I mutter, "Otter claws."

He tries to lift his head from the bed, manages an inch and collapses back down. "What?"

"Oh, it doesn't matter. What matters is Lu Leng. She's barely breathing. Listen to that cough. What should we do?" I know I'm shaking. Guilt for being away from the children scratches up my throat like clawing leaf lizards, their tiny needle claws necessary to grip onto the smooth bamboo as they camouflage themselves as leaves. I clasp my throat. It hurts. Stinging like death is looking for a way in.

Ash manages to prop himself up making all sorts of painful noises that hurt me like porcupine barbs and cocks his ear for the sound of the little girl's breathing. "I don't hear anything," he says.

I swallow and it's like a ball of nails. No. "Salt and stars!" I push back through the bars with no care for noise. As the bar springs back into place, it drags a long graze across my back. I launch at my cot, shoving my arm through the bars to find her hand. It's as cold as a stone at the bottom of a frozen pond.

I squeeze it. I shake it. I pull it. Her whole body follows like a sack of wet laundry. Unresponsive. I push beaver tail slaps. The wide, alertness of a rakka possum. The crack of a baby birds beak through an egg shell. Anything. Everything.

Ash throws his whisper at me. "What is it? What's wrong?"

I don't answer. I look to the roof, slowly bringing the worms over her cage to full light. My eyes are closed. But the glow of purple and pink pierces my eyelids. It's so bright. Brighter than it should be. Because it's the color of my fear.

Ash curses and I hear him trying to rise from his bed. I turn to him, my face drained of anything good, and my heart trying to sap my emotion. I don't want to feel this. But I must.

He *feels* me. His face reflects my grief and hopelessness. I turn back to the sweet, proud Char girl from Black Sail City who put too much hope in Ash and me. Who ran out of time before we could bring her body to the light, dry those lungs and give her a chance. My throat catches on the hot star traveling up from my chest.

I force myself to look at her. Eyes open, drenched in colored light. Chest still. Lungs no longer working. Her expression is not peaceful; it's filled with panic and frozen in a fight for life that she lost. I don't understand how this happened so quickly. My hand drops from her wrist. All Blood bouncing back to me because it has nowhere to go.

I stand, hands covering my mouth, but they can't hold in the scream. It comes out before I can stop it. "Help!" I grip the bars. *Crack, crack, crack!* Like the snap of a noodle cake before it's thrown into boiling water. *Crack! Crack! Crack!* Small fractures appear in the bamboo beneath my fingers, traveling up and down like tiny earthquakes. "Guards! Come now!"

Shadows move, but not as fast as they should. Easing from chairs, twisting their backs, and lazily picking up weapons leaning against the wall.

Ha Fun makes his way to the side closest to Lu Leng's cage. He peers through the bars and dips his chin in a sad but unsurprised way. He turns to his tally wall, arms hanging limply at his sides. He sighs too deep for one so young. Taking up his small sharp rock, he scrapes an X into the stone below his lines that mark the tallies of the days. His shoulders rise and fall slowly, like the unwinding of a drawbridge.

Eleven Xs. Eleven Char children. "You may have to scrub that one out. She could live." I have no right to this hope. That is as clear as the cross on the wall.

How could I have let this happen?

The other children begin to rouse. Yawning and stretching their arms as guards clap loudly down the steps. I bounce on the balls of my feet while Ash scrapes his hair back and stares at me with a stricken expression.

The guards come to me. "What're you screaming about?" Irritated and barely awake, Qi Sha blinks and pokes his spear through the bars.

I point to Lu Leng's graying body. "She needs help, she's… she's…" My words disintegrate like oily paper on my tongue.

Ash pipes up, voice as dry and dusty as an unread book. "She's not breathing."

Qi Sha's expression relaxes. "That's it?" Sho Sen has the decency to look uncomfortable.

My heart begins to throb like it cannot hold the Blood in any longer. I tap my chest. "That's it? Do something! How can you be so heartless?"

He walks painfully slow to the Lu Leng's cage like he's enjoying the torture it creates. Qi Sha squints his beady eyes through the bars and frowns, his face comfortable in its pinched expression. "Doesn't look like there's anything to be done. She's dead." He pokes her lifeless body with the handle of his spear, and I feel bile rise in my throat.

The worms on the ceiling glow brighter than a new planet. A planet the color of sunsets and grief. The children let out sad little gasps and sighs. They do not cry. The reason: Ten Xs before Lu Leng.

"Sho Sen," Qi Sha directs. "Clear her out before she starts to smell."

Ash tries to stand, to get closer to me, but I put up a hand. "Ash, stop. Don't hurt yourself!" I cannot have any more good blood on my hands. Bad blood, on the other hand, I am ready to bathe in. Sho Sen unhooks Lu Leng's cage door and steps inside. My hands wrap around the cage bars like a hungry hantu ghost. The bamboo crackles. "Don't touch her," I warn with fire in my eyes and destruction in my fingers.

Qi Sha flaps his hands at Sho Sen. "Get on with it!"

A sound rumbles the ceiling and causes all the guards to stop in their tracks. It's deep and dark and rocks the foundations of the palace. They look up with knowing eyes. The sound comes again. Rich and metallic. Like the deep, lonely call of a widowed whale.

The young Sho Sen hovers in the doorway as I start at one end of my cage and run my finger along every rod of bamboo. It fissures and crumbles, the cage collapsing as I pull Lu Leng's body into my arms. I await the repercussion. For spears at my throat or Ash's skin to be slashed again, but nothing comes.

One more gong-like sound and the guards peel back like they're attached to strings and are being drawn back to their puppeteer. Instead of explaining, they just leave, shadows disappearing upward. The iron gate locks, leaving us alone again. The wall that separated Lu Leng's and my cage is now destroyed. The door to mine swings open.

I cradle the girl in my arms. She is so small, so soft, and oh so cold.

I send healing frogs, creatures with gills to let her breath under water, spider webs to hold her together, but it's too late. My power won't travel into her veins because they no longer pump blood.

My heart can't break but I'm learning it can crack. And each time, it leaves a dark, sap-filled scar that cannot be erased. I lift the light-as-a-rag girl, holding her against my wooden heart, and carry her to Ash's cell door. Placing my hand on his gate, I crumble the bamboo as if it were weak plaster. I enter and kneel beside him, laying her across the end of his bed.

Tears flow freely from both our eyes. I *feel* his heartache. He *feels* my ache for a heart.

"This cannot continue."

He smooths the hair back from Lu Leng's brow. His eyes lift to mine, full of letting go and sacrifice. "I shouldn't have argued, Luna. You must do whatever is needed to get these kids out of here."

I bow until our foreheads are touching. We are swans pulled by opposing currents. He understands there is no other choice. Even if it means we will never see each other again. "I know."

"Whatever you want me to do, I'll do it." His voice breaks open. "Even if that means leaving you." Blood gushes from a wound we keep picking at. A wound we can't seem to heal.

The staccato clack of wooden shoes carefully treading down the long stone steps is a strange accompaniment to our suffering.

The iron gate creaks, and Soo Si's silk skirts appear, then the rest of her, face shining with a kind of birthday level delight. Hopping down the last few steps like a giddy child, she claps her hands rapidly when she sees me. Her eyes sweep over the broken bamboo, nose scrunching at the sight of Lu Leng in my arms. But it doesn't dampen her enthusiasm as she squeals and jumps up and down. Evil in the very air beneath her feet. "I have wonderful news!"

"Can you not see the dead child in our arms, you—" Ash starts.

"I'd be careful if I were you, traitor Shen." She waggles a finger. "Now, let me share what I have come to share and then you can go back to whatever you were doing." She gestures at us like we're a spill that needs mopping. I think of all the horrible things I want to do to her but I hold my tongue and remember my oath to free these children. She leans into the cage, just the tip of her headdress jangling over us. "The emperor's mother is dead! I mean, we all knew it was coming. Poor woman!" She has the audacity to attempt to wink at us. Her eye paint sticks her eyelid down for too long. "The royal mourning gong just sounded a few minutes ago." She bounces up and down and then points at me. "Now it's time to plan the wedding!"

I could kill her now with one quick touch. This devil deal feels tenuous and uncertain. But I wouldn't get very far with the children and Ash in tow. I must wait.

My tongue slips from its bindings. "Thank you for sharing your *news*, Soo Si. Now leave before I do something we will both regret." My eyes are deathly and my mouth forms a hard line. She takes one look at me, purses her lips, and takes my threat seriously. She steps backward and twirls, sending a puff of heavy floral perfume into our faces. Rushing back up the stairs with a spring in her diabolical step.

This woman offers our only chance. But is it worth taking?

Ash places his hand over mine as we hold the little girl who will never return home. Never feel the salt spray on her face and place wishes on smoke creatures in the sky. "She may be worse than my brother, Luna. There is something especially evil about a person who uses the stones of love to pave their path to power."

I stare out at the dozens of children whose fate I hold in my dirty little hands. "I think you are right."

39

LYE

SKULLS TO REACH THE SKY

"Mei Li Long," I repeat her name and it wraps around my tongue like a warm lempeng. The thin green pancake smeared with coconut jam was our favorite. And because it was cheap to make, we had it often. "You got married?" My eyes scan the brittle-looking crowd then come back to her cut-glass face. She looks as if she may cry but also like she has cried an ocean and has no tears left. "Mei?"

Mei's eyes fall to her dry, wrinkled hands. "I did marry, yes. And I had three beautiful children." Again, I scan the crowd for these young people with whom I share blood. My heart begins to feel charred and feathered at the edges. Choice of words and tense are so important. She said "she had." *Had.*

The villagers encircle us like a loose lasso but keep their distance. Their hands are tightly fisted around farm tool handles, but none seem ready or even capable of attack. Joka looks out upon the crowd nervously, hand to his bamboo neck. Jing Ha covers her cheeks with her hands. The Shen stare between the Keeper and the

Char. Confusion twists their starving faces. I need to say something, but my mouth feels as parched as the land looks. I swallow. I need to remember I mean something to these people.

Char grip their swords and spears tightly but keep them at the hip. I put up a hand. "Place your weapons on the ground," I order my soldiers, and face the crowd. The Char do as ordered and without argument. *You are everything: Keeper, Char, general, peasant.* "Your Keeper has returned. It may seem strange to see her accompanied by Char warriors, but I assure you, we are not here to harm you. In fact, we're here to help you."

Mei snorts along with several other villagers. A farmer who looks as if he's not eaten in days drags himself forward. "Your palace has tripled our orders for exported goods. We work day and night to fill them. We are starving and near frozen because of the emperor, and you expect us to believe you are here to help?" He bows his head as he says this. Even in his anger, he cannot look me in the eye. He still holds reverence for the Keeper. "I don't know why you bring filthy Char to our village, but—" He begins to sway, his tired eyes rolling back in his head. He goes limp and begins to fall. Ipoh launches at the man as villagers gasp. He catches and gently lays the old Shen on the ground, checking for injury. Jing Ha kneels beside the man and places a hand at his temple. She whispers, "Willow bark," which will calm and ease pain as Shen villagers lean in like plants to an open window.

"I am not in the emperor's service any longer. Word travels slow to the northern villages, but the Keeper, Lye Li Koh, escaped the palace many months ago." I gesture around me. "How else do you explain my companions?"

To this there is no answer.

Joka clears his throat. "Believe me, we are no allies to your emperor. He has ordered the death of many of our soldiers. I have fought many Shen in battle. But that is war. We are here because your emperor has violated the rules of honorable battle." He reaches into his pack and the Shen peasants tense. But he pulls out a small notebook and holds it up for them to see. "In this book are the names of Char children the emperor has kidnapped." He opens the pages and runs his finger down the long list of names, reading some. "Re Ri, Gan No, Lu Leng…"

"Children?" a woman asks, her eyes and ears scooping up the information willingly.

Jing Ha straightens and lets her hands fall so her wooden cheeks show. Proud and glistening in the streaky light of a sunset that seems to be promising a different kind of day than there has ever been. "They kidnapped my four-year-old son, Bok Ah." She stares out at the crowd, who seem captivated if not a little unsteady on their feet. The dandelion has been robbed of its seeds, and the stem is as hollow as a straw. "I promise I would never lie about such a thing. Why else would a wife and mother travel to the Shen mainland?"

The villagers nod their sagging heads. They want and need to believe. The emperor has pushed them past their breaking point and now their minds are open. They no longer believe he is without fault or beyond reproach. They already thought he was a monster. This new information just seals the decree with gold wax and a wooden Char stamp.

Mei taps my shoulder and I spin around, revealing my sycamore arm. She stares at it for a moment, mouth dropping open, and then she opens the door to the Koh family home. "I think you best come inside. You've sown a seed. Let us give it a night to take root."

I nod and dig into the clay dirt, addressing my village. "It is clear the emperor has abused his power. I want you to know, I'm on your side." I hope I have it in me, to be split down the middle. A small voice in the back of my mind whispers, *Maybe you were always split and now you are coming back together.*

"How can you be on our side and theirs?" The woman points at the Char as they file inside.

Pulling back my sleeve, I hold my sycamore arm up for them to see. "Because I am the Keeper, but I am also a Char general. I am Element and wood. I am everything, and I'm ready to share my power with you." I step back, letting those words sprinkle down on their heads like the edge of a firework.

I close the door and press my back to it. Concerned Char eyes are on me as I take a deep breath in and thump my heart. They thump their hearts in support. I hope I am ready. For *everything.*

MEI SERVES US tea around the same table we used to sit at as children. Back when Ash and I were crammed in with five other cousins, two to a chair. Our butts were so bony, it wasn't that bad sharing. Ghosts of the past sit in those chairs now: Uncle grumbling as he tried to spread the meal evenly between seven little mouths. Auntie smiling, happy but exhausted. We never went hungry. The meals were small but regular. In treating his subjects as slaves, the emperor has cut the collar instead of strengthening it. He has lost them without realizing it. When you stand on peoples' skulls to reach the sky, sooner or later the people stop bowing their heads to your climbing feet.

I still remember Mei clutching my skirts as they took me away. "Take me with you," she'd begged. Shen soldiers smacked her down. She cried into the red dirt as they placed me and Ash carefully into the royal chalice. My lips lift into a wry smile. How foolishly excited I had been, bouncing up and down on those velvet cushions, dreaming of a new and better life.

The Char drink their tea gratefully and in their Char way, loud and slurping. Their willingness to accept Shen hospitality and her willingness to give it is hope in itself. Mei regards them warily but also with amusement. My presence, my vouch, seems enough to lay a thin ribbon of trust between them.

Mei collapses into the last chair and places her hands on the table. "So, cousin, what have you been up to the last seven years?" She grins, eyes running over the Char convening in her kitchen, and it makes everyone instantly relax.

There's no food to offer, and we pour out our rations to share with her as we tell her what has happened, what is about to happen and plans I didn't even know I had until I stepped foot in my village and saw the stretched faces of people who have had enough and can't give anymore.

I touch Mei's hand with my magicless fingers. "Mei, where is your family?"

Mei's eyes blink back saltwater. "My husband died in the spring trying to fill the new quota of red rice before the season ended." She stares at our joined hands with wonder. She expects a spark of lightning or flame. She was certainly used to it when we were children. But of course there's nothing. "You know how cold it gets when the glacier starts to move. They found him in the water. He died of exposure, Lye." Her lips quiver. "All to satisfy our great and infallible emperor." Her tone turns sour, her shoulder's shake.

Jing Ha searches Mei's face and finds herself reflected. "Your children are in the sky also, aren't they, Mei?"

Mei's head seems too heavy to hold up anymore and it collapses onto her arms. All bravery and humor gone. "There was no food. I gave them everything. I didn't eat for days but they just couldn't, they couldn't—"

Jing Ha does what it seems she was born to do and uses her Earth power to calm and heal. "I know, I know," she whispers, sending something that takes at least some tension out of Mei's razor-sharp shoulders.

I don't know how to feel. Guilt swarms me as well as anger. I abandoned them. I left them in the hands of a someone who could not take care of his people. "I'm so sorry, Mei."

"There are many stories like mine, Lye. The people are drained dry. There's nothing left. Their loyalty is lost. He doesn't deserve it." She whispers that last part, seeming frightened someone will hear her. But the emperor has no friends at this table.

Slowly, Jing Ha works on the grieving widow. "You have suffered through too much."

Mei lifts her head as Jing Ha's power envelops and warms her hurting heart. "How is this possible?" she asks to the Char whose hearts and minds are brimming with sympathy. "The Keeper creates warriors not healers. That is how it has always been. That is the role of the Keeper."

I smile, a soft, not fully formed thing. But my purpose is becoming clearer. "That *was* the role of the Keeper who was slave to the emperor." Power swirls through my blood, but there's nothing destructive in its nature. It is the storm breaking, the sun rising. Creating life and harmony. Balance. "I am my own Keeper now."

We talk into the night as one solitary candle burns to its end. We tell her everything. Of battles. Victories. Losses. And the Carvresses claim to the throne.

"I don't know how I can help, cousin, but I want to," Mei whispers into the dark as Char eyes begin to close and sleep. "I think the village will want to help also. At least, I know they won't try to stop you."

Her Atmosphere reads like secret cranes, huddling close to share warmth against the cold. Looking like they're keeping a secret when really all they're keeping is each other safe. I coast my hands over the air around her. Her Pulse flutters at the corner of her hip. She is Blood. Nothing close to Luna's power, but a comforting, helpful kind of gift.

I know what I must do.

"Mei, come with me," I say, holding out my hand to find her in the darkness. She grips it tightly.

Joka's voice is laced with caution. "Where are you going, Lye?"

"To share my gift," I reply. The Char make way for us.

Joka follows me outside and stands watch as I awaken Blood in Mei. I release my finger from her Pulse, energy passing from my body to hers. The change is instant and the process makes me feel a little lighter, less shackled to the murk beneath the earth's surface. But also—tired.

She bows low, forehead pressing to the earth. "Thank you, cousin. I promise to be worthy of your faith in me."

I stand too quickly and sway. I feel like a hollowed cork tree. Light and airy, lacking stability. Joka stabilizes me, his hands at my waist. "Lye, are you all right?" It is nice to hear my first name spoken instead of "general."

"I am." I steady and straighten. The weakness wearing off quickly. "In fact, I think I am feeling better than I have in a long time."

I scrunch my elemental hand. Something feels different. I'm just not sure what.

40
KI ANAH

SENSES SCRAPED TO BLURS OF GREEN

That something can be deathly dangerous and have restorative power at the same time is not an unfamiliar concept to Ki Anah. Just look at her daughter, who could torture with one hand and save lives with the other. The women are very careful in the way they treat the coral. Light destroys it, so it's wrapped many times over and consumed quickly once taken out. Even then, Ki Anah has nearly broken her teeth crunching down on coral too late. She has been assured the women's size is from years of eating the stuff and she won't become a giant from these small samplings. She takes a last bite, watching in amazement as the coral begins to turn white and die as it's exposed to sunlight. Beautiful, welcome, not-so-warm, but she doesn't mind, sunlight. She moves the small piece around her mouth with her face tilted to the pale-yellow bulb in the sky. It tastes like freshly washed bok choy. Ki Anah blinks hard, suddenly wondering how her house and garden are faring un-occupied. Is it full of rakka possums? Have all her pastes and preserves been destroyed, her plants chewed down to their roots?

Sun taps her shoulder gently. "What are you thinking, Mama?"

"I was thinking about home," she answers as they assemble at the edge of cliff. She doesn't elaborate since she's not in the mood to be teased. Especially not when she steps closer to the group of women who are holding what look like shallow wooden canoes in their giant hands. She peers over the edge. It's more of a steep icy slope than a cliff, but Ki Anah feels dizzy all the same.

Sun and Guen clomp through the thick snow to her side. "Wa! You can see the whole world from here," Guen remarks, the skin of some unknown but very warm animal draped over her shoulders.

Sun ruffles her wooden plaits, the *clink, clank* something Ki Anah is starting to get used to. Wooden hair was never something any Char asked for. Ki Anah shrugs. It has no use. "Maybe not the *whole* world, but definitely a lot of the Shen world."

They stare out over a patchwork of fields, the thick veins of twin rivers cutting the land like lightning strikes. The land looks peaceful from up here. It also looks empty. Ki Anah shivers as she recalls being chased through fields by frightening lizards and farmers with scythes. She knows she needs to get down the mountain, but she's not ashamed to admit she's afraid of what awaits them. She imagines it could all end very quickly if they're not careful.

Shei-Shei nudges her shoulder and Ki Anah twists around. The woman strokes her own arms as if they're not her own. "It is strange to truly feel the cold." The fire tattoo at her eye moves as she talks, and Ki Anah finds herself staring at it. "You know, right down to your bones."

"You didn't feel it when you, er…" Ki Anah pulls the skins she was given tighter around her throat. The cold bites like a villain snake, darting into any crack it can find.

Shei-Shei shakes her head. "When I died? No." She is stunning in her flesh form, with the added depth of a flush to her cheeks and freckles dotting her nose. Ki Anah guesses she must not have been more than twenty years old when she was turned to wood. "I was like any tool or implement that becomes frozen. My moving parts simply stopped moving."

"Not anymore," Guen states, her voice a little edgy. "Now you're like them." She points at Ki Anah and Sun. A slight frown marring her face. "Now you can bleed and die like any old human."

Shei-Shei pulls back, shock and regret clear on her round face. Sun brings Guen into a rough hug and playfully places his hand over her mouth. Her wooden arms bash against his wooden chest. "Ah, Guen, leave Shei-Shei alone. She's been through enough. And you do know she's sorry for what she did to you." Guen's eyes crease. Ki Anah wonders what a bite from wooden teeth would feel like. "You need to learn some manners. That's not how you speak to a princess."

Shei-Shei giggles shyly, covering her rose petal mouth and Ki Anah's head snaps between the two. There's no way on sea or sand she will permit her son to court a Shen princess. She rolls her eyes. Can't just one of them find a nice Char to settle down with?

She breaks the exchange by inserting herself as a barrier. Then she calls to Dianh. "What are these for?" she asks, tapping a thin wooden canoe. They seem too thin to hold them all in the water. "Is there a river nearby?"

Dianh smiles. "Of sorts." The tiger wolf jumps up on the huge woman, nipping at her elbow. Dianh smacks it down with a wallop and Ki Anah winces. "No, Zui-Zui." She points at the ground. "Sit!" The beast abides her. Looking up at its owner like she is the sun and moon.

Ki Anah watches her son, his eyes on the princess Shei-Shei who has re-joined her sisters, standing like a sore thumb among the sculpted women. "If only my own children were that obedient!" she remarks to Dianh.

The giant laughs, loud and hearty, and Ki Anah swears snow falls from branches at the sound. "I wish that too!"

"How many children do you have?" Ki Anah asks, connecting to this mother as all mothers do.

Dianh counts on her fingers. "Five at the moment. I had hoped for six, but I see now that Guen is well cared for." Her eyes slide to Sun and the birchwood girl, playing in the snow, brows raised.

Ki Anah clasps her hands, wringing an imaginary dishtowel. "They are a strange pair, but the arrangement works for them. To be honest, I think Guen has taught my son a few good lessons."

Dianh lays the canoe in the snow, as do the other Dark West women. "Children are good at that, aren't they? Teaching you lessons you didn't even know you needed to learn."

Ki Anah smiles as the cold air frosts her cheeks. Deep green pine needles are shining like urchin spines. It's clean and fresh and wild up here. A beautiful place to raise a family. "They are good at that, yes."

Dianh taps the inside of the strange boat with her foot. "In you get. It's time to send you home." Ki Anah's eyes widen as she begins to understand the method by which they will get down the mountain.

"Oh, this is going to be fun!" Sun crows, beating his chest with his fist. Guen copies the movement and Ki Anah frowns.

The Carvresses shuffle backward from the boats like a flock of birds wary of a tossed stone. Shei-Shei stands with them but appears lost. She always seemed the odd one out, and now she's even more so.

Guen stands on her tiptoes. "What? What is going to be fun?"

Dianh crouches down and cups the little girl's face. "I have enjoyed having you around, girl with the birchwood bones who is born of bravery. But now it's time to for you to continue your journey. I have a feeling there are big things in your future." She stretches her arms as wide as they will go, which is very, very wide. "Big things!"

Guen hugs Dianh, still confused about what is about to happen. She looks to Sun, who points at the wooden canoes. "We're about to go for the ride of a lifetime!" His finger moves down the glacier until it's pointing at the lake below.

Dianh stands and begins talking them through how to "sail" down the glacier as she piles sacks of food into the back. How to steer and slow. How to "land" when they stop suddenly at the base. Sun bounces on the balls of his feet, anxious to jump. "Listen to the woman!" Ki Anah snaps and he manages to stand still. Whether he's taking it in, she can't be sure.

There are four canoes, each tied to a tree with long rope so the women can retrieve them. They split up into groups. Ki Anah, Sun, Guen, and Sifah in one, the other Carvresses dividing into the remaining boats.

Sifah is the strongest and will hold the rudder steady. Sun will help steer.

The Dark West women position the four canoes at the point where the glacier begins to drop. The nose of the boat hovers in mid-air, like an axe about to drop. Ki Anah's eyes slide to the side, to the steep slope below them. The Dark West women's masks slip over their faces, and they count to three.

Ki Anah gulps and grips the sides. She is far too old for this.

Why in stars and sky did she sit in the front?

THERE ARE MANY ways in which this could go wrong, but as the nose begins to lean toward the ground instead of the sky, there's no point in thinking about them. The balance has tipped. The canoe doesn't ease them in, it flies. All they can do is hold on and hope they reach the bottom unscathed.

Sun lets out one whoop and then is robbed of any more noises except grunts of exertion as he digs his sharp tool into the ice to try and influence their direction. Wind doesn't just whip Ki Anah's face, it digs its claws under her skin and tries to rip it from her skull. She wants to scream. Maybe she is screaming. All she knows is her heart is in her mouth and she needs to concentrate very hard not to spit it out into the snow.

Sifah grips the sides, face taut, and curses. *A Carvress cursed!* That can't be a good sign. Guen's body is pressed against Ki Anah's back, sheltering against the biting wind. She's not much of a shelter though, and strands of cold thread through the space around her.

They snake down the mountain, traveling faster than a ship with the strongest wind in its sails.

It's terrifying and invigorating. But mostly terrifying.

Small rebellious pines pop up in the snow like the scene changes in a puppet show. And Ki Anah leans left and right to aid in steering around them. Her senses are scraped to blurs of green, the soft swish of the canoe scraping against the snow, and the powerful wind.

Guen squeals as they head for a larger pine that has challenged the mountain and grown to full height. If they hit it, the wide trunk will crush them.

Sifah jams the slowing pin in and Sun steers them right, but it's still too close. They're going to collide, and traveling at this speed, they will not come out of it without injury. Ki Anah does the only thing she can think and throws her hand out, ready to push off the trunk. Guen, shaking with adrenalin, climbs into Ki Anah's lap and pulls her hand back.

Just as they are about to crash, Guen throws her feet out, pushing off the trunk and sending them sideways. The ripping, grazing sound makes Ki Anah's heart that was in her mouth squash and drop to a lump in her throat.

Guen screams and Ki Anah pulls her back into the canoe, lifting her little feet to survey the damage. The pads are sanded off. Ki Anah doesn't know what this means. But she clutches the child to her breast as they shoot past boulders and saplings.

Sun shouts, "Look down there!"

"What is that?" Sifah asks, impossibly breathless.

"Can we avoid them?" Sun asks, though his tone suggests he already knows they can't.

Sifah thrusts the slowing spike down but it's not doing a thing in the loose, deep snow. "My boy, there's no avoiding anything. We'll be lucky if we can stop this thing before we shoot straight out to sea!"

Black dots move awkwardly across the frozen pond. Clinging to one another for support. There's a party already waiting to capture them. Ki Anah feels a grave digging into her chest. A possible death preparing to nestle there. The only way someone would know they were here was if Ash and Luna told them. And the only reason Ash and Luna would reveal this secret would be if they had been tortured to the point of death. Even then, she is doubtful, but here they are. A Shen welcoming party.

Ki Anah closes her eyes and prays. She will not be taken. She taps the dagger at her side. She will fight to her last breath to protect the others.

She hopes her family will forgive her.

41

LUNA

FAVORS AND INVITATIONS

There's no way to make this right. Right now, in Black Sail City, a mother and father are probably searching for their missing child. They will think they see her as they watch dark plaits clap the backs of Char children crossing their path. They will hear laughter as the young ones play and wish Lu Leng was among them. Their hearts will hope that somehow, she ended up there, simply lost in the chaos of after-battle. But we know the truth: what they hold onto is dead hope. They will never see their daughter again.

The space is in shambles. Children could escape their cages and yet no one moves. They're waiting for us to tell them it's safe. I cup Lu Leng's gray, sunken cheek. They will never be safe here.

"Luna," Ash whispers, voice like a crawling fog over the bay. "Don't give up." I know he's scared I'll retreat to the dark, disconnected place. A big piece of me wishes to, but I'm counting on love to get me through these next moves. I dig my claws into the deal I made with Soo Si like it's the only thing keeping me from falling. Love will give me the strength to do what must be done.

Too many guards clap down the stairs two at a time. They press up against the iron gate and when it's unlocked, they pour into the space like a waterfall of weapons and fear. After my display of destructive power, they've tripled the guard.

"Finally, you understand the threat I pose," I boom, Lu Leng limp in my arms.

They line up at my now shared cage with Ash.

Sho Sen clears his throat and steps forward. "Give us the child." Stern but sad. A dead child should, and does, bring out the humanity in almost everyone. Except for the soulless concubine.

"I will not," I say, clutching her to my breast.

Ash puts a hand on my shoulder and squeezes. Waves on the sand, pulling the grains home. "She's in the stars, Luna."

"But she needs to be put to sea," I say stubbornly, knowing it's not possible. "She cannot rest until then." My arms quiver. My heart beats out the rhythm of a death drum. I stare at Lu Leng's vacant face. *There were so many things you had yet to learn and experience. You barely had time to live before life was ripped from you.*

Guards creep closer and violence breeds in my fingertips. "Soo Si has ordered disposal of the body. We must do as we are told." Sho Sen lowers his eyes, seeming apologetic, not unaffected by the dead girl in my arms.

Ash stands with effort and approaches the guard. "What will you do with the… with her?" he murmurs.

The guard's gaze flicks to the other children. Big plate eyes pressing through gaps in the bars. Grimy fingers slipping on bamboo. "Cremated," he whispers.

"We will release her to you *if* you return her ashes." Ash bargains when he's no position to, but Sho Sen nods.

Ash gently nudges me forward. The guard lifts Lu Leng from my arms and I allow mercy by not killing him. The moment her weight is absent from my arms, my body crumbles. My bones are salt soaked, as my skin trembles with grief and undone promises. I am a thrown ball of string, unravelling until there's nothing left.

They leave as they came, and I fold into Ash's arms, heaving sobs I can't control as he traces circles on my back. "I feel like we're losing," I murmur. Even as I say it I will it to not be true.

"Perhaps we are losing but we have not lost."

HOURS LATER Sho Sen returns, a small jar containing a thin layer of dust at the bottom in one hand and a piece of parchment in the other. Qi Sha snorts and spits behind him.

Ash takes the jar and I take the parchment.

"I know we cannot put her to sea, but if we scatter her into the river, she will find the sea eventually." He wraps an arm around my shoulder and my feelings flood to him. His breath catches as he takes on my grief, my love, and my determination, all in one punch.

"That's a nice idea," I say, wishing there was more I could do.

Together we walk out of our cage. The guards step back, allowing us this one kindness. But their swords are drawn. They won't hesitate to slash Ash's heart if I try something. The Char children chant, pushing me forward. *Things should have turned out better for you, Lu Leng.* I should have done better.

Ash holds my waist, stabilizing a crumbling structure when he's split at the seams himself. We scaffold each other like we always have. "I *feel* you, Luna. This is not your fault. Please, place the blame where it belongs."

I nod, trying to stretch and wrangle the blame from my heart where it sits like drying gum paste. He's right. The blame lays squarely on one person's ornamented shoulders.

Ash hands me the light glass jar. I hold it up to the glow of worms. How can this be all of Lu Leng? It seems so inadequate. We squat at the edge of the canyon—the depth unknown, the crevice completely dark. But I hear the water and feel its anxious, rushing need to join the sea. I feel the same.

I press my fist to my heart and tip the contents. It disappears in the quickest and most painful blink of an eye. "You can go home, Lu Leng."

Sho Sen clears his throat and points at our cell. He has done this one favor. I won't expect any more.

We return to our cage and allow him to lock us in, for what good it will do. The children return to talking quietly among themselves.

I unroll the parchment, and Ash and I read the elegant characters together.

I laugh despite myself. Covering my mouth quickly. "We're invited to the wedding. And it's in two days."

Ash leans his head against mine and I feel the roughness of scabs against my skin. "It doesn't say we, Luna. It only says you."

I've learned we do better when we are together. When we have each other's backs.

Sho Sen lingers while Qi Sha is already stomping back up the stairs. I push the paper between the bars. "You tell *her* I'm not going to her ridiculous event without Ash, and if she has a problem with that, she can consider our deal off."

He nods and finally leaves.

When he's gone, the small humor I found in those black characters on delicate paper disappears like pipe smoke on a windy day. Rage rattles my ribs. Creatures that burrow and break rush to my fingertips. I place my hand on our cage, and it cracks and crumbles to a pile of pulpy chips. Slowly, I step over the rubble and make my way around the edge, touching every cage. Children step back with brutish smiles as I shatter their containment with Blood.

The ceiling hums from power that comes with knowing they cannot and *will* not defeat me.

42

LYE

UNUSED TO HER SKIN

Morning is an eager rooster, crowing at the first sign of light. It comes too soon. The Char uncurl from corners, stretching and cracking wooden limbs. Joka and I are more bleary-eyed than the others. The door opens and Mei enters from outside dressed in a red wool hat and padded coat. Frosty mist tries to push inside, and she banishes it with a slam. She has a fresh flush to her face from the new strength I have gifted to her.

Ipoh rubs his eyes and squints at Mei rushing about the kitchen. "Where have you been, cousin of the general?"

Mei speaks as she fills a pot with water. "I've been talking to the rest of village." She smiles, pulling eggs from her skirt pocket like they're gold coins. "They believe your story and they're willing to help." I'm relieved and a little surprised.

She taps Ying Yi on the shoulder, and he flinches. "Ouch! She has power." I nod. "But she has no tattoo." He shifts his bandaged leg on the chair. I survey his wounds with concern, wondering if he can make the next part of the journey.

"You changed her?" Jing Ha asks, voice pitched high and worried. "— a Shen, but is that wise?"

"Mei is not a soldier. She will use her power to help others. I will hear no more about it," Joka warns, but with a sadness to his voice. "Lye was right to choose her."

It was wise and it was right. "For too long I was forced to gift powers as a weapon. Men and women were selected for their ruthlessness, their anger, their desire to harm." I pick up my pack and sling it over my shoulder and wiggle my feet into my shoes. "I'm not doing that anymore." It's a decree I can stand by. A promise I know I can keep.

The Char tip their chins. If there's an argument inside their cheeks, they keep it to themselves. I have their loyalty. Their trust. That is enough.

Mei spins around, eggs fried with scallions and sesame oil glistening on the plates in her hands. "You're leaving?"

The Char lick their lips and Ying Yi snatches a plate before I can order him not to. "We don't have time to waste. I need to find the Carvresses. We should leave now."

Mei bows her head and shrugs into her jacket while the others pass the plates around, scarfing breakfast like hogs at a trough. "Let me take you to the glacier. But I caution you, cousin, winter has come early, and it has reached the ground."

I swallow. It feels like amber and blood. They have to be there. They just have to. I have not left room for any other possibility.

STARING AT my dainty feet carefully sliding across the frozen pond to the base of the glacier, I don't know why I'm still moving. Stamping my foot down, it's clear the ice is several feet thick. There's no hole or hollow. There's no way we can get in and no way for them to get out until spring. We're too late. If they're at the dragon's heart, they are warm, but do they have enough food? There are many ways they could be in danger. Not to mention the monster tribes of the Dark West. Without Ash to lead them to safe hunting grounds, this plan had a terribly frayed end.

Joka and the others shuffle behind me, slipping and skidding and clutching each other for stability. Mei's giggle is not very subtle. "General, what do we do now?"

I reach the point where the glacier melts into the surface of the pond—the coldest, strangest lava flow—and sink to my knees. I place a hand on the ice, and it sinks through several inches of snow to hard as rock ice. I leave it there, letting it become so cold and numb it begins to burn.

"General?" Joka's voice seems far away. "Lye?"

A hand goes to my shoulder. Warm and comforting. Of my blood and now of Blood. "Lye. Look up," my cousin says with wonder and a strand of fear like the burned black noodle among the perfectly cooked ones.

My eyes lift. My heart jumps. I scramble backward and turn to run but of course it's impossible. Everyone scatters, tripping and falling as they try to reach the edge of the pond to get away from whatever is shooting down the mountain like a star from the sky. "Clear the way!" I shout. Four shapes are coming at us at a lightning pace and they're going to hit with as much force if we don't get out of the way.

Joka is frozen to his place, staring at the long, leaf-shaped structures coasting toward us like tips of broken spears thrown by a giant. I reach the edge and scream, "Joka, move!"

But it's too late. I hear him laugh, the sound full of relief and joy and astonishment. Then I hear the word "brother."

Sun, Ki Anah, and eight wooden heads across four strange-looking boats come into view. I don't recognize all of them. Their faces are peeled back with a kind of jubilant terror as the boats hit the edge of the glacier and fly a few feet in the air before landing on the icy pond. The vessels suddenly seize, and the passengers fly out in a tumble of wooden limbs and flesh. Sluing across the ice like flat stones.

Joka stands up among the chaos unharmed, and I want to fly at him, slap his face for being so reckless. But I must get in line as Ki Anah jumps up, dusts herself off, and storms toward her son. She smacks the back of his head, tears filling her eyes. Then she throws her arms around his neck and hangs there like a medallion. Sun slips and slides toward them, a small child clinging to his arm, and punches his brother's shoulder.

It's wonderful to see. Some parts of the heart have come back together. They fuse to one another like they were never divided.

"Oh Mama, you're alive." Joka exhales a breath he's probably been holding for months.

"Of course I'm alive!" Ki Anah snaps, though the elastic in her voice is half stretched. I sense her story has some sting to it. "I'm a Yan. Yans always survive." The elastic frays. A question she doesn't want answered. There's still a Yan missing and a Yan lost forever.

The Yans pull sacks and packs from the boats and move to the bank of the pond.

Mei's hands are scrunched into fists. Her eyes blink rapidly as she watches the Carvresses straighten their incredible wooden bodies. She knocks her head toward the impressive women as they approach the edge of the pond. "You're telling me these, er, wooden women are Shen royalty?"

The Carvress of Sand Otter Island brushes my sycamore arm as Mei stares. She taps her work and shakes her head. "Ah, I wish I'd had more time. I could have made it beautiful." Her breath smells like pine. I snort quietly. I suppose it's because her mouth is made of the stuff.

I bow. "It has served me well, Carvress. I have no need for embellishment." The scars are plenty. She smiles, grace rolling from her body.

Mei rolls onto her heels with her hands behind her back, and the Carvress twists elegantly in her direction. "And yes, young Shen woman. We are Shen royalty. We are the missing princesses of the Chow dynasty." The way she says it leaves no room for argument.

"The who and what?" Mei whispers.

I know something of the tale. Nine princesses who fled the palace after something happened with their brother, the emperor. But that was hundreds of years ago.

I wave my hand. "I will tell you later." I'm distracted by a Shen among their ranks. A woman with a Fire tattoo. I frown. She doesn't look familiar, and with those remarkable green eyes and beautiful face, I'm sure I would remember changing her.

We gather to assess each other for both injury and rank.

Behind us, curious villagers who followed us mill about, eyes straining to get a look at the strange wooden women and the Char accompanying them.

Sun steps forward from the group and salutes me. "Joka tells me you're the new general." A small wooden hand curls around his leg and my eyes wish to peel back, but I keep surprise from my expression, awaiting what I am sure will be explained.

I bow my head to Sun. "Setsu put me forward."

Ki Anah bows in my direction. "How is my husband?" she asks, voice small and unpinned to hope.

"He is well, Ki Anah. He guards the refugees at the monastery behind Black Sail City." Her whole body seems to deflate of stressful air. "Though I dare say he's not too happy with me. I ordered him to stay."

Ki Anah bows quick. "I am sure you had your reasons, General."

Sun chuckles. A strange sound given all that has happened, but it's not unwelcome. "Have we got a story to tell you!" he says, gesturing at the sky. The small wooden hand is attached to a wooden shoulder, and then a small, pale wooden face peeks out from behind his leg.

The boats begin to move on their own, slowly returning up the slope. Shen villagers gasp and my Char crew jump and curse.

Joka steps back and almost falls on his butt. "Seems we have a lot to talk about, brother!" His eyes move from the boats to the little girl and back again. They clap each other on the shoulder and laugh. I'm so happy for them it's splitting me at the seams. But as they walk toward the village, people parting around them like they're a fallen comet, I feel longing.

My brother is still out there. My family is still one half gone.

One of the villagers reaches up to touch a Carvress. She withdraws and scuttles closer to me. "What is this dark magic?" he says in a dried grass voice.

The Coalstone Carvress stands tall and pats her much jumpier sister, who takes a deep, unnecessary breath and brings herself to smile. Nine hundred years is a long time to be away from home. The Shen woman among them appears a little lost. She seems unused to her flesh, and pinches her arms, comparing their plumpness with the hard boniness of the people in front of us.

I catch up to Sun, leaving Mei behind with the villagers that are closing around us like a lid to a bottle. "Who is the Shen woman with you?"

Sun whispers, "That's Shei-Shei, the Carvress of Pearl Shell Beach."

"H-how?" I manage, voice wobbling with shock.

Sun chuckles. "Well, she kind of died and then a giant Dark West woman brought her back. Seems when a Carvress dies, they return to their flesh forms." Giant? I don't know what to make of this information. But it feels as if it's one of many new things we're about to absorb. Keeping the mission at the front.

Joka counts the heads. "Where's the ninth Carvress?"

Sun's shoulders slump. His eyes lower and he clutches the wooden girl a little tighter. "We couldn't bring her back."

So, one is dead. One is flesh. And then there's this tiny Carvress, who holds her head up proudly, but also ducks every time a villager comes too near.

The Coalstone Carvress stops abruptly, causing the bottleneck of people to bulge. The Char form a protective barrier around the Carvresses. The Coalstone Carvress gently ushers Shei-Shei behind her and addresses the crowd. "Fellow Shen, we are the Carvresses of the Char islands." The villagers step back rather than forward, afraid but in no condition to fight. "We are *also* the missing princesses of the Chow dynasty. I am Sifah, the eldest princess. Please do not be frightened. We are not here to harm you. We are on your side." She gestures at the crowd, repeating my words from yesterday.

The crowd blinks and is quiet. They don't attack. They don't seem to know what to do except to let us continue. Mei breaks from the villagers and comes to my side. With her shoulder touching mine, she seems proud to show me off to the rest of her tribe.

As we walk back to the village, some Shen drop away and others follow. They listen to the Char tell tales. They stare at the Carvresses, searching for a strand of commonality. In Shei-Shei, they find it. She separates from the others and walks among her people. Listening to their concerns and suggesting ways to help. They accept her readily. I think it won't be long before they accept the others.

It's a strange delegation but seems to have clicked together like a wagon that was missing a wheel. Everything, everyone, rolling, rolling toward the palace. I feel it calling like a rusty bell.

Ki Anah tugs my sleeve. "Tell me, do you know if my daughter and Ash live?" she asks, voice broken into pieces that wish to fly across the mainland and dive into the sea.

"They sent us a message. It's how we knew to come here and find you. All I know is they were alive four weeks ago when that message was sent."

Ki Anah bites down on her lip; Atmosphere is of delicate, just-budded leaves. "They must be alive. They must." Joka embraces his mother tightly and it makes me ache. It makes every scar scratched into my sycamore arm pulse like a hundred heartbeats out of sync.

"Yes, they must be," I repeat under my breath. Wasting wishes willingly.

We plod toward the village, snow crunching beneath our feet. "If I know the chancellor, he will keep them alive as collateral. Until he has me, I believe they will be safe."

Mei frowns and stops walking. "The chancellor is dead, cousin."

"Dead?" The air is knocked from my lungs and my feet are frozen. My heart is suddenly paused in its purposeful beat. *Dead.* I'm an empty cotton blossom. One pinch and I am crushed to dust.

Mei nods fervently. "They sent his death notice to the village weeks ago. I guess I'm his only remaining family, so it came to me.

He was killed by a Char warrior. A woman, I believe. I'm sorry, Lye. I thought you knew."

"Luna," the brothers say like a prayer.

I shake my head. "There is nothing to be sorry for, dear cousin." A strange emptiness clouds my mind. A feeling of lost words and missed opportunities. If Luna killed him, no doubt he deserved to die. He was my blood, but brother seems too intimate a word to use in his instance. To put him and Ash in the same category seems almost blasphemous. I feel released and regretful for the chancellor's death. Not grief exactly, but a small, still sadness does creep into my heart. He needed to leave this earth. It's a shame, but there was no saving him.

The edge of huts and farm buildings show ahead. Joka taps my sycamore arm. "What are you thinking?" he asks. His disappointment in me seems to have ebbed these last two days. Whether I can trust him as I did before is unclear.

"That I am glad we no longer have to worry about the chancellor." I can't say more, my feelings are more complicated than the bagua to past emperors' tombs. There may never be an easy unraveling of them. Ash is the only other person who could understand how I feel. I grit my teeth. When I see him again, we shall talk about it.

43
KI ANAH

LIKE RED ENVELOPES

She has been told this is the purpose of their journey, but there are too many Shen. Everywhere Ki Anah turns on this march to the palace, she sees another drawn-down face. Another villager with clothes hanging off them like they're the dummies Char use for training. Though these mouths are not scribbled with anger and there are no tattoos at their eyes. These people are wastelands. Their leader has run through them like a dust storm and blown away hope, leaving only hunger and desolation.

When they traveled to the cathedral cave so many weeks ago, they hid in the canyon. Now they follow the river but march like targets along the top.

She thinks back to when they first met Guen. Ki Anah had no clue to the mistreatment hiding behind the neat village grid. She had assumed all was well. Assumptions, she's learned, are grassy knolls with honeycombed caves beneath. Collapse is not certain but is certainly a possibility.

A villager grazes her cherrywood hip, and she jumps. These Shen's attitudes are peculiar to her. They have shown no aggression, barely a glare, their fascination seems kind of envious. She frowns. That a Shen could envy her seems preposterous.

The Carvresses glide beside them with grace and understanding. They accept and assist, leaning in rather than away, as they realize there is no threat here. Ki Anah watches Sifah kneel to speak to a Shen child. The Carvress smiles and nods, and the girl looks at her with a mixture of awe and mistrust. Sifah shrugs this off as she has with the others. Confident she will win them over. Ki Anah shrugs too, reminding herself the Carvresses are Shen, or were, or partly are. Her head hurts when she thinks about it too much. As does the weight of what happens to the Char if these wooden princesses take the throne.

Her children take to change more easily, but they are young. Their minds are designed to stretch and adapt like wet discs of rice paper. Easily shaped and folded into all manner of dishes.

But she follows the group as they travel toward the palace, gathering disciples. Carvresses hand out wooden limbs like red envelopes at new year. Lye gifting elements like they ride on the breeze and swim in the river. There's much trust involved in making either an elemental or wood change. What if the Shen turn on them? What if all they're really doing is strengthening the Shen to become an even more dangerous army than before?

Joka sidles up to Ki Anah as they walk the bank of the second arm of the river. It sounds desperate, hastily churning toward the palace. She knows that feeling. Her daughter and Char children are captive at the end of this waterway. She wants to run, but she must stay with the group.

"Mama, you look very, er, very deep in thought. Are you all right?" he asks.

She glances up at her tall, lean son with his hair in need of cutting. His bamboo neck is starting to yellow and dry. There's a maturity that wasn't there before, grown from battle and diplomacy. He has always been intelligent, but life and war has educated him in a different way. She purses her lips. She's not sure if she should be proud or upset. "I'm all right. I am just anxious to get to the palace. And I worry…"

Sun with Guen on his shoulders catches up to them. "What are you worried about?" he asks.

Her head switches back and forth at the crowd in front and behind them. "How do we know we can trust these Shen? Your 'friend' the Keeper awards them power, the Carvresses have gifted limbs…" Ki Anah is proud of her Char heritage. By doing this, she fears their traditions could be swallowed by the much bigger mainland.

Furrows like wave ripples form in Joka's forehead. "The Carvresses have only gifted limbs to heal injury and to save lives. Mama, you see how many Shen are close to death here. These innocents suffer for the emperor's greed. And Lye, I mean the general, has only given powers to those who are worthy. Those who will use their element to heal and help, never to harm. And she does so indiscriminate of whether you're a Char or Shen."

Ki Anah crosses her arms over her chest. It's very hard to accept this new way of things and not feel like the Char will be chased out and traditions will disappear. It makes her feel like a relic. "Everything is changing too quickly."

Sun beats his wooden chest. "If you ask me, things can't change soon enough."

Joka rubs his chin, eyes on the girl general in a warm and grateful way that Ki Anah finds discomfiting. "Change is good, Mama. Quick change is even better in this case. We need as many allies as we can get if we are to convince the emperor to let the Carvresses enter the palace."

Ki Anah snorts. "You may be able to change unhappy peasants' minds. But you will need more than helpful, healing allies when you reach the palace."

War is the way of Shen and Char. When they knock on the emperor's door, Ki Anah feels sure he will not simply open it for them. No, they are all marching straight into the points of swords and spears.

She unravels her dark hair with proud slivers of silver running through it, proof of a life well lived, and winds it back into a tight bun at the nape of her neck. It's not that she is too old to believe in peace. It's that she has endured a lifetime of battle and loss, which has taught her nothing comes easy.

Ki Anah puts her head down and marches. She has done her part and now she must put the fate of everything and everyone she loves in the hands of these younglings and the nine-hundred-year-old princesses.

44

LUNA

PLOTS THAT WILL NEVER WORK

bove, where ancient tapestries and gold paint decorates the walls, preparations are being made for a funeral and then a wedding. With a smirk, I think of Soo Si's impatience. I imagine she stomps her wooden heel and rattles her adorned head with frustration at the emperor's mother still coming first, even in death. It's hard to feel bad for the death of a woman who influenced the emperor to do so many terrible things. Actually, it's impossible.

My heart beats steady. Hickory calming. Hickory rationalizing.

Below, children play in the rubble, building forts from broken bamboo. It brings me small joy coated with a heavy basting of sadness because this brings them a pinch of happiness. Char always find happiness in the simplest pleasures.

The removal of bars means I have been hugged so many times I cannot count. I am held almost always. By the children during the day, and at night by Ash, whose warm arms and healing body give me more comfort than I deserve.

I soak it up, knowing my time with them will soon be over. I lean into hickory to help me through. Not to shut out the emotion but to help manage it in small pieces.

The guards strike the iron gate now permanently locked between us and them. I hear it open quickly like a sail in a wind change and children rush up the stairs to collect meals.

One exclaims with pure excitement, "Ai ya! There's a dumpling in our bowls."

I turn to Ash, who sits crossed legged on the floor, playing with one of the younger boys, Bok Ah. He can't be more than four years old. They take turns stacking the broken pieces of bamboo into a leaning tower. As the children stream up the four stone steps to the tray of steaming bowls, the tower collapses, and the boy points at Ash. "Ha! You lose!"

Ash chuckles, a sound like ice melting. "That's not fair. Rematch after you've had your food?" He offers his hand to the boy, who shakes it very seriously.

Bok Ah is handed a bowl by another child. Lifting it to his face, he stares at the shining-with-fat dumpling floating in broth, poking it with is finger like he's not quite sure it's real.

Ash and I wait until all have food and then head up the steps to see what's left. Ash still holds his chest like he's scared his organs will fall out, but he can walk. The healing Blood I've been sending him in his sleep is working. Sho Sen is waiting for us, sharp eyes observing us through the bars. "It's a gift from the emperor's bride. She wishes to remind you of your commitment."

I glare at Sho Sen, his bald head gray compared to the rest of his skin. "I'm aware!" I snap.

I can think of nothing else.

I hear a low growl of slight discomfort. Candlelight catches a shadow, bringing it closer. Four strong legs. A proud snout. Liquid golden eyes, like the milk of the moon that remind me of my lost brother, run straight to mine. Mulia.

Four men hold ropes around her neck but are dragged along the ground as she bounds to the gate to reach me. Her black-as-seaweed claws *clackity clack* on the stones. Behind the four men are two more with arrows aimed at the wolf or me, whoever decides to step out of line first. Ash's eyes widen with fright, and I realize this is his first encounter with the incredible tiger wolf.

"Floods and fire!" he exclaims. "I've heard of the emperor's exotic pet, but I never saw her. Lye described you, Mulia." He addresses the enormous creature, whose ears prick and point to the ceiling. "But I don't think her description did you justice." He extends a hand to pat the wolf's head, and Mulia pulls back, wary. She bares glistening white teeth and I laugh, flicking my fingers and telling her of all the people in this rusty castle, she can trust Ash.

"How did Soo Si get her away from the emperor?" I ask as I run my hands through Mulia's thick gray and black fur. The wolf tiger bears my hand but doesn't lean into it. Her wildness leaks around control.

"She has her ways." The guard's cheeks flush crimson and I don't need any further explanation.

Mulia's heart beats strong and sure. It beats for me and for herself, but it also saves every tenth beat for her master. Despite his ill treatment, she is devoted to him. It competes with my Blood power but only in a small way. A microscopic vein versus a wide artery. My influence is spreading, and I feel sure she will do what I need her to do. I tap my heart with my spare hand, a feeling of regret pulsing over the trapdoors of hickory. Because she will do it, but she won't want to. My other hand rests in Mulia's ruff. A trust I will betray.

"You are a valiant creature, Mulia. And I am sorry for what must happen next," I whisper.

The great wolf stares with eyes like the last slip of the sun before it disappears below the horizon but she doesn't understand. Sniffing my palm, she licks traces of fat from my fingers. The clink of spoons against bowls as dozens of children scrape the last tasty scraps of broth from their bowls makes my choice easier. Sacrifice is not supposed to be easy. But this one is essential.

I release Mulia and bid her to sit.

I take my bowl from the floor. It's barely warm now. A little like my conscience.

Ash places his hand on my shoulder, his finger slipping over my collar to deliver a calm sea. A memory of a home I hope he will get to see even if I cannot. "I *feel* you, Luna." In those words are hidden meanings. He's asking if I'm sure. If I can do this.

To the guard I say, "Tell the emperor's bride thank you for her 'gift' and I will see her at the wedding." Then I flick my hand and tell Mulia to return to the emperor.

The men can't hold the great wolf, and she gallops away, four ropes trailing behind her. *Mulia, wait at the bedroom door,* I urge. *Let them remove those ropes before you enter.*

ASH WORKS HIS arms under my side and pulls me against him. My cool back presses against his warm chest. Spine to sternum.

The children have settled and the space fills with small snores and rattly breathing. Fear of losing another one wraps around my chest like a butterfly python, squeezing and squeezing. I breathe in slowly, trying to calm myself. But Ash knows. He can *feel* it.

"You have doubts about what you must do," he states.

I take his hand and press it against the hickory. His heart beats fast against my back. His breath is ember warm on my neck. "It's murder." Dark nothingness calls me. In that place of shadows and built-up walls, it was easy to do bad things. To simply flick my hand and inflict pain and torture. It became near natural. The dark cradled me like a hammock.

Ash's voice brings me back. And even though what he says is futile, his hope is still wanted. It's like leaves falling to the earth from a great oak tree. They will die and decompose, but in doing so, they nourish the earth so new plants can grow. "We'll find another way, Luna. I don't want to lose you."

Perhaps because I do this for love and for the benefit of others, I won't be pulled under. I'm not sure. I do know it's the only path before us. Ash knows it too, but it helps him to talk as if it isn't. "You will never lose me."

He lays a kiss below my jaw, sending tiny chills of perfect snowflakes up and down my skin.

I let him concoct plans and plots that will never work as his hands coast over my body as if he's memorizing every dip and curve. And when he pauses, I turn to face him and do the same. I want to remember the scars on his chest, the muscles across his back. The slight unevenness to his cheeks created by his lopsided smile.

We have a few more days before it all changes.

Before I become an assassin.

45

LYE

BENDING TOWARD BELIEF

The woman's Pulse pops like a mustard seed in oil at the bend of her elbow. She reads of Air. Purposeful. Disciplined. But also charitable. Like she would feed all the starving peasants on the mainland if she could.

Her hair is streaked with large sections of white, but her face is unwrinkled. She keeps eye contact while I change her when most close their eyes. When I'm done, she takes the longest breath in and then grins, showing several missing teeth. "Thank you, Keeper." Her voice reminds me of a slightly out of tune mandolin. "I always knew I was Air."

I bow quickly and swipe the hair from my eyes. "You did?"

She pats my sycamore arm. Tapping the tally marks with her short stubby fingernail. "Mmhm." She shakes her hair, and it fluffs out like a tamarin's mane. "I'm a hurricane in the kitchen!" She cackles, her chest filled with new energy. Her joy passes to me, a gift I happily receive.

We are changing the world body by body, Shen by Shen and Char by Char. And with every person I change, my body feels lighter. Like I'm floating on a cool breeze or burning to soft ash. Coasting like topsoil over the earth or evaporating like steam. And shedding my skin like a lizard. All elements live in harmony.

At the palace I could change about a hundred Shen in one day. But there would be months before the next influx of potential soldiers. And although this is what I want to do, I'm not accustomed to the faster pace, the greater numbers.

I look up at the jungle-dressed mountains looming large. We're a day's travel from the palace.

Finding my cousin talking to another group of displaced, discontented Shen, I point to the peak, the palace hidden beneath dense green palms and thickly threaded woods. "You think we can do this?" I ask.

Mei's cheeks rise. Her dark eyes have seen so much death, but she thumps her chest like a Char and says, "We must, cousin."

"Where'd you learn that?" I ask, eyes on the fist over her heart.

"From you, cousin. You do it all the time."

"I do?"

Mei grins. "Like the Elements, being Char comes natural to you."

Natural. I never thought of myself this way. It bolsters my resolve.

I squeeze Mei's shoulder. "When we get up there, I don't know what will happen. Promise me you'll look after the vulnerable. Make sure they're safe."

She bows. "Of course, General." Her use of that address when as children she would shove me from the woodpile to win "swamp monster" and kick me in her sleep in the bed we shared makes us both giggle.

THE CARVRESSES WALK in front as if they know exactly which way to go. And I suppose they do. The palace was their home once. I stay in the middle among the hundreds following us. They're not fighters. If I gave them a sword, they'd probably use it to cut a melon or slash weeds. They are farmers and fishermen, wives and washerwomen. They are Shen who have lost faith in their leader because he never gave them a reason to keep it. They're mistreated and malnourished. I shake my head and a strange laugh escapes my throat like a trapped moth, all dry and feathery. This is no army. And that makes me very happy.

It's no army, but it's the backbone of the Shen. The emperor must realize if he doesn't have the peasants on his side, the entire country falls.

Ki Anah stomps in front, shoulders curled inward like she's a baby bird wishing to return to its egg. I move up to catch her and she spins around. Her eyes are red rimmed, though no tears fall. She's a typical Yan. Bravery is woven into their skin. To show vulnerability is to cut that skin open for all to see.

"Ki Anah," I start as the Carvresses signal the group to stop. "What is bothering you?" I pat my wayward hair. I look unkempt and unwomanly. "I sense agitation in you." Her mouth creases into an unhappy fold. "Like roots trying to find a place to settle."

Around us, men and women spread into small camps. Unrolling their somehow both flat and lumpy bedding, and lighting fires. The water is closer to the bank here, and some Shen take rods to the ruffling green grass edge to catch dinner. I breathe in deeply. There's a cool, fresh taste to the air, layered with woodsmoke and peppered with stars, it reminds me of home. My Char home.

Ki Anah wrings her hands, eyes darting to the groups of peasants. "There are a lot of Shen." She points subtly to a group nearby where a man stretches his new wooden leg, twisting it back and forth with a marveling expression. "And now they are Shen with Char magic. I want to believe they wish for change, that we can work together, but—"

We wander to the edge of camp where deciduous trees cling to their last leaves like a scarf being held against a strong wind. A breeze picks up and they lose another layer. Ribbed oak leaves fluttering to the ground. "But." I try to finish her thought. "You are concerned about the threat this might pose to the Char."

Her eyes are on her children. Joka, Sun, and the strange little birch girl, Guen. "There are only Shen to change. It weights the scales out of balance."

I touch her elbow with my elemental hand, holding back my power. It's easier now. Perhaps because I share often, it doesn't build up as it used to. Her Atmosphere is simple. It's of a mother, much like Jing Ha. The difference is in her tight hold to tradition and preservation. It's a worthy Pulse. "I have only changed Shen who are worthy of the gift, Ki Anah. People who have good intentions and won't use their power as a weapon."

She shakes her head. "What's to stop the Shen from completely devouring the Char way of life? You'll take our Carvresses and leave us with no protection. Like I said, the scales are out of balance."

The stars are brilliant tonight. Shining like they know we have a good cause. "Ki Anah, my hope is after this is over, there will be no scales. Balance will come through peace." My legs tremble and I ease myself to the ground. Achieving this balance is sapping my strength.

Ki Anah grips my sycamore arm and helps. Her concern washes over me like the stars have dropped down just to dab my forehead. "I wish I shared your faith, Keeper. Maybe I am just too old for this new way." She checks her perfect bun, straightens her skirts, and sits beside me.

I lean back, arms in the cool grass, looking at the glinting silver sky. One day to the palace and still so much to do. "You know it was your son who suggested this course."

"Ah, Joka," she sings, immediately knowing which son. Her voice cracks a little as she lifts her gaze to the sky. "You know, I think Ben Ni would have encouraged it also. He could see far past the sea surrounding our little island. I suppose now he sees the whole world."

I smile sadly. "He is always in my heart, Ki Anah. I owe him my life and I hope I have done him proud."

Ki Anah pulls her knees up and wraps her arms around them in a childlike way that is so unlike her. "Did you love my son?" she asks. I bite my lip. The question reaching into my chest and scraping away at my battered heart.

I bow my head. "No. I never had the chance." My eyes drift to the other son. The tall, lean one with a bamboo neck and a heart I think could be mine, if not for a hundred obstacles.

She sighs then, a big billowing thing that could boost a slow ship. "I cannot promise I will ever feel comfortable around this many Shen. But I do understand what you're trying to do." She pats my knee. "Just be careful."

"Careful?"

Her fingers come together and pinch my skin lightly like she's sealing the end of a yum cha money bag. "A candle only has so much wick and wax to burn, Lye Li."

My hand shakes and I concentrate on stilling it. "Then I will burn as bright as I can while I can." I turn to her, and my lips pull over my teeth in a grin born from a great idea. "I know just what to do for you, Ki Anah Yan."

She frowns and leans away. "Ai ya! Why are you looking at me like the last piece of crackling on the plate?"

A deep, smooth voice peels layers from my nerves and adds silk to my heart. "Mama, listen to Lye."

KI ANAH'S PULSE is over her womb. Her worried expression and squirming making my job more difficult. Joka kneels in the night dewed grass and holds her hand. Something *has* changed in him. A shift in his demeanor and Atmosphere. Like a storm clearing, his clouds lighten from black to gray to white. Sun is at her other side, with the girl Guen poking at the fire with a stick, seemingly disinterested. His Atmosphere is stranger still. When I first met him, he was full of anger and hatred toward Shen and while he's not trusting, he bends toward belief, ears cupped, eyes open.

He has a father's care cut through half his heart and in caring for a Shen child, he has changed too.

"Mama, be still. You don't want the general to make a mistake, do you?" Sun urges.

Ki Anah huffs. "Maybe *this* is a mistake."

I breathe in, feeling the element pulsing from her womb. She is unsurprisingly Blood. An element that has appeared more and more often since I started this journey, especially in women. "If you don't want to do this, you don't have to," I manage as my strength channels into this one task.

Ki Anah flaps her hand in my face. "No. No. I want to. I want to be able to understand my daughter better. I want to be able to help my family."

I bow my head. "Very well."

Joka watches me closely. Attentive to the movement of my hands and the breaths I take. The way Ki Anah reacts to the sudden flow of power from me to her.

She lets out a small "oh." Like finally something makes sense to her, and then it's over. I release my hand but feel like it's still touching her. Like I've pulled a little out of my own skin.

"Lye?" Joka whispers as Ki Anah twists her hands in front of her face in wonderment.

I lean on one arm, clopping to the ground. "If you could leave me to rest for a moment. Just a moment." The pauses between my words stretch with my labored breath. "I just need some peace."

Ki Anah bows. "I feel new and yet somehow like this was always in me. Does that make sense?" she asks, her Char beliefs laying down their arms to listen instead of fight.

I force a smile. I feel so very tired. "Perfect sense."

"Thank you, Keeper Lye." She bows low. "I will leave you to rest."

Sun scoops up a barely awake Guen and bounces around his mother with excitement. I hear his far away voice asking silly questions like "Do you feel full of claws and beaks?" I'd laugh if I weren't so exhausted.

A soft hand made for mapping cups my face. I have nothing to send its way. I feel like a soup bowl drained of its contents. Joka's kind face hovers over mine. "You're next, Joka Yan," I whisper, each letter from my mouth feeling like a piece of my soul.

He's fuzzy and gray, a shadow in my vision, but his voice is as clear as a pristine lake. I wish I could bathe in it. "No, Lye Li Koh. I am not."

"I thought this is what you wanted?" I manage as my eyes begin to close. I will replenish my energy and then I will change him.

He takes both my hands in his. "I thought it was too. I thought I needed this to be at your level, to be worthy of your love. And maybe that's partly true. Maybe I need to be bigger and better than I am to deserve you, but I won't do this to you." He gestures over the whole of me. "It's taking something from you, Lye. I suspected before Mama, but now I see it clearly. And I won't be the one to take more."

I fight to keep my consciousness. I need to see him, feel him. I shuffle up. "You have certainly proven yourself worthy of elemental power, Joka. When I am better—"

He leans in and kisses my forehead. His lips stay there for seconds I wish had no end. "When you are better, you will have more important things to do than change me."

I blink as the stars swirl. I think love is rearranging them. "I will?"

He nods. "Yes, and I'll be right beside you as you do them. Without an element but hopefully with your heart?"

I smile, a warm slow thing that spreads across my face like the sun over the sea. "Always."

He pulls back, a serene smile on his fine, intelligent face. He lifts his head to the stars, opens his mouth to speak just as something whistles through the air that is only meant to shatter perfect moments.

An arrow plunges into Joka, piercing our single second of happiness. More fly overhead like a flock of confused birds, until all time and space is filled with screaming, screaming, screaming.

46

LUNA

WATERMELON OR BRUISE

Loyalty is a strange, flighty thing in the Shen palace. Of the guards I've seen, their loyalties lie with Soo Si. Bought and bullied. Soo Si doesn't have loyalty-inspiring qualities. I've seen the fear in their eyes at her threats to family and loved ones. She has manipulated everyone's loyalty her way and then secured it with coin.

Sho Sen shoves a handful of black violet through the iron gate, eyes on children playing in the rubble. He regards them in an exhausted, resigned kind of way, like a maid who has entered a room destroyed by her master.

Taking the flowers, I scrunch the petals in my hand. Not all are loyal to Soo Si or we wouldn't need to perform this farce. "Eat it," the Water Shen with tired eyes and tried patience insists. "I need to get back."

I sigh and press the wilted blooms into my mouth. The taste like unripe-ness. Bitter and chewy. He watches me intently. "If the emperor knew about this, he would be very unhappy at how you've 'taken over' this area."

He awaits my open mouth, to prove it has been swallowed. I stick out my tongue and he nods, satisfied. I step back and gesture wide. "You're welcome to come in and set it all straight," I tease. "Or better yet, why don't you tell him all about it?" Ash watches from the lowest step, a warning in his seascape eyes. But we're already in the worst situation. I'm not sure it matters what I say now.

The guard shakes his head and crosses his arms, waiting for the flowers to work. It doesn't take long. A few minutes, and fog creeps over my power. Not blocking it completely but making it harder to access.

"You, traitor," the guard calls to Ash. "You're to come also." I feel a little lift, a bird testing its wings.

Ash grins and as his lips lift, the guard's mouth pulls down. Equal and opposing forces. "But she ate all the flowers."

The guard chuckles cruelly. "We don't need black violet to keep you under control."

Ash turns to the older boy, Ha Fun, whispering instructions and then claps up the steps. He is more scar than skin these days, but he has healed well and there's a cork bounce to his step. "People always underestimate me," Ash says with ridiculous cheeriness.

Qi Sha appears, his knobbly, hateful face sneering as he unlocks the gate and allows us to step through. "More likely you overestimate yourself."

Ash takes my hand as we are pushed up the stairs at the point of a spear yet again.

"I don't know why they want either of you there," Qi Sha mutters as we ascend, the air becoming drier and more fragrant with each level. A confusion of scents. Grieving incense mixed with pungent jasmine, which I like in tea but now reminds me of something rotting.

We reach the ground floor, and it's clear why the two clash. Funeral banners and offerings are being swept into bags to make way for bright pink and gold wedding posters. Gaudy strands of paper blossoms are tacked to the windows while paintings of the emperor's mother are torn in half as they're ripped from the walls. I cringe at the lack of respect. The emperor's mother was no ally, but this feels wrong. I pause to stare at her years ago likeness. Severe, a forward frown like her lips have been drawn together by invisible purse strings. In life and now in death, the woman looks permanently dissatisfied.

Shaded sunlight raps at the windows, held back by gray clouds. Seems fitting for this terrible union. I pause, my heart reaching for a murder bird that cuts the sky with its slicing feathers. But I can't quite reach it. The guard uses the back of his spear to push me, and I stumble. Ash reaches for me and gets a sharp knock to the shoulder. Jaws open within my fingers, desperate to bite down on the two Shen behind us. Qi Sha whistles and another guard joins him, a flame at his eye. He grabs Ash under the arm and yanks him away. He cries out as the Fire Shen sends something hot and burning under his skin.

I could hurt them. I could *kill* them. I'm storing harm like squirrels store nuts for the winter. There's little room left and soon something nasty is going to roll out without my say-so.

Ash shakes his head. I hold back. The guard drags him away. "Where are you taking him?" I shout as I am pulled in the opposite direction.

The spear twists the cloth into a swirl at my back. "Don't worry, little Char. Your traitor is just getting cleaned up for the wedding. Can't have him stinking up Lady Soo Si's big day." *Little*. The word has come to mean something different. It started as endearment, changed to a way to keep me down, and now I feel ownership over it. I am enormous strength and power in a little body. There's *little* I cannot do, cannot overcome. I have *little* patience for these guards.

"So, they won't hurt him?" I ask. A stupid question. The answer will only damage me.

"I didn't say that." He laughs like a screeching bat, and I slap his face hard, adding the snap of a bat's leathery wings to it. He cups his sore cheek, raises his spear, but Sho Sen stops him.

I smile. "You forget. I am a guest of the emperor and his bride."

I am little Luna. I have Yan family blood. I have Blood in my fingers. *Little* do they know how powerful I am.

SHE SHUFFLES into the lavish room sideways to fit an elaborate gold and pink wedding headdress through the doorway. It reminds me of a three-horned water buffalo. Guards flank her but she waves them away. "Don't worry. We have an arrangement. Don't we, Luna?" One eyelid is painted in dragon scale green and watermelon pink. The other side is varying shades of purple like degrees of a bruise. My chin pulls back in confusion. If this is some new Shen fashion, and it's not a good one.

I look down at my red silk nightdress, the gold sash so tight I can barely breathe. They pinned me down to put a test color on my lips, which I have since wiped on my sleeve.

"Where's Ash?" I ask, my head jingling from the two fox hairpins stuck in my hair.

She frowns, creasing her round, white face. "Aren't you going to comment on my crown?" She tips her face left to right. "Don't mind the face paint. We haven't decided which color to go with yet. What do you think?" She caresses her face with gold, ring-crusted fingers.

"Where is Ash," I repeat. Telling her she looks like a water buffalo probably isn't the wisest thing to do.

She pauses, red heat creeping up her unpainted neck, which is several tones darker than her face. "Mind your manners in front of the emperor's bride," she snaps, pointing at me with sharpened nails.

"Touch me," I growl. "I dare you." Heat sparks behind my eyes and flames burn in her hands.

Her finger curls in like a slater tortoise retracting into its shell. "He is safe. Though you may not recognize him when you see him tomorrow. They peeled several layers of dirt from that Shen's skin."

My fists tighten and I step toward her. "As long as that's all you did."

She lifts the jingling crown from her head and places it on the velvet bench at the end of the bed, rubbing her scalp. "Don't threaten me. If you wish to save your grotty little children, you best do as you're told." My fingers stretch, fields of tornado moths buzzing in my capillaries, ready to shred her skin and pull the meat from her bones. She purses her lips and stares, a new kind of evil dazzles in her eyes. "Or I could order them to be disposed of now."

Hickory beats so loud I worry it can be heard through my chest. "No. Please. I will do what you ask." I force myself to relax.

"You should be grateful. I've provided you with this luxurious room. Had you bathed and sent you a fine dress to wear." *Grateful?* This gold and red velvet box they've put me in feels no more comfortable than the damp rock walls of the palace belly. Less so. But I manage to nod my head and shuffle back until I'm sitting on the edge of the bed.

Soo Si scuttles closer and juts her face far too close to my own. "Now, tell me. Purple or green?" She winks her elaborate eyes in turn.

My lips purse with disgust and my eyes roll. "The purple makes you look like you just sparred with a potato-fisted foe and lost."

Soo Si laughs. It's a cackling false thing, like a lying bird's call. "I appreciate your honesty, Char-Shen." Her expression says otherwise. It says *I want to twist your arm until it breaks. I want to scratch your eyes and rip your ears.* She taps her chin. "Maybe you can help me with another task I've been struggling with."

What else could this horrible woman want? "I think you've asked enough of me." The rich, emerald-green bedspread gathers around my small backside as I shift uncomfortably on the mattress.

Her eyes are black as coal but have an oily shine. They dart like a snake. "You need to cooperate. I am not above a little more torture to get what I want," she hisses.

Believing every word, I stand. "What do you want?"

She grasps my shoulder and pinches hard. The grip of something scaly and dark and bent on death. "To lie in a bed the size of a peasant's home, *alone*." she whispers to herself, a squint in her eye that almost looks like pain. But then she laughs, half chokes on the force of it, and barks, "Come with me."

She drags me by my clothes into the hallway. Flying down the stairs like a demon who has stolen wings. The guards chase after us, trying to keep up, but Soo Si is fast and agile. Barely panting a breath as she opens doors and weaves left and right. She finally stops at double doors carved with the Shen symbol of five elements. Air, Water, Fire, Earth, and Blood. I place my hand on the paw symbol for Blood. Feel it like a heartbeat against my skin.

Soo Si orders two guards to slide the large wooden barricade away from the door. It groans and scratches the carvings. Dust floats to the floor. These doors haven't been opened in a very long time.

She pushes and they resist like she isn't welcome. "Hand me a candle," she snaps. A guard retrieves one from the wall sconce.

Small light reveals a great hall full of stacked furniture: dusty painted vases as tall as a person and tapestries laid across marble tables. A furry layer of dust and old air is on every item. I cough. It smells musty and old, like a coffin.

Soo Si beckons me inside. "I would have had one of my own carved, but that takes months. And we don't have that kind of time."

I follow her inside while guards stand to attention at the door. "Yes, I noticed your hurry to get this marriage over and done with when I saw servants hanging wedding garlands over the funeral decorations."

She huffs, winding around tables, avoiding vases painted with beautiful women and cherry trees. Large platters decorated with willows of sadness and regret hanging over crystal clear ponds. "At least I don't have to worry about that drugged old bat any longer. And although the emperor is blue, I have many ways to make him forget." She smiles self-congratulatorily, sticking out her chest, and I shudder at her possible methods of distraction.

I don't know why I'm following this serpent of a woman so I stop. Wondering how much I can fight back and how much I must give. My hand brushes against a tapestry. In the sparse light, I make out Char islands woven into deep, sapphire blue. Green bumps stand out strong and striking with white capped waves hugging the coasts. They're waiting for me to come home. My heart beats like a Char drum, stretching to the sea. I close my eyes and inhale salt air, hear the crash of the waves against the pylons. Memories may be all I will have, but they are full and wild, and almost enough.

Soo Si's irritatingly shrill voice pierces and dashes my dream. "Aha! There they are. Come here, Blood child!"

I walk around the table, finger dragging through thick dust. Soo Si holds her candle up to several large objects, tongue clucking. "Wa! So many to choose from." She taps her sticky red lips with delight.

"What in the stars?" I exclaim. My mind jumps from face to face. I know those carved cheekbones. I have bowed before those wise eyes. I thump my chest, the Char action making Soo Si's nostrils flare. For stacked haphazardly, arms and legs linked together in a precarious balancing act, are the nine Carvresses. Or in the Shen world, the nine Chow princesses. Their perfect faces stare from the backs of nine thrones. Sadness sweeps over me as I find the Carvress of Cockle Fan Island, who fell to her death so many weeks ago.

Soo Si holds her candle to each carved likeness. "Which one looks the most like me, Luna Yan?" She touches their cheeks and pokes their eyes, and I wish I could launch at her and scream, "Get your hands off my Carvresses." But I bear her vanity. The truth being they are not my Carvresses alone. They belong to the Shen too. It certainly feels strange and uncomfortable to think of them that way though.

"Shei-Shei looks most like you." Her younger, rounder face suits the greedy bride and that is all. Soo Si cannot compare to the princesses. The concubine is beautiful, but her pinched, gluttonous heart pulls lines across her forehead and scrunches her mouth. She is wholly unworthy to sit on Shei-Shei's throne despite the Carvress's crimes.

Soo Si's head snaps to me. "Who is Shei-Shei?" Her eyes narrow. I could speak again of the Carvresses and their right to the throne, but I wonder what good it would do.

I climb up to reach the throne, tangled between two others. Si-fah, the Carvress of Coalstone Island, stares proudly. The woman I see didn't know her brother was about to betray her. She didn't understand what her life would look like nine hundred years onward. "This one," I say, tapping Shei-Shei's face.

I hope they are safe. I pray there are things happening outside these sandstone walls that are brighter and better. But these feel like watery dreams. Easily drained away.

Soo Si peers at the carving. Assessing its attractiveness. "She's a bit plumper than me, but yes, this will do nicely."

She claps her hands and the guards come to retrieve the throne.

Weeks ago, I had hoped these thrones would be filled by their rightful owners, even as I worried the Char could lose themselves in the process. But it's been too long. I can't hold out hope that they're coming. It's an empty dream and fret now. A luxury to think about the repercussions of such a takeover. It's not going to happen. The best I can hope for now is Ash and the children to get away safely.

Soo Si jumps up and down gleefully as guards carry the throne from the enormous storeroom. She pinches my elbow hard. "From this throne, I will lead the Shen empire into an age of wealth and power never seen before. Even if I have to work every peasant to the bone to do it." She winks at me like her next words are not the most immoral and conniving ever spoken. "And when those farmers have worked to their last breath, well, there's always their children, right?"

And I am to help her achieve her despicable goal. My stomach bucks and twists. Strange guilt runs charcoal stains across my hickory heart. I never thought I'd live in a world where I felt guilt toward the Shen. But then, I never thought I'd be here in the palace, about to murder their emperor.

47

LYE

A THOUSAND FRIENDS

They were sleeping, dreaming of a better future. The reality of arrows and swords has broken that dream. Shen soldiers killing their own people.

Joka falls to the ground, clutching his neck as Sun rushes to his brother's side. I search for Ki Anah but can't find her. I pray to the stars she has survived. Joka coughs and rolls to the side. The screaming grows so loud it's all I can hear.

I am an empty shell filled with the howling wind of the sea.

"General Lye," Sun says in a too-calm voice. "We're under attack." He takes a hold of the arrow embedded in his brother. "I count twenty Shen soldiers. Five each of Air, Earth, Fire and Water."

Joka isn't moving. I reach for him but can't bring myself to touch. I can't feel the coldness of another dead Yan boy. I can't look at his vacant eyes. It's too much. And it's Joka. *And I just can't.* The screaming grows hoarse, as if it can't sustain itself.

Jing Ha places a hand on my shoulder and I spin around. Her eyes are sympathetic. Earth pulses from her body in wave of warmth and shelter. "General." She peers into my eyes, trying to find something. A pinprick of hope. A flash of leadership. But if Joka is—I can't even think it—"General!" Her voice is harsher now. Like a mother scolding her child. "You need to stop."

Stop what?

Sun hasn't looked up from his brother, but he mutters as arrows whir past our heads, "I think we can be sure of her feelings now, brother." Humor in his voice.

The screaming stops.

I grasp my throat. The screaming was coming from me.

Joka sits up, pushing his brother away. "Don't you dare touch it. I don't trust your clumsy hands." The arrow moves in the bamboo as he talks.

I shuffle toward him on my knees. "You're alive," I manage, embarrassingly throwing my arms in the air.

Joka smiles and points at his miraculous neck. "I am, but could you help me get this out? It pinches." His eyes dart to the riverbank where hundreds of peasants mill, frightened and unprotected. "Quickly!"

"You won't bleed?" I ask, as I grasp the arrow.

Joka shakes his head very carefully. "It's shallow. I won't bleed."

I close my eyes, ears filled with sounds of panic and protection. Mothers and fathers standing in front of their children. Young Shen shielding elders. Char soldiers ordering Shen to get behind them.

I open my eyes and pull carefully. The arrow slides out of Joka's neck like it was lodged in a target not a person. He pats the sappy hole and sighs with relief. His eyes connect with mine and top up my bravery. I stand. "Follow me!" I order to the Char and Carvresses.

We tear through huddled peasants to the frontline. The Carvresses link arms and create a shield and we fall in beside them. Arrows are notched as Shen ones fly at us and land in the Carvresses wooden bodies. We fire but the arrows fall short, piercing the grass. We follow the wooden princesses as they move forward rather than running away. The Shen don't approach, staying out of a sword's reach but now close enough for an arrow. They stand between us and the palace.

I shoot straight into the chest of an Air Shen, red blooming over his white robe.

"Stay behind us, subjects. We will not desert you," Sifah shouts. "We will not retreat either. We outnumber them fifty to one." She steps forward. "Keep marching."

Shen peasants gather behind the Carvresses, chanting a song I haven't heard for a long time. Not since before I was the Keeper. An ancient anthem that was banned from use before I was born. Because it doesn't praise a supreme leader. It doesn't hold one up over all others.

A land of deepest canyons and highest mountains
Of evergreen forests and dust deserts
Beautiful and wild.
Stone and wood.
We owe much to this country
Our debt can never be repaid
But it is our country
It holds our debt in its heart like a promise
A promise we must keep.

Arrows soar like diving peril birds, trying to find their way in. The Carvresses lift their arms and some arrows land deep in their wooden appendages. I know it causes some pain from the small cries that don't match the strong war cry they continue shouting. But they can't stop them all.

People fall. But they are lifted, tended to. I finally find Ki Anah, using Blood power and Char courage to help the wounded. Mei is with her, rounding the elderly and children together and keeping them in the back.

The group keeps marching forward.

The Shen soldiers appear confused and rattled. They stumble back as the group presses on. We fire more arrows, immobilizing several.

The Shen peasants won't surrender. But they are dying. They may think it a worthy sacrifice, but I do not. Even if the palace is at the edge of morning.

Another rain of arrows flies at us. I duck as one clips my ear, replying with my own shot. "Sifah," I call to the tall Carvress with wooden eyes that have turned to stone. "We need to protect the people."

Her chin dips. She knows what I mean. She puts a fisted hand in the air and cries to her sisters. I hand Joka my quiver and bow and don't give him time to speak or to stop me.

"I order you to stay with the peasants. Protect them at all costs."

Joka and Sun bow. Jing Ha salutes. "Yes, General."

The Carvresses charge, swords in hands, and I run beside them. Trying to focus and not get caught in the awe-striking sight of seven wooden women. Fierce and brutal and clear in their need to protect the people streaming toward the Shen soldiers like a wave. A terrible and powerful wave that will wash away any resistance. But lives will be lost. I can't have their blood on my hands.

I turn back as Shei-Shei screams, straining against Sun's grip, "Let me go with my sisters!" He holds her tight. The birchwood girl takes Shei-Shei's hand and the princess goes slack in Sun's arms.

We, women of immense strength and gifts, thud the earth. Our powers baffle soldiers and scatter them like cast seeds. They scramble, they stumble, they fall. They quiver at the hands of the mighty Chow princesses and the girl who *was* everything and nothing. But is now Keeper, Char general, sister and friend. I am so much more than my torturers and captors could comprehend. It feels right, fighting at their side. Like I was always here with these women as their missing piece.

The cork carving blossoms into a complicated tree, with leaves like weather patterns and flames, branches of wood that live long after it has been cut.

I sweep and spin. Sending cracks of lightning and snaps of turtles. I do not kill. I injure and disarm. I follow my fellow warriors' example. Spilling blood is my preference but I am learning a new way.

Mi Asha, ebony dark and rumbling like a storm cloud, holds a Fire Shen off the ground by his arm. He spins like plucked chicken. "Tell the emperor as the sun rises over the rust red palace, the Chow sisters will return home."

The soldiers are disarmed and dismayed. Broken and bleeding. Some run. Some surrender, bowing to the Carvresses like they've found a new god. I call my Char to bind them. We have no time to interrogate, but I ask one question. "How did you know we were here?"

A Water Shen shakes his head, eyes following the wooden women as they throw men aside like sacks of sugar. "You think you could start a rebellion and the emperor wouldn't know? He is waiting for you, Keeper. And so is the rest of his army." His spits at my feet.

"You mean what's left of his army after the battle of Black Sail City," Joka corrects, his finger running over the splinter hole in his neck.

"You mean after we destroyed your city?" The Water Shen smiles gruesomely with a mouth cornered with blood.

Joka swings his fist at the Shen, knocking him out and getting a frozen hand for his trouble. Ki Anah clasps her hand over his fist, taking quickly to the healing power of Blood.

"A rebellion." I roll the word around in my mouth and enjoy the taste.

The Carvresses keep marching. Stepping over bound Shen soldiers and yanking arrows from their arms like they're splinters. The mountain jungle closes around us. Palm leaves stroking our arms and encouraging us to push upward to the palace.

To think I tumbled down this mountain and into the sea, desperate to escape, only to be stomping determinedly back up many months later, ready to force my way in.

There is a difference. Now I have a thousand friends at my back.

48
LUNA

A UNION OF SNAKE AND CHARMER

"Are Shen weddings always like this?" I ask, leaning closer to Ash, who has been stuffed into a stiff, formal outfit with exaggerated shoulders and flaps of blue running down his chest to his knees.

Ash doesn't turn, watching the couple standing at the front of the room. The twelve-inch-high gold and purple hat does nothing to distract from the emperor's bloodshot, puffy eyes. Soo Si looks like a child at a buffet. "No, they're not. For starters, people usually wait until the mother of the groom's body is cold before rushing to the altar." They've placed us conspicuously close to the front, probably so they can keep an eye on us. I shift uncomfortably. We're hemmed in by guards on both sides.

The decorations are clashing and tacky. Pinks and golds mixed with emerald greens and purple. Hastily made silk flowers randomly scattered over benches and above our heads. The only beautiful part of this ceremony is Mulia. She sits at the emperor's side, her head nuzzling his hip, more regal than the bride and groom. The emperor's hands are in her ruff, and he scrunches her fur when the monk lifts his shears to slice a lock of hair from his mane. I reach for Mulia, sensing sadness as she takes on her master's grief. Even if their bond was formed through harsh treatment and kidnapping, there's still a softness to their relationship. It brings a prickle of doubt to my fingertips. A scratch that doesn't draw blood—yet.

There are few in attendance other than army officials. Soo Si's father stands on the opposite side, expression severe and surprisingly disapproving. He eyes the emperor with disgust, and I guess the groom's not helping his case by sniveling and shaking like a toddler.

"So there's no shell?" I whisper, receiving a poke with the point of a dagger from the guard at my side.

Ash wiggles in his fancy Water Shen dress. "Shell?" His hair is tightly braided, and it looks… odd. Unkempt and wild is all I've ever seen on him. I suppose this is what he looked like when he lived at the palace.

The monk drones. Humming a prayer I don't understand. "At the end of a Char wedding, the elder pours sea water over the couples' joined hands from a shell the couple finds on the beach together." I close my eyes, remembering the last wedding I attended. Sea spray salting the bride's simple raw silk wrap. The couple actually looking like they loved each other. Ben Ni squeezing my hand and gazing all romantic at the pair. I breathe out slowly. Trying not to detach myself from the memory. Pain accompanies joy and that doesn't make the memory any less beautiful.

Ash bows his head as the monk cuts a piece of hair from Soo Si's dark bun and she hisses at him to be careful. "I like that. Very Char." He lifts his head and turns slightly so I see the waves breaking in his ocean eyes. "Maybe we can have a hybrid wedding. Combine traditions."

I blush and then the blush dies. Dropping from my cheeks like a disappointing sunset. There's no wedding in our future. Only separation. But I force a smile. His finger brushes against my hand and I allow the warmth and promise to fill me. Even if it's false and will drain away like a broken dam.

The pagoda is enclosed and cold air bats at the canvas walls. There's no music, only the flat monotone of the monk in front. He holds the two pieces of hair to the sky and then binds them with a silk cord.

The emperor releases Mulia and clasps hands with Soo Si, whose smile is as sweet and treacherous as rancid syrup. I pity him gazing at her with admiration and promise. He pins things on the concubine he shouldn't. He mimics her actions, bending to her like an obedient servant awaiting instructions. That thorn of doubt works deeper into my skin.

Yes, he is weak, pathetic almost. But is he deserving of death?

I remind myself, whether influenced or not, he ordered attack after attack on our people. He trusted and authorized the doctor and the chancellor to torture. Whether he knew about the children or not, a bad leader comes in many forms. Ignorance of what one's delegates are doing could be one of the most dangerous of all.

The monk takes their joined hands and lifts them over his head, pronouncing them married. "Long live the emperor and empress!" the small group shouts. At the word "empress," Soo Si's lips stretch into a feline smile. Mulia growls, giving off an Atmosphere of distrust. The new empress's eyes dart to the creature. She whispers something to her husband, and he tugs on the tiger wolf's collar hard and stomps on her paw. The tiger wolf whines and lies down.

The wind outside protests too, howling and moaning and— humming?

Ash's hand grasps mine and the guards are too distracted by the sound of several sets of footsteps thudding against the stone outside to notice. Everyone, including the imperial couple, twist to the entrance of the pagoda. Dirty and injured soldiers stream past, words fly up and to the sky before I catch them, but then a Fire Shen runs through the center of the space, leaving muddy boot prints on the plush carpet. He falls to his knees at the royal couples' feet.

Soo Si steps forward. "You better have an excellent excuse for interrupting the royal wedding!" she spits between her clenched fangs. Torture dances in her eyes, sharp and unforgiving.

The bowed soldier, robes of orange, fire pulsing from his fingers, and blood streaming down his face like paint, approaches the empress on his knees. She steps down from the altar, leaving her husband standing there clueless, so the soldier can whisper in her ear. Her painted-on eyebrows rise high. "Already?" she exclaims, and gathers her skirts, stomping hurriedly down the aisle. Her husband trails after her, elegant but empty. Theirs is a union of snake and charmer. We all know the snake is simply biding its time to strike.

Just as she's about to exit, she curls around suddenly and points at Ash and me. "Take the prisoners to the throne room, now!"

WE'RE SHACKLED and dragged through the palace, hope and fear colliding like reed stems in a storm. I strain to see out the window. At least a hundred Shen soldiers holding shields higher than themselves are linked together in a barrier cuff around the palace. If there is someone out there, they won't be able to get through.

I exchange a worried glance with Ash, unsure of what this means, and if it changes anything at all.

49

LYE

WAIT

It looks dirty," Ki Anah states, a disapproving gaze running up and down the dark, bloodlike stains creeping up the stones of palace. "Like dried blood."

"It's not, is it?" Guen asks, birchwood bones rattling with worry.

I smile a half moon smile, waiting for the shadow to lessen. "No, it's not blood. It's iron leeching up from the soil."

Joka's concerned voice coasts over my shoulder, lips so very close to my ear. "Well, they definitely seem to know we're here." He points at the growing line of shielded soldiers doing what they've been trained to do: create a protective band around the palace.

I feel like a mirage standing in front of the place where I granted powers that were used only to rage horrible war. Earth, Water, Wind and so much Fire sent to kill but often extinguished themselves. All in the name of the emperor. I bear death on both sides, so heavy it almost crushes me. As soon as the sun moves, I shall dissolve.

The Coalstone Carvress places a wooden hand on my shoulder. "It has changed since we fled so many years ago, but not as much as I would have thought. Tell me, Keeper Lye Li, what is this emperor like?"

I describe the young man I came to know. Cruel when surrounded by cruelty, kind when surrounded by kindness. Weak and reliant on others to make decisions. Spoiled by privilege and position. The Carvress nods her head like she is very familiar with this type of man. Her head tilts to the earth with sorrow, a small dewdrop of sap wetting her splinter eyelashes. "I see. Not much has changed at all."

When we chased the soldiers to the edge of the jungle, we let them enter the palace to deliver our message. Their response collars the palace.

Over a thousand peasants settle among the evergreens and moss. They're used to basic living conditions. They know how to live off the land.

I stand on a rock and address the camps of families and villagers. "Thank you, my friends, for coming this far with us. I bid you to wait now. Wait until we can devise a way into the palace that avoids bloodshed."

Someone shouts, "What if we're attacked?"

The Carvress of Black Sail City answers, "Then we will protect you."

I shake my head. We can fight off twenty soldiers, but even a depleted Shen army contains hundreds of trained soldiers. I watch the villagers, some possessing Char and Shen powers, kneeling to flatten the ground to build a shelter, or reaching up to gather the few frosty berries left on the trees. I shiver. We cannot stay here indefinitely.

The Yans huddle around me as the barrier grows in front of the palace doors and dark heads of archers gather over the parapets. Sun points at the lines of Shen peasants taking over the forest like spot fires. "Even I know this would be a one-sided fight not worth fighting. We have the numbers, but these are not soldiers."

Joka's hand finds mine. I send anxious paddling feet at him. A duck desperately scrambling to get to the edge of the pond before it freezes over. "That's the point, brother. They're not warriors. They're farmers with their families. They have the most to lose if this doesn't work."

I sigh. "Thanks for reminding me."

Mei, accompanied by a woman, softly interrupts our meeting. I turn to a middle-aged face. Crinkles in the eyes and dark, sun-kissed skin. "Ga Lo has some news to share, Lye."

"Keeper, I mean General, I mean—" She stumbles over her words. Being everything means people don't quite know how to address me.

"Lye Li is just fine." I smile.

She bows quickly. "Lye Li. More are coming."

The rest of the group spin around. "More?"

Guen swings Sun's arm, her pale, birchwood eyes have fire in them. "More Shen, more peasants?" she chirps.

The woman nods. "The miners to the east heard about the Chow princesses' wish to claim the throne. They've also heard the Keeper is awakening Elements in humble peasants. They want to help."

A heart bird of red smoke rises in my chest. Something bigger than hope: destiny. "How many?" I want to simply ask *how*, but I don't want to test our fortune.

She stares at my sycamore arm, fascinated rather than disgusted. A green aura of desire floats about her unkempt head of hair, black as bats and thick as a horse's mane. "I can't be exactly sure, but it must be thousands. These last few months the Shen have suffered greatly because of the palace's endless demands." She holds up her hand, fingers crushed and mangled. My lips press with sympathy. "Trampled by my oxen," she explains. "To keep up with orders, I had to plow at night." Her head falls in shame. "I knew better, but I was so tired. So very hungry. I needed to meet the harvest requirements, or I wouldn't get my rations."

Mei places a hand on her shoulder squeezing. "This is not your fault."

I tilt my head and smile. "Mei is right. None of this is your fault."

The Carvress of Cockle Fan Island blinks at the woman and bends down to her. "I can help if you would like." The Shen woman looks to Mei, who has quickly become somewhat of a leader, for reassurance. Mei nods and they walk away. A wooden hand is in the woman's future.

My eyes lift to the palace again. A tight barrier surrounds the building. It's standard protection procedure. Even though we outnumber them, many would die if we attacked and I can't let that happen. I cannot become more scar than woman. As I scan Shen Atmospheres, faint from this distance, unease ripples through the forest. A deer walking on thin ice. They are hesitant, and none of them are trained to kill their own.

I step toward the eight-foot-high shields. Sunlight bounces off the metal like violent starbursts.

One foot and then another.

Someone catches my arm. "Lye Li Koh, wait!" Wood tightens like a trap.

I shake my head. "What good will waiting do?" I throw my sense outward, trying to latch onto Luna and Ash, but I can't get past the row of soldiers. Soldiers who read of confusion like ants that have had their line disturbed and don't know which way to go. "I've waited long enough." I need to see my brother.

Sifah steps closer, her voice is a lullaby to my anxiousness. "At least wait until more Shen arrive from the east. With greater numbers, we have more power to negotiate." She nods to the cuff around the palace. "They are also waiting. Let's not give them a reason to move closer just yet."

The Carvresses all nod their heads in agreement.

I am forced to comply. I know they are right. But in my mind, I storm the palace. I walk right up the emperor, take him by his purple silk collar, and demand to see my brother and Luna. When he refuses, I torch his insides until his eyeballs turn to charred pieces of coal.

50
LUNA

CANNOT WAIT

A stone rolls down the mountain. Its pace too fast and its path too unpredictable. Something is happening, but from our guarded positions in the throne room, I'm not sure it moves fast enough to change our fates. We're living in a horrible but very real bubble. Any dreams of floating out and over this situation is just that: a dream.

The emperor strides into the room in streams of wedding gold and purple silk that remind me of a dying orchid. Mulia flanks him, as does a senior officer. Soo Si clatters behind them on wooden heels, cheeks punched with rouge, waxy face paint melting as Fire grows within.

"We should attack, should we not?" the emperor asks the Earth officer as he climbs the stairs and sits in his throne like a child on a toy he's scared will be taken from him. Soo Si scrambles to take her place beside him, gathering up her skirts and plonking into her throne. Wiggling her skinny butt like she's settling into a nest. Shei-Shei's face floats above the pinched-faced concubine, making her look plain by comparison.

"But most of them are Shen, emperor," the Earth Shen replies hesitantly.

The guard, watching us and ready to grab our chains should we become unruly, becomes distracted by the conversation.

"You're right," the emperor says, scratching his perfect chin. "We should not kill our own." Mulia straightens. I throw test strands of control, asking her to tilt her head to one side. She abides.

The Earth Shen officer shuffles closer, then turns to Ash and me kneeling on the carpet warily. "Your imperial majesty, may I approach?" The emperor nods while Soo Si looks like her eyes might pop out of their sockets. Her plan is unravelling as her control falters.

Soo Si leans forward, headdress slipping over her forehead. "You may approach and address both your emperor *and* empress."

He climbs the platform and whispers something in her ear that causes her to half rise from her seat like there are strings pulling from above. But then she swallows slowly, composes herself and passes the information on to the emperor. He doesn't hide his panic well. He turns to his wife. "What do you think we should do, my love?"

Ash and I *feel* each other's confusion. Two stories are playing alongside each other. But we only know how to read the one in front of us. The one that reads *kill the emperor and free the Char children.*

Soo Si's eyes narrow to me as she says, "I think you need a moment to calm yourself, darling. Whatever is going on outside the palace walls is not your concern." She flicks a jeweled hand, bangles jingling like warning bells at the pigsty door. "Let the army take care of it. Today is our wedding day and I have a very special gift for you."

Ash's eyes are sea storms, his lips as flat as an unreachable horizon. His chin twitches, neither yes nor no, because he knows it's too late. There are no plans left to make. This is it. I reach for Mulia, wrapping my influence around her consciousness tightly. I test it again by opening and closing her jaws and lifting her paws one by one. She can't resist me. I overpower and consume her will. Her lips curl, teeth showing in a peculiar, uncontrolled smile, like a demon who knows only violence.

"But they are my subjects," the young man dripping in opulence and wrapped in weakness starts, gripping the edge of his throne like it may float away. "I'm not sure this is the—"

Soo Si rises with her temper. "You're never sure! You have the will and strength of an earthworm," she spits. "At least an earthworm serves a purpose!" The officer steps back quickly, like he's watching a powder keg about to explode. "If there are Shen farmers protesting out there, threaten them. Kill some to keep the rest in line. There!" She stomps her foot. "Problem solved."

The emperor half frowns at her insults, half slackens like he's relieved she's taking over. My lip curls. He is the most pitiful, pathetic creature I've ever met. Soo Si is right; he has less worth than an earthworm. Anger bubbles like boiling mud. *I hate him.* Ash keeps his eyes on the royal pair. Expression level but his fists are tightly scrunched. His Atmosphere is a wall of ice, a shield against what is to come.

Yes, the emperor is despicable and undeserving of the throne.

I flick my fingers subtly and Mulia rises from her place beside the monarch and pads quietly behind the two thrones.

Soo Si smiles toothily, sickeningly excited about the moment ahead. I almost expect her to clap with giddy glee. I suppose she may afterward. After I kill him. Bile rises up my throat. He would execute his own people. He would listen to this vile woman and allow her to influence his every decision. His weakness shames his country. He cannot, should not, be leader.

Mulia's cobalt claws extend. Between the throne legs, she leans back on her haunches, ready to pounce. Ash shuffles closer. Our shoulders grazing. I *feel* him telling me it's all right. I have his support.

I close my eyes, heat and death and power swirling about my heart. But it beats strong. It lets murder in as it would love. It is the unbiased observer. Disconnected from moral judgement. I murmur to the beautiful tiger wolf, "I'm so sorry." And then my hickory heart rules so I can do what I must. I flick my hand. A blur of gray and black, and the tiger wolf attacks. Ripping open the jugular in one awful and awe-inspiring move. Blood flowing like a freed river.

Yes, I hate him.

But her hate will destroy our world.

Ash gasps and the emperor is struck dumb, mouth opening and closing. A fish taking its last breaths.

There's no scream. Soo Si is dead in gurgling seconds, blood decorating her wedding gown as vivid and vulgar as the tacky garlands hanging over the throne. Her plan, our deal, dying along with her.

I release Mulia from my influence and she licks her blood-soaked lips, shaking her head like she has a bug in her velvet ear. She places a paw on the emperor's lap, leaving a streak of red on his wedding robes. He stares down at it and then at me, a realization finally coming on its own.

He points shakily, while the guards gape and gasp. "You did this."

Mulia growls at her former master. Even though I released her, a closeness has formed between us, something that winds over the top of the emperor's bond, because it is formed from respect.

I don't deny his accusation. "I did you a favor."

Ash stands. "Listen to her!" His eyes beg, his body is straight and proud.

The guards look in confusion from us to the throne, uncertain of which direction they need to run.

The emperor clutches the dead empress's hand and pulls. Soo Si's body slides from the throne, painted eyes still open. I turn away. I know it was the right thing to do, but I can't look at her lifeless face without regret. Violence and death should never be easy. My heart beats like a clock, but I feel around it. I let anguish in.

With his wife hanging from his grasp, blood waterfalling down the throne steps, he orders me to death with the flick of a hand.

The guards spring to action, taking up my chains and dragging me away. I slip and fall but they continue to pull me like trawling bait. I allow it. My hands dry but feeling soaked in blood. Behind me, Ash yells, "Wait!" At the first thud of spear shaft whacking flesh, I fight to look back. Guards club his barely healed body. Turning scars to wounds. My fight snaps back like a bow string. I kick and scratch, not fighting for my own life but fighting for his.

"Ash!" I scream, running toward him but unable to overpower so many men at once. They yank the iron hard, and I fall, chin first, splitting the skin and my heart.

I am dragged from the room, eyes blurry with tears and murder, but my focus is Ash's eyes of brightest blue and a saltwater smile. He speaks words I *need* to hold on to. Words that follow me even though he can't. "I'll be right behind you."

I'm slammed against the doorframe, just as I *feel* him sending me a message: A memory of Ash as a child, coming home to a mother with open arms. He wishes me to get the children now.

The emperor asks a question I cannot make out, and brief exchange follows before Ash's voice, loud and clear and *oh so* slow, tells the story of a scheming concubine. I'm sure he won't believe Ash, but it's not about that. He is buying me time. Words are the coins and Ash is counting them out into the emperor's palm piece by piece.

I call to Mulia while the emperor attention is on my love. I sense her padding behind me, tongue out, droplets of the empress's blood soaking into the carpet. Her golden knife eyes on the four guards' backs.

51

ASH

A NECESSARY KNIFE TEST

The emperor holds his bride awkwardly. Pressing her limp, red-spattered hands to her chest only to have them slide right off again. The shock of the change in plans brews like a hungry cloud over my head. Luna killed Soo Si. When she had the chance to kill the emperor, she didn't do it. It was clear Soo Si was the greater evil. She had nothing but greedy, dark intentions for the Shen. Luna is an eclipse to a black sun. She blocked the greatest evil.

I breathe in a sigh of relief as I watch the tiger wolf softly slip behind the emperor and out the door. Luna will get the children. They will have a shot. At least I can give them that.

I glance down at the sniveling, lost emperor. I wonder what will become of him without his shadow influence. With the way he stares into her dead eyes, I'm guessing he will seek to replace her. He's like a bird to a buffalo's back. A parasite. Unable to survive without a beast to do his dirty work.

The emperor turns to me, seeming to just realize I'm still here. "Shen traitor, explain what she meant. How could this…" he attempts unsuccessfully to stifle a cry, gesturing to the blood and carnage surrounding the throne. "Be a favor? You have one minute before I condemn you to death like the girl."

"I don't need more," I reply, trying to sound firm, confident. Everything he is not.

He lifts Soo Si's body, her hair pins jingling happily atop her lolling, lifeless head, and hands her to a remaining guard. "Take my wife to the infirmary." His hands drop. "And tell *her* she may enter, unarmed and alone." His mouth twists at that last word, and I wonder who he's talking about.

He settles into his throne as I'm dragged forward and dumped at his feet. The chains dig into my skin, but I'm used to working around such things. I think of the room I shared with Luna; the chains did nothing to strangle what grew between us. I think now there is no chain, weapon or obstacle that could.

"Leave us," the emperor orders with his eyes red and his chin tilted as if ashamed of his own grief. The guards depart, and he opens his palm and invites me to speak as he wipes away a thin tear.

I begin. "Emperor, Soo Si, your bride, was plotting to murder you." The emperor's eyebrows rise slightly, and he begins pulling the decorations from his head and fingers, letting them fall like discarded pebbles to the floor. *Tink. Tink. Tink.*

"You're a liar," he says, surprisingly calm. "She loved me. I was ready to give her everything. She had no reason to."

I need to take my time. Stall like the wolf waiting for the rest of its pack. Give Luna as much time as possible so she can get away safely. "You heard the way she spoke to you just before her death. She despised you." I look up into a confused expression. An "I don't want to believe it even though I know it's true" expression.

I *feel* Luna slipping out of reach. It's a good thing since it means she's closer to the children.

"I am the emperor. One cannot despise the emperor. It's against the law. My ancestors were chosen by the Elements. The first emperor was a Keeper." He stands angrily. "Soo Si *loved* me."

His voice compresses, smaller and smaller like a bird underfoot. "She loved me."

I bow my head, knowing my words are twisting a knife in his heart, but they are necessary. "She did not love you. She loved power. And you stood in her way."

"She's *just* a woman. She wanted only to be my wife. To please me." I try not to, but a sour laugh escapes my lips, and the emperor's face twists to a scowl.

I push the dagger in as far as it will go. "Emperor, she murdered your mother. She had half the guard in her pockets. She has made you a fool."

Flames light in the emperor's eyes. Shame. Grief. Betrayal. He is losing face. He is losing respect. To him, this is unacceptable.

Luna, please. *Go.*

52

LUNA

GO

Mulia wishes to growl as she witnesses my mistreatment, but I ask her to stay quiet. To make as little noise as possible while she rips into the guards' ankles and tosses them against the wall. She lunges, a stunning crack as she breaks the first guard's leg and sends him flying across the hall.

Qi Sha barely has time to gasp before he too is disabled in a bone-crunching, blood-spurting way. They roll about, moaning as I get to my feet and snatch the keys to my shackles. The unlocked chains hit Qi Sha's chest with a satisfying thud.

"I will let you live if you shut your mouths." I stretch my fingers wide. Qi Sha snarls and unsurprisingly, his lips pull back ready to shout. Sho Sen clamps his hand over the soldier's mouth to stop him. "I guess I will shut them for you." I kneel, hands on both their bare legs and send sleeping viper venom. For Qi Sha, I add a deep fang bite. Their eyes close and they are silent.

I look back, willing Ash to appear. *Right behind me. He should be right behind me.* I *feel* him, repeating those words. But they're just words. His footsteps are not echoing down the hallway. His eyes are not on mine. I can't breathe but I must. I want to scream but I can't. My fear must be folded into bravery right now. My heart must pulse forward and down to the belly of the palace. Mulia stoops, front legs folded, nose pointed to the ground almost as if she is bowing to me. I run my hand over the gray diamond between her ears, between her shoulders, then grab her ruff and swing myself onto her back. The great beast's ribs expand and contract under my legs. Her fur is as soft as duck down at her skin and as bristled as wire on the outside. She puffs air from her black nose. She is terrible and powerful and ready to maul. I press into her fur and whisper, "Run, Mulia."

I sense Ash pushing me on. *Luna, go.* We press on. Galloping levels, Mulia taking the steps flights at a time, tongue hanging out, panting like a pup, until I *feel* him no longer.

A sorry guard gets caught in our descension and Mulia snaps, taking a piece out of his arm without breaking stride. She is magnificent and I'm privileged to be carried by her strong legs.

The iron gate vibrates with the sounds of frightened, hungry children.

"Luna!" they shout. "Ash!"

"Everyone come to me now!" I yell, wrangling with the large bunch of keys, trying to find the right one. They stream up the stairs, stopping suddenly at the sight of the terrible Mulia, blood staining her muzzle. "Ah *tidak masalah*, it's okay, I promise. She's on our side."

One child reaches through the bars to touch the great wolf and I remind Mulia to be gentle. She licks the little girl's hand, making her giggle. It's a wonderful sound, but a sound we have no time for. The lock finally opens, and children swarm us like blood fish around a rock.

"Where are we going?" Ha Fun asks.

Deep breath in. Hickory times my words like seconds. Saying them out loud makes a statement I must live up to. "We're going home."

The children cheer. They slip and fall as they pant like their lungs have forgotten how to breathe. But they are stronger than anyone gave them credit for, and they follow me as I ride Mulia to the ground level. The older ones are carrying or holding hands with the younger ones, helping them along.

We make it to the carpeted levels, and we are a glorious stain on the nice fabric. I half hope the children are really working their grimy feet into the velvet, leaving a mark no one can remove.

They blink and stall, sunlight harsh on their eyes.

We are up. We are out.

Mulia lifts her muzzle to the sky and howls.

Outside, interlocking shields surround the palace. I swallow what feels like bone fragments and knife blades.

We are not free yet.

53

LYE

EVERYTHING CHANGES

"Look!" Guen points at two long shields parting slightly, exposing shadow rather than light. The opposite of breaking clouds. A guard slips through the gap, his shoulder almost clipped as it closes again.

He takes a few steady steps toward us, though they become less steady as he gets closer. He stops twenty yards from the edge of the jungle. "Keeper! The emperor will see you!" he shouts. "Alone and unarmed!"

I step forward, ready to go, ready to offer anything, *everything*, to see the Char children, Luna and Ash freed, and the Shen with lives restored. The villagers' voices rumble and ripple down the mountain. *This is dangerous. This is a trap. Don't go,* they warn.

But I *am* everything.

I am not nothing.

Fire, Water, Earth, Air, and Blood course through my veins. I am never unarmed. No trap can contain me. I gaze at the archers lining the parapet walk. But an arrow can pierce my skin.

Sifah places a hand on my shoulder and nods her elegant head, seeming to read my mind. "We will protect you, Lye Li Koh."

I step out from the trees like I'm shedding a robe. Wind dances through my cropped hair. I know my skin has darkened and my freckles shine like black stars across my cheeks. But the guard recognizes me instantly, and his knee folds on instinct. "I will come unarmed, but I will not come alone."

The Carvresses gather, creating their own small shield around me.

To the ground the soldier shouts, "That is not what the emperor wants."

The guard gapes at the seven wooden women and Shei-Shei. Her Fire tattoo catching the light and reminding all who watch that the Carvresses, the princesses, are Char *and* Shen. He tumbles backward, eyes like a vampire owl, unblinking. We walk past him, and I tap his head lightly. "I no longer care what the emperor wants."

As soon as we're in range, arrows rain down.

They pierce the Carvresses like they're moving target practice. Arrows twang as they lean over to protect my blood-and-flesh body. Shei-Shei hides with me in the cocoon of wooden armor. Her earthly green eyes connect with mine. "This is the part where we change everything," she murmurs, hopeful and hunted.

I nod, hunched over, toes crossing the red painted squares of the palace courtyard. "This is the part where we accept nothing but the throne."

Some of the Carvresses straighten for a moment as arrows chip their skin, making Shei-Shei and I visible to those looking down from above. Shei-Shei's beautiful face lifts to the sky, eyes like emeralds, counting the soldiers sprinkled across the top of the palace. "There are too many," she says, tracing a line from tower to tower.

An archer shouts, "Hold your fire!"

Taut bow strings relax. Soldiers mutter in confusion.

The Carvresses hold tight around us, but something has changed. Shen archers point down at our wreath of wood and element. While we look up, shielding our eyes from the glare reflecting off the copper roof.

Shei-Shei blinks and straightens. "What's happening?"

I shrug. "I don't know, but they're not shooting. That has to be a good sign, right?"

Sifah plucks an arrow from her forearm, throws it on the ground and grumbles, "Perhaps they have run out of arrows."

I watch the soldiers. "I don't think so; it's something else."

The cuff of shields has relaxed also, tilting as Shen peer through the gaps. The pointing fingers are all in one direction: Shei-Shei's.

54

ASH

BLOOD DRAINED,
TEAR STAINED

"L ies! Lies! Lies!" the emperor shrieks, voice climbing the walls like cat claws down a chalk board.

My shackled hands rest on the top step. I'm so close I can smell sweet wine on his breath and count the small beads of sweat forming across his brow. He is grief and panic. Doubt and rage. He glares like I am to blame so I glare right back. If that's what it takes to hold him here while Luna finds a way out, so be it.

"I speak the truth, emperor. Soo Si came to us and struck a bargain. If Luna used her Blood power to make Mulia kill you, she promised to release the Char children."

He freezes in his hand wringing and foot stomping, eyes twitching. "Now I know you are lying." He wipes his nose with his sleeve and then seems horrified by it, holding it up and away from the arm of the throne. "There are no such children here."

I shake my head as pity washes over me for a man who has allowed himself to be led. Has opened the palace doors to evil. His ignorance baffles me. "You kidnapped and tortured Char children. They have been beneath the palace for months."

His Atmosphere is shaking like a corner rat. With no escape the only way out is to attack. "How dare you accuse me of such a crime! Kidnapping children violates all rules of war. I would never—"

He quivers with suspicion and so much fear. There's no trust, only anxiousness. A jumpiness to his motions. My pity turns to anger as I think of the emperor lying clueless in his fluffed-up bed while Lu Leng was dying in the dirt. "How can you have not known?" I challenge. "How could you be so ignorant of what was happening in your own palace?"

The emperor's lip curls. My words are having the desired and dangerous effect of pulling him into an argument. All to give Luna time. "I am the emperor. I command others to do work in my name. Why should I know every silly little experiment that goes on within these walls?"

"You call kidnapping and torturing children a silly little experiment?"

Aghast, he shakes his head vehemently. "No, of course not! But I chose people to carry out my will. I trusted—"

I laugh bitterly, rattling my chains at the blubbering man. "Maybe *they* chose *you*." I point at what must be a diamond-crusted heart, only capable of looking pretty and deflecting. "They chose the gullible emperor who would fall for any scheme. Who doesn't have an original thought in his pretty little head. What did she call you? An earthworm?" I throw my words like spears. "Even an earthworm has a stronger spine than you."

He stands, silk slippers almost touching my hands. "How dare you question your emperor's choices!" He shakes. He shudders. A flag in a changing wind. He flicks his hair like there are still voices in his ear, or maybe he wishes there were. He's on his own now. No one to blame, no one to make his decisions, and it terrifies him.

"Well"—I tap my chin—"a leader is only as good as the people he surrounds himself with." I glower, my eyes as heated as balls of fire. "And you chose a murderer, a torturer, and a snake," I spit.

A face of empty death. Blood drained, tear stained.

There's no one to witness. No one to stop what comes next.

I *feel* Luna again. A force like no other. She is strong and brave and full of love. Her warmth surrounds me, providing a shield nothing can penetrate.

At least before I go, I get to know I saved her.

55

LUNA

ABOVE GROUND

Sunlight and salt. Hope and horror. We made it above ground. The children scream and point behind me, and I dig my heels into Mulia's side gently. She swings around and I can't breathe, I can't speak. Relieved and confused, I wish to fall at their feet and shake them senseless.

The Carvresses walk down the main hall of the palace in a tight circle, looking like a cracked open sea urchin for all the arrows sticking out of their backs and shoulders. The children snuggle together, sharp squares of sunlight from the iron lined windows heating their pale faces. Just like me, they're unsure what to make of the view before them, but Sifah, my Carvress, opens her arms wide and exclaims, "Char children, don't be afraid. We are here to help you."

Several soldiers flank them at a distance. All eyes are on a Fire Shen who's face I saw only moments ago, carved into a throne. I tilt my head but don't have time to ponder for long.

The women spread out as children rush at them. And strangely, amazingly, the Shen soldiers do nothing.

And then there she is. My hickory heart wishes to crack and bleed but settles for a solid, reassuring beat. Whatever ill feeling was between us is cured—by time or circumstance it doesn't really matter. I dismount Mulia and run at my sister, my friend, Lye. Throwing my arms around her neck and burying my face in her shoulder.

"You're here," I whisper, feeling enough weight lifting from my shoulders to be shared.

Lye looks down on me, smile soft and wary. "Did you doubt me?"

"I doubt everyone." I laugh a short as a sail snap. I need to ask her so many questions about my family, Black Sail City, but first we need to get Ash.

Pain like no other scrapes across my stomach and I collapse like a broken chair. "Ah."

56

LYE

ASH, ASH, ASH

Luna crumples to the ground. Hugging her stomach like she's just been punched. She lifts her palm to her face like she expects it to be coated in blood.

The incredible tiger wolf whines and leans down to lick her face. There's so much to ask. So many things I want to say to the girl with the hickory heart but when she whispers, "Ash is with the emperor," all must wait.

Something is very wrong. "Where?"

Luna pulls herself back to standing and swings onto the back of the impressive creature. "We have to get the children out first," she says in a voice as strained as a boat rope in a storm. She and the tiger wolf turn to the guards pinned against the wall. The creature growls and they put their arms up.

A child laughs. A strange sound to hear in the palace.

An even stranger noise bellows outside, and we look to the windows. A horn that reminds me of a howling of sea wind and bird shrieks. Mi Asha exclaims, "They're here!" The cuff begins to wobble, and shields fall.

Beads to a broken necklace are clicking into place, one by one.

"Mama!" Luna cries. "Sun, Joka!" The names are music on her tongue. A change is occurring but it's not what I thought it would be. There are no more arrows, swords clashing, or blood spilling. The Shen outside don't fight. They don't even push at the soldiers. They talk to them. They point at the Char children's grimy faces smudging up the palace windows. Soldiers shake their heads, dismayed, and shields that were once rigid and impenetrable slacken. Thousands of Shen swarm the palace grounds, my Char crew at the head. I smile like my brother, with half my face. Thrilled at the scene before me but until I can share it with Ash, the thrill only goes part way up the mountain and tumbles back down.

A little boy shouts, "Mama!" and breaks away from the Carvresses, squeezing through the slightly ajar door and running into the crowded square. I hold my breath, awaiting an arrow to skewer the boy in his tracks. I close my eyes. There will be a scream and then nothing.

Nothing.

Nothing.

My heart beats *Ash, Ash, Ash.*

I open my eyes to Jing Ha embracing the small boy who must be Bok Ah. Ki Anah, Sun, Joka, and Guen push through the broken barricade toward the palace, focused on the Char children who are more rags and bones than flesh, but still so strong. The young Char push the door open, light streaming across the blood red carpet, and run into the square. Unbelievably, Shen soldiers allow them through.

Mei aids Ki Anah and the others to encircle the other children and gather them close. Mei has brought grace and pride to the Koh family, where I felt there could only be shame and destruction. I pass my trust to her that she can look after the children.

My eyes connect with Jing Ha with her arms tight around her little boy and she salutes. The reunion pushes me into the palace and to my own reunion.

Luna takes one heart breaking look at her mother and brothers through the window, waves her hand, and turns away.

Ki Anah watches her daughter ride away with pride and desolation.

Joka mouths the word *go*, and I follow Luna.

One is missing. And we must find him.

57
LUNA

DON'T LOOK BACK

The underside of the dragon is revealed, legs and arms kicking and flailing. Everything has turned upside down until I don't understand the world anymore. Shen and Char laying down their weapons, mixing together. Nothing will be the same now. I clutch my stomach—the pain is beginning to cool and numb, which is not a good sign. *Hold on, Ash, please. Don't leave this world right when it's getting good. Right when a place has been made for us.*

I clutch Mulia's ruff as she bounds up the stairs to the throne room. The Carvresses click and clack behind me. Wooden shoulders knock against each other. My mother is out there, my brothers. We have crossed oceans and countries. How is that we are in the same place and still not together? My heart cracks and stretches like steam to a boat builder's plank.

Lye is at our tail. I sense her blood rushing like a flood. Her heart trying not to fail at the thought of her brother—I shake my head. No. I will not allow thoughts of bad things and terrible ends.

This is not how it happens. I now know how much I love him, and it's far too much to let him die for me.

Shei-Shei, miraculously and unexplainably flesh, breaks from the Carvresses to be at my side. Mulia's lip curls as she matches our pace. Her face is etched in my memory as the woman who broke me apart. Wooden or not, her actions pulled my soul from hickory. I owe her my pain and my healing. How she came to be flesh again is a mystery I hope I will have time to solve later. After. After I save Ash.

We reach the closed doors of the throne room and Mulia's claws dig into the floor with a ripping sound. Two guards cross their spears over the entrance, but their hands shake. And when Shei-Shei approaches, head lifted high, regal as only an ancient princess can be, their lids pull back in awe mixed with alarm mixed with recognition.

"Let us enter," she commands as the Carvresses arrive behind her, beautiful and magical. Grain lines and knot holes. Char and Shen in a perfectly brutal package.

The spears pull back a few inches, like a second hand ticking backward. The guard on the left, his wavy lined Air tattoo moving as he speaks. "Your face. It's you." He turns to his counterpart. "It's her. From the throne."

The other guard shifts nervously, and his spear drops with his knee. His forehead scrapes the ground. "Forgive us, princess."

Shei-Shei pretends she knows what's going on and waves her hand. "You are forgiven. My sisters and I wish to enter, at once." She turns to her sister. "Since when is the throne room on the second floor?" The sisters exchange displeased expressions.

I shudder. I *feel* cold. I *feel* a playback of sun-blessed memories in his mind. Touches of gold and kisses of starlight.

Ash, don't look back. Look forward.

I dismount Mulia, and Lye's hand is suddenly in mine. I feel no element from her. On my part, all I'm projecting is fearful, hiding creatures. Things that blink moon eyes from tree hollows and under rocks.

The Carvresses allow us to go first, heads bowed like we're already at a funeral. We place our hands on the door and push.

58

ASH

MODE OF THE LIVING

He rushes to the window and presses his hands against the glass, looking more like a hungry child than an emperor. Something has changed out there. Something that increases his breathing and makes him run a trembling hand through his hair, his headpiece falling to the floor.

This is good.

This is what we needed.

I can't speak but I listen. The emperor counts thousands of Shen peasants gathering in the square. "There are Char there! Char at the head of the crowd. Char and Shen working together. What is this deception?" he blathers. "Char children? Stars! You were right?" he spares me one glance as brief as the beat of a murder bird's wing before returning to the window. Disbelief turning to shame when he sees dirty, ragged Char children running from this rust-red prison. "She *was* lying to me."

To him, I am nothing.

"She was supposed to come alone," he remarks, eyes glued to the window.

Minutes slide by like beads across an abacus.

I press my hand against my stomach, trying to hold in everything that's trying to spill out, but it will do no good. It hurt like a thousand burning irons when he stabbed me, but now I feel no pain. All I feel now is calm and sad. Strangely hopeful that even though I won't get to see it, our world is changing. Our way is ending. There may be peace between Shen and Char for the first time in almost a thousand years.

I wish I could laugh at the way the emperor dances about in a panic. But laughing feels like a mode of the living—and I am dying.

59
LYE

PROMISES

The doors open like an ancient spell book, and the scene is horrifying familiar. A desperate, selfish man clad in fine silk and gold, and a kind, brave boy lying in a pool of blood at his feet.

The emperor takes an intimidating step toward me, knife in hand. "Keeper." He utters the title like a threat and a prayer.

I do not bow but step to him as he did to me. Luna rushes to Ash's side, her tears saltwater to blood. She holds her hands against his, pressing and pressing. Trying to stop blood that keeps on coming. "Oh Ash, you can't. You promised," she whispers.

A shiver runs through me as I slip on my brother's blood. Wooden feet on the polished floor behind me punctuate my moves. "Lay down your weapon and surrender, emperor."

"The… children?" Ash asks between wet coughs.

"They are safe." Luna strokes his hair and looks up at seven pairs of pained, wooden expressions and one flesh one.

Ash closes his eyes.

I lunge at the emperor, whacking the knife from his hands and kicking him swiftly to the ground. I can't look at Ash. I just can't. If I see no life in his eyes, I won't be able to do what needs to be done. I will give up. I will surrender. I will sink to the earth and never get back up. The Carvresses flock around me, heading for the frightened, shaking young man, who seems younger by the second.

The emperor glances from Shei-Shei to a throne with her face on it and back again. "How can this be?"

They move closer as he stumbles back, murmuring like sisters to a brother, "You have done a bad thing."

"I was scared." His voice quivers and reaches for their understanding.

"We know." They form a circle around the emperor, nodding their beautiful heads. "Now you must atone for your crimes."

He sniffs. I cannot see him from his huddled position, surrounded by his ancestors, but I think I hear the words, "Forgive me."

There are not enough shells in the ocean or leaves on the forest floor to count the number of crimes he must make up for. Forgiveness is as out of range as the moon.

Luna's grief-stricken scream could reach it though. Long and bloody and loud. She stands and storms, scooping up the knife and hacking at the emperor's throne. When it doesn't yield, she kicks it over and uses her foot to smash it apart.

I force myself to look at my brother. Ash is turning as gray as his namesake. I want to comfort him, I must. I step toward his body and Luna brandishes a large piece of wood threateningly at me. "Don't you dare say goodbye."

I pause. "Luna," I whisper but her eyes are fire. Her mouth grim and determined.

She shakes the hunk of wood at me. "He is not dead yet, and one of you is going to fix him. Now!" She shows no hesitation, no veneration as she marches up to the circle of Carvresses and yanks one by the arm. "He has given everything to help you. Fix him now!"

She dumps the wood in the Carvress of Abalone Island's cedar hands so violently the Carvress buckles from the force. She doesn't bow. She doesn't wait. With my help, she drags Ash under his arms to the window, sunlight burning through the mist and streaming over his pale, blood-drained face.

The Carvress bows. "It may be too late."

Luna clutches Ash's hand fiercely like she would happily walk through hell for my brother. Like maybe she already has, and if it meant he would live she would turn around and do it again. Her Blood power calls like a siren over the mountain and birds fly against the glass as monkeys shriek in the jungle. Everything rises like an orchestra, all creatures at her will. "It won't be."

I try so hard not to cry. This lump in my throat keeps rising and falling, rising and falling. "H-h-how can you be sure?" I tremble and reach for my brother, palm sweeping over the coldest forehead. He is Water turned to ice.

Luna's golden eyes lift, stony and convinced. "Because he has never broken a promise to me."

60

KI ANAH

WOOD AND BLOOD

The Char children are safely in the jungle. Joka handed the notebook to Mei, Lye's cousin. The girl has leadership and compassion born into her bones. Just like Lye. Ki Anah takes a steeling breath. Char children are being cared for by Shen as if they were kin. She never thought she'd live to see such a day, but then it's quite difficult for her to be surprised these days.

Sun whispers something to Guen and she frowns. But then she embraces her adopted father and pushes his wooden chest. Not angrily. More like, what are you waiting for, go! She stomps her birchwood foot and retreats to the forest, arms open to the children in need.

Joka joins his brother, striding shoulder to shoulder. They will follow their mother as she heads for the palace doors.

Ki Anah has done her part. Now she needs to be with her daughter.

Animals stream around her, snagging on her skirts, and she has to keep lifting her feet to avoid stepping on various rats and bugs that scamper for the door. Her Blood sense pulses at the presence of all these critters. It is both foreign and comforting because she also senses their loyalty to Luna. They give her a path to follow.

The shield barricade has collapsed. Whispers of returning princesses bounce from mouth to mouth, ear to ear. The Shen peasants have broken the shield line into smaller pieces. Pieces that don't seem to care as she walks right past them and into the imposing building.

She supposes the world the Shen knew has been ripped apart too. She passes many stunned expressions as peasants relay the Carvresses origins and the history that has brought them back to the palace.

She overhears a peasant talking to a soldier of her new Elemental power. The idea that the Keeper gifts her power to those deserving is a strange concept for the soldiers. But then, everything about this is strange. She sets her chin. Strange but better.

Joka places a hand on Ki Anah's shoulder, his fingers brushing the exposed skin on her neck. It sends a flurry of motherly warmth and worry his way in the form of a duck hiding her chicks beneath her wing. He pulls back, exclaiming, "Wa! This is going to take some getting used to." She frowns. It certainly will.

Her sons pick their way through the trail of animals rushing for wherever Luna is. Piles of bugs lie dying on their backs, little legs pedaling. She sniffs the air, acrid chemicals burning her nostrils. Sun swears as he accidentally steps on a yellow chipmunk. It squeaks and squirms, thankfully not injured. Ki Anah rolls her shoulders as she senses the animal's discomfort, and they sound like rocks under her skin.

The zoo of scampering creatures is slowing them down and Ki Anah sets her mind on the animals. They begin to part and weave around their feet rather than getting caught under them. "Is that you?" Sun asks eyebrows raised.

Ki Anah nods. "I think so." She tries to hold control but it's difficult, and the animals part and close in, part and close in.

They can move faster though, threading through hallways and large carved arches. Heavy tapestries hang from the walls depicting

Elements and the Shen's greatest warriors, and it baffles Ki Anah to think she is now part of this Shen tradition.

She is not powerful like Luna, but she is part of the wheel.

When she reaches two ajar doors flanked by two confused-looking guards, spears lying on the ground as they peer curiously into the room, Ki Anah stalls. She's apprehensive of what she might find, because the animals have stopped. They gather at the door but dare not step over the threshold. Sun and Joka stand behind her.

She raps her knuckles on the open door gingerly. "Luna, it's your mother. You in there?"

When no one answers, Ki Anah steps inside. If it's possible, her whole being gasps at the sight: Wood and blood, a boy who is lost, and the women who mourn him.

61

LUNA

TAKING BACK WHAT IS OWED

The Carvress of Abalone Island whispers the last incantation, hovering over Ash with a pearlescent shell necklace hanging from her neck. The light around us turns golden and almost thick. I look down at what was once an open, bleeding wound, to a smooth wooden plane of ashwood. It makes me want to laugh in a desperate, hysterical kind of way that the thrones are carved from ashwood. *Of all things.* But there's nothing funny about this.

I tap his cheeks. I wait for breath, and blood to rush. "Ash," I whisper. His eyes remain closed. I want the sea blue. I want the storm and crashing waves. Anything. Everything.

The empty and bewildered emperor sits on the floor before the eight princesses. They look with grief and pity upon the man draped in purple silk spotted with crimson with a crown laying discarded in a puddle of blood. He deserves disaster. He deserves to be shredded and pecked apart until he is nothing but a sorry skeleton. Ash is leaving me. The only way I know how to bear such a weight is to call upon beaks and claws to create suffering.

Lye kneels with me as glass shatters and birds fly into the room. Everyone shields their faces as they screech and swoop about the room. Lye's hand shoots out, grabbing my wrist. "You need to control it, Luna. Don't go back to that place. Don't let darkness take over." She smooths Ash's golden-brown hair from his face lovingly.

"Breathe!" I shout. "Live!" *You promised. You let me believe you could keep it.*

Hickory slides, blood pumps. *Why am I always the one left behind?* It can't bleed but my heart feels like its drying up and flaking away. Like Ash. *Like* Ash. Birds circle, and all eyes lift to the ceiling.

"Little Luna," they say.

No.

A voice I've run from. A voice I've argued with a thousand times. A voice I wish to hold onto and never let go of. "Luna," she says as she runs to me, her heart pumping differently. Her love familiar. Mama falls to her knees, takes one look at Ash, and lifts her fist. Brings it down hard on top of Ash's chest.

My mouth falls open. Lye reaches out to stop her, but Joka and Sun grab my arm. "Wait," Sun says like he knows something we do not.

She bangs on his chest four more times. Each pound hurting me with its hollowness and giving me foolish hope at the same time.

On the fourth punch, Ash's eyes fly open. He coughs and his hand flies to his chest. He rolls to the side. Breathing. *Breathing!* He glances up, a smile halfway to heaven. "I know you disapprove of me, Ki Anah," he manages. "But that seemed a little harsh."

Lye covers her mouth, tears streaming down her newly freckled face. "Oh brother, you're alive."

Ash's hand coasts to his stomach, fingers tracing the ashwood edges. "It would seem so." He pulls up to half sitting, his head still in my lap. He looks at me, *feels* me. Eyes like the sea taking back what is owed. "Kept my promise, didn't I?"

I lean down and kiss his cold mouth, not caring that my mother and brothers are watching. I can't care about anything except those saltwater lips and the boy who helped me save the world. "I never doubted."

Mama clears her throat pointedly, and I pull back. "Where did you learn to do that?" I ask, hand fisted.

She straightens and says proudly, "The birchwood girl, Guen, taught me." There's so much I don't know. So much I need to tell her. So much I *owe* her.

The birds settle, forming a line atop Shei-Shei's throne. The flesh Carvress steps up to the platform and inspects it, turning around to face us so her face and the carved one are side by side. The likeness is identical.

Arms and hands are linked. We are together. We have survived.

It seemed impossible and yet here we stand.

I wish to stay here in this warmth and joy for a moment: Lye's forehead touching mine, my mother's hand at my back, and my brothers' grinning faces gazing down at me. And Ash, living and breathing in my arms. Promises we've held out to the future feeling closer than ever before.

But then the emperor's usually smooth voice turned all bumpy and uneven, asks a question: "What is it you want?"

62
LYE

EVERY ELEMENT

"What is it we want?" I repeat. The question stretches far beyond the palace, over fields of rice and wheat, and oceans and islands.

The emperor sits slack under a window, either too cowardly or too weak to stand up and look outside. If he did, he would see a disbanded army and people desperate for change. But he simply stares at the roomful of women, blinking back self-pitying tears.

Shei-Shei steps away from her throne, which has drying blood on it, and frowns. The Carvress and princess looks to her sisters, whose heads swing from face to face a little unsure. We got here. We stand in the throne room. But what comes next?

Ash and Luna hold tight to one another, that part is the one strong known. There will be no separating the two. My brother finds my hand and squeezes and quite suddenly I feel like their bubble has grown large enough to fit me inside. Without a word, he conveys that separation from me is not an option either. My family will be by my side now. Forever.

Sifah coasts forward, eyes running along a platform that once held ten thrones, one for each of the nine princesses and one for the prince, then she turns to the lump of silk and sweat, the emperor. "Nephew, your time as leader is over."

His lip quivers but he doesn't argue. "Will you kill me?"

"I'd very much like to," Luna murmurs and the birds perched on the throne flap their dark wings.

The great tiger wolf lifts her head and whines, taking her place beside Luna. Luna places her hands into the magnificent creature's ruff, as natural as if the huge wolf was a family pet. Ki Anah's eyes widen, and she retreats a few inches. I sense she'd like greater distance. I'm impressed at her ability to bend and bounce back. In fact, I'm impressed by all the people I've chosen, Shen and Char.

Sifah shakes her head. "No. It is not our way. It is not the Shen way. At least not when I sat on the throne."

The emperor lets out a long breath packed full of relief but then follows it with a nasty sneer. "And what? Now you think a bunch of silly women can sit upon the throne and rule? There's a reason there have only been emperors since your departure. Women are too—"

Luna strides to the emperor, glances at Sifah who nods permission, and swings a powerful, jaw-cracking punch, knocking the sniveling man unconscious. Ash snorts and the Yans clap. Then we turn away from the pile of finery that did nothing to hide his flaws, thinking of him no longer.

Joka speaks, fine voice running a velvet cloth over my heart. *Can we finish what we started? Can we even begin?* "Will you sit upon the throne again, Carvress? I mean Princess Sifah, I mean—"

Sifah laughs and bows her wooden head. "Both titles are correct, and both are equally important."

"Does this mean you won't desert the Char, Carvress?" Ki Anah asks, her question fair.

Sifah traces Shei-Shei's carved face at the top of the throne. "We have served the Char for nine hundred years, Ki Anah Yan. We would never abandon them."

Ash sighs impatiently, always ready to take on the next challenge. "So, what do we do then?"

All royal eyes fall on me. A gaze that both lifts me from the floor and shakes me like a ragdoll.

The Carvresses form a line, standing across the steps, staring down at the rest of us from where thrones will sit when they take their place. Regal and imposing. Magic and magnanimous.

Ash makes a strange noise. Like he knows something the rest of us don't.

"When our brother stole our power, every Element transferred to him, and he became the first Keeper. It was the consequence of his deception. He could gift Elements to others, but he could not use the power at full strength. He chose to give it only to warriors. To men and women who were trained to harm. When he died, his power did not pass to his heir. It was born to a soldier's child that he had awakened. A child with the potential for great love and sacrifice."

My heart begins to pound in my chest like a drum. Though not a war drum. Something else entirely. A beat of unity and celebration.

The Carvress of Abalone Island, Princess Ce Lia, continues. "And every time a Keeper passed away, a new one was born stronger and with more capacity for love in their heart than the one before."

I shake my head. I am not what they say. I have done terrible, terrible things. I was cruel and dark. I led so many to kill, so many to die. I brought a great nothing to the world and though I have strived to overcome my failings, I'm not there yet.

Ash leans into me. "Sister, listen."

I lift my sorry head.

Mi Asha bows to me. To *me*. "The Keeper has a higher claim to the throne than the Carvresses. You hold all our power. All our love. You are—everything."

I am everything.

The room changes color, or maybe my eyes see things in a different light. Either way it is bright and golden and full of promise.

I shiver and straighten. *Can I do this? Rule the Shen empire?* It seems preposterous and nonsensical, but I can't deny the rightness of it. Like all my Elements have slotted into their places on the wheel and it can finally move. Breaking free of the tangled vines and rust that held it static for an age. I've been chasing this feeling my entire life. I laugh. To think it was here on the throne all along.

I bow low to the Carvresses. "I may be everything, but I've learned I am nothing without the people I love. Char *and* Shen people." I beckon them. They climb the stairs gathering in a messy, upturned group that barely fits on the platform and is perfect in its mismatched-ness. "I cannot rule alone. For this to work, the two lands must find a way to lead together."

Sifah lowers her head and smiles. "That is what we were hoping you would say."

63

SETSU

AN IMPOSSIBLE THOUGHT

Setsu would have sailed to the ends of the earth to see his family again. Sea air kisses his worn cheeks and whispers strange hope in his ears. He gives a satisfied grunt. Lucky for him, he only has to sail to Bird Cage Island.

When the heart bird flew into the dining room of the monastery, a tiny scroll attached to its leg, Setsu knew the message was for him. He snatched it from the hands of a fellow soldier before they could finish reading Setsu's name.

The message was simple and mysterious. Saying only that the war was over and to sail to Bird Cage Island in one week.

The week was torturous for Setsu, and he may have knocked a few men into walls as he swung his shoulders down the covered walkways. Grumbling and groaning and being as disgruntled as a hoarder bear who has lost his collection of bones. He couldn't help it. The message was signed "your family." But what did that mean? Were they all together? Luna too? And why meet on Bird Cage?

He asks himself these questions over and over as the borrowed boat bounces over ghost waves. Waves with no crest or break to them, just a small rise in the water, like a ghost is trying to push its way up and out. Setsu snorts. He doesn't care how many ghosts escape as long as they push him closer to shore.

Long, thin curved rocks jut out of the water like a cage. If he could go faster, he would, but he is at the mercy of wind and sea. He curses, swiping salt from his moustache. Momentarily, he wishes he had the kind of power, Shen power, that could influence the current. A strange and impossible thought.

Bird Cage Island is covered by clouds when the sun shines on all the sapphire water surrounding it. The cloud moves and pulses, almost like it's breathing. With a squint, Setsu shields his eyes, realizing the cloud is an enormous flock of moon-sun birds, twisting and turning in circles over the land. His eyebrow arches and his oak hand pats the sword at his hip, preparing for all manner of danger when he lands.

The boat flies across the last half mile as if the wind is being blown solely into his sails. He steels himself, but Setsu Yan could never prepare for what he's met with as his boat hits the sand bank. He jumps from the boat.

Knee deep in water, waves lapping at his tree trunk legs, his mouth drops open like a winding castle bridge, slowly and with effort. Four Carvresses sit beneath the shade of coconut palms, while lines of Shen snake away from them like an octopus's tentacles. His hand wraps around the hilt of his sword and he takes another few steps. He watches, disbelieving, as freed Shen prisoners from the battle of Crow's Nest Island bow to the Carvresses. What is this trick that makes them appear as if they both respect and need them?

This is some dark magic, some spell about to turn darker still. Setsu closes his eyes and visions of past battles run across his mind until all he sees is red.

His sword slides from its sheath, metallic and slicingly sharp.

"Setsu!" A voice like malt syrup and the finest plum wine.

"Papa!" A voice that almost brings him to his knees for how much he has missed it.

Two Yan women splash through the water and fall into the barrel-chested man's arms. Fitting there like missing buttons and buckled armor. Setsu's sword drops into the water and sand rakes over the blade, hiding it as the tide pulls out. But Setsu can't seem to care. He lifts Luna and Ki Anah up and carries them to shore, heart bursting with a relief-coated joy he had begun to think was unattainable. As he embraces them, his body fills with feathered nests and warm furs. He hugs them tighter, wonder pecking at his heart. Knowing there are many stories to be told. And his ears are bursting at the thought that he will hear them from his wife's and daughter's lips.

Joka meets him on the shore with Lye by his side in imperial Shen dress. Sun clutches the hand of a small wooden girl, who stares at him with a very familiar "don't underestimate me or you'll regret it" kind of attitude. And then there's a Shen boy with a Water tattoo whose eyes never leave Luna.

There is much to explain. But for now, all Setsu wishes for are arms wide enough to hold his whole family together and never let go.

Over Bird Cage Island, the moon sun birds switch to sun and stay that way. With salt air streaming through their wings, they race beak over claw high into the sky.

If you have enjoyed reading

THE GIRL WITH THE SYCAMORE SCARS

please consider leaving a review.
It helps readers like you connect
with books they'll enjoy!

Don't miss these other titles by

LAUREN NICOLLE TAYLOR

"Lyrically written, this powerful and at times painful read captures the reader and does not let go."
—Booklist, starred review

In 1953's post-WW II Japanese internment camp era, two teenagers facing extraordinary hardship collide at a time when they need each other most. Their stories, a collection of events, are each on their own harmless. But together, one after the other, they change the world.

Nora's struggles are just beginning, and she must now become Kite—a stronger, more independent version of herself. Kettle must accept that he is also Hiro: a Japanese American with every right to happiness and freedom. They must rely on each other, otherwise it's their future in jeopardy, along with the fates of the street kids in their care.

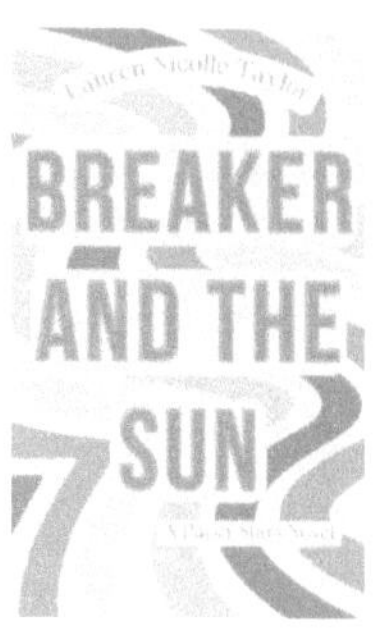

A recently returned Vietnam vet struggling with PTSD and a high-achieving Chinese-French immigrant find solace in the Catskills at the Ugly Tree, where they find themselves lulled toward an enchanted, peaceful sleep.

ACKNOWLEDGEMENTS

Firstly, I'd like to thank my family. Writing a book is a very quiet exercise for me and my family is not quiet. So, they had to put up with me moving from room to room to find the impossible 'quiet space' in our renovated train station home during the multiple lockdowns of 2021. Shushing and sighing whenever someone opened a cupboard door or popped their head into ask me a question.

To the mixed Asian community. When I say I'm part Chinese, Indonesian, Thai, French, Scottish and Irish it can seem like a lot to process. But you feel me. You welcomed and accepted me into the subculture of 'mixed'. I felt heard. I felt validated. I hope this book shows that.

To Emma and Hannah. Thank you for believing in this mixed Asian fantasy. Writing a book from my multiple Asian backgrounds could have been a dealbreaker and I had been told by others to simplify. But I was writing in my own voice. That seemed pretty simple to me. You saw and championed its uniqueness and I'm so happy the Hickory Heart series found a home with Owl Hollow.

Lastly, a huge thank you to my agent Jessica Schmeidler. For being the best agent an author could ask for. Always on the lookout for opportunities. Always the first to read my new work, offering awesome critique whilst maintaining my voice. Always cheering me on when I doubt myself. Good communication is key between author and agent and I'm so grateful to have that with Jessica.

LAUREN NICOLLE TAYLOR is the bestselling author of The Woodlands series and the award-winning YA novel *Nora & Kettle* (Gold Medal Winner for Multicultural fiction, Independent Publishers Book Awards), which is the first book in the acclaimed Paper Stars series.

She has a Health Science degree and an honors degree in Obstetrics and Gynecology. A full time writer and artist, Lauren recently moved from Australia to Canada with her husband and three children for a new adventure. She is a proud hapa and draws on her multicultural background in all of her novels.

Lauren is represented by Golden Wheat Literary.

Find Lauren at http://www.laurennicolletaylor.com.

#HickoryHeart
#TheGirlwiththeSycamoreScars

facebook.com/TheWoodlandSeries
twitter.com/LaurenNicolleT
instagram.com/laurennicolletaylor